PRAISE FOR
PUDGE & PREJUDICE

Written with wit and considerable insight into the highs and lows of first love, this coming-of-age twist on the Jane Austen classic had me laughing out loud, singing '80s lyrics in my head, and cheering on the brilliant, yet self-deprecating heroine. *Pudge and Prejudice* is a joy to read from beginning to end!

LORIE LANGDON, author of *Olivia Twist* and the Disney Villains series

Allison Pittman will have readers laughing (and singing) on every page of this delightfully tenderhearted novel for all ages. In *Pudge and Prejudice*, she not only offers a brilliant, modern retelling of Jane Austen's classic, she taps into the best of the human spirit through the witty yet hopeful lens of a quirky and often "unseen" teenage girl. With spot-on voicing, Pittman crafts a particularly savvy character who learns that beauty really is soul deep and that she's got something of value to offer her new town. Try not to sing along as you read this sweet story. Dare you!

JULIE CANTRELL, *New York Times* and *USA TODAY* bestselling author of *Perennials*

What a delight! In *Pudge and Prejudice*, Pittman appeals to the young and the young-at-heart, bringing Jane Austen's masterpiece to radiant life in a 1980s Texas high school. Packed with names and references from all Austen's novels, Jane-ites will relish this new young heroine. Pudge will steal your heart and—as she finds her Darcy—take you right back to the thrill of first love.

KATHERINE REAY, bestselling author of *Dear Mr. Knightley* and *The Printed Letter Bookshop*

Full of spunk, wit, and '80s charm, *Pudge and Prejudice* is a retelling so immersive and unique, it stands on its own, a masterpiece that would cause even Jane Austen to reach for a boom box. A. K. Pittman dazzles with her rich voice and attention to detail, making this book a brilliant addition to the YA space. Truly, I cannot wait to read what she writes next!"

CAROLINE GEORGE, author of *Dearest Josephine*

quintessence: *the most perfect example of a quality or class: EPITOME*

Pudge and Prejudice *is the quintessence of what a Jane Austen retelling should be.*

Austenites, rejoice! This is the P&P adaptation we've been waiting for. With a fresh and sparkling YA voice that is certain to draw in readers of all ages, A. K. Pittman has refashioned the most ubiquitous of all Austen characters and storylines into a setting and style so innovative and yet organic—a Texas high school in the 1980s—you can't help but wonder if this is somehow what Jane had in mind for Darcy and Elizabeth all along. Readers will wonder why there were no hair scrunchies, Swatches, and pegged jeans at the original Netherfield ball. I can't remember the last time I loved a book as much as I love this one. It's an instant classic I will return to time after time.

BETHANY TURNER, award-winning author of *The Secret Life of Sarah Hollenbeck* and *Hadley Beckett's Next Dish*

Equally funny and poignant, *Pudge and Prejudice* is a brilliant nod to a classic work while still remaining true to '80s pop culture and appealing to modern teens. The only explanation for how Pittman managed to have both my teen daughter and me laughing and identifying with Elyse is that the author is a magician. The interplay between the three sisters is spot on. The connection between Jayne and Elyse is sweet without being syrupy, and the somewhat competitive if protective relationship between Lydia and Elyse is a picture of the best in childhood sibling rivalry. Even better, the small-town Texas setting lays out every single pop culture reference and nostalgic event of the '80s that makes me want to run for my scrunchies and Walkman. Truly every reader, young or old, will find something to love in this quick read. Well done. Well done.

JANYRE TROMP, editor, and author of *That Sinking Feeling*

Pudge and Prejudice is the Jane Austen adaptation we've all been waiting for! Set in the 1980s, *Pudge and Prejudice* is ripe with cultural references that will delight both young readers AND their mothers. We'll all be wishing we could bust out our Walkmans as we follow Elyse Nebbitt into the murky waters of her new Texas high school, where her beautiful older sister, Jayne, becomes the instant "It girl" and her younger sister, Lydia, makes a fool of them all. Meanwhile, Elyse finds herself both fascinated by and exasperated with Billy Fitz, the popular, brooding boy skulking around school. Laugh-out-loud funny, sweet, poignant, and timely, this book is a delightful throwback to the classic tale that we all know and love. Allison Pittman has honored Jane Austen well with this wonderful novel.

KELLI STUART, author of the award-winning novel *Like a River from Its Course* and *A Silver Willow by the Shore*

I'd never imagined Austen's *Pride and Prejudice* set in a 1980s teen world, but Pittman makes it work with expert skill that all ages will adore. Between Elyse's internal monologues, hysterical teen antics, family drama, and the references to all-things-'80s, this book will have you chuckling, cheering, and smiling as Austen's classic takes a clever turn into the world of scrunchies, high school, and first loves. Move over Bon Jovi and Cyndi Lauper. *Pudge and Prejudice* is a delightful hit at both the funny bone and the heart.

PEPPER BASHAM, author of the Mitchell's Crossroads series and *My Heart Belongs in the Blue Ridge*

Does the world need yet another Austen adaptation? Yes. Yes it does. And the world needs this one. *Pudge and Prejudice* is a book with snort-laugh inducing turns of phrase, nostalgia for days, and all the heart you could ever want in a story. Add to that characters who feel like friends and the delightfully sincere narrative voice of Elyse Nebbitt, and the novel shines. An absolute joy!

SUSIE FINKBEINER, author of *Stories That Bind Us* and *All Manner of Things*

Nostalgic yet on trend, *Pudge and Prejudice* is equal parts smart and relatable. Allison Pittman's voice shines with wit and charm in this story that will delight mothers and daughters alike. Grab your scrunchies and your '80s tunes for this can't-miss romance!

ASHLEY CLARK, author of the Heirloom Secrets series

Humorous and heartfelt. Jane Austen would be utterly delighted in this *Pride and Prejudice* adaption by Allison Pittman!

TERI WILSON, bestselling author of *Unleashing Mr. Darcy*, now a Hallmark Channel original movie

With its relatable characters who steal your heart, nostalgic '80s references, and hilarious, soul-stirring voice, *Pudge and Prejudice* will be your favorite read of the year. If A. K. Pittman's name is on the cover, I'm reading it.

JENNY B. JONES, award-winning author of *A Katie Parker Production* and *I'll Be Yours*

a novel

A. K. PITTMAN

PUDGE & PREJUDICE

wander
An imprint of
Tyndale House
Publishers

Visit Tyndale online at tyndale.com.

Visit the author's website at allisonkpittman.com.

TYNDALE and Tyndale's quill logo are registered trademarks of Tyndale House Ministries. *Wander* and the Wander logo are trademarks of Tyndale House Ministries. Wander is an imprint of Tyndale House Publishers, Carol Stream, Illinois.

Pudge and Prejudice

Designed by Jacqueline L. Nuñez

Edited by Sarah Rubio

Published in association with William K. Jensen Literary Agency, 119 Bampton Court, Eugene, Oregon 97404.

Pudge and Prejudice is a work of fiction. Where real people, events, establishments, organizations, or locales appear, they are used fictitiously. All other elements of the novel are drawn from the author's imagination.

For information about special discounts for bulk purchases, please contact Tyndale House Publishers at csresponse@tyndale.com, or call 1-800-323-9400.

ISBN 978-1-4964-4282-6 (hc); ISBN 978-1-4964-4283-3 (sc)

Printed in the United States of America

26   25   24   23   22   21   20
7   6   5   4   3   2   1

*For Beth—who has been my friend through cruel
summers and winters with hazy shades
Who never, ever let me stop believin'
And for Rachel—my friend who was willing to take me on as
an agent (and Bill, who knew it was time for me to fly . . .)
And most of all, for Mikey—who knows all of my
true colors, and will keep on lovin' me anyway*

If you're lost, you can look and you will find me
    Time after time
If you fall, I will catch you, I'll be waiting
    Time after time

Cyndi Lauper
"Time After Time," *She's So Unusual* (1983)

I cannot fix on the hour, or the spot, or the
look, or the words, which laid the foundation.
It is too long ago. I was in the middle before
I knew that I *had* begun.

Jane Austen
Pride and Prejudice (1813)

candor: *unreserved, honest, or sincere expression* : *FORTHRIGHTNESS*

Elyse Nebbitt's **candor,** *while refreshing, would also prove to be a most troublesome feature.*

It is a truth universally acknowledged that a teenage girl in possession of a double-digit jeans size must be in want of a diet. I'm just not a part of that universe. All my life—my chunky, pudgy, soft-bellied life—I've always found something I needed more than a smaller waist. Like to read more books, to learn more words, to know the personal satisfaction of guessing the grocery total before the cashier *beeps* through all the produce. You know, things that matter.

I am the Saturn of my solar system, only instead of a body surrounded by floating chunks of ice, I have a single, soft, rippling ring. Nothing a few celery sticks wouldn't cure, according to my mother. Not all girls are *naturally* thin, Elyse, she tells me. Every day. Followed by, Boys aren't likely to take the time to search for inner beauty.

To the universe, being thin means being *right.* In my case, it would mean my mother was right, and boys were right. If I've learned nothing else in my fifteen years, it's this: I would rather stand my ground in all my wrongness than step one foot into someone else's idea of right, even if it means I'm sometimes left standing alone.

Then September of my Sophomore year, 1984, my entire universe changed.

My father ripped our family up from our mediocre life in Phoenix to pursue an equally mediocre job in Texas. Northenfield, Texas, to be exact, where he would spend his days doing something called Property Management. Actually, his company had given him three choices: Someplace, Ohio; Somewhere, California; and here. But Ohio was too cold for my mother's taste and California too expensive for my father's salary.

And so, Northenfield, Texas.

Texas.

It's not like I was expecting cowboy hats and gunfights. I watch *Dallas*. So I knew it had cities and towns, just like we drove through on our way here. I knew it couldn't be much different from what we were used to in Arizona, but the view from behind the U-Haul wasn't exactly promising. When we finally came into what would be our "town," I counted one string of fast-food restaurants and two scrawny strip malls. There was, however, no lack of churches. One after another lined the streets. Methodist, Baptist, First Baptist, Southern Baptist, Lutheran, Sanctification Baptist—each differentiated only by the name and the quippy message on the sign out front.

> BIBLE CLIFF'S NOTES: SIN, BAD. JESUS, GOOD.
> DID YOU "FALL" INTO SIN? TIME FOR
> BACK-TO-SUNDAY SCHOOL!
> GOD BLESS THE BADGERS

This last one I wouldn't understand until we drove past Northenfield's one enormous High School: HOME OF THE BADGERS. So at least I could rest easy knowing my future classmates and I were blessed by the congregation of Sanctification Baptist Church. When I had a chance, I'd suggest we visit there first, just to keep all of our interests under one roof.

Our street was in a perfectly average neighborhood, if on the downside of shabby. Older houses—all of them with porches and swings. Rough green yards, huge trees. Like everybody on the street had agreed that they would tidy up later.

"It looks so *normal*," I said to my older sister, Jayne. She and I were in the second seat of the Station Wagon—Mom driving, following Dad, who was solo in the U-Haul. Somehow, after six hours in the car, Jayne managed to look beautiful, her blonde hair in symmetrical, fluffy feathers, her skin miraculously sweat free, her clothes unrumpled to catalog perfection. Some would think this would conjure up some sort of jealous spark in me, but it's really more of a sense of wonder. Being jealous of Jayne would be like being jealous of a butterfly, who has no more control over its beauty than Jayne does. Everything about Jayne is *effortless*. Not just her beauty, but her kindness, her goodness. In a way, we are everything each other is not, so we stick together in our weak spots. And that's important, because in this family, you need a hand to hold in our spinning vortex of chaos.

The moment the big truck turned onto what Mom called "our" street, Jayne and I each rolled down our windows, trying to guess which would be "our" house. There was no sign out front, and since it was the middle of the day, plenty of driveways were empty. But then, the huge truck with all of our worldly possessions drifted to a stop, and Dad hopped out with all the fanfare a middle-aged man could muster. Mom pulled precariously into the narrow drive, and we were home.

The house.

Our place in Phoenix looked like every other house in Phoenix. Small, square, tan. A front yard full of rocks. Little rocks, big rocks. But this—it looked like something out of one of Mom's movies-of-the-week, where the story is about some young woman inheriting an old house, then there's a montage of painting and hammering with some hunky carpenter before—*voila!*—the essence of quaint Victorian architecture is restored. But we had a dad who, as far as I knew, didn't own a tool belt, and a mom whose housework didn't extend beyond doling out chores to me and my sisters. So, really, I didn't know if the house was sadder to see *us* than we were to see the house. While I knew it was nothing more than two stories of brick and wood and windows, I swear I saw it take a deep breath and sigh as we piled out onto its lawn. Never before had I felt compelled to apologize to a domicile. But for the time being we belonged to each other.

We are what has been called a "sprawling" family. Mom and Dad, Jayne and me, and three other sisters besides. Yes, five of us. Five Nebbitt Girls. Jayne, as I have mentioned, is beautiful, but that's not nearly an accurate-enough descriptor. She is sixteen, a Junior, and looks pretty much like she should be in the pages of *Mademoiselle* magazine. "Five Quick Fixes to Take You from Tolerable to Tantalizing!" Our younger sister Lydia is thirteen and also pretty, but in a much more cautionary way. And by "cautionary," I mean—lock up your little brothers. Between her long, spiraled hair, her short shorts, eye makeup, lip gloss, and—um—figure, she could pass for at least seventeen. But the only thing "seven" about her is her grade. As in, *seventh*. But only because she had to repeat kindergarten. I know for a fact Mom finagled the rules to enroll her in eighth here in Northenfield.

There are two others, too. Mary and Kitty. The Littles. One is six and one is eight; one likes to read and the other likes ponies. I don't know much beyond that. They're always just kind of *there*, you know? Filling chairs at dinnertime, using the last of the toothpaste, hogging the TV. Jayne and I love them, of course. The way you love a pet—not like a puppy or anything, but more like a couple of hamsters that can capture your fancy for an entire afternoon before becoming nothing but rustling, squeaking noise you have to remember to feed.

My parents lump us into two groups: the big girls and the little girls. I am, of course, one of the big girls. Two years older than Lydia, one year younger than Jayne, who also happens to be my best friend.

The Littles, even though they'd been relegated to the backward-facing third seat of the Station Wagon, managed to be the first ones out of the car, climbing over Jayne and me, squealing with delight at the yard and the trees. Perfect for a Swing! Or a Tree House! Or a Fort! In the backyard, if there was a backyard. They ran in circles, tumbling over each other, getting leaves and grass in their hair, and laughing because they had to Pee!

I swear the house looked at me for help.

Jayne and I unfolded ourselves out of the car. For me, it was a slow, sweaty process, pulling my T-shirt away from my back and waving it to make a breeze. No one would ever believe we'd come from a shared experience. She wore a pair of pink jogging shorts and a tank top and looked like she could have been a model for an ad for the Diet Pepsi she was drinking.

"So this is it," she said, offering me a sip.

I took a swig. Normally, I hate the taste of diet anything, but I felt a need to build up courage. Apparently Mom did, too, because her hands were still gripping the wheel.

"Is she ever going to get out of the car?"

Jayne took the can of soda back. "I think she's as freaked out as the rest of us."

Dad jangled a set of keys above his head and was all, "Hey girls! Let's check out the new digs!"—like any of us ever talk like that. But it was sweet how he included Mom in his *girls*, because that seemed to do the trick to get her out of the car.

"C'mon," I said to Jayne. "I want to see the charm on the inside."

We followed Dad up the stairs while Mom rounded up the Littles. The only Nebbitt not on the front lawn was Lydia, who remained in the front seat of the car. Arms folded. Face pouting.

"I am, like, not getting out of the car? Okay?" She had perfected the vernacular of the Valley Girl, even though we'd never spent more than a week in California.

Dad shouted something to her about not being able to have her choice of room because the sluggard shall not inherit the desirings of her heart—but no proverb would ever get Lydia to do anything she didn't want to do.

The house had a big porch that went all the way from one end to the other, with five shallow steps leading up to it. The wood felt soft and worn, and my first step felt like the latest of a thousand. My mind went to every classic old movie I'd ever seen—all the porch swings and suitors and moonlit nights. But there was no porch swing here. Instead, there was this long wooden board with little rocker-like things under the four legs. The minute Mom saw it, she did this annoying little hand-clappy laugh and squealed something about *never having seen one in real life* and *here on our very porch* . . .

Dad had no idea what the thing was, and neither did I. Mom's been known to get just as excited over a really good dish of pudding, so I was ready to ignore this, too. But Mom wouldn't take another step before educating all of us on the joys of the Joggling Board.

Most people, see, are allowed to have nice, normal furniture on their front porch. A bench. The aforementioned swing. Maybe a little table for lemonade. Not the Nebbitts. We inherited this thing. It's huge—like, ten feet long. And the deal is—according to Mom's rambling explanation—a girl sits on one end, a boy on the other. Then, somehow, you rock—or, *joggle*—the board, and the motion scooches you both to the center, where I guess you share a kiss? I don't know. It's something Mom learned about on PBS. And, legend has it, nobody with a Joggling Board on their porch will ever have an unwed daughter in the house.

The whole time Mom was telling me this, I was watching Lydia get out of the Station Wagon. She was wearing a pair of white satin shorts that barely cleared the top of her thighs and a Dr Pepper T-shirt that, besides being cut in half, was at least two sizes too small. It's not what she was wearing when we left the Shady 8 motel that morning—Dad would never have given his blessing—so she must have changed in the car. Mom thinks she is adorable. I think that if anybody looks like they belong on a Joggling Board, it's my sister Lydia.

Right then, though, Dad was too excited about the new house to give much thought to his daughter's indecency. He took a deep breath, uttered one of his trademark Nebbitt family prayers—part Scripture, part sitcom, and part phrases he remembered from his quote-of-the-day calendar—and swung open the screen door, declaring a little WD-40 would work that squeak right out.

Now, I don't know if it's technically possible to fall in love with a house. But given my prospects for romance, it's a much safer bet than a boyfriend, and whatever faded paint and broken screens might have been visible on the outside, the inside was pure charm. Worn down, overstuffed, dust-in-the-daylight enchantment.

Dad gave the instruction to take off and explore, which Jayne and I did while Mom got the Littles to the bathroom. We ran upstairs first, instinctively knowing it would be our domain, and found four rooms attached by crooked hallways, with shadowy alcoves where a girl could disappear if she wanted to. Jayne and I claimed our bedroom, reserving the rights of the eldest to choose the one with a sixteen-paned dormer window that looked right out onto the front yard. No closet to speak of, but two four-poster beds, a big armoire, and a chest with ten drawers. I mean, we had a U-Haul full of furniture and stuff, but this place was semifurnished throughout, like a bonus.

Back downstairs, however, Mom wasn't nearly as pleased. She has this way of sniffing and talking out of the side of her mouth, and she was wandering from corner to corner performing this exact ritual, saying there'd be mice, for sure, and what a bear it would be to heat and cool, and since we were only baby-sitting this place on the whim of the owner—well, who knew when we would be thrown out onto the streets?

But then, Mom can complain about anything. The world is full of delights she can ruin with a single, shrill word.

Meanwhile, Jayne and I flew up and down the stairs, bringing our bags in from the Station Wagon, and even crawling around in the U-Haul for the few boxes we had clearly labeled. Lydia, banished to the small, slope-roofed room, was lying flat on her back on the floor, declaring she wouldn't lift a finger to seal her own fate.

I was mid-trek with a box when Mom hollered from the car that she was taking the Littles with her to the grocery store to get a few supplies and dropping Dad off at the office where he had a blah-blah meeting with some-whozit-body about setting up a new whatever, so Jayne and I would be in charge of helping the movers.

Movers? In what way was I even remotely qualified to supervise a bunch of movers?

Dad said to relax, it was just a few boys from the High School who needed to get community service hours.

"Like, *criminals*?" I asked.

Before he could answer, Lydia came tearing out of the front door, propelled by the powerful promise of Boys. Movers, criminals. Whatever.

As if for the first time, Dad noticed her outfit and declared she would do best to help Mom at the grocery store.

Knowing the cavalry was on its way, Jayne and I sat on opposite ends of the Joggling Board—careful not to joggle—and enjoyed a refreshing beverage rescued from the watery ice in the family travel cooler. The slightly crisp breeze of late September made the front porch more comfortable than the stuffy inside of the house, and it gave us a chance to survey the neighborhood, not that there was much to see.

"I don't even want to think about school." I took a handful of soggy-ish, trip-worn Cheez-Its and joggled the box down to Jayne.

"Oh, c'mon, Pudge," she said, using the nickname I'd worn since I was a toddler and made myself sick after eating half a pan of Christmas fudge. (When Jayne asked me why my tummy hurt, I famously said, "I ated too much *pudge!*" Adorable, right?) It was our secret, this name. Only Jayne was allowed to call me that, and from her sweet lips, it never sounded like an insult. Or felt like one. "You'll make friends. People love you."

"No, people love *you*. I get the residual affection."

"You're silly. But, if you really want something to worry about, get this. While you were asleep, Mom let it slip on the drive that the school isn't a regular High School. It's a Junior High and High School combined. Not, like, in the same building? But right next door."

She bit a tiny cheese cracker in half and chewed while the meaning sank in.

"So," I said, the horror slowly dawning, "Lydia . . ."

"Same campus. Same clubs. Same everything. Maybe Mom could homeschool us with the little girls?"

"Yeah, because that wasn't a complete waste. We're lucky we can read."

"You can do more than read. School won't be any problem for you, brilliant one. I'm the one with terrible grades."

"You're exaggerating. They aren't *terrible*. And even if they were, nobody would care because you're so beautiful and charming."

"You don't get scholarships for being charming."

"Well, you don't get boyfriends for being smart."

"Then I guess we're doomed to a long life with Mom and Dad. We'll have to put all of our hope in Lydia."

I raised my can of Orange Crush in salute to the idea, then took a long, tepid sip. Might as well enjoy, since Mom's grocery run wouldn't include any sodas or snacks. These were special occasion road-trip food. Soon it would be back to canned vegetables, tuna casseroles, and bun-less burgers—Mom's ideas of healthy family cooking. When the little girls whined for a cookie, she'd tell them such things weren't a part of Elyse's diet. Ah, yes. Elyse's diet. A constant refrain and reminder of every extra pound. None of them were ever *my* diets. I would never willingly subject myself to weeks' worth of cabbage and grapefruit. During the month or so before moving here, I'd lived on nothing but rice cakes, carrots, and Pepsi Light, listening to Mom go on and on about how wonderful it would be for me to start at a new school with a whole new figure. I guess neither of us factored in my old school's cafeteria cheeseburgers and chips.

Jayne and I stayed quiet. Moments like this were such a rare occasion in our household, I think we were both ready to soak in the peace. Then, from out of nowhere, a sound I never expected to hear in Northenfield, Texas. The rumbling car motor, yes, that was common enough, but singing out over it was the sound of an electric guitar. As it came closer, I realized it wasn't just any guitar, but Neal Schon's. As in, Journey, and we were hearing the unmistakable guitar solo of "Don't Stop Believin'." In only a matter of seconds, we could put the music together with a car—Camaro, late seventies model, midnight blue. Sweeter than sweet. And, shock of all shocks, it came to a screeching, rumbling, rocking stop right behind our U-Haul.

There are those moments when you get the opportunity to stop and have a short talk with yourself and say, "*Hey, self! Remember this. Make a note. Get rid of the brain space you're using to remember your lines from the fourth grade play and make room.*"

This was one of those moments.

The music played on to the end of the song, then disappeared when the engine cut. The doors opened, and two boys got out. One looked like sunshine—blond, curly-all-over hair, tall, thin, green IZOD shirt with the collar popped. The boy with him, everything opposite. Dark, straight hair, parted in the middle and feathered to the sides. Jeans, Ramones T-shirt, Converse high tops.

Jayne and I set our soda cans on the Joggling Board and stood up, because it was pretty obvious they were headed to the front porch. The dark one hung back a little, but Preppy Boy took one look at my sister and smiled like a kid who'd found a Transformer under the Christmas tree. A new boyfriend for Jayne? Well, that would be a matter of time, as in 5 . . . 4 . . . 3 . . . 2 . . .

prepossession: *an attitude, belief, or impression formed beforehand : PREJUDICE*

When meeting new people, one must not allow a negative **prepossession** *to color one's opinion; to do so will taint all future interactions.*

ONE OF THE GREAT IRONIES of being the chubby girl on the scene: you literally take up more space than any other person around, and yet you are somehow invisible. To be fair, the minute Charlie Bingley (Green IZOD Shirt Boy) met Jayne Nebbitt, the entire neighborhood could have been swallowed up by muddy underground aliens and neither of them would have noticed a thing. It's like they formed a bubble of true love around themselves, impermeable to nonbelievers. And, by nonbelievers, I mean, of course, me and Billy Fitz.

Yeah, Billy Fitz. If I had it to do all over again, maybe I wouldn't have laughed at his name, but it sounds funny, doesn't it? *Billy Fitz.* Like the way you might describe a goat with seizures. *He's got himself a bad case of the Billy Fitz.* But while I like to think I laughed because his name had that distinctive, funny ring to it, truth is, I laughed because just the sight of this beautiful boy caused my polar extremes of anxiety and poise to collide, tie themselves into a knot, and expel themselves in a distinctly barnyard sound that I tried to pass off as a snorting response to a perfectly fine name.

Anyway, Billy didn't have the same sense of humor, because he looked straight through me—not over me, not around me, but literally *through me*—and said, "Bing. What did you get us into?"

Like my sister and I weren't even there.

"You need the community service points for National Honor Society," Charlie said, never taking his eyes off Jayne. "I'm just here to help out."

"*Helping* implies there are others doing their share of the labor. I don't see anybody else here."

"*We're* here," I said. I wanted to say that I was a shoo-in for National Honor Society, too, but there was still no indication Billy Fitz knew I was standing there. I didn't want to startle him.

"Don't worry about it," Charlie said, his spell still unbroken. "You girls don't lift a finger. We'll get started, you just show us where everything goes."

"You don't think we should wait until Mom and Dad get home?" Jayne is a lot of things, but adventurous isn't one of them.

"Like they'd be a lot of help," I said. In fact, if we hurried, we could get the job done before they even came back.

And so we worked. Keeping priorities straight, we unearthed my boom box and found a Top 40 station to keep the music going. REO Speedwagon, The Cars, Billy Idol—aka everything our father would forbid us to listen to if he were home. The boys were the souls of efficiency, with Charlie motivated to impress Jayne, and Billy motivated to get away. My sister and I helped, too, of course. Jayne knew exactly where every box and chair and lamp should go, so she kept to the front door and foot of the stairs, pointing and directing and encouraging. I was more of a workhorse, running back and forth with whatever I could easily carry. Jayne carried a few things too—throw pillows and candy dishes and such—but she somehow remained perfectly put together, while I sort of disintegrated over the course of the afternoon. By the time the last bed frame came out of the truck, only about half of my hair remained up in my scrunchie, and I could feel a big ol' sweat stain on the back of my T-shirt.

"What do you know?" Charlie said as the four of us stared into the empty truck. "We still have an hour before practice. What do you say we head down to Dairy Queen? My treat."

Before Jayne or I could say anything, Billy piped up. "Not a good idea, I think. Coach will kill us if we're late, especially since we skipped seventh and eighth to come here in the first place."

So he's rude, and a truant?

"Come on, Fitz, there's plenty of—"

"Besides. Everybody from school is going to be there."

That's what he said. What he *didn't* say was that whatever their standing might be in the Northenfield, Texas, social community would be seriously jeopardized if they were to show up with these two outsiders in tow. Jayne, maybe, not so much, but the wild-haired, chubby, sweaty-faced sister? Not a chance.

"It's all right." Jayne jumped in. "We should be here when our parents get back anyway, right, Elyse?"

"Exactly," I said, trying to sound all fresh and breezy.

"All right then," Charlie said. "Are you starting school tomorrow?"

"I think so," Jayne said. "At least I hope so. Nothing else to do, is there?"

"Excellent," Charlie said.

Thus ending their first date, they began a slow stroll back to the house, stranding Billy and me at the foot of the U-Haul ramp.

"So," I said, not at all awkward, "your car. Is that a '79?"

"Seventy-eight."

"Awesome." Topic depleted.

He had a leather fob on his key chain, and he flapped it against his thumb impatiently, keeping his eyes on Jayne and Charlie, who were giggling together while the sun shone its glory upon them.

Not that Billy wasn't beautiful, too. Like, Tom Cruise with a better nose. He ran the hand that wasn't flapping his key chain through his hair, and it all fell magically back into place.

"So," I said, valiantly soldiering on, "any advice for me for starting school tomorrow? Words of wisdom for the new kids?"

He pulled a pair of Ray-Ban Wayfarer sunglasses—yep, Tom Cruise—out of the front pocket of his jeans and put them on before looking at me.

"Be careful who you try to hang out with. In this town, kids have already pretty much decided who their friends are."

Seriously? No (1) "Be yourself"; (2) "Check the bulletin board for clubs"; (3) "I'll introduce you to the school welcome council." Or even, "Hey, come sit at my table at lunch." Nothing but a warning?

"Duly noted. So, Charlie said something about practice? You guys play football?"

"Yep."

Apparently some invisible person in the branches above my head had also asked a question, because that's where he directed his answer. A lesser mortal might have given up on the art of communication by now, but not me. There are simple, if unwritten, codes for behavior that create acceptable conversation, and Billy Fitz wasn't following any of them. He wasn't going to get away with that on my front lawn.

"I hear High School football is like a religion here. Is that true?"

"Nope. Religion is like religion here. Football is football."

"Insightful," I said, and he gave the littlest shake of his head, like I'd gotten to him. I had a distinct feeling that Billy Fitz wasn't used to being the victim of even the tiniest dig. "What position do you play?"

Now he looked down at me and folded his arms. Even with the Ray-Bans between us, I sensed real eye contact. "What do you know about football?"

"I know you have the puny build of a running back and the arrogance of a quarterback. So, one of those. Am I right?"

His top lip did this flicker thing, not quite to Elvis proportions, but close. I chose to log it as a smile and tried not to die.

"Quarterback."

Should have had money on it. "What about Charlie?"

"Kicker. He actually plays soccer."

I looked over my shoulder at Young Love and First Love. "My sister used to play soccer too."

And then, in perfect unison, Billy Fitz and I both said, "Figures."

It was like scoring some sort of victory, and I would have made more of a fuss about it, but right then our blue Country Squire Station Wagon turned the corner, and long before she pulled it into the driveway, Mom was hanging out the window and saying *Hellooooo* in a way that can only be described as tootling.

Charlie was off the porch like a shot, at the ready to open the car door for Mom and introduce himself as she stepped out. She repeated his name three times, like she was running it through some sort of computer program, and then asked if his family wasn't the same family whose name appeared on several car dealerships we'd passed on our way into town.

"That's my father's company, yes," Charlie said.

You've seen that cartoon where the fat guy and the skinny

guy are stranded on a desert island and the fat guy imagines the skinny guy is a hot dog?

Charlie Bingley = skinny guy.

Mom was still licking her lips when she zeroed in on Billy Fitz and made her way down the driveway, her purse dangling from her extended arm, asking who this might be?

"That's my friend Billy," Charlie said, right by her side. "Billy Fitz."

She called him *Charming Billy*, as in that stupid old song, and if that wasn't enough, she started in on who were his parents and what did they do/own. Never mind that he was obviously uncomfortable, fidgeting with his key chain and looking at the ground.

Finally, I said, "Mom!" hoping that would be enough to make her stop. I looked to Jayne for support, but she just gave me this helpless shrug. Adorable. Useless, but adorable.

"It's okay," Billy said, clenching his keys in his fist. "My dad is a computer systems analyst."

Mom made a sound that meant she was impressed.

"He's not living here right now, though. He's got a three-year gig at Oxford."

"As in, England?" I said, obviously hoping to impress him with my grasp of geography.

Mom made a sound that meant she was still impressed, but sad. Because it must be so hard on his mother—

"Yeah. Well, not too hard. She's dead."

Mom clucked, and I swear was about to say something along the lines of *poor baby*. Luckily, Charlie spoke up. "He practically lives with us. We're like brothers. Unofficially."

"Speaking of which," I said, hoping to bring about conversational rescue, "where are the other girls?" Normally, I wouldn't care, but hey, it changed the subject.

Turns out Mom had left them at the store, with the groceries, because Safeway wouldn't take an out-of-state check. That meant each of us would have to empty our purses for whatever cash we had to contribute. Not at all embarrassing.

"We'll leave you to that," Charlie said, though for a moment I was terrified he would volunteer to chip in.

The three of us stood on the porch, waving, as Journey blared through the open window with the roaring of the Camaro's engine. Mom did that smiling-out-of-the-side-of-her-mouth thing, saying something about expecting better manners from a half-orphaned abandoned child. I gave her the fourteen dollars and fifty-eight cents I had in my wallet and went upstairs to start unpacking.

Minutes later, Jayne joined me, and we dug into the first box, labeled SCHOOL SUPPLIES. Notebooks and binders and a big plastic box full of pens and pencils and such.

"I hope we have everything we'll need for tomorrow," Jayne said, with the nerve to look nervous.

"What are you worried about? You already have someone to carry your books and walk you from class to class. Five more minutes on the porch and you would have had your hand in his back pocket."

"Stop it." She threw a stuffed panda for emphasis. "He was just being friendly. Texas is the friendship state, you know."

"Well, nobody told *his* friend."

She made a frowny face. "Sorry. But you heard what he said. I feel bad for him. He's cute, though. Maybe after you get to know him a little bit—"

"Forget it. I have a hard enough time with *nice* guys."

"I'm sure he's nice deep down."

"Like, Australia, maybe."

She found the box with our bedding and began unloading and unfolding sheets and blankets.

"Well, this will cheer you up. We happen to have arrived

during Homecoming week. And we're invited to the dance this Friday night."

I tucked a sheet around the corner of a mattress. "We're here ten minutes and you already have a date?"

"Not *me*, silly. *We*."

"Like, me and Billy?"

How I hated the little bit of hope that worked its way into the question, when I was trying so hard for casual, like, whatever. Even worse was the tiny bit of pity when Jayne said, "No, not exactly. *We*, as in the family."

Okay, maybe *that* was worse.

"It seems," she explained, "since everybody in town went to this High School, Homecoming is for the masses. They all go to the game, and the dance after is in the city square. They have a band and everything."

"So, the little girls, too?"

"Yes."

"And Lydia?"

"Yes." A bit less enthusiasm.

"Dad will never go for it."

"Mom will insist. And she'll go on and on until he decides he doesn't care, and then he'll give in and we can go."

Her bed was made already, and she'd flopped down on it, with her feet kicked up to the ceiling. I knew her head was full of strings of twinkly lights and stars and blond curls.

I sat on the edge of my own, still-unmade bed. "I'll start working on my pleading right away."

Jayne flipped to her stomach. "Thanks! And you'll have fun too. You'll see."

"I don't know about that." Then another thought came into my mind too horrible to contemplate. The fear must have shown on my face.

"What is it, Pudge?"

"Mom. You know she's going to wear the go-go boots."

Jayne knew enough to look a little frightened herself. "She wouldn't. It's a street dance, country music, probably."

"Oh, she will."

"Don't be ridiculous. Of course she won't."

deportment: *the manner in which one conducts oneself :*
BEHAVIOR

The youngest Nebbitt sister's deportment *was an*
embarrassment to the entire family.

OF COURSE SHE DID.

But that didn't happen until Friday, after our first half
week at Northenfield Texas High School, home of the Mighty
Fighting Badgers. And how pathetic is it when your mother's
white patent-leather, square-heeled go-go boots are almost the
highlight of the week?

Meanwhile, we begin with Wacky Wednesday.

There really ought to be some sort of rule against enroll-
ing new students during a school's Homecoming, especially if
said school indulges in theme-dressing throughout the week.
For our Badger debut, Lydia, Jayne, and I opted to go neutral, with jeans and polo shirts and Reeboks. Jayne's hair was
swept up in its perfect feathers, Lydia's was a shining mass of
copper spirals, and my own dark tresses were contained in a
purple scrunchie. For all of our efforts, we were rewarded with
the distinction of looking like freaks, because everybody else—
like, even the teachers and the middle-aged woman working
the front office counter—was decked out in wackiness. Girls

wore plaid skirts with polka-dot tops and mismatched socks and shoes; boys wore their pants inside out and their grand-fathers' Hawaiian shirts and oversized sombreros. We stood out like well-manicured thumbs.

And so it was in every class—finding a desk, moving because it was someone else's desk, the teacher's introduction to a disin-terested class. At least that was my experience. No doubt Jayne was immediately folded into a lab group in chemistry and invited to read the role of Laura Wingfield in the class study of *The Glass Menagerie*. In the middle school wing, Lydia was probably jump-starting the puberty of every boy she passed in the hall.

I, meanwhile, walked into a timed writing in my AP English class (a deconstruction of Thomas Moore), a battle with my Trigonometry teacher (yes, even though I'm a Sophomore, I'm in the right class), and I don't even want to think about PE again until some future therapist insists I do so.

The first friendly face came in World History where they were working in groups creating maps of tyrannical conquest. I was ushered straight to the group assigned Attila the Hun, and that's where I met Lottie and Collin.

Lottie—short for Charlotte—was a sweet girl with thick glasses (like, really thick, not joke-thick for Wacky Wednesday) who immediately shook my hand, expressed great excitement that I came with my own set of colored pencils, and invited me to join her and Collin for lunch. Collin embraced the wackiness of the day by wearing a red clown wig, mismatched Nikes, and what I presumed to be his mother's nightgown.

"I'll have to check with my sister," I said.

"Oh, she's welcome to join us too." That was the end of chitchat; Lottie was all about the work, and for the remaining forty-five minutes, I could believe that moving here might not be the worst thing that ever happened to us.

So, Lottie was the first friendly face. The most familiar face belonged to none other than Billy Fitz in battleground Trigonometry. His Wednesday wackiness consisted of an inside-out shirt, plaid golf pants, and white suede loafers. The shoes, actually, were kind of awesome.

"So, tell me," I said, sliding into the desk across the aisle from him, "how much am I going to regret this?"

"Depends on how smart you are." He was tapping his pencil on the corner of his notebook.

"I was pulling a B back home, but the teacher was close to retirement, so maybe he wasn't as invested? This guy seems intense. Is he? Like, are there tutorials if we need—"

"You know what really helps?"

He was leaning way over, beckoning me close to whisper. That's when I noticed he had flecks of gray in his blue eyes. "What?"

"Not talking while he's trying to teach. Why don't you try that for a while?"

The two kids in front of us snickered, and I think my face turned as pink as my polo. I opened my cat-in-a-field-of-daisies spiral to the next clean page and dove into the problem the teacher was working on the board.

On Throwaway Thursday we were supposed to wear our oldest, most worn-out, outgrown, full-of-holes, trashy items. Not a problem for the Nebbitt sisters, as Mom made us keep absolutely everything until it had been passed down and worn by the youngest sister, although Lydia did need a quick tutorial on the different meanings of the word *trashy*. Old T-shirt? Acceptable. Jeans ripped just below the back pockets? Not. Thursday was also the day I aced a Trigonometry quiz, opened my locker on the first try, and discovered that Collin, with his long strands of greasy black hair, was marginally less creepy in a clown wig.

Finally, Friday.

A new sound joined the usual buzz of the hallowed halls of Northenfield Texas High School—a tinkling of bells like dozens of newborn angels or a wandering herd of tiny cows. These were attached to enormous flowers—like, chrysanthemums the size of a human face—strewn with ribbons and streamers floating down to the human shin. The ribbons bore the school name written in puffy glitter glue and were festooned with tiny charms and bells and buttons. These, for the non-Texan, are called "Homecoming Mums," and the girls wore them with swaggering pride. Well, sometimes staggering pride, especially when the ribbons got caught up in their Nikes. Cheerleaders dressed in uniform, football players in jerseys, and all other Badgers in black and purple. Class time was cut in half to accommodate an hour-long Pep Rally, pregame tailgate barbecue, and a mad dash for seats two hours before game time.

Jayne and I gladly bore the burden of representing the entire Nebbitt family at the game, Lydia being far more interested in getting ready for the dance and neither of my parents having ever watched a game on TV. We sat alone, since Lottie was with the Pep Squad (more about that later) and Collin was in the band, but eventually the seats around us filled. We cheered when everybody cheered, jeered when they jeered, and I think I might have scored a few potential friendship points by explaining the Neutral Zone Infraction call to the group of girls from my English class who had yet to say a single word to me. And while we didn't exactly participate in the conversations, I don't think we were total outcasts.

That didn't happen until the dance.

Here's the scene: hundreds of happy Texans, awash with joy over a hard-won victory, gathered in a roped-off parking lot in front of a white-domed courthouse. A flatbed trailer served as a stage for a five-piece band made up of two science teachers, a custodian, an assistant principal, and some guy on slide guitar.

What Charlie had told Jayne about the family atmosphere was right—little kids and old people milled around, ringing cowbells and dragging coolers. The crowd was small enough to see everyone but big enough to get lost in, and I concentrated on the latter, knowing Mom and Dad and the Littles might be showing up any minute.

The whole town might be invited, but there was definitely an area designated for us, the kids, the subjects of the crowned King (Charlie Bingley, no less) and Queen, a girl named Katie Berg wearing the world's most carefully engineered strapless royal purple gown. Here we mingled and here Jayne danced, putting to good use everything we learned from watching a secretly rented copy of *Urban Cowboy* one night last year when Mom and Dad were out at a Property Management wingding. She two-stepped, she waltzed, she Cotton-Eyed-Joe'd with a host of different boys, but most often with Charlie.

Lydia made the rounds, too, wearing her tightest jeans and a Badger T-shirt (I'm still at a loss as to how it came into her possession) custom tailored, having been shredded into beaded fringe just above the waist.

Me? I sat on the low brick wall bordering the courthouse lawn and listened, toes-a-tappin'. Lottie sat with me, explaining bits and pieces of Northenfield town lore. Like the slow-burning Sonic/Dairy Queen rivalry for Friday night teenage patrons and the underground movement among the students to work shorts into the dress code and the scandal that had rocked the town to its core when she was in seventh grade.

"It was his father," she said, leaning in close so I could hear. *His* father was Billy Fitz's father. No need to name names, because I must have been staring at him for at least two songs. He was standing with a group of football players, all of them wearing clean jerseys and 501 jeans, but he was the only one who didn't look like he was celebrating. Even though, off in the distance, you could clearly see the scoreboard still shining a 17-point victory, he stood apart, one hand in his pocket, the other holding a root beer.

"What scandal?"

"This woman in town was hopelessly in love with Mr. Fitz and couldn't handle his rejection."

"Before or after his mom died?"

Lottie looked at me admiringly. "So, you *do* know a few things! Been doing homework on the local hero? Do you like him?"

I rolled my eyes, hoping to communicate, *Are you kidding?* "I've never met anyone who was such a perfect combination of *Cute*, *Jerk*, and *Jock*."

"Don't forget *Rich*," Lottie said.

"Well, maybe that explains the other three."

The band was playing a song called "Crying My Heart Out Over You," and the dance floor had been whittled down to a bunch of old people who could dance to such mournful music. All of us kids were getting restless, but when the final sad note drifted away, the drummer clicked his sticks above his head, counting off *One! Two! One-two-three!* and the singer—I swear, next year, when I take Physics, I will see always and only this image—Mr. Eaton, belted out, "*Just take those old records off the shelf!*"

A cheer went up among my generation, and the dance floor flooded with kids—coupled and not—to celebrate the miracle of old-time rock 'n' roll. Lottie and I weren't exactly part of the tide, but we did hop down from the wall and sort of move, I guess, in a quasi-rhythmic way. The crowd of football players, too, had dispersed, save for Charlie—who now held Jayne's hand—and Billy. In a none-too-subtle gesture, Charlie pointed over towards me, obviously trying to convince Billy to ask me to dance. Billy's feelings about such were equally obvious. He shook his head, shook it harder, then turned and walked away.

"I guess that's a big fat no," I said to Lottie, who had watched the whole thing beside me.

"I wouldn't take it to heart. Girls put so much emphasis on boys and what they think, always wanting this boy or that, like having a boyfriend is the most important thing that will ever happen to them in High School."

"Let me introduce you to my mother sometime," I said. "I'd love to see you two debate the issue."

"Oh, don't get me wrong. I think it's great to have a guy to go to movies with and such, but there's no use mooning around over the captain of the football team when there are plenty of other perfectly suitable boys out there willing to share their popcorn and buy you an Ocean Water."

"Suitable, as in Collin?" The kid himself was slinking his way in our direction, beckoning Lottie for a dance with his long, bony fingers.

"Better than standing forever on the sidelines." She set her soda can on the wall and went to join Igor, leaving me alone.

Realistically, I know there were a few eyes in the crowd not focused on me, but it didn't feel that way at the time. I put on a brave face, singing along with the band like I was at a concert, and figured I'd blend in and blend away with the exiting dancers as soon as the song ended. Jayne took a second to send me a piteous glance, which I laughed off like, *Hey, no big deal*, and I thought for a moment the Nebbitt family might survive its first social outing with a modicum of dignity. That's when the crowd parted—well, not parted, exactly—but formed a big circle, and in the middle of the circle a couple was dancing like nobody was watching. Or like everybody was. The guy was decked out in a cowboy shirt, Wranglers, and boots, and while he was technically dancing, meaning he was moving in some sort of orbit around his partner, it was the girl who garnered all the attention. She was bouncing and spinning and—okay, no other word for it—*writhing*, all encouraged by the guitar's solo. Her face was obscured by a mass of long, curly hair, but nobody was looking at her face. Only that body—every move enhanced by a swirl of her shredded, beaded T-shirt.

Oh, Lydia.

There was still a chance that we could escape total humiliation. Nobody knew her, nobody knew us, nobody could play a Bob Seger song forever. But then, out of the crowd, wearing his blue polyester pants and favorite Christian T-shirt (a crossword puzzle, shaped like a cross that spelled "Jesus, answer" in the boxes), Dad walked right up to my sister, gently took her by the upper arm, and spoke to her, something like telling her it was time to go.

She looked mortified, her partner looked terrified, and I couldn't decide whether I should just be happy that at least nobody was paying attention to me. The couples filled in the void left by my sister's gyrations. In the silence after the final chord, Dad found both Jayne and me, raised his hand, and shouted that it was time for all of us to go home.

importune: *to press or urge with troublesome persistence*

Once stranded, Jayne's only hope of survival was to importune *her sister for rescue.*

TWO WEEKS AND SIX DAYS LATER—Thursday night, right during the first fifteen minutes of *Family Ties*—the phone rang, and Mom answered it. Nothing extraordinary there—Mom almost always answers the phone. It's easier that way, for all of us. Otherwise, we'd spend the first five minutes of every conversation letting her know exactly who was on the other side of the line and what they wanted. Plus, *Family Ties* was one of the few shows that met with parental approval *and* had a cute actor. No ringing telephone could compete with Michael J. Fox, not even in Lydia's anticipating ears.

Still, when we heard Mom's long, lyrical *Hellooooo, Mrs. Bingley*, Jayne and I tore our eyes away from the Keatons on the screen. Mom walked out of the kitchen, stretching the yellow phone cord all the way into the living room, and mouthed *MRS. BINGLEY*, as if the neighbors three doors down didn't hear just who had dialed our number a few minutes before.

I muted the TV, grateful for the first time in my life that I had no such option for my mother. Still, her side of the conversation was too cryptic for true comprehension, even if its volume made me wonder if she somehow thought Mrs. Bingley was deaf. Or ninety. Or both. All Jayne and I heard was, Yes, Yes, Of course, Indeed, and a finale about something being our pleasure before Mom scuttled into the kitchen, hung up the phone, and returned with an expression that could only be described as triumphant.

Jayne, it seemed, through the powers of Mom's compliant negotiations, had a babysitting job.

Now, I must explain that for girls like us, meaning girls without access to a family's unlimited credit card, babysitting jobs are the absolute key to functioning normally within our society. Movie tickets, new jeans, cassette tapes, magazines, lip gloss—all those things cost money, and until you're old enough to snag a paper hat and make shakes at Dairy Queen, that money comes from sacrificing the occasional weekend to take care of somebody's kid.

It's a delicate thing, being new in town. Establishing clients, building trust. It's one of the best reasons to go to church, so you can hang around the nursery looking trustworthy. Or a girl can take a stroll around the neighborhood, chase a ball that some kid kicks into the street, return it with a smile, and hope a parent pokes a head out the door for an introduction.

But there are rules. One being that you don't babysit the younger siblings of your friends, because that just reinforces the fact that you need money more than your friend does, because otherwise, well, why isn't *she* babysitting? And Two, you really, really don't babysit the younger sibling of a cute boy. One that you like. And one who might possibly like you back. Now, I—of course—have never had the opportunity to put this rule to the test, and it was too late to bring Mom up to speed on the delicacies of booking.

As if all of this wasn't enough to justify the look of horror on

Jayne's face, Mom's further explanation had us clutching each other's hands for support. To spare anyone the inconvenience of shuttling back and forth to deliver the girl, Jayne would ride the bus—the BUS—to the Bingleys' house after school the next day. And stay there for the entire afternoon and evening.

We might not have been the richest kids in school, but we were lucky enough to live within walking distance, sparing us the daily humiliation of climbing those steep steps of shame to be hauled back and forth on some dilapidated yellow monster vehicle. The bus was for kids who had neither the car nor connection to get a ride.

"I'll go for you," I offered, ready to spare my sister shame on all levels. "I'll even let you take the money." We did that a lot, splitting the pay for an evening's work.

But Mom butted into our negotiations, stating that Mrs. Bingley had asked for Jayne specifically. Figures. They always wanted Jayne. Probably looked at me and worried I'd spend too much of the evening raiding the fridge.

"It's Friday night," I said, still speaking on my shocked sister's behalf. "There's a game, and we were going to go. You know, trying to fit in. Make friends, all that stuff?"

Total waste of words, though, because Mom had given hers.

Finally, Jayne found her voice. "Can't I please just take the car? It's so much easier if I can drive myself there and back. That way nobody has to be bothered—"

Here Dad piped up, surprising us as he always did whenever he showed a bit of interest in our lives. On this occasion, he served up a sober reminder that Jayne didn't have a Texas driver's license, and that we didn't have a car to spare, and that he was far more interested in how the TV family would unravel their conflict, seeing how ours seemed to be settled.

The next day, in the midst of a sea of students decked out in Northenfield Texas High School purple, I watched my beautiful sister climb onto BUS #38, helpless to do anything to rescue her. She found a seat near the front and looked out/down at me with such a forlorn expression I was tempted to climb up with her—to be someone to talk to if nothing else. At that moment, though, the bus spewed a fume-filled cloud of black smoke around me. By the time my vision and lungs cleared, she was gone, as were most of the kids. Gone to their cars, or to the Pizza Hut to have dinner before the game, or to the stadium/band hall/locker room to prepare for their role in the evening's entertainment.

So I walked home.

Lydia lagged about half a block behind me, and I could hear her giggling with the two Freshman boys who'd been flirted into carrying her books. These were smart, non-football connected kids who would spend the rest of the afternoon doing her homework on our front porch. Unable to listen to yet another "*Algebra? As if . . .*" I took my Walkman out of my backpack and put my headphones over my ears. The cassette inside was The Go-Go's, and I listened to the squeal of the tape rewinding to my favorite song. It fit the moment, lyrics about kids getting out of school, though I had no hope of hanging out and being cool. The steady thrum of empowered women pounded in my ears. *We got the beat. We got the beat.* I thought of poor Jayne—no beat, there. Shuttled off to assured humiliation. And Lydia behind me, giggling like a stupid twit, when I knew very well she needed attention more than tutoring. Leaving me. The cheese stands alone. Well, walks alone.

It was Friday night. Friday night at home with Mom and Dad and two little sisters. Three, counting Lydia, who was sulking in her room—grounded for another dress code violation at school. Friday night, when every other normal person was sitting, or standing, or cheering, or marching, or playing on a football field. In a particularly cruel twist, I could actually hear the sound of the game—the band, the crowd, the announcer. That last one, not perfectly. Like when you're almost out of radio range and the words keep going in and out. But the sharp staccato of the drum line was crystal clear.

But, hey. Who needs peer group camaraderie when you've got Friday Night with Mom and Dad? Hours and hours of it, stretching out longer than that long, long couch—the one not *quite* long enough to hold everybody, so you end up with part of your butt slipped between the cushions. Who needs a greasy bag of yellow popcorn when you have your mom's special snack of Ritz and Cheez Whiz? Who needs to watch a cute boy in tight pants run like something beautiful on a green field when you can watch the latest slap-fight in evening gowns on *Dallas*?

Now, I could have gone. Dad even asked—with that tilted head look of concern that he gets—if I was sure I didn't want to go. *Hang out with the kids? Be with your friends?* But it wouldn't be a lot of fun without Jayne, and the two friends I'd made at school—Lottie and Collin—wouldn't be able to sit with me in the stands. Lottie was in Pep Squad, what the popular kids called the Cheer-Sitters, meaning she was allowed to wear a cute uniform and paint her face and sit with other Cheer-Sitters in the stands and wave pom-poms wildly in support of the Cheer-Leaders on the field. And Collin was in band, fulfilling his role as a euphonium phenom.

And so I was sitting on our butt-pinching couch watching two women with big, shiny dresses throw things at each other in their bigger, shinier houses when the phone rang. Mom muttered through her Ritz-Whiz and hoisted herself up from the couch, only it didn't ring again. She came back and was in the middle of voicing the ingenious observation that it must have been a wrong number when it rang again. Twice, then silent. Then again.

"Want me to get it?" I asked, because I had pretty good idea who might be on the other end.

Dad, ever my protector, decided if there was some nut job making prank calls, he'd give him a what-for. He got one foot in the kitchen by the third ring, and then it stopped.

Bingo.

The phone stayed silent after that, and I bided my time until a commercial aired, when I announced an urgent need to go to the bathroom. I ran upstairs to the telephone in the hallway after a quick stop in my room to grab the Strawberry Shortcake address book where Jayne had recorded the Bingleys' phone number in her perfectly rounded script. Technically, it is listed as *Mrs. Bingley*, a babysitting contact, but *Charlie* is written right beneath it in heart-shaped parentheses.

One ring, and Jayne answered, "Hello? Bingley residence."

"It's me."

"Oh, Elyse. Thank goodness. I need you to get over here. Now."

"Well, all right-y." As if that was even a remote possibility.

"I'm se-se-se—" And then as close to explosive a sneeze as our Jayne can get. "Serious."

"Ah," I said, understanding. "They have a cat."

"Thr-thr-thr—"

I assumed she'd eventually get to *three*. I lowered my voice to the timbre of a *Dallas* villain. "And just what do you want me to do with these cats, dear sister? You know animal cruelty is a crime in this state."

"It's not just the cats. This girl, the little sister? She's a beast." At this point her voice muffled as she put her hand over the mouthpiece, saying, "No, Caroline. For the last time, we are not watching *Miami Vice*. I don't care how cute Don Johnson is." Then back to me. "So? Come over? Help me with this kid?"

"That depends. Can we watch *Miami Vice*?"

She answered with a sneeze. "As long as I don't have to be in the room with her or the c-c-cat*sssss*."

"One last thing, oh evil genius sister. Wait, make that two. How am I supposed to get out of here? And how am I supposed to get over there?"

"Don't say anything. It's Friday night. *Falcon Crest* and the one night they stay up late to watch *Nightline*. Just kiss 'em good night, go upstairs and-and-and—"

"Out the window? And, *Gesundheit*."

"That's what the tree is for, right?"

"Are you giving me big-sister permission to sneak out and *lie* to our parents?" Normally, Jayne took her responsibility of setting a good example very seriously.

"Just this once. You know how they are. Tell them I'm sneezing and Mom will come over with a humidifier or something and scream at Mrs. Bingley for having a house amok with allergens."

It was a scenario too probable to ignore.

"So how am I going to get there? Steal the car?" I was only half joking.

A silence—a little too long—and then she said, "It's not *that* far."

"Oh no." Because I knew exactly what she was thinking. "I can't ride the bike there."

The bike, known in our family as the Two-Wheeled Monster. One of the blessed few of Dad's projects ever to achieve functionality. He'd built it from parts picked up at yard sales and— so help me, I'm serious—Spring Cleaning trash heaps. When we complained, he said we'd get a new one as soon as we biked a hundred miles on his hard labor, at which point he produced a little log book and attached it to the handlebar with a neon green pipe cleaner.

"You'll log on five more miles. At least."

"What do you care? You have a driver's license. You don't need a bike."

"Elyse, please. Please! You should see this house. I know she's going to pay at least twenty-five dollars. It's yours, every bit of it. Just—*No, Caroline. We are not going to play with your mommy's makeup*—seriously. Save me?"

Nobody can say no to Jayne, so I tore a page from the *X*s in the address book, scribbled down the directions, and looked up, straight into Lydia's eyes.

"Don't say a word," I said, with all the big-sister authority I could muster.

Ten minutes later, I'd kissed Mom and Dad good night, planning to allay their suspicions by saying I was bummed about missing the game and just wanted to go to my room when a weird twinge of conscience pricked me, and I decided to give truth a fighting chance.

"Mom? Dad? I just realized I'm supposed to help Jayne with something. Would it be okay if I rode the Monster over to Bingleys'? It's not far."

The brilliance of this particular jab at truth is that I spoke it right when two women in heavy makeup were on the TV, fighting each other in their poufy evening gowns. Honestly? I don't even know if my parents heard the question, or if the vague gesture Dad offered was one of permission or not. But I'd done my daughterly duty, and they didn't say no. Still, I wasn't going to call attention to myself by leaving through the front door.

Ignoring the possibility of a broken neck or torn jeans, I successfully crawled out of our bedroom window and down the sprawling oak growing too close to our house. Dad had declared the thing was a threat to our plumbing and that the first thing on his agenda was to dig it up. Knowing his follow-through, I figure the littlest sister will be doing the same thing to sneak out and meet her boyfriend in 1998.

We keep the Monster parked at the side of the house, unchained, in hopes that somebody poorer than us will eventually pedal it away. This might have been the first time I'd ever been happy to see it waiting for me. I threw my leg over the patched-up banana seat and grasped the mismatched handlebars. According to Jayne's directions, it shouldn't be more than a twenty-minute ride.

Once out of view of the house, I turned on the blinking safety lights attached to the front and back and switched on the little transistor radio attached to the purple woven basket. With a few twists of the dial, I found a station playing a decent song and turned up the volume loud enough to drown out the sounds of the game.

The air was almost cool as I rode, but not so much that I wished for a jacket or anything. In just a few minutes I was out of our neighborhood and pedaling past a long strip of shops—Dry Cleaners, Kinko's, Doughnuts and Sandwiches—none of which were open. Cyndi Lauper's "Time after Time" came on the radio, and I sang aloud.

I considered it an anthem to my sister, and in moments of pure silliness we'd sing it out loud to each other, confirming our solidarity through pop music. We would look for each other; we would find each other. Sometimes it seemed we were caught in some kind of alternate existence—given to the wrong family, victims of some cruel brain transplant that made us so different from our siblings. And our family made us so very different from anyone around us. Not just because we were poor; I knew lots of poor kids with perfectly normal parents. But because we were weird. Bohemian gypsies with the social graces of goats, never wanting to invite friends over lest that be the day Mom decided to see if all of her go-go dancing outfits still fit (they didn't), or Dad felt like recruiting everybody into an impromptu reading of *The Taming of the Shrew*. (That happened once.)

Once I got past the strip mall, the houses got larger—brick facades and well-groomed lawns. Little lights lining the walkways. I stopped singing and concentrated on the street signs, turning left on Netherfield. The porch light was on at 75817. I walked the Monster up the drive and stashed it behind the bushes before ringing the bell.

"Oh, you're a lifesaver," Jayne said the minute she opened the door.

She was bathed in a golden light from inside the house, and I immediately felt unworthy to walk in, and probably wouldn't have if she hadn't grabbed my sleeve and yanked me over the threshold.

Never before did I know a house could smell pretty. *Good*, maybe, if there were cookies in the oven, or *clean* if someone had just finished a mop job with Lysol, but *pretty*? It was like the whole place was perfumed.

"Come on." Her voice echoed, even though it was little more than a whisper. Jayne ushered me through a broad, bare entry hall, and then into a living room—sunken—with carpet that felt like clouds beneath my Reeboks. The furniture looked like something in a magazine or a TV show—everything matching. No piles of laundry, no Fisher-Price toys, no unfinished books or forgotten school projects or tall plastic glasses full of abandoned Coke. The television sat deep inside the wall, with folding doors on either side. On the screen, two men dressed in pale suits were running and jumping into a convertible before squealing away to synthesized music. *Miami Vice*.

"You caved?"

Jayne shrugged. "She said her mom lets her watch all the time, so who am I to say?"

"And where are the filthy Beasts of Benadryl?"

"Laundry room."

At the sound of our voices, the little girl sitting enraptured by the images on the screen turned around. She was dressed in pink, frilly pajamas, her hair in one thick braid down her back. Pretty, I guess, until she scowled and said, "Do you mind? Some of us are watching."

"So that's the other beast?" I spoke out of the side of my mouth, but well within hearing.

Jayne hushed me too and said, "This is my younger sister, Elyse."

"Why is *she* here?"

"Just to keep me company."

In this light I could see Jayne's reddened eyes and nose and reached into my backpack.

"Here," I said, slipping her the small bottle from our medicine cabinet.

"Are those diet pills?" the beast, Caroline, asked.

"No!" We spoke in unison, but Jayne continued. "They're allergy pills. I'm allergic to cats." Then she popped two in her mouth and swallowed.

"*You* should take diet pills," Caroline said, looking straight at me.

I wanted to say that she should take silent pills, or something equally clever, but she'd already turned her face back to the TV, and I'd have to battle for her attention.

"Come on," Jayne said, taking my arm in hers. "Let's go into the kitchen. Tons of snacks."

I followed, loving my sister for not thinking I needed to take diet anything.

Only one word can describe the Bingleys' kitchen: *perfect*.

The floor was cleaner than most of our dishes, the counter-tops wide and shiny and free of unopened mail and school field trip permission slips. Crumbless toaster. Crystal bowl full of brightly colored fruit. On the downside, according to the Bingley refrigerator, Charlie and Caroline had never colored a picture or gotten a gold star on a single school assignment, nor had the Bingleys ever been to any interstate truck stops. But all of that could be forgiven after opening that freakishly uncluttered door.

There, in neat rows, was every kind of soda can imaginable, all lined up and categorized. Jayne grabbed one for each of us, along with a couple of big, juicy apples from the bottom drawer. Then she opened the side freezer to reveal an entire shelf stacked with frozen pizzas, alphabetized by toppings.

"Unbelievable," I said through one juicy bite.

"It's all so civilized, isn't it? Look, even the Tupperware is labeled. *Roast pork. September 5. Eat by October 31.*"

"What fun is that? How would anyone ever win the 'Guess that Meat' game?"

Jayne wrinkled her nose indulgently before pulling out the third pizza from the top. "Thick crust cheese?"

I agreed, and we both took on the task of preheating the oven. This stove had more buttons and knobs than every appliance in our house combined. Satisfied we weren't in danger of blowing up the place, we dialed up the desired temperature and were opening the box when we heard the sound of the front door opening, followed by Caroline's squeal of delight.

coach-and-four: *a coach with four horses designed for three passengers*

The additional passengers made the journey in the coach-and-four *stifling and uncomfortable.*

"High five!"

Charlie Bingley stood in the middle of his living room, palm raised in the air as his little sister jumped in vain to slap it, squealing, "Too high! Too high!"

Billy Fitz was with him, and after making a sound like a bear, he scooped the little girl up and lifted her to within high-fiving range. Then, still holding her, he held up his own hand for a slap before setting her, giggling, down.

In summary: bratty Caroline Bingley is the luckiest girl alive. Case closed.

"Did you win? Did you win?" She was all prancing, simpering, as if the spirit of Rebecca of Sunnybrook Farm had suddenly invaded her body.

"Of course we won," Charlie said, smiling as big as a goalpost. "Was there ever any doubt?"

"The other guys never stood a chance." This was Billy, in a moment of unguarded joy. He'd lowered himself to Caroline's height, and punctuated the word *chance* with a bop of his finger on her nose.

To review: luckiest girl, ever.

"Well, of course they stood a chance." This, *this* is how I chose to insert myself into the conversation. We'd been standing by, completely unnoticed in the wake of Caroline's newly discovered impishness. At my comment, four sets of eyes—the cute, the gorgeous, the little, the sisterly—all *whooshed* in my direction. Charlie looked amused, Jayne mortified, and I fully expected little Caroline's head to start spinning and spewing at any minute.

But Billy. He cocked his head back in challenge, and so doing, flipped his still-damp bangs out of his eyes. "What do you mean by that?"

"Well . . ." I looked to Jayne for help. Total waste of time. "I just mean that, you're a High School football team, right? Playing another High School football team. In that alone, there's some expectation that you will be equally matched."

"Are you aware that their starting lineup consists primarily of Sophomores? That they don't have a single Senior playing on their entire team?"

"No, but—"

"Or that none of their players weighs more than two hundred pounds?"

"Well, how could I—"

"Did you spend five hours last week locked in a room with a bunch of football players watching the video of every game they've played so far this season to pinpoint their weaknesses?"

"Nobody invited me."

This reply surprised him, and I think he might have actually laughed if the timer on the oven hadn't beeped.

"What's that?" Charlie asked, his attention whipping toward the kitchen like a puppy presented with a new sock.

Jayne turned and started walking toward the kitchen, speaking over her shoulder. "I hope you don't mind, we cooked a pizza. I know it's late, but we hadn't eaten—"

"Mind?" Charlie zoomed past me, practically knocking me down like some poor underweight lineman.

That left Billy, Caroline, and me. A cozy little trio. Little Miss Lucky had wrapped her whole body around Billy's letterman jacket arm.

"We usually go out to eat with the guys after the game," Billy said, sounding oddly apologetic. "But tonight, *for some reason*, Charlie wanted to come straight home after we showered up."

I forced the image of Billy Fitz in the shower straight out of my mind, because I didn't want to melt all over the Bingleys' pristine white carpet. *The Reason*, he and I both knew, was Jayne, and we could hear the sound of the two of them laughing and mangling the lyrics to Duran Duran's "Hungry Like the Wolf." In fact, when we walked in, Charlie was holding a gravy ladle like a microphone, the sleeves of his letterman jacket pushed up to his elbows, his hair worked into a ridiculous spike, singing,

> *The pizza is round, my stomach is loud*
> *Because I'm Hungry Like a Wooooolf.*

Normally, it is my pettest peeve to hear people destroy song lyrics. Like, if you don't know the words? Just hum for effect. But now Charlie was crouching on the kitchen floor, prowling around just like Simon Le Bon in the video, and we all laughed. Even Billy, a little.

"Well," I said, because I am apparently incapable of allowing myself—or anyone else—to simply enjoy a good time, "I guess since you guys are home, you can watch the kid? We can go."

"Go?" Charlie leaped right out of character. "Why go? Stay, eat."

Jayne snickered. "You sound like a caveman. *Why. Go. Stay. Eat.*" At which point he launched immediately into a dead-on Captain Caveman impersonation, turning the ladle into a club which he mock-pounded on his own head.

"They're goofy," I said over my shoulder, speaking like some sort of indulgent parent.

"Yeah," Billy agreed, but when I looked at him, I could see he was not nearly so approving. "Hey, Bingley!" He unwound Caroline from his arm and went to the other side of the island to disarm Charlie of his ladle. "What do you say we cut this up so we can eat?"

With the ease of familiarity in this kitchen, Billy opened a shallow drawer, produced a lethal-looking pizza cutter, and went to slicing the pie into eight perfect portions. Is there nothing this guy can't do well? Charlie took four cans of Coke out of the fridge.

"What about me?" Caroline asked from the doorway. Obviously, she had the math skills to realize she was about to be left out of the party.

"It's bedtime," Charlie said, the affable high-fivin' big brother nowhere to be seen.

"It's only ten o'clock."

"Ten o'clock. Bed."

"But it's Friday." The day of the week stretched out— *Fridaaaaaaaaaaaaaay*—in an obnoxious whine accompanied by a stamp of little bare feet. I loved that she was losing this battle.

"Go watch TV. In Mom's room."

"But I'm *hungry*. Jayne didn't make me anything to eat."

My sister clapped a hand to her chest, like some mortally offended heroine in hoop skirts. "That's not true. You had a whole box of macaroni and cheese, and a corn dog, and a Sprite, and—"

"Here," Charlie interrupted, shaving a thin sliver off one slice of pizza and handing it over on a napkin. "Take this, and this"—he offered a little package of white-powdered doughnuts—"and this"—a half-empty pint of chocolate milk—"and go upstairs. Now."

Caroline juggled her snack with a scowl, but dutifully disappeared.

"One down . . . " Billy said, with his brow raised meaningfully at Jayne and me. Charlie punched him in the arm.

"Where are the plates?" Jayne did this adorable figure-skater-like spin as she asked.

"Who needs plates?" Chuckles was back. He positioned the cans of Coke on the island top, shoved the pizza to its center, and plopped a roll of paper towels beside it. "Dig in."

Despite some not-so-subtle maneuverings from Billy to have it otherwise, we ended up with Jayne and Charlie on one side, Billy and me on the other. Throw in a red-checked tablecloth, candlelight, and a kid from orchestra with a violin, and we might have had a double date.

Jayne offered to take the smaller slice, and the rest of us *dug in*. Through chomps and strings of cheese, Charlie filled us in on every detail of the game. For every play, it seemed, he took special care to mention Billy's heroism.

"What about the halftime show?" Jayne asked. Bless her heart.

"We don't get to see much of that," Charlie said with adorable indulgence. "We're in the locker room."

"Oh, that's right." She knocked the heel of her hand against her forehead. "I didn't think."

"And the cheerleaders?" I asked, you know, just for a little self-torture. A bit of sauce had dribbled on my chin (according to Jayne's frantic dabbing at her own), and I wiped it away. "How were they? Did they allow for proper inspiration?"

"I didn't much notice," Billy said. "Too busy winning the game."

"But I'm sure you notice them in general, right? I mean, that's what they're there for, isn't it?"

"I'd say they're more for the crowd."

"Don't be ridiculous. It's the traditional male/female role. Hunters and Gatherers. You guys go out and hunt down that football, bring back the victory. Meanwhile, the women gather all that school spirit. Wear those short skirts and sparkling white Nikes. Just bubble all over at your presence."

Billy leaned on one elbow, turning himself fully toward me, making Jayne and Charlie disappear.

"You have a problem with cheerleaders?"

"Not at all. It just seems unlikely for you to have 'not noticed' them. When, in fact—"

"What fact, exactly?"

"Fact," Charlie said, forcing his way back into the conversation. "Billy here has never dated a cheerleader."

I swallowed a swig of Coke and feigned a choking shock. "Really?"

"Me either, for that matter," Charlie continued. "I like a nice, normal girl. Pretty, though." He looked at Jayne, who dutifully looked away. "And sweet. And nice."

Nice. Sweet. Pretty. My sister in three words.

"What about smart?" Billy asked.

Now, I have no idea what was churning around in the minds of anybody else at our little pizza party, but at that moment, every part of my body turned into a globby mozzarella mess. Because he didn't look at me. At all. But it was the *way* he didn't look at me. Like, he was trying really, really hard *not* to look at me. Which made me think that what he was trying to say was something along the lines of, *Yeah. Nice, sweet, and pretty are great. But smart? That's what does it for me.* And, of course, from there, one could only acknowledge the fact that I, Elyse Nebbitt, was not the prettiest, not the sweetest, and—sorry to say—not the *nicest*[1] girl around. But, in this company especially, the smartest.[2] Ergo, if Billy Fitz likes smart girls, and I am a smart girl, Billy Fitz likes me.

That moment—that realization—lasted exactly thirty seconds before little Caroline, her face smudged with so much pizza sauce and powdered sugar that she looked like some tragic child in the court of Marie Antoinette, pitter-pattered back into the kitchen, with the excuse of not wanting to throw away "food trash" in the upstairs trash can.

"Smart girls are usually ugly." She directed her comment right at me, and I knew the little snipper had been listening on the other side of the door all along. "Don't you think so, Charlie?"

"Caroline, GO UPSTAIRS."

"No, but really. You were talking about that yesterday, weren't you? About how sad it was that smart girls couldn't ever be as pretty as pretty girls?"

My face burned, and pizza had never looked so unappetizing.

"Go upstairs now, Caroline, and wash your face."

"We should go, anyway," Jayne said, hopping off the barstool.

"But," Charlie said, fishing, "you're babysitting. You should probably stay until my mom gets home. Isn't she supposed to pay you?"

---

[1] To clarify: by "nice" I'm talking about my interactions with people in general. My willingness to do good deeds, sacrifice the last Fudge Graham cookie to a little sister, loan you a pencil because you were too stupid to bring one to math class. That kind of nice. As for the other meaning of NICE GIRL, well, there just hasn't been the opportunity to not be nice in that way, even if I wanted to.

[2] Again, to clarify. My sister Jayne is a smart girl. Good grades, hard worker. But she has to work a lot harder for those grades than I do. So, by default, I claim the title of smartest.

Caroline snickered at that. Little monster. Everybody knows that *poor* smart girls are a whole other category. I looked over at Billy, but he wasn't looking at me. At all. And not in the meaningful *not* looking way. Just, not.

"It's fine," Jayne said, holding out her hand as if Charlie himself were offering a twenty. Which, thankfully, he wasn't. Because that would have killed us both. "Next time. Or, whenever."

"How are they getting home?" Billy asked, bypassing us altogether. "I didn't see a car."

"Jayne rode the bus," Caroline said, with the implication that doing so could be equated with crawling her way up out of a sewer pipe. "And I don't know how *she* got here."

"So that bike is yours?" Billy asked. How cruel is it that, when he finally acknowledges me, I want to crawl onto a bus with my sister? Or under one. At this point, it really doesn't matter.

"Well, you can't both ride home on a bicycle," Charlie said. "We'll take you."

"No!" Jayne and I spoke in unison.

"I mean," Jayne took the lead, "we'll be fine. We've done it before."

"Besides," I said, "you can't leave this precious one home alone."

"I could just take you," Billy said. "You can put your bike in the trunk."

"Or I could take them," Charlie said eagerly. "And I promise to be careful with your car."

"Or we can all go," Caroline said. "And I promise not to tell Mom that you let me eat pizza and doughnuts in her bed just so you could be alone with a girl."

There was a momentary stare-down between Charlie and Caroline, during which I knew I was witnessing a battle for the ages. Charlie blinked first and told his little sister to go get some shoes on.

Since we hadn't used dishes, there wasn't much of a mess to clean up, but Jayne attempted to anyway, until Charlie finally grabbed her hands before they could run water into the sink and said, "Magda will get this in the morning."

We were a solemn company heading out to Billy's car, too much so to appreciate the humor of watching him try to wrestle the unfortunate Monster into the trunk. (And by Monster, I mean the bike, of course. Not Caroline. More's the shame.)

Billy got behind the wheel saying, "Charlie, you have shotgun." Which I'm sure hadn't been *Charlie's* plan at all. Jayne and I got into the back seat, with Caroline wedged between us. In an odd quirk of mine, I immediately inhaled deeply, experiencing the '78 Camaro on an olfactory level.[3]

"It's leather," Billy said, meeting my eyes in the rearview mirror.

"And no food allowed," Charlie said. "Ever, right?"

"Right."

"Except if we get ice cream after we drop them off," Caroline said. "That would be fun."

"We won't," Billy said decisively. I leaned my head against the glass of the back window and smiled.

The moment the engine roared to life, music exploded from the speakers right behind my head. Boston, "More than a Feeling." More than anything, I wanted to follow the lyrics—to hide in the music. To forget the day. Only, in some ways I knew I'd never forget this day, and with each passing moment in Billy's car, I didn't want to. I found myself thinking about the girl I'd been only minutes before. The smart girl Billy Fitz might have (probably didn't, but *might* have) liked. And how she'd slipped away, back into the poor, not-nice, not-pretty girl in the back seat with her sister. In the front seat, Charlie was

---

[3] OLFACTORY: sense of smell. See? I told you I was smart.

trying to lighten the mood, impressing us with a painful falsetto meant to match the vocalist on the song.

Slipped awaaaaay—ayyy-aaaaaay—

Jayne laughed appreciatively, but then we all got quiet so as not to spoil the beauty of a perfect guitar solo. That was when I felt a tug on my sleeve, and Caroline Bingley stretched up to whisper in my ear.

"He's never going to like you." Her breath was hot and smelled like a sick combination of pizza, sugar, and milk. "So you might as well not even try."

civility: *a polite act or expression*

Elyse found the new boy's **civility** *refreshing, especially as it stood in stark contrast to the rudeness of the other boys.*

SEVENTH PERIOD, Trigonometry, believe it or not, was my favorite class of the day. Advanced Placement English was the most fun (Oh, really, Mrs. Pierson? Nine chapters of *Wuthering Heights* by Thursday? Done.), and World History the easiest (Open-note quiz over the factors contributing to the decline of the Roman Empire? Obviously Mrs. Baxter hasn't seen my notes. They could be a personalized textbook.). And with Chemistry something like a lobotomy with beakers, PE creating fodder for nightmares and therapy, and Spanish an endless conversation about *la comida*, Trigonometry won out as favorite for giving the perfect amount of challenge and the greatest feeling of reward for a good grade earned.

It helped, too, that Billy Fitz was in that class. We'd almost gotten to the point of comparing answers. He lent me a pencil, and I swear the grooves around the tip came from his own perfect teeth. Once, and I can't be totally sure, I think he was about to ask if I wanted to get together to do our homework, but that might have been wishful thinking. He said, "So"—right before the bell rang, cutting off the rest of his question.

All of that, of course, was before the infamous impromptu Friday Night Frozen Pizza Party (FNFPP). He didn't talk to me after that. Didn't look at me. Wouldn't check his Swatch to give me the time of day. Then again, he wouldn't be caught dead in a Swatch.

"I don't know why it bothers you so much," Jayne said. It was early in the morning, and we were sitting on the Joggling Board, waiting for Charlie to come pick her up. Apparently an important stage of the High School pseudo-courting ritual consists of being driven the three blocks to school even though you'd get there earlier if you walked. "I didn't even know you liked him."

"I don't. I mean, he's good-looking if you like that athletic movie-star kind of thing. But he's kind of a jerk, too. You know. Rude. Like he thinks he's better than everyone else. Which, maybe he is, but that doesn't give him the right to be such a cretin."

"Do you want me to talk to Charlie?"

I glanced sideways at her. She couldn't even say his name without making a goofy grin.

"Of course," I said. "Because that wouldn't be humiliating at all. Look, I don't like him."

"Pudge . . ."

"Okay. Maybe I did, at first. But then, why in the world should I waste my time on a guy who doesn't like me, right?"

"Right."

The smooth sound of Charlie's silver Fiero brought an end to our conversation, and she gave me a quick hug, saying, "Want to ride with us?"

I tried not to roll my eyes. "It's a Fiero, sis. No back seat."

"You can share with me."

"No, thanks. You go and have fun. See you at lunch?"

She lifted her brown bag in affirmation before skipping down the steps, blonde tresses flying behind her. Charlie, ever the gentleman, came out from his side of the car and, holding the door for Jayne, called to me, "Want to ride with us?"

I shook my head in disbelief, stood, and leaned against the porch railing to call back, "It's a Fiero. No back seat."

"You could share a seat with your sister!"

I suppose the comment justified the measuring look he gave to my sister's teeny-tiny behind, and then me. "Maybe?"

Those two were made for each other. Together they could conquer the world leading armies of koalas on unicorns.

"No. Thanks. Have fun. See you at lunch."

He waved, handed Jayne into her seat with—I swear—a bow and a kiss on her hand, and then they were off.

I didn't mind watching her go, really. He was a nice guy; she was a nice girl. They were a cute couple—even if they weren't officially a *couple* yet. How the powers of Northenfield Texas High School officially determined such things was lost to me. Tonight would mark one week since the FNFPP, and so far he had called her on the telephone three times, bought her a Wednesday Warm Cookie in the cafeteria at lunch, and—this I heard from three different people in study hall—used her name on a vocabulary quiz when asked to give an example of somebody who might be described as *lissome (adj.)*. That, I admit, touched my calloused heart, and I didn't even tease her about being in a Regular English class where they wasted precious time and paper on vocabulary quizzes. For all I know, poor Charlie might have used her name to describe something that might be considered *byzantine (adj.)*, just because the word sounded pretty.

This morning was the second in a row that he'd taken her to school, and if it weren't for the fact that our team had an Away

Game in San Angelo, all signs indicated that the two of them might have enjoyed an actual date.

I was pondering that very thing when our screen door burst open and a whirling blast of my sister Lydia set the softly cooing doves in our trees to scattering.

"Do you feel that?"

Her hair, a mass of perfectly spiraled copper springs, came to a floating rest over the sparkling headband she wore across her brow. With tight white jeans, a fuchsia-colored spandex top, and matching Reeboks, she looked like she was about to flip a switch on a boom box and teach an aerobic dance class for Mrs. Schenkman across the street.

"Feel what, exactly, Lydia?"

"Not exactly feel, maybe, but—" She stopped, closed her eyes, and drew in a breath deep enough to grow another cup size while raising her hands above her head. Then, slowly, she let it out, and when her exhalation was complete, she turned to look at me, her eyes rimmed with deep purple mascara. "How about now?"

If anything, I was more confused and said so.

"There's a new boy on the street." With that, she grabbed my arm and pulled me inside, hushing my protests as we slipped up the stairs, past the Littles who were still in their nightgowns, watching PBS in pursuit of a math lesson.

"What are we doing? We'll be late for—"

"Shh!"

We came to my room, and she dragged me straight to the window. "Now, wait."

Ornithologists awaiting the appearance of the rare golden-cheeked warbler wouldn't have had the stillness and patience of my usually flaky-as-a-biscuit sister. Every time I budged or fidgeted, she redirected my attention, and within a minute or so, I gained a respect for her I could never have imagined.

"There," she finally said, her voice full of triumph and awe. "What did I tell you?"

I had to put my forehead up against the window to get the right angle, but there he was. *New* didn't even begin to categorize him. I'd never seen him anywhere. Not at school, not at church, not around town. I hadn't noticed a moving van on our street, and Jayne hadn't said anything about seeing a new kid in the registrar's office, where she worked as an aide during her study hall time every day. And yet, there he was, walking down our street, right in front of our house, with a backpack slung over one shoulder, obviously heading for school. He was tall and thin—more like lanky—with dark curly hair cut short over his ears, but long enough to touch the top of the popped collar of his baby-blue oxford shirt. He wore shorts, too, which I'm pretty sure went against Northenfield's dress code, except these were plaid, and almost down to his knees. Those, combined with brown loafers, made him look unlike almost any other boy in school. The lack of socks alone would be a topic of conversation across campus.

"Who is he?" I asked.

"I don't know," Lydia said, pulling me away. "This is the first I've actually seen him. Now come on, if we hurry we can follow along behind, but close enough that he'll hear us and turn around."

In that moment, I swear my little sister was doing advanced mental math. Calculating rate of speed and distance, factoring in possible impediments like Mom asking why we hadn't left yet or if we'd remembered to put carrots in our lunch. Impressed, I followed her lead, and by the time we hit the sidewalk, New Boy was a consistent five squares ahead of us. Still, there was little chance we would get his attention, because by then he had bright yellow headphones covering his ears.

Sure enough, we followed him right to the hallowed halls

of Northenfield Texas High School. Well, before the halls, we melted into the pods of people gathered on the steps and on the lawn. Lydia brought us to a halt near one of the trees—the Big Tree—surrounded by stone benches. We climbed up on one of the benches so we could surmise which group he would join. Jocks? No, though a few of them offered one of those thumb-hooking handshakes as he walked by. Same with the Brains. He neither acknowledged nor was noticed by the Ag kids, but a gathering of Pretty Girls greeted him in chorus. The easy, obvious answer, of course, was that he would align himself with the Preppies, but they spent their before-school hours in the Library reading the New York newspapers, so there'd be no way to verify.

"Don't you have to get over to the Junior High School building?" I asked Lydia as we watched him disappear behind the double-front doors.

"All the boys there are awful. Like children."

"And yet—" I gave her a gentle nudge off the bench, and a ready-set trio of those awful boys was there to catch her.

Thus unencumbered, I moved to blend in with the other kids, through the doors and in the halls. I went straight to my locker, stashed my lunch and afternoon books, and took a quick look in the square mirror mounted to the inside of my locker door. The mirror was something I'd inherited from the previous owner, who—according to the butterball writing next to it—would love John Medina 4-ever. I hoped they were happy, somewhere. As for the face looking out of the glass today . . . she was having a good hair day. Bangs under control, thanks to a few minutes spent with a curling iron, and the Dr Pepper Lip Smacker giving just the right amount of shine to her lips.

I grabbed my stuff for English and slammed the metal door shut, taking time for one last look around for Jayne. It seemed weird, not wishing each other an Awesome-Possum Day. Like it was jinxed from the get-go. But she was somewhere far more awesome than locker 1221. In the parking lot, maybe, leaning against Charlie's car like it was no big deal while talking to other people with vehicular clout. Or they might be walking slowly, hand in hand, not caring if their love put them in danger of a first-period tardy.

I, on the other hand, was in no such danger, as I would be in my desk, early, with enough time to copy down the class agenda and homework before the first bell. Other early nerds roamed the hall with me, basking in the approving glances of the hall monitors. No passes needed here. My footsteps echoed in the stairwell, and Mrs. Pierson's welcoming door awaited. The woman herself was nowhere to be seen, as usual, but she trusted me to be in her classroom alone.

Except, I wasn't alone.

Again, there he was. The boy from this morning. Baby-blue oxford shirt, curly dark hair, yellow headphones, backpack. All of it cuter than it had looked from my second-floor bedroom, and all of it piled in my desk. *My* desk.

Now, normally, I would rather throw myself into a pit of fire than open up a conversation with a boy. But this was my desk. And before anybody tries to brush it off as "just" a desk, let me explain.

1. It is clean. No history of heavy metal bands or long-lost loves or horrible poetry have been scratched into its surface. Unlike my History class where, every day, I have to look down at the Neanderthal philosophic musings of some kid who carved *Life Is Hate* surrounded by what I'm sure he thought looked like lightning bolts.
2. It is on the outer aisle, along the window. Which means

not only do I have the occasional opportunity to glance out at something green, I'm also spared the rush of bodies at the dismissal bell.

3. Under the window is a bookshelf lined with books—all of which are free for the borrowing. When I'm bored (which, in this class, isn't often, but still happens), I can peruse the titles and plan my next conquest. If not for this shelf, I would never have been introduced to the literary genius of Margaret Atwood.

This isn't the kind of desk you get on your first day of school. You can't just saunter in and claim the by-the-window graffiti-free desk. I myself had started in the middle row, three seats from the back, behind a girl who had her hair moussed and teased so high I didn't even know Mrs. Pierson wore glasses for the first few days. No, this is the kind of seat that you get through strategic maneuvering. Winding around like that Centipede game. I had to rook my way into it after two kids transferred, one became homebound with mono, and another dropped into Regular English when she discovered she'd have to read books quietly inside her head. Lottie almost took it from me, and might have, too, except the day it turned up free, she wore clogs to school, and I wore Nikes, so it was a matter of who could get to it first without tripping.

And now, this guy?

He looked up and smiled. His lips were thin, so the smile looked like a doodle, and by the time I was next to him, tapping my ear to get him to lift his headphones, it was gone.

"Is there a problem?" Nice voice. Really nice voice. Some people, when they're listening to headphones, tend to speak really loudly to compensate. Like they think they need to be louder than the music we can't hear. Not him, so we had the first sign that he wasn't a total idiot.

"You're in my seat."

He pulled one side of his headphones away from his ear, and I could hear REO Speedwagon on the other side. Another good sign.

"I beg your pardon?" Polite, too. This might be more difficult than I thought.

I tapped the desk surface. "You're in my seat."

"I didn't know Mrs. Pierson assigned seats."

"She doesn't, officially. But this is mine."

He made a show of examining it from all angles, and I promised myself that if he said, *I don't see your name on it*, I was going to deck him. Instead, he made a very grown-up face and nodded slowly. "I can see why you'd want it. No graffiti."

"Exactly."

"Next to a window. Outside aisle."

"Yes, yes. All of that. I get here early every day so I can claim it."

"Not early enough this morning, though. Obviously."

I looked at him through narrowed eyes. "You're new."

"You're right."

"You can't just come in and take somebody's desk."

"True." By now he had pushed the stop button on his Walkman and was giving me his full attention. "But it seems the nicest thing to do is to offer the best desk to a new student. It's the law of hospitality. The cornerstone of civilization."

"Ah. But the laws of chivalry dictate that you should offer it to me. You won't always be new, but I'll always be a lady. In fact, you shouldn't even be sitting in my presence."

His eyebrows danced up, clearly pleased with my banter, and he stood—more like, unfolded himself—slowly, and with exaggerated grace. "Your desk, my lady."

I gave a passable curtsy, saying, "Thank you, m'lord," before sliding into the seat.

"And, with your permission, I shall take that which is directly behind you."

"I will allow it."

It was Collin's. He'd survive.

The moment he sat down, I was thankful that, for once, I didn't have all of my hair wound up in a scrunchie, because I knew the back of my neck had to be as red as the ink from Mrs. Pierson's pen when she wrote *encouraging* notes on our essays. I felt I'd somehow gained the upper hand. If *I* wanted to talk to *him*, all I had to do was turn around and talk. Which I did.

"I'm Elyse, by the way. Elyse Nebbitt."

He held out his hand. "Gage Wickam."

We said *Nice to meet you* in a perfect chorus, then laughed self-consciously.

"So, Elyse Nebbitt. What are we currently studying in Advanced Placement English?"

I held up my battered paperback. "*Wuthering Heights.*"

"The Romantics. All that unbridled passion. Unchained, unchecked literary rock and roll. I and I alone am the center of my universe. Away with you, stodgy scholars of the Enlightenment. Let me rip my beating heart from out my breast and present it thus to you, for in it resides my soul."

"Something like that," I said, thinking he deserved this desk far more than I. "Have you read it?"

He pulled his own well-worn copy from his backpack. "They told me when I registered."

"So why did you ask?"

He looked away and sort of deflated a little bit. "Just making conversation. I already knew your name, and I'm not always comfortable talking to people. Seemed like a safe topic."

"You don't seem shy."

"Not shy, just—guarded."

"Well," I said, wanting to rescue him from this pit of

vulnerability, "the class is good. Mrs. Pierson is cool. And if you need any help catching up . . ." I trailed off, waiting for him to swoop in with something gallant. Instead, he shifted uncomfortably and turned his attention to the tiny, perfect script framing the edges of his desk.

"Whoa—what is this?"

I didn't have to read it to know. "That's my friend Collin's work. What you have there are the lyrics to 'Bohemian Rhapsody.' It starts here"—I pointed to a spot in the middle of the pencil well—"and then sort of spills out."

"Admirable."

"That's one word for it."

The bell rang to allow the masses entrance to the building, and within a few minutes, the room was filled, including Collin and Lottie. Lottie took her regular seat next to me, but Collin hovered for a moment, and I felt like I was trapped in a television rerun.

"That's my seat," he said, peeking out from underneath his greasy dark bangs.

Again, Gage stood, but this time he just held out his hand and said, "Dude. It's mine now."

Collin, barely tall enough to reach Gage's shoulder in the first place, slumped into something smaller.

"Cool." He moved around to the desk behind Lottie—one of those ancient wooden things with a writing surface almost too small for a piece of paper.

We made introductions all around, and by the time the bell rang to start class, it seemed like Gage Wickam had been here all along. Mrs. Pierson breezed in, pulling her familiar gray cardigan around her shoulders, and, after calling us to attention, asked, "Who can tell me about the distinguishing characteristics of the Romantic movement?"

She was met with our familiar good-natured grumbling, but

then I heard a shifting in the seat behind me. Mrs. Pierson called on Gage, seeming pleased and surprised, and an answer flowed behind me. It was everything he'd said before, though somewhat refined, and I glowed with the fact that he'd said it all to me first.

intrepidity: *the quality of being characterized by resolute fearlessness, fortitude, and endurance*

With stone-faced **intrepidity,** *the football players boarded the bus, ready to do battle with our Area enemies.*

AFTER SCHOOL, I waited at the Big Tree with Collin. The usual fleet of yellow School Buses lined the circular drive, the usual kids hanging out of the windows. But today, at the end of the line was a bus covered with banners.

In a beautiful show of solidarity, Cheer-Leaders and Cheer-Sitters stood side by side, creating a tunnel out of their waving pom-poms. Lottie was among them, and when she happened to catch my eye, I sent her an enthusiastic thumbs-up for a job well done. Just behind the Wall of Cheer, select members of the marching band played our school song; those not chosen to play waited in the less-decorated bus.

"Our conquering heroes, right?"

It was Gage Wickam, starting up a conversation as if we'd been palling around together all day long. I managed to hide my shock with what I'm sure was a totally casual-sounding "Oh, hey." Standing on a bench like I was, we were nearly eye level with each other—me, a little taller. "Yeah, heroes, I guess."

"Think they go through all of this for the basketball team?"

"I wouldn't know."

"They don't. Or baseball, or volleyball, or any of our other teams that manage to make it into state playoffs. Watch, these guys will wipe out before Area, and they'll still have cupcakes in their lockers on Monday morning."

"You seem to know a lot about all this for being the new kid."

He shrugged, shifting his backpack. "I'm not exactly new. To the school, yes, but not the town. I lived here a few years ago."

"Where'd you go to school?"

But before he could answer, the band hit one massive note, and the drum line exploded. The Pep Squad girls launched into a syncopated spelling of V-I-C-T-O-R-Y punctuated by our school's initials. Everywhere around us, kids whooped and hollered, while Gage and I took a moment to engage in a look where each promised the other that he and she found all of this just a little ridiculous.

The noise doubled as Coach Bell—a square-set muscle of a man who looked like a humanoid bulldog stuffed into a purple windbreaker—emerged on top of the Team Bus (yes, *on top* of the bus) with a megaphone. Somehow, his voice transcended the band, the drums, the cheers, the hoots, as he made all kinds of promises about the terrible, truly terrible things our boys would do on the football fields of San Angelo. Then, one by one, he announced each player's name, and the girls raised their pom-poms as if the sheer force of their shaking would sprinkle both spirit and victory on the heads that passed beneath them.

"George Nighting!" And this huge guy jogged down the line of girls, their pom-poms barely high enough to brush his shoulders. Coach Bell insisted his boys dress up even for their Away Games, and Nighting's neck spilled out over the collar of his dress shirt, the tiny knot of his tie dwarfed by the massive lump of chin above it. He looked, to me, like he'd make the perfect big brother—somebody to fight your battles, defend your honor. Jayne and I had often wished for a brother, even a younger one. Somebody who might bring a little sense into the house. Someone for Dad to talk to, if nothing else.

Next came, "John Willow!" and frankly, I was surprised to find our Pep Squad still standing after he ran his course between them. Even *I*, the girl who kept just one toe in the NTHS gossip pool, knew the swooning power he held over the entire female population. This week, he was supposedly dating one of our cross-country girls who had twisted her ankle slipping in the locker room shower. Personally, though, I thought he was just using her as an excuse to get out of class five minutes early to carry her books. "Mark my words," I'd told Lottie and Collin at lunch, "the minute she gets that cast off, he'll be on to someone else."

"Frank Churchill!" Now, *he* caught my attention, because while I'd heard his name nearly every day at school over the announcements ("Frank Churchill, representing NTHS at the Future Business Leaders of America economics competition"; "Frank Churchill, NTHS athlete of the week"; "and the winner of ten free Sonic chili dogs is . . . FRANK CHURCHILL!"), I'd never actually seen him in person. And now, I finally had a chance, assuming I could get the perfect break in the pom-pom wall, to get a glimpse—

"Billy Fitz!"

And Frank Churchill passed by, unnoticed.

Now, it's not like I'd never seen Billy Fitz before, but I'd never seen him looking quite like this. Jeans, yes. Levi's 501, to be exact. And polo shirts, T-shirts, a gray cardigan on this one morning when it was kind of chilly. I'd seen him in his football uniform, his letterman jacket, and even in an apron and goggles one time when I delivered a note to Mr. Castellano's Chemistry II class and they were in the middle of a lab with all kinds of things smoking in the beakers. But now here he was, wearing a suit that made him look like a television lawyer. While the other boys were in compliance with shirts and ties, he was the whole package—shiny dress shoes and a jacket. I was glad he hadn't been in Trigonometry earlier (the players are excused from afternoon classes on Away Game days). The pressure of being in the presence of all that masculine beauty would have stripped away everything I know about numbers.

I felt myself rising up to my toes, and as I did, it happened. He looked at me. Not over in my general direction, but *at* me. His eyes plus my eyes. Four eyes. Math intact.

And then—I'm not sure what came over me. Perhaps it was the throbbing of the drums, the trumpets and flutes and tuba joined in harmonious school spirit, the not-at-all annoying repetition of our school name . . . All of this swept over me, softened my hardened high-school heart, and I raised my hands above my head, clapping, letting out a joy-fueled shout of his name.

"Billyyyyyyyyyy!"

I was not, of course, the only one shouting, but while the rest of the rabble had fallen into a rhythmic "*Fitz! Fitz! Fitz! Fitz!*" my ululation rang high and loud above the rest. And he smiled. Not a big smile, but a small one, which was infinitely better. A big smile would have had to acknowledge everybody gathered to shout his praises. This was small. Private, just the slightest lift to the corner of his mouth, accompanied by a tiny shake of his head, because he knew I knew he knew he didn't really deserve this level of adoration. Even if he was a quarterback.

"You like him?" Gage asked, nudging my hip with his elbow, a move that almost cost me my balance on the wall. That's when I realized that when I lifted up my hands, my shirt had come up to reveal a strip of soft, white skin, peeking around the top of my jeans like a rippling border of frosting on a cake.

I dropped my hands and looked at him. "No." My tone totally implied, *Don't be silly*.

"I mean, it's fine if you did. I'd understand. Most girls do. Everybody does."

By now, Coach Bell had announced the next player, and Billy had his foot on the first step into the bus. When I glanced over to give him a final wave, to grab that last delicious bit of his attention, I found myself facing a completely different image. No shy smile, no hint of self-consciousness. Worse, he wasn't looking at me anymore, but at Gage. And the look wasn't pretty. His nose wrinkled, his lip curled, and if he hadn't been wearing a multi-hundreds-of-dollars suit, he might have played Red Rover through the lines of the Pep Squad girls and leaped over the crowd to get to us. Him? Us? Unclear, but worse yet, when he did look at me again, he seemed . . . sad. No, not sad. Sad would have been great. More like, disappointed. In me.

One more name called. "Walter Elliot!"

Billy disappeared into the bus.

"Wow," I said, hazarding a glance at Gage. He stared straight ahead, hard. "I guess not *everybody* likes him."

"No, they do. The truth is, not everybody *knows* him."

Still, Gage didn't look at me, and we stood in some strange solidarity as the rest of the team was announced, with Charlie— a mere kicker, after all—the last name called. He loped betwixt the pom-pom arch, offering a loose-armed wave to all. On the other side, near the band, I saw Jayne's head bopping up and down as she jumped. Once Charlie was on the bus, Coach Bell shouted a few more violent promises as the girls piled in with the players and the band made its way to the back of the fleet.

We, the student body, were dismissed.

Gage and I stood still in the midst of the milling crowd, his unspoken accusation of Billy lingering between us. I wanted to ask more, if for no other reason than to give myself permission to feel relieved at Billy's disinterest. But Gage looked almost like he'd gone into another place inside his head, and the muscle at the corner of his jaw was working in a way that might have been menacing if I hadn't noticed he'd popped a Tic Tac just as we started talking.

I was trying to find the right way to ask him if he wanted to walk me home—walk home with me. Walk home together. Walk together. Leave—when I heard Jayne calling to me above the buzz of our disassembling student body.

Watching Jayne run is kind of like watching a shampoo commercial. Her hair flies golden behind her, and the surrounding area turns into a field of daisies. I knew introducing her to Gage would probably seal myself in second place, but I did it anyway, and he seemed appropriately unimpressed, especially when she delivered her news.

"Charlie asked if I'd like to go to the game with his mother."

"Charlie Bingley?" Gage asked, clarifying, but nothing more.

Jayne nodded, then turned back to me. "The players get two tickets for their family members. She's driving to San Angelo, and he said I could ride with her. That it's okay with her, so she'll have someone to talk to. And he wants us to get to know each other."

For this last bit, she squeezed my hands and jumped up on the bench with me so we could exchange a squeal-y, sisterly embrace. Gage had the decency to look away.

"Wait a minute." My math skills kicked in. "*Two* tickets? But what about the bratty sister? Doesn't she need a ticket too? Unless"—my jaw dropped in horror—"you said I'd babysit. You didn't, did you? Because if you did—"

She laughed. "No, of course not. I wouldn't do that. Caroline's using Billy's ticket. Because," her voice dropped to a whisper, "you know, he doesn't really have anyone to give it to."

"Oh." My elation at my sister's coup deflated, and not just

because Billy hadn't thought to ask me. Why should he, after all? But because he didn't have another soul besides that horrible little Caroline to give his ticket to.

"Anyway," she stepped back and resumed her full volume, "do you think Mom and Dad will let me go?"

"Let me think." I tapped my chin as if deep in thought. "Will Mom and Dad consent to let you spend a few hours in a BMW with the mother of a nice boy who also happens to be an heir to multiple car dealerships?"

"Elyse . . . "

"Do you want me to help you ask them? Or do you want me to tell them after you're long gone?"

She bit her bottom, perfectly glossy lip. "He did say his mom would be here to pick me up right at four."

"Here? At the school?" I thought about Mrs. Bingley, whom I'd never seen outside of the silver-framed glamour shot on the mantel. Perfect, honey blonde, pearl earrings, flawless manicure, and a smile white and frozen, like an Eskimo Pie that couldn't be bothered with chocolate. I could see why Jayne wouldn't want her to pull up in front of our ramshackle little house, let alone get trapped in a flattery-filled conversation with our mother.

"Yeah . . . " Jayne's furtive look confirmed my hypothesis. "As of now, I might not have time to go home and change."

"I'll tell them," I said, and she hugged me again, declaring me the best sister ever before disappearing into the crowd.

Gage hadn't said a word during our conversation, and now he looked up at me, one eye squinted, like he was trying to figure out a puzzle.

"So your sister's going out with Charlie Bingley?"

"Sort of, I guess?"

"Well, that explains it, then."

"Explains what?"

He held out his hand to help me down from the wall, grasping my arm just below my elbow. And, shock of all shockers, didn't let it go once my feet hit the ground. In fact, he moved his hand down, past my wrist, until he was holding mine in this comfortable, loose embrace—one I could get out of easily enough if I wanted to, but I didn't. Not just yet.

"Explains you and Billy, whatever's happening there."

"There's nothing happening there."

"Because he and Charlie are like brothers, and you and Jayne being sisters—"

"There's nothing happening." I squeezed his hand, feeling this irrational need to reassure him, and a little flattered that I had to. "He doesn't like me. At all."

"That's impossible." With one little tug, we were walking together. "Who wouldn't like you?"

We didn't talk for a while, which was good, because if I had to express my thoughts out loud it would be nothing but *He'sholdingmyhandHe'sholdingmyhand* at a steadily increasing volume. I wondered if anybody else noticed. If that girl from PE who made thunder sounds while pointing at my thighs was around here somewhere, watching me walk away with the newest cute boy. Or if my sister Lydia might pop up and be forced to eat every mean, teasing word she'd ever said. Instead, I looked up to see the Team Bus roaring out of the circle and Billy's face looking out the window, just long enough to spot us before looking away.

At that moment my JanSport backpack slipped off my shoulder, leaving me no choice but to walk with twenty-eight pounds of books hanging off the crook of my elbow or let go of Gage's hand to adjust the strap. I chose to let go. When my backpack was settled again, I kept my hand on the strap, holding it in place. I didn't want to give him the chance to not hold it again.

"So," he said, casually, as if we hadn't just shared the most intimate physical connection of my life, "looks like we're both free tonight."

"Yep." I tried to match his casual tone. You know, just a gal.

"Would you, maybe, want to hang out? Or, maybe, go out? Wait, are you allowed to go out on a date?"

Holding my hand. Asking me out. In the course of ten minutes this guy had picked me up, spun me around, and dropped me in a land I'd only imagined. One that I'd convinced myself I didn't care if I ever visited or not, but now kind of wanted to see. The shock of his question—no matter how stumbling its posing—left me without an answer. So, stalling, I asked my own.

"Why would—I mean, why wouldn't I be? Allowed, that is. To go out."

He shrugged, a move that was already familiar. "I don't know. I guess after listening to that conversation with your sister—"

I didn't want to tell him that I had no real answer, because the subject had never, ever come up. Therefore, I decided to answer it myself.

"I'm allowed."

He gave me a soft bump to my shoulder, knocking me out of my path for half a step.

"So, how about if I pick you up at seven?"

This, *this* was happening. We might have been two teens on a TV show. I knew this script. It was my turn to say something flirtatious and clever.

"You don't know where I live."

"I will. After I walk you home."

triumph: *a victory or conquest by or as if by military force*

Armed with mousse and a curling iron, Lydia achieved **triumph** *over the unruly mop of hair.*

ANY FEAR I HAD that my parents might not allow me to go on a date at the tender age of fifteen promptly disappeared the minute I told my mother that I'd been asked out. I don't know if she could have looked more surprised if I'd told her that I had just found a million dollars while rescuing possums from a drain pipe for which I'd been named Texas Woman of the Year for life. The combination of shock, elation, and pride in her approval was a little insulting, actually.

"Yes, Mom. Me. A boy asked *me* out for tonight. Can I go?"

There'd been the usual questions about whether he came from a nice family, what his parents did for a living, if he seemed to be a young man with a future—all of it a little formal and tedious for a Friday afternoon conversation. Besides, I didn't have the answers, really. If she'd asked me about the color of his eyes, his preference of loose-leaf paper over spiral, or even the feel of his hand in mine, I could have kept the conversation hopping until Dad got home from work. So, I told her what I did know—that he was newly returned to town and that he seemed like a nice boy who needed a friend.

"It's nice to be able to show some hospitality," I said. "Like Charlie did for Jayne." And I took that opportunity to tell her that Jayne was going to the Away Game with Charlie's mother and sister, at which point Mom's face got all goopy. I think she'd been in love with Charlie on Jayne's behalf since the day we moved in, always calling him *such a nice boy*, though she never had taken a shine to Billy, whom she always referred to as *that other one*.

Anyway, with her permission granted and Dad's sure to follow, I had a date. And only three and a half hours to get ready for it.

If I had to name any dark spot in this picture, it was the fact that Jayne wasn't there to share it with me. She wouldn't know until after the fact, so I'd miss out on the fun of anticipating with her. I needed someone to help me a little here. Coach me on what to do and say. She didn't have *much* more experience than I did, but her preference for those silly romance novels she read all the time made her more than an expert in my eyes. And then there was the matter of, well . . . *me*. Jayne might be the only person to use *Pudge* as a nickname of pure affection, but she was also the only person who genuinely overlooked what the rest of the world saw as a flaw in my figure. She appreciated me as is, without the *if only* that everybody else seemed to attach.

MOM: Elyse, sweetie, if only you'd lose a few pounds. Not much. Maybe ten, fifteen. You'd be so much happier.

DAD: Darling, if only you'd learn to comport yourself more like a young lady. You're too big to be running around the house like some overgrown puppy.

LYDIA: There might be some potential there, if only you'd put some effort into it.

BILLY FITZ: [sound effect: crickets]

Without Jayne's guidance, I appeared to be on my own, an option only slightly less terrifying than asking for Mom to help. Luckily, the Littles' science lesson of bringing in damp leaves from the backyard had resulted in a nasty snail infestation in the kitchen sink, and all of Mom's attention was taken by prying the slimy things off the dishes and handing them to the squealing girls to repatriate them under the porch.

Alone in my room, I turned up my radio as loud as I dared, Blondie singing "Call Me" in the background while I sang along, wondering just how it would feel to be covered with kisses. Like, *covered*. The lyrics that followed talked about rolling around in designer sheets, which seemed too risqué to sing out loud, even for a girl brave enough to go on a date with a boy she hardly knew, so I resorted to humming until the chorus where I shouted, "Call me!" exuberantly into an invisible phone.

It occurred to me that I hadn't given Gage my phone number, so he *couldn't* call me. Like, if something came up—like in that episode of *The Brady Bunch* where Marsha has to cancel a date with that line, *Something suddenly came up*. If something suddenly came up, and Gage had to cancel, he couldn't. I'd just be left here, waiting, like some pathetic girl. I stopped right there in the middle of my search for the perfect outfit and went over to my desk, where I had a little wooden box I'd bought as a souvenir from our family's one and only trip to Knott's Berry Farm when I was twelve. In it was a pad of paper, also from Knott's Berry Farm. It looked antique, with sepia-toned scrolls along the border, and my name in what was supposed to be old-fashioned script at the top. I tore off a sheet and, in my best, clearest handwriting, wrote my phone number. Just in case he ever asked, I didn't want it to be on some scrap, or written halfway when the pen died, or some other such disaster.

But then, how pathetic did this look? He says, "By the way, I don't think I have your number . . ." and I whip out some ready-written theme-park souvenir script? Like a calling card from some Henry James heroine? *I know nothing, less than nothing. I need Jayne, and she's Away.* I shoved the slip under the blotter on my desk and returned to the task at hand.

What to wear.

If I had any saving grace here, it was the fact that Gage had only seen me in one outfit, so anything was fair game. I could wear my dark Gloria Vanderbilt jeans with my pink polo shirt, or my faded Levi's with my white polo shirt, or my red jeans with a black polo shirt. The only dresses I had were ones with church-mandated ruffles, which seemed presumptuous for a first date. Everything else seemed predestined to create an only date. Not even the brown corduroy pants, long plaid skirt, or pale blue silk blouse offered any hope. Jayne's side of the armoire was tempting, but while I technically could get myself into some of her clothes, the strain created on the fabric didn't guarantee that I'd *stay* in them for the entire evening.

There was only one source of hope in the house, and with desperate times calling for desperate measures, I braced myself to call in reinforcements. Luckily, I didn't have to humble myself too much, because the moment I opened my door, there she was.

Lydia.

"Mom says you have a date." She seemed genuinely pleased, so the shock must have worn off.

"Yeah, I do. With that boy we saw this morning."

She clapped her hands and did a kind of twizzle-spin in the threshold. When she stopped, she asked, "What are you going to wear? Because, you know, you have nothing."

"That's why I thought you might, you know, help."

"Let's see." She pushed me aside and went to the clothes-strewn bed with the authority of a surgeon called in to perform the world's first emergency wardrobe transplant. "Nothing." Then, to the armoire, where she flicked through the hangers saying, "Nope. Nope. Ugh, no. Nope." Then, back to me, hands on her hips. "How is it that we are even related? Does Mother buy you nothing? Is that what you do all day when you say you're studying at the library? Do you really go sifting through the trash bins of abandoned department stores? Because this is awful."

I held up my jeans defensively. "These are Gloria Vanderbilt." My sole claim to a designer tag.

"Do you know who else wears Gloria Vanderbilt? Mrs. Rivera. My math teacher. Those are teacher pants. Those are *math* teacher pants. You can wear those when you want to figure out quadrangle equations—" *Aw, poor Lydia. She tries so hard.* —"but you CANNOT wear them on a date."

"It's all I have."

She stepped back and studied me, tapping her perky little chin. It was the hardest I'd ever seen her think.

"You need something completely different."

"Okay . . ."

"I mean, you need to *be* something completely different. Catch his attention, you know?"

"So, like, the corduroy?"

"There's no excuse for even *possessing* corduroy pants. Unless you're, like, a farmer. Are you a farmer, Elyse?"

I couldn't personally make the connection between corduroy and farming, but then I didn't live in Lydia's world. "No, I'm not a farmer."

"So, what are you?"

"What am I?" I paused long enough for us both to doubt that I had an answer.

"None of this"—she waved her arms over the clothing casualties strewn across my bed—"is you. Or at least, not who you want to be, obviously. Who would want to be this?" She held up a pair of faded purple drawstring pants with elastic at the ankles and the plaid shirt I always wore with them.

"They're just clothes."

"Close your eyes."

I did.

"Now, tell me. How do you *really* see yourself? How do you want *him* to see you?"

Lydia's voice, when disconnected from her overly glossy lips and constant petulant expression, took on a mesmerizing, wise quality. I tried to think in adjectives alone, idealistic modifiers: Pretty, Sweet, Girlfriend. But then I realized, those words were all Jayne. I always got the twist on those words: Interesting, Funny, Buddy. But now I had this chance to come up with something new—some merging of both my truest and undiscovered selves. I didn't have to be what Gage wanted; besides, I didn't have a clue what he wanted, or if he wanted anything at all. For all I knew, I could wear the same outfit I'd been wearing when he asked me out, and he might not even notice. And I didn't have to succumb to Jayne's romantic pressures, because she'd be planning not only what I was going to wear on our first date, but also what I'd be wearing in our engagement photos. Lydia, I'm sure, doubted I'd see even a *second* date with Gage, and she relished the power of taking Jayne's place in this moment.

How did I want him to see me? The more the question rolled through my brain, the more I knew that *him* wasn't Gage at all. I thought about Billy Fitz, and the tiny smile he'd sent me, picking me out of the crowd after school. And the way his face had soured when he saw Gage. And the way I'd gone on with my life after, unfazed. Not exactly strong, but not weak, either.

"Cool," I said, relishing the syllable. "I just want to look cool." I opened my eyes to Lydia's enthusiastic approval.

"Cool we can do. When is he picking you up?"

"Seven."

"That gives us . . . "

"Two hours." I didn't want to waste any time waiting for her to do the math.

"Perfect. You go shower. I'll meet you back here with the perfect outfit. Do you trust me?"

I looked at my purple pants. "Do I have a choice?"

She ran toward the door, but before leaving she looked back and said, "And for Pete's sake, shave your legs."

And that's how I ended up wearing my father's cashmere sweater on my first date.

Here's the whole outfit: a pair of thick, black tights, with the feet cut off, and rolled up to the middle of my calf. The footie part of the sock was hidden inside my shoes—a pair of black dress shoes Mom had bought from a bargain bin for two dollars, not realizing they were boys'. My father's cadet blue cashmere sweater, too small for his latest girth, but long enough to hit me just above the knees, then hiked up a little thanks to a wide, black belt that gave the illusion that my waist was at least two inches smaller.

Before putting any of this on, I'd spent a good ten minutes with my head between my knees as Lydia worked through my damp hair with a blowdryer, scrunching and unscrunching the curls in her nimble fingers. The result was a wild mass, soon tamed by a lace stocking-turned-headband. (I didn't ask where the lace stocking came from. Some things are better left unknown.) Then, makeup, including expertly applied eyeliner, raspberry-colored lipstick, and a generous splash of Jean Naté perfume.

"Lydia, you are a genius." Truth, without a hint of irony. I don't know if the sweater transformed me, or if I transformed the sweater. Either way, the worn, soft material clung to me on top and fell into soft folds below. "You sure Dad won't mind?"

"Slip away fast and he probably won't notice. Besides, I rescued it from the donate basket before we moved."

Slipping away turned out to be easy, as the doorbell rang at 6:58, leaving only two minutes for Gage to step inside, meet my parents, and slip away before the opening shenanigans of *The Dukes of Hazzard*. Mom complimented his shirt—a crisp white oxford with a Brittania logo on the pocket—and Dad asked just enough questions to ensure that his daughter's escort was unlikely to be both a basketball player *and* a serial killer. Then we were hustled out the door.

"My aunt let me borrow her car," Gage said, and I understood the sheepishness of his admission when I saw the vehicle parked in front of our house.

"Is that a Gremlin?"

"It is, indeed. But it's that, or walking."

"Drive on."

When we got to the car, he opened the door for me, saying, "By the way, you look cool."

So, you know, a perfect start.

The Northenfield Cineplex offered three movie choices: something called *Teachers*, *The Terminator*, and *Stop Making Sense*, a concert movie with the group Talking Heads. That would have been my choice, but I could hear Jayne's voice whispering on the wind, telling me to let him choose. He's the guy, he's buying the tickets (I assumed, though I had my own crumpled five-dollar bill just in case).

"*Terminator?*" he asked. "I heard it's good."

"Sounds great." Because, by then, with his hand on the small of my back guiding me up to the ticket window, it did. Without question, he bought our tickets, and two oversized sodas, and a medium popcorn to share. I tried not to calculate the expenses, and I worked very hard to take one nibble of popcorn to his every two. We were early enough to see every preview, commenting on what looked good and what didn't, and I couldn't help but wonder if we'd see any of them together.

When the movie itself started, we placed our drinks on the floor, and by the time the screen was filled with a naked Arnold Schwarzenegger, Gage was holding my hand. He leaned over, and while Sarah Connor clocked into her waitressing job, stroked my sleeve with his other hand and whispered, "Is this cashmere?"

"It's my dad's," I whispered back.

My reply had an amusing, if unintended, consequence: he drew back a little and said, "Oh. That's cool."

If I ever have the opportunity to write a review of *The Terminator*, it would go something like this:

> Arnold Schwarzenegger rides a motorcycle and shoots guns, while Gage Wickam, who smells like spice and lime, holds my hand and reminds me over and over how time travel works.

We stayed through the ending credits—at my insistence—while people crawled over us, trying not to knock over our half-empty soda cups. Finally, we were the only two people in the theater, besides the workers in their shiny gold vests, ready to gather trash and scrape the floors before the late-show audience filed in. I recognized one of them from Trigonometry, though he gave no indication of recognizing me, not even when the lights came on full strength.

Unlike the animals who had watched the movie with us, Gage and I gathered our trash, though we had to let go of each other's hands to do so.

"Are you hungry?" he asked as we made our way into the aisle.

"A little." I lied. I was starving. My one-third of a medium popcorn had been my dinner.

"What time do you need to be home?"

"Not for a while. Maybe midnight?"

We dropped our trash in the enormous rolling bins, and he took my hand before we made it into the lobby.

"Dino's still the place to go around here?"

He was referring to Northenfield's homegrown pizza parlor. Red-checked tablecloths, candles burning in jars covered with long, waxy drips. Pizzas came in one size, and sodas came by the pitcher. It was the place to be and be seen by all the school kids on Friday nights and by all the church kids on Sunday nights. Saturdays were for families—parents and children. Social suicide for teens.

"It is," I said, not mentioning that I'd only been there once, on a Saturday night. With my parents. And little sisters. Wishing I had a bag to put over my head.

There were more cars in the parking lot than when we first arrived, which meant some extra wandering around time. The night was cool and crisp. There might have been a moon, but with so many light posts and bright, shining marquees, who could tell? When we finally found the Gremlin, Gage took the keys out of his pocket and unlocked my door, joking about who would ever bother to steal this hunk of junk anyway. I laughed—not because his joke was funny, but because his face was so close to mine, and then all the light went away, because he kissed me.

It was a quick kiss, I suppose—I didn't have any others to measure it against—but not so quick that I didn't have time to record every millisecond. His lips on mine, his hand on my face, thumb stroking my jaw. The taste of popcorn and Pepsi. A break away. A quick return, and then the cool night air between us.

"I didn't want to spend the whole night wondering if I'd have the courage to do that."

"It's okay," I said, stopping myself from rising to my toes so he could do it again.

"Still hungry?"

"A little," I lied, again. This time because I couldn't imagine using this same mouth to eat a slice of Dino's cheese pizza.

We didn't talk on the drive. A song by Spandau Ballet played on the radio, the lyrics perfectly filling the Gremlin's tiny space, reassuring: "This much is true."

At the restaurant, we got a table by the window, one reserved for "dates," according to Dino's Unspoken Code of Seating. After a brief discussion, we settled on a pepperoni and mushroom pie and a pitcher of Mr. Pibb.

"I only have five dollars," I confessed, thinking his impressive display of cash had to come to an end sometime.

He produced a credit card. "Dinner's on Aunt June."

And so we added cheese sticks.

It seemed the kiss loosened our tongues, and conversation whizzed back and forth through the flame of the single candle between us. We talked about books we'd read, ones we hadn't read, and ones we wanted to read. We learned that neither of us had ever seen *The Maltese Falcon* and both thought *Casablanca* was overrated as the greatest movie of all time.

"Clearly," I said, dunking a stick of breaded cheese into a small dish of warm marinara sauce, "that title will soon be given over to the subtle dramatic masterpiece known as *The Terminator*." I pronounced the movie title in my best Schwarzenegger, which admittedly wasn't good, but he laughed anyway.

"Next time, you choose."

"How do you feel about period pieces? Women in long dresses. Accents. Subtitles."

"Accents *and* subtitles? What is that? Like, italics?"

He said it just as I filled my mouth with burning cheese, and I laughed and yelped simultaneously, fanning my gaping maw as the steaming, stringy remnant seared my chin. You know, like a lady.

Across the table, Gage's face twisted into disappointment. Disgust, really, and my heart started to break, until I realized he wasn't looking at me. Rather, he was looking *behind* me, and when I turned around, I saw why. Apparently, everybody was back from being Away, and Dino's was about to fill up with football players, cheerleaders, band members—and their dates.

Jayne, looking shocked, sent a pretty wave across the restaurant, then a not-so-subtle hint that I should apply a napkin. Immediately. I did, but not before Billy Fitz saw me. And by the time I'd cleaned my face, he was gone.

Chapter 8 (b)

interlude: *an intervening or interruptive period, space, or event*

Between chapters, the author created an **interlude** *to provide some backstory for her character.*

THE RIDE HOME WAS SILENT TOO. But not the companionable kind, like when we were riding to Dino's, fresh from a kiss, listening to the perfect song. This silence was full, like there wasn't any room for words, because the ghosts of all the unspoken ones were packed in the space between us. And the only way to clear the air was to poke them.

I drew first.

"So," I said, as the Gremlin shuddered to a stop at a light, "what's the deal between you and Billy, anyway?"

"The *deal*? There's no *deal.*"

"Fine. Don't tell me if you don't want to."

The light turned green, and Gage started to talk. Telling me everything, giving details to what I only knew in broad strokes.

Billy Fitz's mother died when he was in sixth grade. Cancer, they said. Vicious and fast-growing. Afterwards, Billy's father, a computer programmer who traveled all over the country setting up data management systems for various companies, had to take a job here in Northenfield to take care of his son, thinking Billy'd had enough upheaval in his life.

"But he doesn't live here now, right? Why?"

"I'm getting to that," Gage said, switching off the radio to escape a love song. "Mr. Fitz ended up working for the school district, teaching some computer classes at the High School and doing some stuff for the central office. That's where my mom worked, and that's where they met each other. After a while, they started dating."

"How long of 'a while'?"

"Just a few months. Their first official 'date' was the High School Christmas concert. I couldn't figure out why Mom was dragging me to this thing, but then there was Mr. Fitz and Billy, and we all sat together and went to Dairy Queen after."

"That sounds nice."

"It was totally weird. Awful."

"Why?"

"Billy Fitz was already this small-town star, you know? Always made the All-Star Little League Baseball team, always won all the Field Day races. Once he did the entire Bicycle Rodeo course on a wheelie. After his mom died, every woman in town was bringing him Dino's pizzas and chocolate cake. Girl Scouts gave him ten boxes of *every* type of cookie. That was in the paper—he had them all stacked up on his pool table. Oh, yeah. He has a pool table in his house. *And* a pool. And a TV in his bedroom hooked up to a speaker system so that it sounds like you're in a movie theater watching *Buck Rogers*."

"So his dad and your mom—they started dating for real?"

"Yeah."

The acknowledgment came out small, something he clearly didn't want to claim. I can't imagine what it must be like to watch your mother *date* another man. I remember Lottie telling me about the scandal that had rocked the town, and my stomach clenched up, anticipating details to come. Gage told me how Mrs. Fitz hadn't been dead for even a year, so the whole town seemed to have an opinion about the relationship at first. But the people who worked with Gage's mother, Lorraine, knew the two hadn't even met before Mr. Fitz started working for the schools, and soon enough the gossip died down. He was just lonely, you know? And he had this little boy to raise, without a lot of history of spending time raising him in the first place. So, when he meets this woman who also has a little boy about the same age, it seemed logical that they would come together as a family. *The Brady Bunch* without the annoyance of a sister.

A missing piece of the puzzle poked out at me.

"So," I said, staring out the window as we drove past the darkened theater, "do you mind me asking . . . where is your dad?"

"You can ask. Everybody else does, and when they do, Mom tells them he died in Vietnam. Which he might have if—as Aunt June will tell you—we're thinking of the right guy."

Apparently, things between Mr. Fitz and Gage's mom were going well, and the only problem with the Happily Ever After business is that the two boys hated each other. Mostly, it was a matter of Billy hating Gage. Here was this kid from nowhere, whose mother was a high-school dropout secretary thinking she could just swoop in and take his mother's place. Not that she moved into the house. That wouldn't be good. But they were over there all the time, cooking dinner almost every night. Disappearing upstairs for hours at a time while the boys watched football in the family room.

I shuddered. "Gross." It was bad enough thinking about parents dating, let alone . . .

"You have no idea. We went on a 'family' weekend to Six Flags. Billy and I got our own room. Do the math."

In the beginning, Billy had been grudgingly accepting. Not

friendly or anything, but quiet. When they all went to a movie together, Mr. Fitz and Lorraine tried to get the boys to sit next to each other in the row in front of them so they could talk to each other. Then, once the movie started, Billy would move—sometimes five or six seats over—just to make them mad. When Gage and Lorraine started going over to the Fitzes' house, Billy wouldn't let Gage go into his room, claiming "stuff" had gone missing the last time he was there. Just general jerk stuff, pretty normal for a spoiled rich kid.

"But it got worse?"

Gage was driving slower, almost as if he was delaying our arrival home. "Way worse."

Now, remember, Mr. Fitz is some kind of computer genius, right? And after a while, he got totally bored working for the schools, and he started getting all these out-of-town jobs. Like, for a week or two. Mostly at different universities. Sometimes they'd go visit. When he had a short-term contract with UCLA, for example, they all flew out and went to Disneyland. But mostly, while he was gone, Gage and Lorraine basically lived in the Fitzes' house. Lorraine slept in Mr. Fitz's bed, and Gage got a guest room with poster privileges and a new bedspread.

"Awkward," I said.

"Awful."

"And this went on for how long?"

"Almost three years. Until Billy was in ninth grade, I was in eighth."

"Wow. And they never thought about getting married?"

"Oh, Mom thought about it."

Lorraine was almost everything a wife would be to Mr. Fitz. While he was out of town, she took care of the house, paid the bills, took Billy back and forth to school, helped him with homework. Even went to parent-teacher conferences on Mr. Fitz's behalf. She moved out of the little house she and Gage lived in, and they stayed with her sister June during the times Mr. Fitz was in town—times that were becoming more and more rare. Whenever she brought up the subject of marriage, however, Mr. Fitz "wasn't ready." But if she issued an ultimatum of any kind, or even when she *said* it was over and refused to talk to him for weeks at a time, he'd get an opportunity to go do some work with MIT or Harvard or something and ask her to bring Gage to the house, and they'd have a heart-to-heart when he got back.

Fascinating as all this was, I wanted to know more about the boys. "How were you and Billy getting along during this time?"

"We weren't. He started calling my mom all kinds of horrible names, which meant every kid in school was calling my mom horrible names, which meant my mom lost her job. She pulled me out of school, and Aunt June paid for me to go to St. Bart's, since we used to be kind of Catholic."

It was during one of these times when Lorraine was waiting for Mr. Fitz to come home for a heart-to-heart that she met Lt. Mark Denley, a handsome Air Force recruiter making the rounds through Texas High Schools. (TRUTH: All Gage said was, "That's when my mom met Lt. Denley." All superfluous details are of my own invention.) They met in the St. Bartholomew cafeteria, shared a first meal of stale bakery cookies and watery punch, and he asked her to go back to San Antonio with him two days later.

"Whoa!" I was impressed as much with my own reverie as his sparse detail.

"Yeah."

"So, obviously, she went?"

"Not right then, obviously."

When Mr. Fitz came back from his latest adventure, Lorraine was waiting for him in the living room with a chicken shish kebab dinner and a bottle of wine. (Gage and Billy had been sent out to the movies with enough money for two features, popcorn, soda, candy, and arcade games.) While Mr. Fitz went on and on about this huge system he'd installed, and how they wanted him to go overseas somewhere to do pretty much the same thing, Lorraine knew it was now or never. She would either have to be his wife, with all the perks that entailed, including traveling *with* the man who would be her husband, or this needed to end. Forever. So she told him so, and when he tried the same old thing, about how maybe they should wait until the boys were out of High School so they could truly forge something new together, she lost it.

"That would have been four more YEARS!"

"Exactly."

Gage turned into my neighborhood and brought the car to an absolute crawl.

She left right then, kebabs on the skewers and everything, and went to the theater. She waited in the parking lot until Gage and Billy walked out, then drove to the front and told the boys to get in the car. But Billy refused, saying he'd rather walk than be seen in that old hunk of junk. So after Lorraine made sure he had a quarter to make a phone call to his dad, she and Gage went home. The next day, she withdrew her son from St. Bartholomew's, and the day after that, they packed all that they could in the back seat of the car and drove to San Antonio. Within a week, Lorraine was Mrs. Lt. Mark Denley, and the three of them lived in a quiet neighborhood near Randolph Air Force Base.

"How . . . romantic?" I said, not at all sure if that word came close to applying.

"I guess."

"But, then . . . why are you back here?"

"Lt. Denley—Mark—got transferred to Ramstein Air Base

in Germany. Sounded fun, since I hadn't made any real friends in San Antonio. I mean, I wouldn't know anybody in Germany, either, but Mom said the school would be full of other kids like me. Air Force brats, so they knew how to make friends."

We were in front of my house now, the Gremlin rumbling beneath us.

"So," I ventured, because I had to say something, "how did you end up back here?"

"Just . . . didn't like it. Everything was weird. Like, a whole different language."

"Silly—you were in Germany!"

"Not that. The whole culture. Who was what rank. Who's an officer. And all these rules. Crazy stuff. I wanted to come home."

"Here, home?"

"The only one I know."

beau (sg); beaux (pl): *a frequent or regular male companion in a romantic relationship*

Elyse, Jayne, and Lottie sat around the table and chatted about their beaux.

I REPLAYED THIS ENTIRE CONVERSATION to Jayne late that night, as we sat up whispering in bed while the rest of the house slept soundly.

First, though, of course, I filled her in as to how, exactly, it came to be that I was at Dino's on a Friday night with Gage Wickam, and she told me of all the excitement of being at an Away Game with the finest of Northenfield Texas High School society.

"So that's why you two didn't come join us at the big table at Dino's," she said at the conclusion of my tale.

"Exactly. I mean, I knew Billy could be kind of a jerk, but this shows a whole different side. Selfish, you know? And hateful."

"Weeeeell," Jayne drew out the word, preparing to be generous, "there are always two sides to every story. It could be that Gage was kind of a toot himself. He's a year younger, right? Maybe he was a total brat."

"No." I tore off a piece of breadstick Jayne had brought back wrapped in a piece of foil. "You didn't see when he was telling the story. Totally hurt. Billy *humiliated* him in every way possible." I could still see his face, illuminated by the dashboard light of his car. He'd stared straight ahead, only glancing over at me when I asked a question. And that's when I'd seen the true pain of sharing something that he'd carried alone for so long. "That's probably why he had such a hard time making new friends. Billy Fitz made him feel like he was worthless."

"Hmm." It's the sound Jayne makes when she wants time to think before committing to an opinion. "I suppose it's possible. But maybe Billy was just trying to protect the memory of his mother."

"Or maybe he just wanted his father to himself. And, anyway, that backfired on him, because now his father is working in Oxford, and Billy has nobody."

"He has the Bingleys," Jayne said, picking flecks of parmesan cheese off her breadstick. "I mean, he has his own house here, but he lives with them. That wouldn't be possible if Mr. Fitz had married Gage's mom, right? He seems happy there."

I felt myself puff up in defense. "And I suppose that's all that matters? That Billy's happy?"

"Of course not," Jayne soothed. "What matters is"—her expression turned mischievous in the glowing green light of the clock radio—"did he kiss you good night after baring his soul?"

"He did," I said, remembering it. We'd been on the front porch, bathed in the glow of the porch light Mom and Dad had so handily left on for us. It had been deeper than the kiss in the theater parking lot. More *important* somehow, because we shared a secret. Or, what I took to be a secret. Even though I didn't say so to Gage, I'd promised myself not to share his story with a single soul other than Jayne. He had a fresh start here, since Billy had nothing to hold over his head. I wouldn't do anything to jeopardize that, and I asked Jayne to honor that promise too.

"Of course," she agreed. "It's nobody's business."

"Speaking of nobody's business," I said with a comic waggle of my eyebrows, "where are you and Young Charlie on the kissing scale? I have two to report. And you . . ."

"I really, really like him, Pudge."

"Really?" I feigned shock. "Because it's kinda hard to tell . . ."

"And I think he likes me."

"Well, duh. Anybody within a mile of you two can tell that. So, has he kissed you?"

Even in the clock light I could see her blush. "Tonight. For the first time, actually."

"Where?"

"Right on my lips."

I slugged her.

"Oh, in his car. We pulled up just as Gage was driving off. Perfect timing."

"Perfect, indeed."

"He asked me—right out loud—if I'd consider myself his girlfriend."

We squealed a silent, sisterly squeal, kicking at the mattress like two Irish dancers.

"Why didn't you tell me?" I scolded. "Letting me go on and on about Gage, and you had the big news all along!"

"That's important too," she said. "And, do you think—does he consider you to be his girlfriend too?"

My excitement for her remained constant, but my own deflated, just a bit.

"I don't know. I'm not sure, exactly, how all this stuff works.

I mean, it seems like he likes me, but then, when he was talking, I felt more like a friend. Or . . . therapist? But mostly friend."

Jayne patted my leg in that way people think is comforting. "Maybe that's what he needs most of all right now."

As it turned out, whether or not Gage Wickam considered me to be his girlfriend depended entirely upon the moment. We walked to and from school together nearly every day, and he was always nice about letting Lydia walk with us. Sometimes she and I would walk together, hashing out the latest trauma from home, like the Littles' annoying piano practice, while he followed behind, listening to the music on his Walkman. Sometimes he and I walked together while she danced in circles around us, peppering Gage with questions about San Antonio and Germany, and if he didn't agree that airmen were sexier than soldiers. (For the record, he had no opinion.)

Other times, he and Lydia would walk side by side, talking about—of all things—clothing and fashion and designers. Gage always wore the best, according to Lydia—like he came out of a magazine or something. Sweaters tied around his shoulders, expensive loafers, designer jeans and shirts and, apparently, underwear. I know this, because one morning, bold as anything, she asked him, "Boxers or briefs?" And, without missing a beat, he said, "Calvin Klein." I didn't understand the significance of his answer until later that afternoon, while we (Lydia and I) were helping the Littles color the flowers on yet another homeschool science worksheet.

"Can you imagine?" Lydia said, carefully tracing the word *conifer*. "His underwear probably cost more than my entire outfit. He's, like, the perfect boy."

"Hmm." I borrowed Jayne's noise, but added, "He is pretty special."

On the flip side, the kissing, the hand-holding, the telling me I looked cool—all of that fell into sharp decline after our date. As in, it didn't happen. Unlike Charlie and Jayne who were—almost literally—inseparable. They had perfected that whole arms-around-each-other-while-walking thing. He carried her tray at lunch, her books between classes, her backpack before and after school. She baked him cookies, wrote him notes, decorated his locker with sparkle stickers, and even let him pick out *his* favorite flavor for her Bonne Bell Lip Smacker. (7-Up. Go figure.) They talked on the phone for twenty minutes—the maximum time allowed by Dad—every evening, even after he'd driven her home from school and they'd talked in the car for at least an hour before Mom went outside and said he'd either have to marry her or go home. When she wasn't *with* him, she was talking *about* him, and if I didn't love my sister so ferociously, it all might have made me a little jealous.

But I did love her. I *do* love her. And every time I did start to feel the slightest twinge of green, the utter happiness on her face turned it right back to my normal pinkish hue.

Someday, I thought, *Gage and I might be like that*. It would just take a little time. In the meanwhile, we did our homework together, sometimes. Ate lunch together, most days. And even had another "date" or two, meaning we spent one Saturday night in our kitchen, listening to the entirety of Casey Kasem's *American Top 40* countdown while I made brownies, and I went along when he volunteered to chauffeur Lydia and two of her friends to Black Light Skate Night at the roller rink in the basement of the Methodist church.

"So, is he your boyfriend or not?" Lottie asked one day at lunch. Gage was at another table—one populated with Junior

Varsity Basketball players—and hadn't sent so much as a glance in my direction.

"I don't think so," I said. Lunch that day was the peculiar perfection known as School Cafeteria Pizza—rectangular in shape, thick in texture, sausage-y in flavor, and unmatched in deliciousness. That, and a double serving of canned peaches, a glop of chocolate pudding with sprinkles, and a tall Styrofoam cup of red drink made Fridays my favorite cafeteria day. "I guess I'm officially a one-date wonder."

"Well, how do you feel about that?"

"I dunno." But I did know. I felt silly, and awkward, and foolish, and nine.

"Then do something about it. A girl can't just sit around and wait for a boy to decide if he's going to commit himself to being her boyfriend or not. Look, being part of a couple is a key to survival in this school. You've got too many Friday nights ahead of you to risk spending them alone."

"That's easy for you to say. You have Collin." Who, at the moment, was busily defacing Lottie's math textbook with a love poem. Later, at book check-in time, she would have to pay sixteen dollars for the gesture.

"Do you think that just *happened*?" She didn't even attempt to lower her voice.

"I guess so," I said. "Like Jayne and Charlie. One glance and—"

"The real world is not like Jayne and Charlie. Look—" she dug around in her purse, produced a dollar, and handed it to Collin. "Go and get us a couple of fried fruit pies from the snack bar."

Collin looked up, tilting his head back to see her through the fringe of black hair covering his eyes. "What's that?"

"Hostess pies at the snack bar. Two of them. Apple?"

This, to me, and I nodded.

"Apple for Elyse and a cherry for me."

He looked at his unfinished verse. "But I've only got four lines left."

"And the snack bar's only going to be open for five more minutes. Go."

He took the dollar with a fawning gesture, and scuttled (really, there exists NO other word to describe his movement) to the table at the far end of the cafeteria where the Booster Club parents sold Hostess snacks and ice cream bars to earn money for banners and foam fingers to Boost School Spirit.

"Now." Lottie leaned across the table, her face twisted into something like a general giving the final instructions to the troops before launching into battle. "Do you think Collin would be my—or anybody's—*first* choice in a boyfriend? No. Of course not. Maybe not second or third, either. But we can't all sit around and wait for the perfect boy to come along and couple us up, now can we?"

"*Couple us up?*"

"Be realistic. I'm not going to get into the specifics of population, even though I could, because I work in the administration office during sixth period and can check all the files while the ladies are at lunch. So, while the numbers of girls and boys at this school might actually work in the girls' favor, the desirability between the two populations is completely skewed."

"Skewed?"

"Meaning. For every decent, cute boy here, there are between three and five equally matched girls. Meaning if you're not willing to "date down" a little, you run the risk of being completely alone until graduation."

"So, you consider yourself to be 'dating down' with Collin?" I looked at the poem he was so diligently scratching into the front cover of her book. Greasy little monkey though he might be, my heart broke just a bit for him. "Does he know?"

She blinked her eyes very slowly, and her voice took on the tone and tempo of a sock puppet. "Collin and I are guaranteed dates for every foreseeable dance and banquet for the next three years. Winter Ball, Homecoming, Band Recognition, Prom—next year, when we're Juniors—unless he can swing us a favor with Katie Berg. And in between, movies, concerts, whatever I want. We each buy our own tickets, of course."

"Of course."

"At this stage, it would be silly to keep up that kind of pretense."

"What kind of pretense, exactly?"

"Wooing. Romance, trying to make some sort of impression."

"Right? Because who wants wooing and romance?" I looked over at the Varsity Athletes' table, where Jayne and Charlie were sharing not only a chair, but a Fudgsicle from the snack bar. So disgusting I couldn't stop myself from sighing.

"Of course every girl wants that, but it's completely unrealistic to think that's what life is going to bring, particularly because most boys are completely incapable of producing either. I say, if you have Gage anywhere close to nibbling your hook, you need to reel him in."

She said the hook-nibbling line just as I took a bite of pizza, and I nearly gagged. My spluttering and choking served not only as my response, but also as a means of attracting the attention of just about everyone in the cafeteria, including Gage and Billy. Gage lifted his eyebrows and sent a comical, *Are you okay?* look, though he made no move to save me if, indeed, I'd been dying in my blue plastic chair. Billy looked genuinely concerned for about half a second before shaking his head and returning to the sketches in the spiral playbook he always carried around. Charlie and Jayne were too wrapped up in the dab of chocolate ice cream on each other's noses to have even noticed that I was still battling the hunk of pizza crust lodged in my throat.

"I'm sorry," I said, after a long sip of red drink. "What was that about hooking my nibble?"

Lottie (also, I might add, unconcerned with my possible need for Heimlich intervention) rolled her eyes. "Don't be obtuse. It's unbecoming. I'm just saying that if Gage likes you— even just a little bit—you need to capitalize on that. Boys don't turn into boyfriends acting on their own behalf. You need to nudge him a little. Be ever present. Make him see you as his only option and *dating* as the only option for the both of you."

"Lottie, you can't trick somebody into being your boyfriend."

"Not *trick*. Just capitalize on the practicality of the relationship."

Before I could ask if she even *liked* Collin, he arrived, two Hostess pies in hand, plus a Twinkie he'd purchased with the change.

"They didn't have any cherry, so I got you a lemon. Is that okay?"

Lottie made him squirm for a split second before smiling and saying, "Of course. That's fine. Good job."

He looked genuinely pleased at her approval and proud to accept my gratitude. He sat down and was resuming his poetry when Lottie tapped the table for his attention.

"So," she said, "for Neewollah, you're going with me, right?"

"Of course," he said, and his face lit up with a grand idea. "I thought we might go as Popeye and Olive Oyl. I have my dad's shirt from when he was in the navy."

"No," Lottie said.

"You're right, of course," Collin said. "Terrible idea. My hair's too long, anyway."

"We're going as Gilligan and Ginger from *Gilligan's Island*. I have a hat from Knott's Berry Farm for you and a slinky, sparkly dress for me." She turned to me. "I even have false eyelashes. We'll be perfect."

"What is this?" I asked, finding myself outside yet another Northenfield, Texas, circle.

"Neewollah," Collin said, aggressively underlining key words in his poem. "It's *Halloween* spelled backwards. It's what the teenagers here do instead of Trick-or-Treating."

"Everything's backwards," Lottie said. "It's the one dance a year where the girls get to ask the guys. Instead of dressing up in something fancy, you can either wear a costume or dress like a tattered Bumpkin."

"There's prizes for both," Collin said.

"But nobody cares about the Bumpkin prize," Lottie said.

"You're right. They don't."

"So." Lottie was talking to me again after putting out yet another possible Collinization of Opinion. "You need to ask Gage to Neewollah. Before somebody else does."

"I don't know." I broke off a flaky corner of the Hostess pie and let it melt in my mouth while I considered. "I've never asked a guy out before."

"It's the perfect thing. The perfect time. Tickets go on sale next week."

"Do I have to pay for those, too?"

"*You* will. But Collin will buy his own, won't you?"

"Of course." Poor kid, didn't even look up.

"But they're not too expensive," Lottie went on. "It's not like Winter Formal or Prom or anything like that. Just something to do in October that isn't stupid football. Ask him."

"How?"

"Just say, 'Hey, Gage. You want to go to Neewollah with me?' Easy."

"And if he says no?"

"Easy, too. You shake his dust off your boots and move on. Aim a little lower." Luckily, Collin didn't see the meaningful way in which Lottie inclined her head in his direction.

I spent the rest of the day worrying, rehearsing, convincing, worrying (more), and finally, deciding to follow through with Lottie's advice. It was yet another Friday (hence, the school pizza), and a Home Game, which meant yet another Pep Rally, which meant my afternoon class only lasted about fifteen minutes, but then who needs Trig anyway.

We poured into the gym, my fellow Badgers and I, under the watchful eyes of the faculty members charged to keep our Spirit somewhat under control while we were under one roof and on the clock. The band played a recognizable tune: Sister Sledge, "We Are Family." The Cheer-Sitters kept to their designated section in the bleachers, pom-poms waving in rhythm, and the Cheer-Leaders flipped and tossed themselves all over the gym floor. The girls' volleyball team sat in a sad little row of metal folding chairs. Some attempt would be made to affirm that this gathering was for their benefit, too, as they had a game, too. Somewhere.

I looked for Jayne's hair in the crowd and found her, dancing in place, frantically waving for my attention. Head down, I elbowed my way through the crowd, knocking away the girl rumored to be Frank Churchill's latest girlfriend for the privilege of sitting next to my sister. For the next thirty minutes, I listened once again to the announcement of our team, name by name, save for Frank Churchill who was on the injured list. Apparently he requested our prayers to keep his brothers strong as they went out to KICK SOME TORO TAIL. I remained neutral during the battle for the spirit stick:

We got spirit,
Yes, we do!
We got spirit, how 'bout you?
JUNIORS!!!!!

I tried not to cringe in empathetic embarrassment when the faculty skit included watching Mrs. Pierson try to loop a lasso around Señora Benavidez, our Spanish teacher, who was supposed to be a bull? Or something? I joined in the polite applause for the volleyball team, wishing them all the best during their thirty seconds of recognition. And, finally, I stood for the school theme song and tried not to look too amazed at the fact that Jayne could sing every word.

Throughout all of this I scanned the crowd for Gage. He'd be on the other side of the gym with the Freshmen and Sophomores, unless, like me, he'd gone rogue to sit with an upperclassman. Nowhere. I trained my eyes to detect his most likely subgroups. Preppies. Lesser athletes. Even the smart kids, who sat in the uppermost bleachers, getting a head start on their weekend homework, caring nothing for Toros, nor their TAILS.

He was nowhere to be seen in the gym, so the minute the final note of the school song rang out, I told Jayne I'd catch up with her in a few and immediately started wedging my way through the crowd and outside to see him walking toward the Big Tree, coming from the direction of the Middle School building.

"You missed the Pep Rally," I said, making it sound like he might forever be haunted by this lost opportunity at school spirit rejuvenation.

"I was doing some tutoring at the library here."

"Fun." And, really, I was a bit envious. "Jayne's going to walk home with us. Charlie has to stay here until the game."

"So, she's cast down among the lowly?"

"Something like that." I figured I had at least fifteen minutes before she'd be finished saying her final goodbyes, but Lydia might be bounding out of the eighth-grade crowd at any moment. It was Now or Never (well, maybe Now or Monday, but Monday seemed pretty far away), so I took a deep, strengthening breath and said, "Gage?"

"Yeah."

There, that part was done. "Can I ask you something?"

"Sure."

So far, so good. "Well, I was wondering if you'd be interested, at all, and I understand if you don't, with me. Or, again, at all. But I was thinking. More, like, wondering, I guess—"

He laughed. "Are you asking me to go to Neewollah with you?"

"Yes!" I almost collapsed with relief. "Although, now, since you asked, I probably jinxed the whole thing."

"No, it's fine. We're cool."

"*We're cool?*"

"Absolutely. I'd like to go with you, of course."

I tried to be worthy of the cool facade he bestowed, but inside I was a raging machine fueled by confidence and glee. "Do you have any ideas for costumes? Or, do you want to do costumes? Because we could just go with the hillbilly look, too. If you'd rather."

"I think we have time to work out those details." For all that his conversation seemed to be in tune with me, he kept his eyes above my head, scanning the crowd much as I'd scanned for him earlier.

"Looking for someone?"

"Oh, just Mrs. Pierson, to sign off on my tutoring hour."

"She's probably recovering from her Pep Rally Mortification Ceremony."

I followed with a quick description of her antics, during which he interrupted me midsentence saying, "That sounds crazy," with such condescension I declined to pursue the reenactment.

We stood in an odd, awkward silence before he asked if Jayne and I were going to the game tonight.

"I guess so. Want to come with us?" Look at me, one Neewollah invite and I'm breaking every rule of social order.

"Nah. I wish, but I need to help Aunt June with some stuff around the house."

"On a Friday night? Poor Cinderfella."

"I'm going to be asking her for some new basketball shoes in a few weeks. Got to build up that good favor, you know? But maybe we could go into town tomorrow? Get some costume ideas?"

"That would be great!" I felt like my enthusiasm would somehow bring him back to my level—equal us out a bit, like we were on that first (and so far, only) date. And it must have worked, because by the time Lydia found us for the walk home, he was his smiling self. Jovial and joking, asking me to show the both of them how Mrs. Pierson had chased Señora Benavidez with a lasso made of jump rope.

We were still within sight of the school when Jayne called to us, and the four of us walked in a solid square formation. Gage and Lydia in front, Jayne and me in back. Crisp leaves skittered around our steps, and when I mentioned I was chilly, Gage untied the sweater from around his shoulders and handed it back to me.

They—Gage and Lydia—walked ahead while Jayne and I stopped so I could put the sweater on.

"Wasn't that sweet?" I said, my whisper blending in with the wind in the trees. "I think I'll wear it tonight to the game."

"It's a good color on you," Jayne said. "But—"

"I know. It's not the school color."

"That's not what I was going to say." We resumed our walk, now a full ten sidewalk squares behind the others.

"What were you going to say?"

"Just . . . be careful."

"Of what?"

"Of wanting too much, maybe? You know, Billy really doesn't like this guy."

I brought the sweater sleeve up to my nose and inhaled the sweet scent of Clean Boy. "Last I knew, Billy really doesn't like me, either."

relinquish: *to withdraw or retreat from : leave behind*

Lydia had her arms linked with two boys, and neither
seemed willing to relinquish *his claim to the next dance.*

IT WAS LIKE A TEEN CARAVAN TO ABILENE, but when all the other kids veered off to go to the mall, Jayne, with her newly minted Texas license, steered the Station Wagon to Seconds Away!, the giant thrift store. She and Charlie were going as Romeo and Juliet, and she figured with an old prom dress and just a few special touches, she would look like Miss Junior Verona 1595.

"What about Charlie?"

"Sweater vest," she answered, carefully checking the mirror. "And I turned one of his mother's pleated skirts into bloomers. Looking for a puffy shirt today, but he's in charge of finding his own tights. I'm not about to mess in that business."

"A boy who will wear tights for you? He's a keeper."

Her face went all dreamy behind the neon green sunglasses. "Isn't he, though? It's like we were made for each other."

"You do remember, though, how it ends? *Romeo and Juliet*, I mean? Be careful of the punch at the party. If you pass out, that'll be one sad date."

Jayne laughed, but Lydia, a languid mass of boredom

sprawled across the back seat, used her foot to *bap* the back of my head.

"Why do you have to be the killer of romance?"

I flipped down the visor and caught her eye in the mirror. She had all her ringlets captured in a side ponytail and a pink terry-cloth headband stretched across her grumpy brow. She'd been sullen ever since she'd learned that our first stop would be at Seconds Away! before joining up with some of the others at the mall for lunch.

"Sorry," I said, trying hard—no, *really* hard—not to come off as too condescending, "I'm not the one who created the couple most likely to participate in a murder-suicide pact rather than wait for two days to see how things worked out. That was Shakespeare."

"You think you're so smart." Lydia was checking *her* makeup in *my* mirror, so I edged to the side to give her a little more room. "No wonder no boy wants to go out with you."

I turned in my seat. "Um, not to completely blow your theory out of the water or anything, but the reason we're going on this little jaunt today is so that I can get an outfit for my date."

"It's Neewollah. You asked him, so it doesn't count."

"But my date is with a guy who asked me out on a date before already. So it does count."

"Do you know how infuriating you are?"

"Both of you. Stop," Jayne said, bringing an effective end to the budding argument. "I have to make a left-hand turn."

We'd all spent enough time with Jayne behind the wheel to know such an occasion called for utter silence and stillness on the part of all passengers involved, and it gave me time to second-guess every moment of my life between the time Gage asked me out and the time I asked him—each one ticking away with the rhythm of the helpful blinker.

There'd been the perfection of the first part of the first date, the magic of the first kiss (and the front-porch encore), the unveiling of his story, and that awkwardness that had existed between us ever since. But, there'd been an *us* to be awkward, right? He hadn't detached himself or drifted away. Sometimes he seemed like a real boyfriend—although one overwhelmed with chivalry and chastity. And other times, he seemed like nothing more than a companion to walk back and forth to school with. We'd gone to one other movie, sat together at one football game, and I once tagged along while he went on an errand to buy floor wax for his aunt. (Because apparently, being a girl, I would instinctively know what kind of floor wax to buy.) Then there was the fact that when I asked him to go to Neewollah with me, he'd said, "Of course."

At the time, I'd been so excited about his response, I hadn't thought to search out the subtext. That kind of insecurity doesn't usually rear its head until moments of utter quiet, like waiting in a stuffy, radio-free car for your newly licensed sister to make a left-hand turn. But now, nothing about our impending date spoke highly of romance. We didn't have a cute "couple" costume—I'd been too afraid to suggest one, and he didn't seem to care. When I suggested we go the Country Bumpkin route, though, he shot me down, as that was the agreed-upon costume choice of losers.

"I trust you," he'd said, when he called to say he couldn't go shopping after all. That his aunt had a slew of chores for him to do. "You can figure this out for both of us."

You know who else could figure this out? Lydia. And there she was, in the back seat, having agreed only after a fair amount of protest, which she voiced once Jayne had successfully navigated across two lanes of oncoming traffic and stopped the car reasonably within a single parking space.

"I still don't think it's fair that I can't even *go* to the dance I'm getting you ready for."

"School policy," Jayne soothed, gathering up her purse. "High School students only. You guys get your own dance in February."

"I can name at least a dozen High School boys who would go with me."

"Trust me," I said. "They'd go with you anywhere."

Any other girl might have been insulted, but Lydia simply acknowledged the truth with a giggle, and the three of us headed into the thrift store.

It was, I suppose, pretty well organized as far as thrift stores go. Big signs hung from the ceiling with words like FURNITURE!!! BEDDING!!! KITCHEN!!! It smelled like a thousand houses piled under one bright fluorescent roof. Jayne led the way to a back corner, where a single, overstuffed round rack contained abandoned gowns crammed into one multicolor lump. With a homing instinct I could never possess, my sisters disappeared within and came out clutching hangers full of discarded fashion. These were whittled down to three possibilities, and the first one Jayne tried on turned her into an Elizabethan teen—or it would, given Lydia's talent with a needle and scraps.

"Now, you," Lydia said, after dispatching our sister to find an appropriately puffy shirt for Romeo.

"I hate costumes," I said, cringing under her scrutiny. "It's hard enough wearing regular clothes."

"Maybe Raggedy Ann? Or a baseball player?"

I felt somehow smaller *and* fatter with each of Lydia's suggestions. We could dress in black with big white dots and go as a couple of dominoes. Or we could dress in black and glue a bunch of metal stuff on us and go as magnets. Or we could dress in black—

"Am I sensing a theme here?"

"Black is slimming," Lydia said. "Unless you think you could do something with this." She held up a pink, frothy gown that should have been mercifully put out of its misery in 1972.

I was just about to comment that the dress would make me look like a giant pile of frosting when a familiar face appeared from the CHILDREN!!! section of the store. Gage, tall enough to peer over the racks, was scanning to the left and the right like a thrift store lifeguard. Mortified, I was ready to dive into the pink tulle, but he spotted me, raised his hand in greeting, and made a beeline toward us.

Books are always talking about the heart soaring, and I tried to get mine to soar across the racks of polyester pantsuits and abandoned sweaters, like maybe he was coming to my rescue with a plan to somehow turn us into Heathcliff and Catherine. Instead, I was given a premonition about how the process would now be inconceivably more awkward.

"Your mother said I'd find you here," he said when he was close enough to pinch a fingerful of fabric. "I finished my stuff early and called your house, but the three of you had already left."

I gave what I hoped was a flirty, fun punch to his arm. "I thought you said you trusted me."

"I do," he said, standing closer, his back to Lydia. "But it was wrong of me to put this burden entirely on you. We're going as a couple, after all, aren't we? It's a decision we should make together."

"Any ideas?"

He stretched his arms out. "Thousands of them. And a full twenty dollars. Let's go."

After instructing Lydia to return the pink monstrosity to the rack, he placed an easy arm over her shoulders and mine, and the three of us navigated the store together. As if on cue, the song over the speaker system blared Duran Duran, "Hungry Like the Wolf." No surprise, that song was everywhere. Inescapable, like it was on the ground hunting all of us. Hearing it reminded me of that night back in the Bingleys' kitchen, Charlie being goofy and Billy being . . . *there*. I thought about how good he was with the terrible Caroline. Patient. Indulgent. And would Charlie be friends with someone as selfish as Gage described?

For the moment, though, I tucked the doubts aside, because the song had inspired Gage in a completely different way. The chain of thought went something like this: Hungry like the Wolf . . . Big Bad Wolf . . . Red Riding Hood and the Big Bad Wolf. It was a brilliant moment, really, when Gage and Lydia hit on the idea at the same time, leaving me no option but to declare it perfect. We found a loopy, hand-knit red cape and a man's mohair sweater, complete with long, horsehair epaulets. We'd hit a treasure trove of forsaken fashion, a mish-mash of hippies, beatniks, and disco babies. Before long I had a shimmery red sequined dress, Gage had somewhat suede-y pants, and we even found a cute basket so I could carry my lip gloss and emergency phone-home money. The final touches? An enormous flannel nightgown, glassless wire frames, and a shower cap.

"Grandma, what beautiful brown eyes you have," Lydia said, batting her eyelashes with an attempt at innocence that might have fooled Gage, but not me.

He broke into a grin that made me think she'd turned into a tasty treat. "The better to look you over, my dear."

She pretended to swoon, then squealed and ran down the aisle toward BOOKS!!! He chased her, caught her up in a big, animal embrace, and carried her back where I was waiting with the mohair sweater draped over my arm. Already the itch was unbearable, and I didn't think there'd be much slow dancing in our future.

Once again, thanks to the talents of my little sister, I was ready for a third official date with Gage. The red dress, basically a bunch of shine with straps, had been tucked and pinned around me perfectly. She'd scrunched and fluffed my hair and clipped the hood in to frame it. Back in the SHOES!!! section of the store, we'd found a pair of sparkly red high heels that weren't exactly comfortable, but Lydia assured me the pain they produced would remind me not to be so schlumpy in my shoulders.

Jayne was a dreamy Juliet with her hair in soft ringlets and her dress perfectly disguised as an Elizabethan gown. When Charlie arrived at the house to pick her up, Mom made the two of them pose in front of the fireplace, in front of the tree, in front of his car—and that was before she discovered the balcony-like possibilities of the front porch. Then it was Jayne, her hand extended to a kneeling Charlie, with Mom's instructions to *imagine the moonlight* punctuated by the pop of the flash.

Seven fifteen, and Gage still hadn't come to pick me up, and I began to worry that I might have misunderstood the extent of the role-reversal of Neewollah. Was I supposed to pick *him* up at *his* house? If so, that's something we probably should have discussed during the afternoon's shopping, but he hadn't said a word. Mom told me not to worry, Dad promised to take me himself if the boy didn't show, and Lydia remained locked behind her bedroom door, still pouting at her exclusion from the festivities. She'd taken the hallway phone into her room, and sounds of muted, complaining conversation seeped through the door.

It was seven thirty, a point where I was about to trade in my sparkly heels and red cape for slippers and sweatpants, when the doorbell finally rang. Mom shouted over and over for me to go upstairs, not let him know that I'd been waiting. Unless his tardiness could be explained by some explosion that robbed him of his hearing, he heard every word.

Rather than going up to my room, I positioned myself at the foot of the stairs, one hand on the bannister and the other on my hip in a pose Lydia assured me made my waist appear two inches smaller. This also gave me the perfect vantage point to see Gage on the front porch before he could see me. I had a host of clever greetings that I'd been practicing in my head for the last ten minutes. I decided to go with, *My! What an inaccurate watch you have!*

Dad swung the door open with a terse greeting, and I allowed my pose to sink into something more like Little Blob Riding Hood. On the porch there was no boy disguised as a Wolf disguised as an Old Woman. No mohair sweater, no suede pants, no nightgown. There would be no evening full of flirtatious leaning in, the better to see me. Or stolen kisses, the better to taste me.

"Elyse," Gage said, after properly acknowledging my mother, "I am so sorry. Can you ever forgive me?"

It wasn't until then that I realized I'd backed up the stairs, and stood on my own balcony, with my Romeo beseeching from the floor. Only, he wasn't dressed like Romeo, either. He wasn't dressed like anything, really. His outstretched arms poked out from a red flannel shirt, sleeves rolled to the elbows. It was tucked into a pair of dark blue jeans—Wrangler, I would guess, without even looking at the tag—which were, in turn, tucked into a pair of heavy work boots.

"It's okay," I stammered, then spoke quickly to cover my mother's haughty disagreement. "I mean, if you'd rather go as Bumpkins, it's okay. Just give me five minutes to change. I have something—"

"No." He compelled me to stop with just the power of his

voice. "I'm not a Bumpkin. I'm the Lumberjack, see?" Gage struck a pose meant to be manly, holding an imaginary axe and furrowing his brow.

"You mean the Woodsman?" Even in my shocked state, I couldn't just let that kind of inaccuracy slide.

"Yeah. Whatever, I guess."

"You should have called," I said, holding my ground. "I might have worn something a little less . . . red."

In response, he walked (stomped—the boots) to the foot of the stairs and took my hand. "You look beautiful. And if you'll let me, I'd love to rescue you."

This bit of romance sent my mother into a fit of approval, and with just one quick snapshot at the front door, I hustled us out to his car, hoping to regain lost time.

"You just wouldn't believe how uncomfortable that sweater was," he said as he drove. Not too fast, but with a weird sense of nervous urgency that made me think he was wanting to regain the minutes too. "So I had to scramble for something else. And then, it hit me. Lumberjack."

"Woodsman," I corrected. Again.

"Yes. Of course. Woodsman."

"You know, the earlier versions—the original, in fact— didn't have a Woodsman. He came along in later tellings to alleviate the fear of the children."

"Is that so?"

Is that so? Of course it was so, and how could a boy who matched me point for point in our AP English class not know that? I continued to fill the car with one-sided conversation about the presanitized goriness of fairy tales—witches eating eyeballs, trolls making bridges out of goblin intestines, flesh turning into spiders. All that good stuff. For his part, Gage gave just a few grunts in acknowledgment that I'd said anything at all, which I chalked up to the necessity of concentrating very hard on the road, as the street was full of children darting back and forth with their bags of candy.

"We could have walked," I said, "since it's just at the school."

"Everybody else will have a car," he said, and by *everybody* I knew he meant Billy Fitz.

It was full-on dark when we arrived, lights streaming from the row of windows high on the wall of the gym. Even from the parking lot we could hear the *thump thump* of the music, and I knew any foray out onto the dance floor would only happen after I ditched the shoes in a dark corner. My first steps on the uneven asphalt were wobbly enough for Gage to take my arm and tuck it in with his.

"See?" he said, bending low to whisper even though he didn't have to. "If I was wearing that sweater, you wouldn't be able to stand having me hold you close like this."

I said nothing, but tucked myself a little closer, feeling my hip brush against his as we walked. I fished our tickets out of my little cloth-covered basket and handed them over to Mrs. Pierson, who had come to fulfill her chaperone duty dressed as Dorothy from *The Wizard of Oz*, ponytails and all.

"No Wicked Witch?" Gage asked, flashing his own wicked smile.

"I'll save that for your Brontë test next week," she answered without skipping a beat.

Inside, the lights had been dimmed to an acceptable level, and the dance floor teemed with every imaginable coupling. Neanderthals and Space Aliens. Soldiers and Hippies. Boys dressed as women; girls dressed as *Women*—as in, the opportunity to put on a slinky gown, high heels, and enough makeup to make someone mistake you for an oil painting close up. And, of course, the Bumpkins. These were mostly kids who were there without a date. Ripped jeans, plaid shirts, straw hats. As Gage steered me to a table along the back wall, I realized how easily he could be mistaken for one of them, instead of my specific counterpart.

I shouted, "You should have brought an axe!" above the din of the music.

"Why?" This, he shouted, too, but then, as he pulled out my chair, he leaned in close enough for me to hear his words *under* the noise. "Am I going to have to fight you off?"

His breath tickled against my neck, and I squirmed and giggled in a way that I would have mercilessly mocked, had it not been my own shivering flesh. In a final, brief gesture, Gage kissed my cheek and announced he was off to fetch snacks and punch, taking my basket with him for ease of transport.

The chairs at the table were empty but pulled to ramshackle angles, meaning their occupants were on the dance floor, or otherwise occupied in or around the gymnasium. Left to myself, I sat back and took in the room, scanning from one end to another, looking for familiar faces beneath masks and wigs and enormous pieces of foam cut into whimsical forms. Neewollah seemed to be the great equalizer of the High School scene—hard to tell who was what when everybody was someone else. Except for Katie Berg, Homecoming Queen, newly reinvented as the Queen of Hearts—hair sprayed red and piled on top of her severe-featured face. She wielded a heart-topped stick and screeched, "Off with your head!" to anyone who appeared to be on the verge of conversation.

The budget for Northenfield Texas High School wouldn't accommodate a real band, so the stage was occupied by a DJ currently spinning A Flock of Seagulls' "I Ran," and I quickly spotted Jayne and Charlie engaged in the most artless of dancing. I could imagine clouds above their heads. They were meant for beaming lights to shine upon them. A living embodiment of the aurora borealis. As the last note faded away, Charlie scooped

Jayne up for a spin, then set her down for a kiss. Hand in hand, the two of them walked off the dance floor, heading straight for me.

"You made it!" Jayne said, her tiny feet skipping on the last few steps. "We've been looking for you." She collapsed, breathless, in the chair that Charlie held out for her, and he plopped himself in the next. "I'm glad you found our table!"

"Yes," I said, trying to match her enthusiasm. Much as I love my sister and have grown quite fond of Charlie, the two of them here meant only one thing. Costumes might hide the outer appearances of cliques, but kids weren't streams to be easily separated, and wherever Charlie Bingley landed, Billy Fitz couldn't be far behind.

Then, as if materialized by my very thoughts, there he was, emerging from a sea of Bumpkins and Surgeons and Punk-Rock Muppets. Billy Fitz, wearing a white shirt with leather lacings dangling from a wide-open collar. It had billowy sleeves and gave him the look of a man who had fallen off the cover of one of those horrible romance novels Mom kept hidden in the basket of toilet paper rolls in the bathroom. Instinctively, I looked to see who he'd been dancing with—probably some cheerleader with a bodice ready to be ripped. But he was, as far as I could see, alone. And, when he looked at me, his eyes, too, did a flicker to the right and the left. Perhaps ascertaining my own lack of escort? If so, then the flicker of a smile might mean that he was glad to see me alone—a double-edged conclusion that should make me feel either irritated or intrigued.

No sooner had the smile appeared than it was gone, replaced by the guarded expression that I'd come to associate with Gage's proximity. The plastic cup of punch confirmed it, and when I looked up to say, "Thank you," I noticed Gage was making no move to sit with me.

"I hope you don't mind," he said, after a brief *Hey* to Romeo,

Juliet, and Regency. "I told Mrs. Pierson I'd sit at the ticket table for a few minutes. Give her a break."

"You can do that?" I tried not to be too awed at the power such a position suggested.

"Well, you know." He puffed his chest to fill the flannel, sending a clear, nonverbal *Nice shirt, Pirate Boy*, over to Billy. "Just for about fifteen minutes or so. I don't want to leave my Little Red alone here. She might wander into the jaws of some Big Bad Wolf."

What might have been cute and flirty in a dark corner of conversation sounded just . . . odd, in the full hearing of friends and family. Jayne and Charlie managed a not-too-creeped-out chuckle, but Billy narrowed his eyes and looked around, saying, "What wolf?"

"It's an expression," Gage said, clearly flustered, and with one last assurance that I would survive without him for fifteen minutes or so, he left.

And Billy sat down, leaving one empty chair between us.

"So, what is your costume?"

"Little Red Riding Hood," I said, twice. Once, not quite loud enough, and the other time in an effort to shout over his smirk.

"And he—"

"The Woodsman."

"What happened to the Wolf?" This question from Jayne, who had taken a brazen sip of my punch.

"He said it was too itchy."

Immediately, I regretted my betrayal of Gage's inability to withstand the onslaught of coarse fiber, because Charlie came back with, "He's twitchy?"

"ITCHY!" I yelled, accompanied by a fanatic scratching of my own arm.

They all nodded in understanding as the music changed.

This time, a Foreigner song—a ballad—and by the third line of the first verse, the dance floor was filled with swaying, costumed couples, surrounded by a sea of single Bumpkins. I tried to shut my mind from the longing in the lyrics. All about waiting too long. Looking too hard. And that hope—that it's only a matter of time before finding that someone you can love. I thought Gage might be that person, but there I was, waiting.

"It's too bad your boyfriend isn't here to dance with you," Billy said during a long instrumental interlude that stretched into the chorus.

"Well, somebody has to take the tickets, you know."

"You shouldn't let him do this. If he's your date, you should be dancing with him."

My little red cape suddenly felt like it was made of Gage's abandoned mohair, the weight of it turning the back of my neck and shoulders into a sauna. I took a (hopefully) casual sip of punch to keep myself cool.

"Who brought you? Why aren't you dancing with her?"

"I don't dance," he said, answering only one of my questions.

I imagined his lips speaking the song's lyrics, in which he proclaimed to be waiting for a girl like me to come into his life. Then I shook some sense into my hood. "Why do you hate him?"

"Who?" And, knowing I would know he knew, "I don't hate him. I'm just acquainted with him. Well acquainted. More acquainted than anyone should have to be."

"I know. He told me."

This must have piqued his interest, because he scooted over to the empty chair and leaned close. "Told you what?"

The heat spread to the front of my neck and what all Jane Austen fans would know to call a *décolletage*, meaning every visible inch of my skin was the same color as the dress. "You know. About you, and him. And . . . before."

"Before."

"Yes. Before. Which is why I think it stinks that you're so rude to him now, when all he wants to do is fit in again. It's hard, you know, being the new kid. And it's not his fault that your father—"

Whatever I had in mind to say after that was lost as Billy grabbed my hand and, heedless of my wobbling heels, pulled me onto the dance floor, dragging me right past Queen Katie Berg, who didn't seem happy at all with what was about to happen.

We didn't drape across each other in a true slow-dance embrace. He kept one of my hands in his, brought the other to rest on his shoulder, and his own rested in the curve of my waist, so artfully designed by Lydia's tailoring touch. My nose was inches from his chest, and he smelled like soap. Clean and—somehow—*blue*.

I tilted my head back, nearly toppling on my heels. "So, were you thinking pirate? Or some kind of Lord of the Manor?"

He looked down at me, puzzled.

"Your costume. I think there's a wealth of psychological data behind people's choice of costume."

"It's a shirt."

"But it's never just a shirt. It's—"

"Shh . . ." He used our joined hands to press a finger against my lips. "Don't talk. Just dance."

I nodded and let myself be held a little closer, both of us moving half a beat slower than the tempo of the song, swaying along with his lead. I closed my eyes for just a moment, bringing all of my sensations only to those points where I was touching Billy Fitz. Our hands, his chest, my waist. No sparks, but tiny points of fire, while the rest of my cells glowed like embers. Gage and I had been closer than this—physically. When he'd held and kissed me, I'd been pressed full up against him and felt nothing. I mean, pleasant and all, but if Billy Fitz found one more touchpoint, I knew I'd combust, leaving nothing but a glob of molten red sequins on the floor. Should that bother me? Yes, it *should* bother me, knowing that within the chest beneath my hand beat a cold, cold heart. Still, it's not like Billy and I were going to exit the floor à la Charlie and Jayne. Soon enough those final notes would fade. Until then, like the song said, there was nowhere else I'd rather be.

"It's not just in costumes," Billy said when the song ended and we were standing still on the floor. "There's always more to any story." He took his hand off my waist but held mine with the other for a second longer before vanishing into the crowd.

I'm not sure exactly how long I stood there, but sometime in the lines of the next song—which song, I had no idea—Jayne was at my side asking if I felt all right.

"Yeah," I said. "Just lost in thought. Looking at the costumes."

"Well, brace yourself to feel a little less 'all right.'"

She gripped my shoulders and forcibly turned me to look at the gym entrance and the new arrival that seemed to be causing quite a stir among all the guys lining the walls in their Country Bumpkin Bachelor glory. Lydia—*our* Lydia—wearing a pair of cutoff jeans rolled up to the Point of No Return and a red-checked shirt knotted high enough to show a stomach as flat and inviting as the Great Plains. Her hair was fashioned into two loose, long braids, and her ratty straw hat looked like a refugee from an afternoon of fishin' and skinny-dippin'. Daisy Duke, in all her gloriously underaged flesh.

The DJ played "Cotton-Eyed Joe" (which I know only because he bellowed, "COTTON-EYED JOOOOOOOOOOEEEEEE," and everybody whooped and ran for the dance floor like it was littered with twenty-dollar bills). Before she even got her well-worn boots into the paint, Lydia had a dance partner on either side, arms looped in hers, leading her to join the whoo-pin' bunch of kids on the floor. One of her escorts was name-less but familiar—a boy from my Spanish class whose country outfit wasn't a costume; he'd probably wear the same clothes to school on Monday. The other, though, was more familiar, and with his red flannel shirt, looked more comfortable paired up with my little (*eighth grade!*) sister than he did with me.

"Should we do something?" Jayne asked, leading me back to the table before we were run over by a stampede of enthusiastic boots.

"Like what?"

"How did she even get in here? It's supposed to be for High School only."

I didn't bother answering her question. It would dawn on her soon enough. Me? I already knew, the knowledge in my head prodded by the feeling of a punch to my stomach.

Where did you come from?
Where did you go?
Where did you come from,
Cotton-Eyed Joe?

Lydia and *el chico* and Gage stomped, forward and back, shouting something every now and then. My sister looked like she'd been dancing to this all her life, but unless she'd lived a secret honky-tonk existence I knew nothing about, this was her first time to participate in this Texas tradition.

How can she do this?

I'm glad I kept my question to myself, if for no other reason than to appear somewhat less pathetic to my happily-ever-after older sister. Together, we went back to our table and sat down, with no sign of Charlie or Billy anywhere nearby.

"I guess someone did have to take the tickets," Jayne said, her tone dripping with a suspicion and distaste usually reserved for our parents.

"There's always more to a story," I countered, quoting a boy I knew I wasn't supposed to trust.

esteem: *the regard in which one is held; especially : high regard*

Billy Fitz grew in the community's **esteem** *with each new victory.*

AS IT TURNED OUT, the second side to the story was fairly sweet and simple. Gage, a little freaked out by the overwhelming itchiness of the mohair sweater, had called our house, ready to beg me to reconsider our costume pairing. I have a distinct memory of the phone ringing, but I was caught up in the adventure of applying my own eyeliner at the time and had shouted for Lydia to get the phone.

Which she did.

Apparently, with all the calmness and finesse of a seasoned hostage negotiator (or maybe fashion negotiator?), Lydia was able to bring Gage to a calm, happy place, and remotely walk him through his closet, unearthing all the elements for the Woodsman costume. (Luckily, an old boyfriend of his aunt's had left a pair of construction boots behind.) So touched was he by Lydia's clearheaded decisiveness, he had offered to finagle a shift at the ticket table to let her in, provided she could sneak out of the house without our parents' knowing. (Luckily, an old television programmer scheduled an airing of *Casablanca* to hold their attention while Lydia slipped out the front door.)

All of this Gage explained to me in the back corner of the gym, while popular tunes brought every other kid out onto the dance floor in a frenzy. By the time he finished, the first few notes of "Almost Paradise" were luring couples out of the shadows—Gage and me among them.

Dancing with Gage chased all memories of Billy from my mind. I mean, I looked up, and it was Gage's face—narrow and soft. My mind literally said, *This is Gage. This is Gage. You are dancing with Gage.* The repetition brought me to the truth, and my mind was all okay. My body 98.6 all over. I smiled a little, knowing I was smiling at Gage. And I kept my eyes locked on his, the swirling colors of the disco ball creating a dizzying aura behind his head. This was very important—the eyes and the smile. Because, if I closed my eyes—even for a second—he went away. Like, the very idea of him disappeared. The smile was to let him know that it was okay. Really, really okay what he did as a kindness to my sister. A kindness to my sister was a kindness to me, right?

And it was important, too, that I kept close to him with my eyes and my smile, because every bit of me below that was numb with memories of dancing with Billy. My heartbeat was slower, my hands blissfully dry, my feet firmly on the ground, feeling the unforgiveness of the gym floor firmly under each step. If I closed my eyes, I'd be back in Billy's arms, and who knows—with a mouth like mine? I might even say something stupid like, *Oh, Billy . . . how divinely you dance.*

So I danced with Gage, forgiving him with each step, and as Mike Reno's voice stretched out that last "*Paradiiiiiiissseee*," the glaring lights of the gym came on, signaling to all of us that the night was over. All the bits that had been hidden in the dark—ripped remnants of streamers, sequins and scraps of costumes, empty punch cups and chip bags—all of it shone clear in the glaring light.

"I guess now I get to take you home?" Gage said, taking my hand.

"Lydia, too, I suppose." I mean, we couldn't let her just walk.

"Probably the safest thing for us to do."

She had amassed a gathering of would-be volunteers—the who's who of the unattached student male bodies, a host of athletes, science geeks, and honor students. At the moment, she was leading them in some incredible form of chase, and they snaked among the tables, heedless of the mermaids and princesses that got in their way.

"She's going to get herself in trouble," I said. "She's not even supposed to be here."

"I'll take care of it."

Gage dispatched himself to the scene, cutting in front of a boy dressed as Elvis Presley, and took Lydia under his wing. What he said had an immediate, soothing effect, and he motioned for me to follow them out to the car. I signaled back but went to find Jayne and Charlie to let them know I was leaving.

"So, is he your date or hers?" Jayne's voice came the closest to sneering that I've ever heard.

"There's a good explanation," I said, but before I could tell her more, Billy's glare cut me right at the throat.

"The school has a social order for a reason." His words were directed at Charlie, but totally intended for me. "And if some people can't behave themselves, maybe they need to just stay home."

"Come on, Fitz," Charlie said with the kind of wide, open smile that would make him a dream model for a toothpaste ad, "nothing wrong with bending things up a little bit."

"I'll see you at home," I said loud enough that both boys would be certain sure that I hadn't heard a thing.

Something incredible happened after Neewollah, and it happened to Billy Fitz. And it happened every Friday night, on our own Home field and Away. The boy, according to Brent Callaghan's *The Final Score!* on the nearest local news station, was, among other colorful adjectives,

Unstoppable,
Magnificent,
A Fitz of Nature (Really. I did not make that up.), and
Perhaps the Greatest High School Quarterback of Any
     Generation.

He was on the front page of the local paper every Saturday morning. The Tastee Freez created a special ice-cream sundae in his honor, featuring a football-shaped caramel balanced high atop a mound of mint chocolate chip ice cream. His jersey number (16) became the price of a root beer (his favorite) at the mini-mart. The Dee-lite Donut Shop created a maple-iced croissant called a Flaky Fitz. The movie theater offered a Friday night "Fitz Five" special which, for five dollars, included a movie ticket, popcorn, and soda for those who chose to fill the seats of the theater rather than the local bleachers. And one church (not ours: we'd finally settled on First Baptist, the blandest of the Baptists) chimed in with Fitz, Faith, and Fellowship, featuring a play-by-play recap with Billy himself in the basement.

Huge stretches of butcher paper lined the school hallways, with "Throw a Fitz!!!" painted in thick, purple acrylic paint.

The same message spread throughout town, painted on storefront windows and on the Specials chalkboards of the cafés. And somehow, the entire town adopted the phrase "throwing a Fitz" as a means of denoting great success or accomplishment. Examples:

Man A: I'm going to ask my boss for a promotion.
Man B: Really? Well, walk in there and throw a Fitz.

Or:

Woman A: Your hair looks beautiful!
Woman B: Thank you. Yes, Charlene at the Cut-n-Curl really threw a Fitz.

And, at school:

Teenager A: How'd you do on that test?
Teenager B: Fitzed it! (with optional chest bump, depending on level of jock-ness)

Mrs. Pierson tried to get in on the craze with a psychological experiment in which she scrawled a giant *F* across the top of a high-scoring paper, denoting the "Fitz-ness" of the analysis. Unfortunately, not many honor students possess such a sharp sense of irony, and after a flood of classroom tears and (so I heard) an avalanche of angry parental phone calls, she stopped the practice and relabeled the papers, with ten bonus points added to make up for the grief. Not mine, though. I was happy enough to know that the paper earned a 97 in her grade book, and I proudly displayed the *F* on our refrigerator, only to have it engulfed in a sea of homeschool penmanship practice.

Our cheerleaders became known collectively as the Mrs.

Fitz, with each girl proudly wearing the title Bedazzled on the back of her game-day jersey. From there it became yet another label of social status. Pretty, thin, and popular girls were known collectively as PMFs (Potential Mrs. Fitzes). The rest of us fell somewhere in a range of TMFs (Total Misfits—yes, I know the acronym is inaccurate, but that's hardly the biggest issue). This phenomenon was explained to me by none other than Caroline Bingley, who ended up in my care at a football game when her mother had to work late. It wasn't a bad deal, actually—Mrs. Bingley paid for my ticket and our snacks, plus an extra ten dollars for the privilege of listening to the kid explain throughout the entire second half why she was a PMF, even if she was only ten years old.

"Because we're the same. And he's my brother's best friend. So we fit. And everybody else doesn't."

"Ah," I said over a cheer that indicated something Fitztastic had happened on the field. "Hence the prefix, *mis*-, to be applied to everybody else like me."

"Yes, because you'll never get married. You'll always be a Miss."

"I was referring to the Old English, and the definition of *mis*- to mean bad, or wrong."

I never knew that a ten-year-old was capable of withering someone with a glance, but I learned the truth in that moment. Her stare was enough to melt me, even with the sharp snap of autumn crisping the air between us. For—I swear—a solid minute, she chewed a single piece of soft pretzel, until it must have absolutely liquefied in her little mouth and seeped down her little throat, because when she opened her mouth again, it was gone, and she hadn't swallowed. I watched. Creepy.

"Just you wait. He'll go off to college, come back, and I'll be all grown up. Then he'll marry me. Because he's my brother's best friend."

"Well," I said, playing along, as if I cared, even though I didn't. Really. "I'm his best friend's girlfriend's sister. Doesn't that count for something?"

"No." And for the first time, I saw just what it would look like to see an evil queen sip hot chocolate.

The only people in town who seemed completely unaffected by the Fitznomenon were Gage, me, and Billy Fitz himself.

Poor Gage.

I know every time he saw a sign saying TGIF—Thank God It's Fitzday—he was hauled back to those days when he was the sad, lost kid, living in big Billy's shadow. Now that shadow stretched across every inch of his life. No place was safe. (Did I mention that the word "Boys" was replaced with "Fitz" on certain bathroom doors? It was.) Rather than walk around with a posture of defeat, though, Gage attempted to actively ignore the Fitzness all around. Doing so gave an odd, disconnected air to his presence. Like an actor in front of what is obviously a screen with a giant, fire-breathing lizard behind him. He didn't go to any football games. Or pep rallies. Or donut shops or cafés or dry cleaners. We walked to and from school together without remarking on the signs that adorned every other front yard.

On to Area!
On to Regionals!!
On to State!!!

The closest we came to talking about football (Fitzball? Someday, mark my words), was one brooding afternoon when Gage said, "There are other sports, you know."

"I know," I'd said. "Charlie plays soccer, too."

And that was the end of the conversation, because of course he'd meant basketball, his sport. His, and several other boys', I might add. (And girls', but that's an entirely different battle.)

They'd already begun their practices in earnest. In fact, they'd played three games before getting a score announced after the Pledge of Allegiance in homeroom. But it wasn't the same. When the football players wore shirts and ties on game day, the cafeteria complied with stain-free food. Alfredo sauce on the spaghetti, for example. Or chicken with white gravy. No such concession was ever made for the basketball players. Sloppy joes. Enchiladas. Anything requiring ketchup.

It was a Thursday afternoon just before the Thanksgiving holiday when I found myself facing a nearly empty cafeteria, with not a friend in sight. The entire basketball team, Junior Varsity and Varsity, were Away at a tournament, taking with them the entire band and Pep Squad. That meant Gage (my sometimes companion) and Lottie and Collin (my daily bread-breakers) were gone, leaving me the choice of wedging myself in at the Jayne-and-Charlie table or getting a bag of Cheetos à la carte and heading for the library to catch up on homework. And, by homework, I mean reading. Quiet moments were impossible to come by at home, with little sisters running around, an older sister mooning around, and parents who were unable to function without a television blaring in the background.

For all the shallow qualities of Northenfield Texas High School, its library stands as a testament to literary pursuits. The room is shaped like a half-circle, with bookshelves fanning out from a central area where tables and chairs are set up for individual or small group study. The center portion of the rounded wall is a series of floor-to-ceiling windows looking out onto the unspoiled fields behind the school. Here there are plush reading chairs, comfortable enough for curling up, but mobile enough to move into groupings, should the occasion allow. And then, in corners throughout, more chairs, fat cushions, even overstuffed bean bags—all of which are, through the miracle of paranoid architecture, in direct view from the vantage point of Mrs. Berry's desk, which sits on an elevated platform at the front.

She smiled at me when I walked in, and I held up my bag of Cheetos in a gesture of full disclosure. She scowled, and shook her head no, but then I spotted none other than Billy Fitz sitting at one of the tables in the far corner, nose buried in a three-ringed binder. I lifted the bag of Cheetos and inclined my head in his direction, whispering, "They're for him," at which point Mrs. Berry became much more welcoming of my snack.

To keep the ruse alive, I had to make my way over toward Billy's table, then veer sharply to take my place across from him at the opposite end.

"Here," I whispered, stretching the open bag across the expanse. "Don't ask questions, just take a few."

Amazingly, he complied, reaching his long fingers inside and extracting a modest handful of puffs. "Thanks." And then he returned to his reading. I placed the open bag in front of me and rummaged around for my novel, prepared to venture on without any further conversation when he asked, "What are you reading?"

I showed him the book cover. *Christine*, by Stephen King. "Have you read it?" Somehow, it seemed safe to assume he was a reader.

"Saw the movie."

Okay. Maybe not.

"My parents wouldn't let me see the movie," I said, instantly feeling stupid. Little Caroline Bingley probably saw *Christine*. Caroline Bingley would probably scare that car to death.

"It was good," Billy said. "But the book is probably better. They usually are."

So, hope that he's not a complete Neanderthal after all. "What about you?"

He held up the notebook, showing pages upon pages of diagrams and scribbled notes. "Playbook."

"Oh," I said, extinguishing anything else I could possibly say on the matter.

He gave me a brief smile that was more about acknowledgment than humor, and we each popped a Cheeto into our mouths. It occurred to me—he's tasting what I'm tasting while I'm tasting it—and the universe became incredibly small and important in that moment.

"Thanks," he said. "I was hungry."

"Should have had lunch."

"Can't stand it down there these days. Too much noise." His nose was buried back in his book. "I don't even know what they were serving today."

"Hamburgers." And, before I could resist, "And Fitz fries."

He looked up, eyes narrowed, and threw a Cheeto across the table, which I managed to catch within an inch of its hitting my nose.

"Sorry," I said, though I wasn't, really, because now he was smiling for real, and chuckling loud enough to warrant a warning *shush* from Mrs. Berry.

"Maybe I could borrow that book when you're finished?" He wasn't exactly whispering but had lowered his voice to an acceptable level of library fuzz.

"It's the library's," I said, wishing we had the kind of money that would let me browse through Hastings and leave with an armful of anything I wanted. "So you'll have to borrow it from them. But I'll put in a good word for you."

"Thanks," he said, playing along. "And if you want, you can borrow this one. But you'll have to be patient. I won't be finished with it until after Christmas."

Because next Saturday was the Area Championship. Two weeks later, the Saturday after Thanksgiving, was Regionals.

And two weeks after that, The Game. State Championship. The hopes of our school, our town. And, here in the corner of the library, the hero who carried those hopes and threw them down the field was hiding in a corner, memorizing the plays. Funny, though. He didn't look like much of a hero right then, not with his hair flopped in his eyes and his Texas Longhorns T-shirt sporting a tiny rip in its collar. He looked weary, maybe worried. And something else. Like, confused, as if he couldn't put all the pieces together.

"That's okay," I said, releasing him from any further conversational duties. "I'll wait for the movie."

It was one of those moments, one of those rare, wonderful glitters of time, when you say just the right thing at just the right moment, with just the right amount of flirt and fun. It's what the French call the *bon mot*. Literally, the good word, but more. Like a perfect scoop of ice cream, or a giant, luminous bubble that floats out of sight before it bursts. I could feel the twinkle in my eye. If my hair had not been somewhat confined to a scrunchie, I would have given it a flip over my shoulder before walking away. He was going to say something else. I could tell. There was a definite fidget in his seat and an intake of breath, but I wouldn't allow it. Wouldn't let him burst my bubble, or sully my *bon mot*. I'd fitzed the Fitz, and on that note, I dropped my novel in my backpack and stood, leaving my open bag of Cheetos on the table.

Chapter 12

rencontre: *a hostile meeting or a contest between forces or individuals : COMBAT*

When different social circles collide, a rencontre *at a party is more painful than pleasant.*

ACCORDING TO JAYNE, who had become the authority in all that is football, it was the biggest, most important victory of the season.

"More than the State Championship?" I asked. "Because isn't that, like, the *big* win?"

"This is the game that gets us there," she gushed. Yes. Gushed. Words gurgling out of her like orange soda from a fountain. "Area Championship. We've never made it this far in the playoffs. Ever."

"We?"

"Our High School, silly."

"Ah. For a minute there I thought you were some kind of invisible angel on Charlie's back when he kicked that winning touchdown."

"Field goal." She corrected. *Good girl.* "And wasn't that the most thrilling moment?"

It had been. Less than a minute to go, our team two points down, and that ball making a perfect arc through the goalpost.

Within seconds, Charlie was hoisted up on the shoulders of his teammates, and I swear I thought time was going to freeze and the sky would fill with rolling credits like the end of a movie.

"So, you see? That's why you should come." Jayne was continuing the line of reasoning that had started this conversation. A big victory meant a big party—at the game hero's home, no less. And since it had been a Saturday afternoon Away Game, everybody had gotten back home at the tip of dark. Starting in one hour, the whole school invited. Presumably, that meant me, too.

"I'm just not much of a party person. You know that. Neither are you, I might add."

"It's not going to be wild or anything." Her eyes met mine in the mirror, where she was re-curling her hair, twisting new perfection upon perfection.

"I'd have to change clothes."

"You look fine. Jeans and a sweater, right? Done. It's not like this is prom or anything."

"I wouldn't know anybody."

"Correction, you'd know almost everybody. Including me, and I promise not to leave your side."

"I don't suppose Gage would be welcome." I watched as the familiar shadow of dislike passed over Jayne's pretty features. We'd settled on a silent agreement of noncommunication where he was concerned. When he showed up at the front door, she swept herself into the kitchen. When he called, she held the receiver out to me like it was something she'd found at the bottom of a trash can. And if the two of us were walking together in the hallway at school and Gage came our direction, she suddenly changed course, like she just remembered her locker was on fire.

"Everybody's invited, so anybody can come."

"And I'm lumped in with *everybody*?"

Jayne sighed and turned around. "You're my sister and I love you, and believe it or not, I think there are a lot of other people who like you too."

She said it with such a mysterious little smirk, I twisted myself around and sat up on the bed. "People like who?"

"Oh, I don't know." She turned back to the mirror. "People. They think you're funny."

Funny. What every girl wants to hear about herself. I flopped back down.

"That you say clever things in class. Make the teachers laugh. Witty, you know. Smart."

Clever. Witty. Smart. It got worse and worse.

"Great," I said, thumbing through a discarded *Seventeen* magazine. It was from July of the previous summer, picked up for a dime at the Friends of the Library rummage sale. The alluring headline WHAT SMART GIRLS SAY ABOUT SNACKS had proven to be nothing more than a three-page editorial for fruit. "I suppose I'll be called upon, then, to bring the life to the party? Maybe start a rousing game of Twenty Questions? Trump them all by making the answer something elusive like 'frosted kiwi slices'? That would be clever and witty, wouldn't it? Of course, given the company, I should probably stick to something they'll actually get. Like, 'football.' Or, maybe, well . . . 'football.'"

Jayne set the curling iron down on the bureau and turned to face me again, this time her expression one of true disapproval.

"Really, Pudge, do you have to be so mean? You might find out that you're misjudging a lot of people here. A first impression isn't always the one that should be the most lasting. People aren't always what they seem to be."

People. Again. "Like who?"

She shrugged. "I'm not going to say anything out of turn, but Charlie's one of the people you're talking about. And he's—"

"Smart?" I challenged.

"Sweet," she said, and I knew I'd been forgiven for my insult. "And you know Billy's super smart."

"And he hates me." I recalled the moment in the library when it seemed there might have been a crack in his facade, but then remembered how I'd sealed it up with my clever retort. Ah, yes, such a clever girl.

"Like I said," she was facing the mirror again now, coaxing her curls to life with her fingers, "people aren't always what they seem."

Her comment intrigued me, enough to bring me up off the bed and over to our closet, where I listlessly moved one hanger after another down the length of the rack, just in case there'd been a spontaneous generation of fashion since the last time I checked. You know, something a girl might wear to a party where *everyone* was going to be.

Jayne looked at me in triumph. "I knew it. I knew you'd change your mind."

"You're forgetting one thing," I said, grasping for the last bit of rope that might save me from the ultimate show of social awkwardness. "It's already after ten o'clock. What in the world makes you think Mom and Dad will let us go?"

Jayne's smile spread up and out, like one of those cartoon cats trying to keep the bird trapped within. "Charlie's mother is the biggest realtor in Northenfield. His dad owns a fleet of car dealerships. Mom would deliver me over there at midnight with two goats and a pound of cheese if she thought it would help Dad's chances of getting work in her properties. They gave us a one o'clock curfew."

My jaw dropped. "As in, one a.m.?"

"The very same. And"—she dangled a set of car keys—"we drive ourselves."

Now this—THIS—was a new development. No ploy of

babysitting. No ruse of getting a ride to an Away Game with the player's mother. My sister was being thrust head-on into a special rite of the teenage mating system. A party, in a home, with dark hallways and darker bedrooms and—I don't know . . . closets and such. And with blessings to stay until the clock turns over. Why not open the gates to the lion's den and toss the girl right in? Throw the virgin overboard into the teeming sea of sex? Why, we didn't even know if the shindig would be properly chaperoned, or—

And then it all made sense.

"You can't go if I don't go, can you?"

She deflated a little. "C'mon, Pudge. I really *do* want you to come. You'll have fun, I promise."

"What are we, *Taming of the Shrew* all of a sudden?"

She looked at me with a blank stare that totally justified my earlier comments, but I couldn't hold a grudge. As much as I loved my sister, I loved even more the idea of having a future favor to call upon, should the occasion arise.

"Will you French braid my hair?" (That wasn't the future favor, by the way.)

"Sure, but fast."

Ten minutes later, my frizz had been relegated to a thick plait, with curled tendrils framing my face. Large, purple-and-black polka-dot hoops dangled from my ears—heavy, but cute, and perfectly matched to the long black-and-purple sweater that reached nearly to my knees. I'd switched out of my jeans and into a pair of black leggings—all of this at Lydia's instructions. I'm pretty sure all of her helpful fashion advice came as a bid to be included in the party, but she'd already crashed more than her fair share of High School events. Tonight, unless she crawled out the window and walked across town, she'd be stuck at home with Mom and Dad watching the late, late, late movie on TV.

"Well, you look perfect, anyway," Lydia said, resigned. She spoke to both of us, but the compliment rolled off Jayne, who rarely looked anything less. Tonight she wore a pair of snug-fitting jeans and a baby blue fuzzy sweater, cropped to reveal such a perfect hint of flat stomach, she'd have to slouch until we made it to the other side of the front door.

"The whole town will have a party when we win the State Championship," Jayne said reassuringly. "You'll be able to come to that one for sure."

Lydia just pouted in reply.

"One more thing," I said, "and I'll be ready to go."

I scooted past her to the phone in the upstairs hall and dialed Gage's number by finger memory in the dark. It rang once, twice, and by the stealthy tone of his, "Hello?" I knew I'd probably waited too late to call.

"Gage? It's me, Elyse."

"It's"—pause, rumble—"ten *thirty*. Is everything all right?"

"Everything's fine. I'm just—Jayne and I are going to a party, and I wanted to see if you wanted to go too."

"A *party*?"

"You know, people, music. Punch, maybe. Pizza . . . chips." I wracked my brain for every teenage-party scene I could remember from a lifetime of television and movies. At the moment, all that came to mind were those cheesy beach movies from the 1960s, with girls in oversized bikinis and guys fake-surfing with perfect hair.

"I know what a party is. You're going *now*?"

"Yeah." I laughed nervously. "Getting sprung special by the parents. So, do you want to go? Jayne's driving. We could pick you up."

"Whose party?"

"Umm, Charlie's? I mean, it's at his house, but everyone is going."

"Everyone."

"Apparently, yes. Even me, so, everyone. Not like, 'everyone who's *anyone*,' ha-ha." (I actually pronounced "ha-ha." Like I was writing him a letter from camp.) "Just, you know. The gang."

I could *feel* his smirk winding through the telephone cord. "The gang, eh?"

"Do you want to go? We could pick you up. Ten minutes. Have you home by one. So, you know, just a couple of hours. Could be fun."

"Fun for EVERYONE!" He sounded like one of those announcers from a commercial for some wacky children's toy. Like a Slip 'N Slide, or a new version of Twister. Then he dropped the act. "I suppose *everyone* includes Billy Fitz."

"Probably, yes. Since he's Charlie's best friend and all. And it's kind of a party to celebrate winning the football game. And he's a football player. So, yeah. Probably him, too."

"I never took you for a Fitzer."

"I'm not a *Fitzer*," I said, suddenly feeling like my honor was at stake. "I'm going with my sister, and I thought I'd see if you wanted to come along. Thought it might be fun."

"Sorry, sweetheart. I don't consider standing in line to kiss the class ring of the Famous Billy Fitz to be exactly *fun*. Besides, I doubt Golden Child Charlie would even let me through the front door. But you should go. Take some notes, so that if I'm ever accepted, I'll know how to act. Okay?"

I think what bothered me most was how very *relieved* I felt. Not until then did I admit to myself that I'd waited until the very last moment to call him, with a secret desire that the conversation would end in just this way. Not that I didn't like Gage. I did. He was still my sometimes-a-boyfriend-but-sometimes-not-depending-on-his-mood-and-circumstances guy. But tonight seemed like an opportunity to break free—not only from my parents' normal, stringent rules, but from my relegation to being the girl on the outside.

"Okay," I said. "And if it makes you feel any better, I'm planning to have a mediocre time at best. Because, face it, I'm basically going so there'll be someone to turn the hose on Jayne and Charlie, right?"

My ruse was wearing thin, so I said a quick "Good night" and hung up the phone, turning to see Lydia standing behind me. Arms folded, disapproving.

"You shouldn't go if he doesn't want you to."

"He's the one who doesn't want to go. I, on the other hand, am perfectly capable of doing exactly as I please."

"You're lucky he even *likes* you."

I dropped my voice to a whisper, suddenly aware of the littlest sisters sleeping just beyond the closed door.

"Thank you so much. You're just as capable of making me feel beautiful on the inside as you are of making me look beautiful on the outside."

Before she could untwist my words to see if she'd been given a compliment or not, I was down the stairs where Jayne waited, slumped, at the front door.

We had to park half a block away from Charlie's house. The street was lined with every kind of car imaginable, and part of me was glad the old family Station Wagon was far enough away that the connection between it and us was broken by the time we reached the edge of the Bingleys' perfectly clipped lawn. Every window of the house shone with light, and shadows moved behind the shades. I could feel the *thump thump* of music through the sidewalk and remembered the complicated stereo system hidden within the living room walls.

"Is his mother okay with this?" I asked, practically shouting over the sound of the party spilling through the front door.

"She's in Dallas," Jayne said, sharing a little piece of information I'm sure our parents didn't know. "Taking Caroline to spend the whole Thanksgiving week with their father."

Just then the door flung open, and two blondes in tiny denim skirts and sweatshirts flung themselves out with it. One looked up long enough to say, "Oh, look, it's Jayney and the sister!" before remembering how invisible I was supposed to be and pretending not to have seen me at all.

Inside, the pristine, white living room was packed with color. Neon, denim, black, not to mention a nearly solid wall of purple letterman jackets standing side by side in front of the television, watching a videotape of one of the previous games. They yelled at the tiny versions of themselves, as if they hadn't lived those very moments.

"TAKE IT! TAKE IT! 40-35-30-25-20-10 . . . TOUCHDOWN!"

"It's a blast already," I said, before noticing that Jayne, despite her promise of less than thirty minutes ago, was *not* by my side.

Great.

I spun a slow circle, looking for anyplace to land my social anchor.

Jock . . . jock . . . cheerleader . . . jock . . . beauty queen . . . jock . . . jock girlfriend . . .

Lottie.

We saw each other and made our way through four make-out sessions, one couple fighting about where they should go for their make-out session, three boys performing an air guitar solo, two girls assuring each other they looked totally pretty tonight, and one kid trying to find out if there was any cucumber in the dip, because he's allergic. Speaking of—those poor cats. I hoped they were locked in the laundry room again. Otherwise, they'd be positively trampled.

"Not surprised to see you here," Lottie said as soon as we were close enough to shout-speak.

The music was too loud for me to surmise whether or not I'd been insulted. "What does that mean?"

"You know. You're still such a fish, swimming around in the sea. This is a prime tank. Like one big net drop of the best of the best."

"You're ridiculous."

She raised an eyebrow. Like, honest to Pete. One eyebrow. I thought people only did that in books. "Where's Gage?"

I tried to raise my own, but probably looked more like someone trying not to lose a contact lens. "Where's Collin?"

She cocked her head (yes, again, like she was a spy or something) behind her. "Getting me a soda. The fridge is full, do you want him to get you something?"

"No, thanks. I'll get my own. I know where the kitchen is. I've been here before."

She looked sufficiently impressed, and I tried not to give off too much of an air of superiority as I brushed past her on my way to the kitchen. I saw Collin—striving to hold three cans of soda, so Lottie must not have specified a flavor—out of the corner of my eye and gave him a little nod of a greeting. That alone made me feel confident, like I belonged. I *knew* someone. I already *talked* to someone.

Once in the kitchen I wormed my way through a wall of bodies to the refrigerator, saying, "Excuse me . . . pardon . . . can I just . . ." until I'd wedged the door open to reveal at least six dozen cans of Coke, Pepsi, Dr Pepper, Mountain Dew, Lemonade, Sprite, Orange Crush. Basically, my mother's nightmare. I grabbed a Coke, popped the top, and took a sip, pretending to be a welcome part of the conversation happening around me. Four guys, all wearing faded jeans and T-shirts with the sleeves cut off, shouted a debate punctuated with pointing fingers. Something about a music video, and whether or not a guy had really been killed in one of the explosions. Fascinating stuff.

"You know," I said when a pocket of silence allowed, "it's really unlikely. They don't use real explosives on sets like that. Can you imagine the liability? Pretty harmless pyrotechnics. Flash paper. You probably handle more dangerous stuff at the Fourth of July picnic."

I took a sip of my Coke, confident I'd won my way into their conversation with my repartee, until one—I think I recognized him from the back row of my History class—closed off their circle by repositioning himself right in front of me.

Luckily, no one else cared enough to notice my gaffe, leaving me to my own devices. Lottie had already found someone more socially advantageous to talk to, so my next order of business was to fulfill my role of chaperone and find my wayward sister.

My short stature made it impossible for me to see through or above the crowd, no matter how high I craned my neck or stood on my toes. Besides, that particular posture made me look more like a freak than anything, so I decided to take on the cool, casual persona. You know, just a gal at a party, looking for the one she came with. Separated by time and space and music and noise. I couldn't remember a time when I'd shared such a small space with so many people yet felt—Cliché Alert!—so completely alone.

I found myself at the foot of the staircase leading up to the second-floor landing, and figured, if nothing else, that would give me a better view of the party below. Bird's eye, if you will. I took the steps slowly, and backwards, mindful not to spill my soda, as at this point it was just as likely to land on somebody's head as the white carpet.

When I got to the top, I moved along the rail, surveying the kingdom below. In a moment of pure silliness, and frankly to see if anyone would take notice, I held my hand out, queen-like.

Shocker, no one responded.

A hallway to the left of me, another to the right, and there I was, stuck in the middle, surrounded by clowns and jokers.

I scanned the crowd, looking for curly blond hair—hers or his. Or a flash of blue sweater. But saw nothing. I turned my back against the railing and took in my immediate surroundings. The landing had been fashioned into some kind of game room, complete with a pinball machine and beanbag chairs, all of which were occupied. Two hallways jutted out from it. One closed door had a line of girls attached to it, so it must be the restroom. There was a chance, I suppose, that Jayne had made a beeline for the potty, to fix her face or whatever, so I waited long enough for the current occupant to come out. Rather, occupants, as the same two girls who accidentally acknowledged us on the front porch opened the door, took one look at me, and immediately began the process of un-seeing.

"Hey!" I called out, hoping to grasp the last bit of their memory. "Have you seen my sister? Jayne?"

"As if," they said—in freakish unison, I might add.

I had to face the possibility that my sister—and her boyfriend—might be hidden behind one of those closed doors, and a battle waged within me as to just what I should do about it. Barge in? Play the voice of righteous indignation in an attempt to save my sister's virtue? Or trust that same virtue to remain, shall we say, intact? I counted four doors in all and realized I had a seventy-five percent chance of making a total idiot of myself by interrupting some strangers' tryst.

Luckily the odds were improved somewhat when the closest door on the left burst open, and a girl I recognized from Chemistry popped her head out, exclaiming, "Everyone! Get *in* here! This kid has *two* Barbie DreamHouses *AND* an entire *suitcase* full of clothes!" At this point, I was nearly trampled by a modest stampede of High School girls eager to relive their childhood with better toys. It was a safe bet that Jayne wasn't in that room, as neither of us had ever been bitten by the Barbie bug.

I stepped aside and found myself at the top of the hallway jutting to the right. One door was ajar, meaning I wouldn't have to knock, or, worse, rattle the knob to determine if it was locked and *then* knock. Nope, just a normal, expected casualty of a party crowd. Walking down the hallway, swiggin' a soda, when *oops!* Some clod bumps right into me, sending me stumbling into the door, over the threshold and . . .

I acted it out, just like that. As if I were following stage directions. I even included an indignant "Hey!" to my invisible bumper. Stupid plan. Stupid, stupid idea. Because, of course, no. My sister wasn't in this room with Charlie. This wasn't even Charlie's room, which I would have realized if I'd bothered to notice that the door on the *other* side of the hallway had a big sign that literally said, CHARLIE'S ROOM. Which made me wonder if the poor boy got lost often.

No, I didn't stumble in on Charlie and Jayne. This was much, much worse.

The room was dark—sort of. I mean, there wasn't any kind of a lamp lit, but there was some light coming through the window. Not moonlight, either, because that would have been too perfect for the moment. Just light, shining up, creating a soft, aqua pond, and Billy Fitz sitting on a beanbag in the middle of it.

"Shut the door," he said, sounding only mildly surprised.

"Sorry!" I scrambled backward, in case a girl was behind the door, or hiding under the bed or, I don't know, suspended from the ceiling behind me.

"No. Come in, stay. Just shut it behind you."

I did as I was told, but not before taking a final peek out into the hallway, not sure if I wanted to make sure nobody saw me come in here, or that everybody did.

"I—I was looking for Charlie. I mean, Charlie and Jayne, of course. I can't find them anywhere downstairs and—I hope it's okay that I'm here. At the party, I mean. Not, you know, in *here*. Because I wasn't looking for *here*, per se."

"*Per se?*"

"Yes. It means, 'itself.' Like, I wasn't looking for this *room*."

"I know what 'per se' means. I just don't think I've ever heard anyone say it."

"Oh." I couldn't tell if he was mocking me or admiring the vocabulary that was sure to net me a perfect SAT score. "Well, anyway. They're not here, and you are—obviously, wanting to be alone. So, I should go find them."

"Unless they obviously want to be alone." *Now*, for sure, he was mocking.

"Well, who better than I to prevent some crime against her virtue?"

He laughed at that, and I felt a physical tug at my core, that place where your tummy tightens up, beckoning me to laugh with him. But I didn't. Not just because it's ridiculously corny to laugh at your own joke, but because I was afraid the sound of mine would drown out the sound of his, and Billy Fitz's laughter provided the first moment of welcoming comfort I'd felt since Jayne parked the car.

"Relax, Great Aunt Elyse." He stood, giving me a first-ever-view of someone leaving a beanbag chair in one fluid motion. "They're in the backyard. Come look for yourself."

He took the Coke can from my hand, which I might have deemed rude, but our fingers brushed against each other in the gesture, making the cold condensation dissipate in the darkness.

He reached past, setting it down on the dresser behind me, then beckoned, again. And I followed, again, until we were side by side, foreheads pressed against the cool glass. I could see, then, why the light was blue. It wasn't a porch light, but light from a swimming pool—too cold for swimming, but the stillness of the water created a diffused beacon that drew kids to its side.

"Over there." He took my hand in his and pointed them in a singular direction, to where I could see Charlie and Jayne, their heads bent together as they studied something in a corner between the porch and the pool house. "Charlie has a bunny."

"Of course he does."

And Billy laughed again. He let go of my hand, but I kept my finger touched to the glass. It was like watching something on a television screen—all those kids, milling around. Music spilled from the house and up through the floor, the first few chords of "Jump" by Van Halen. Billy was standing so close to me that, if it hadn't been for the pane of glass against my head and hand, I might have just done that. Jumped. If only to bring a burst of air into my lungs, because I'm pretty sure I stopped breathing the moment he said the word *bunny*.

"Hey. I really like your hair like that."

Nope. That wasn't going to resuscitate me at all. Not even enough to say *thanks*. Especially once I made the mistake of turning my head—the very one with the hair he liked—to see that he was looking straight at me.

"I mean, usually, it's all kind of"—and he did this thing with his hands, turning his fingers into actors cast in the role of playing my hair, in a wild dance all around his head—"but this. It's all . . . together. Nice."

Ah, now I had breath. "Ummm . . . Thank you?"

"What I mean is, I can see your face. And your face is nice."

"It's a French braid."

"Is it? Well. Cool."

"*Merci*," I said, and then immediately wished I hadn't, because it made my whole face freeze in this awful, kind of toothpaste commercial smile which I kept for about half a second too long before regaining my senses. "Well, I guess I'll leave you to your . . . thoughts?" I was backing away as I spoke, slowly, in case he wanted to reach out, touch my arm and stop me.

He didn't.

"Have fun, Elyse."

I stopped of my own accord. "C'mon, Fitz. You know if that were possible, you'd be down there too."

"Not my thing."

"Really?" I took a moment to look around the room. It was nice. Polite, as if somebody had carefully combed through the Sears catalog's Boys Room pages and bought one of everything in some sort of masculine tartan. A gym bag on a straight-backed chair by the door, a neat pile of books and papers on the desk in the corner, and a single photograph on the bureau, right next to my abandoned Coke can. Even in the dim light, I could see it was a picture of Billy, probably from a few years ago, with a man who must be his father.

"That's my dad," Billy confirmed. "At Oxford. I went to visit him last summer."

"Oh." I filed away a reminder to feel intense jealousy later at being able to *visit* someone at *Oxford*. "So, is this your room?"

"More or less. I stay here pretty much all of the time. Mrs. Bingley's cool, and she's a way better cook than you'd expect."

"My mom's a terrible cook. So, you know, you're better off not coming to our house at all."

"Yeah, but"—he paused to run his fingers through his hair. The same fingers that, only moments ago, engaged themselves in a wild pantomime to my outrageous curls, ploughed their way through his perfect, thick, well-behaved locks, leaving a satin-y ripple that somehow straightened out to stick a perfect ten-point landing across his forehead—"I could if I wanted to, right?"

"Sure. I mean, you've been there before. With Charlie and Jayne. We're the house with the off-brand corn chips. So, I was just joking. You're welcome. Not like, *Thank you. You're welcome.* But you. Are. Welcome. Anytime you want to come over with them."

"What if I weren't with them?"

"Why? Why wouldn't you be?"

"Because I might want to be there just to see you."

The song, "Jump," was still playing, David Lee Roth screaming, "*Jump! Go ahead!*" and every cell in my body was obeying, because my insides felt like a hot bottle of Sprite in the hands of a majorette. Twisting and flipping, ready to explode the moment I opened my mouth. So I didn't.

"I know, I know. It's weird, right?" There he was again, raking that hand through that hair, only now he added pacing to the routine. "Because it's the middle of football season, and I don't usually think about girls at all during football. I mean, I don't have to, because they're always just . . . *there.* You know? And not just any girls, either. We're talking girls that, if I weren't some kind of—I don't know quite what word I'm looking for—"

"Star?" I offered, just to see where this was going.

"I guess. I mean, these days. Literally, today, I could go downstairs and get any girl at this party. Any girl I want. I could just"—he snapped his fingers, the same fingers that, well, we all remember. Enough about the fingers. "And I could have her."

"So why don't you?"

He looked at me blankly. "Why don't I what?"

"Why don't you"—and I snapped. "Why are you up here by yourself?"

"That's just it. The crazy part. The part that doesn't make

sense. I'm downstairs, surrounded by all these girls. And, as insane as it sounds, I didn't want any of them. All I could think about was you."

I could feel the fizziness inside of me settle with each word. Like opening a Christmas present, and it's in a box that is perfectly suited to hold a pair of cool designer jeans, but it turns out to be a yellow sweatshirt with an iron-on transfer of a panda.

Dislodging my feet, I put myself square in his pacing path. "Just what are you saying?"

He sighed, like the weight of the world was moments away from being lifted from his shoulders.

"I'm saying, Elyse, that I like you."

"You like me."

He put his hands on my shoulders, like a TV doctor about to deliver terrible news. "Yeah, I do."

"And just why is that—what did you say? *Insane? Weird? Nuts?*"

"Because you—you're not like other girls."

"Really? Because I got an A in Honors Biology, and I'm pretty sure—"

He took a step back. "I mean you're not—not what most people would think a guy like me would go for. Not like any girl I've ever liked before."

"Are you speaking in some sort of compliment code? Because nothing you're saying is particularly pleasant to hear."

"I'm not saying this right. None of it. Listen, for one thing, you're a Sophomore."

With a postgraduate IQ and vocabulary, but whatever.

"And I can talk to you," he went on. "And you don't care about all of this"—he waved his hand in the general direction of the party downstairs—"stuff. You're not even a part of this world. Not a part of *my* world. They're all such shallow, superficial people. But then I met you . . ."

Yes, yes. Now it's making sense . . . And I started to build up a little. I suppose it would make more sense to feel all fluttery when the most important boy in school is confessing how much he likes you. But I didn't. And I wasn't burning, either, like I did when we danced. I stood very still, feeling the fuzz of my sweater against my hands. Not frozen, not melting, but utterly calm. We have a picture magnet on our refrigerator of Jenny Lake—our souvenir from the world's most tedious road trip to Wyoming. It's a beautiful picture, though, with the mountains clearly reflected in the surface of the water. I felt like that mountain, somehow *seeing* myself in his words. His voice held me there like a shore.

". . . and all of a sudden, none of this even mattered."

Now, you kind of had to be in the room—in the moment, sharing it with us—to grasp the significance of *this*. The *this* was not the party, the crowd, the gym bag full of football equipment, the sounds of raucous laughter floating over the music. No, the *this* was me. I know, because as he said it, those hands—the much-aforementioned magic football hands—were tracing a vague outline. A silhouette, if you will, of me.

My head filled with every word he seemed incapable of saying.

My nice face didn't matter.

My out-of-control, frizzy hair didn't matter.

My fat didn't matter.

But it was there, every unspoken *this*. I was something to be overcome. Like, a stunt girlfriend. A dare to himself. If I wanted to keep standing, I had to look away. Without turning my head, I glanced over at the window. I could see two smudges on the glass where we'd pressed against it, and below them, a faint reflection of myself. Actually, ourselves. Billy and me. I don't know that I'd ever seen an image of myself next to another person, other than Jayne, of course. My photo album was filled with pictures of my sister and me, side by side at the beach, under a Christmas tree, first days of homeschool in our pajamas. It was always pudgy Elyse next to skinny Jayne, and it always felt normal, because that's who we were. Who I was. And as long as I was free from my mother's voice, I was fine. But now, seeing us—me and Billy, fresh from a moment where there seemed like there might actually be such a thing as a Men-Billy—I saw what he saw. Sure, it was fine for him to like me; his mountain to climb was to like *us*. And I wasn't about to be anybody's moral victory.

"Elyse?" he said, finally. "Are you okay? Say something."

"Oh," I said, fighting for every syllable, "is this the part where I'm supposed to, like, throw myself at you in gratitude? You know, poor, fat girls like me can't usually get so much as a *Hey* from the likes of the great Billy Fitz. Am I supposed to feel grateful? Humbled? Should I be swooning right about now? Do you keep smelling salts in your gym bag?"

He stood unfazed, even as my words became loud and shrill.

"You're right. I am different from other girls. I don't need to be validated by you. It may shock you to know that I haven't been pining away, waiting for you to come to this great epiphany of yours."

"Of course you haven't. I know that."

"Then you should also know that not every guy out there sees me as some great charity case. Like, an experiment to create a new median on the social spectrum."

His face twisted into a smirk. "You mean Gage?"

My heart was pounding as I glanced over at the photo on the bureau. "He told me everything. How your father treated him. How *you* treated him. Everybody thinks you're this great guy. Do they know?"

"They don't know everything. I've tried to protect him."

I laughed—this evil kind of *guffaw* that, in any other

scenario, would have been followed by my throwing a drink in his face. "Protect *him*?"

"Yes."

"How full of yourself are you? How can you possibly fit a helmet over that enormous head?"

Now, I could tell, he was irritated. He hooked his thumbs in his belt loops and tapped his fingers (Yes, I know. The fingers again.) on his pockets. He looked at the ceiling, at the floor. But not at me. "I'm sorry. I shouldn't have said anything. I should have known."

That's when I knew something—maybe something that could have been incredible—was slipping away. I couldn't take back anything I'd said, and neither could he. Through the lingering cloud of our convexplosion, one phrase rang clear in my head.

I like you. And everything else after that seemed . . . stupid.

"I should go," I said, resuming the journey I'd started seven lifetimes ago.

"Yeah." He was at the window again, his back to me. "And would you shut the door, please?"

I managed, somehow, to keep my *nice* face a mask of nothing special as I elbowed my way through the crowd upstairs. Better to be ignored completely than to be the chick who just ran out of the bedroom all red-faced and snot-nosed and gasping for air because she just used all of her breath saying stupid, stupid things.

Once downstairs, I began my worming journey toward the back door, when I ran headlong into Jayne.

"There you are, Pudge!"

"Don't call me that," I hissed. Yes, hissed. Teeth clenched, the whole works. I brushed past the hurt look on her face. "We have to go."

"Wait! Come out to the backyard. Charlie has a bunny."

Hard to believe there was a time when that sentence sounded whimsical and sweet.

"No, Jayne. Now."

"But it's early."

In that moment, she looked like a bunny herself, nose twitch and all. I grabbed her arm, feeling the last bit of me draining away.

"Please. Find Charlie, say goodbye. Kiss the bunny and meet me at the car."

"What is it? Elyse? What's wrong?"

I reached for her purse and dug out the keys. "I'll tell you later. Everything. I promise. I just—I have to go."

To my credit, not a single tear was shed until I was out of the house, past the party on the porch, and halfway to the car. By the time I arrived, though, my hands were shaking so much I could barely fit the key in the lock. Once inside, I slammed the door and laid myself low in the seat, the world confined to what I could see through the windshield. Nothing but sky and stars.

solace: *to give comfort in grief or misfortune :* CONSOLE

Who better to **solace** *a brokenhearted Elyse than her beloved older sister?*

THE NEXT DAY WE WERE HIT with an unexpected spate of wet, cold winter weather. The sky stayed gray from dawn until night, casting a dull light through the window, making me feel like I was trapped inside some 1950s photograph. To match the mood, I kept the radio tuned to an oldies station and let the room fill with lyrics none of today's brain-dead kids could ever understand.

For most of the morning, Jayne threw question after question at me, all of them ripped from a book titled, *Just What Happened Up There?* I dodged them long enough, mostly because I had a few questions of my own, since Jayne was hardly her usual, bubbly love-puppy self. So, when that old Leslie Gore song came on, and we heard "It's my party, and I'll cry if I want to," we decided to spill our guts to each other.

"You first," Jayne said, unraveling a cinnamon roll she'd snuck up from the kitchen. We'd been given dispensation to skip church that morning. (*Just this once, please? It is so cold, and we're so sleepy, and we promise not to ask again until after Easter . . .*) The cinnamon roll was what had been left in the kitchen following the typical Nebbitt-family-Sunday-school-time-crunch breakfast. The rolls and half a gallon of chocolate milk would normally have been one of my favorite breakfasts, but with each bite I saw Billy, his hands tracing a vague outline of my figure, and I could barely bring myself to swallow any of either. Good thing I had a lot of talking to do, and I spilled the whole story, starting with the moment I stepped into the room and saw him on the beanbag.

"So, he likes you?" Jayne said, apparently editing out the rest of the scene. "Like, *likes you*, likes you?"

"Apparently." I took a swig of the chocolate milk, right from the carton.

She snapped her fingers. "I knew it. Charlie told me I was crazy, but I have a head for these things. I *knew* it. Oh, Elyse, this is perfect."

No doubt she was picturing a year's worth of double dates—movies, prom, the four of us cozied up in a Dairy Queen booth. Four burgers and two orders of fries.

"Yeah, well," I said, "maybe not as perfect as you think. I didn't exactly ride off into the sunset with him, you know?"

"But you like him, too." She said it as fact, and until then, I don't think I'd ever considered the possibility of that truth. Not that it mattered. I could go to him now and throw myself at his feet, and he'd leap right over me.

"Even if I did," I said, speaking around a mouthful of sweet bread, "I think he's over it. Besides, I have—"

"Don't say Gage."

I bristled in defense. "I was going to say *pride*, but, okay."

She pouted. "Sorry. But there's just no comparison."

"No. There isn't. Now, you. Why are you such a gloomy goose? I mean, the two of you got to play a real, live game of

Pat the Bunny." I said it with a wicked grin that she managed to ignore.

"He's leaving."

"What?"

And then, there were tears. Hers, not mine, and like the selfish beast that I am, I just then realized she'd been crying when we found each other at the party last night.

"He's—he's going to Dallas, to stay with his dad for Christmas."

"Oh." The dawn of understanding brought my level of pity to a reasonable scale. "But that's still, like, a month away. And then, just a couple of weeks—"

"Tomorrow."

"What? But if they keep winning, there's still four more weeks of football. There's four more weeks of *school*." Priorities, you know . . .

Jayne wiped her eyes with the cuff of her sweater. "He says they worked it out with the school, so he can spend a whole six weeks with his dad. Like, homebound or something, and he gets to take his finals when he gets back in January. *January!*" According to her pronunciation of the month, 1985 might signal the end of the world, and she stood up and paced the length of the floor between our beds. "He says it doesn't matter about the football thing, because he's only a kicker, and they can get some Freshman to do that. And he gets to spend all this time working with a private soccer coach, and he might even be able to play on a club team this summer. *All summer!*"

And now she was back on the bed, flopped down beside me with enough force to knock the rolls off the plate.

"I don't understand why he's just telling you now, though. It seems sudden."

"It is. He wasn't going to leave until after the State game. Or, at least after Thanksgiving, since he was here for that. But,

I don't know, his parents swapped out all the holidays, and Mrs. Bingley is going to take Caroline to Disneyland for Christmas. Billy said it wouldn't be a big deal—"

"Wait, *Billy* said? Why does Billy get a say in this?"

She looked at me, her wide, wet eyes blinking with incredulity. "He's captain of the team. He's Charlie's best friend."

My eyes stayed nice and dry, and narrowed with suspicion. "When did these two put their knuckleheads together to come up with this timeline?"

Jayne shrugged. "Over this last week, I guess. Just waiting to get the team into the playoffs."

"And Charlie doesn't want to be a part of the final victory?"

"He doesn't care that much about football," she said, offering a weak smile. "Or, as he insists on calling it, *American* football. So I can't blame him for wanting some extra time with a special trainer. I just wish—"

I interrupted her before the tears could start again. "So, are the two of you going to spend today together? A long, sweet goodbye?"

Blonde waves crashed around as she shook her head. "We said goodbye last night. He says he has too much to do. Packing and stuff. And then he's leaving first thing in the morning."

She crumpled, right before my eyes, my sister who rarely went more than five minutes without a giggle or a joke or an off-key chorus to a cheerful tune. Now the radio played something sad and slow, scratchy lyrics about true, teen love, and it was just too much for both of us. I got up and moved across the room to the radio, thinking I needed to change the music to some mindless Go-Go's or Paula Abdul before the two of us dissolved in a puddle of pity.

Speaking of puddles, rain was pouring outside. Like, literally pouring. I know people say that about heavy rain all the time, but this was like a giant bucket being dumped from the sky. The street was empty, as it should be. Sunday morning and all. After church would be lounging and naps. Football.

The rain turned the window into a solid sheet of water, obscuring everything—trees, houses, cars parked on the street. But then there was one car *not* parked on the street. It was driving, slowly, past our house. No amount of deluge could disguise that car. Billy's Camaro, meaning Billy must be inside. Driving off and away, until he got a few houses down, where he pulled into a neighbor's driveway, turned around, came back, and parked. Right in front. And then, beyond all logic, the car door opened, and Billy himself stepped out.

I turned to Jayne. "Be right back."

"Where are you going?" In the time I'd taken to glance out the window, she'd opened her box of Charlie mementos and was studying a photo of the two of them taken at the Neewollah dance.

"Downstairs. Taking advantage of Dad not being home to kick the furnace up a notch. It's freezing up here."

"Good idea," she said, knowing our father's parsimonious personal temperature.

I slipped my feet into a pair of moccasins and crept downstairs, regretting that I didn't have time to change out of my sweatpants and Phoenix Zoo T-shirt. The sweatpants sat low on my hips, and the T-shirt was left over from a seventh grade field trip. What had once been loose and baggy now, well, *fit* . . . leaving no room to hide. But I didn't have anything to hide from Billy anymore.

I opened the front door just as Billy was about to knock. The result? His knuckles *this close* to my nose. Surprised, we both backed a step away, and I swear his gaze lingered a bit too long on my faded psychedelic tiger before coming up to meet my eyes.

"Oh, hey," he said, stuffing his hand into the pocket of his letterman jacket. I've noticed he wears his jacket better than anybody else who has one. It's not an ornamental garment, some walking canvas for patches. His looks soft and worn, conformed to his body. A part of him.

Just something I noticed.

Moving on.

He was also wearing a hat, which was unusual, but given the rain, not surprising. It was a Northenfield Texas High School baseball cap, also perfectly broken in. The minute I stepped out onto the porch, though, he took it off and ran his fingers through his damp hair, leaving little furrows, with one tight clump of strands arching to a point right above his left eyebrow.

Again, just something I noticed.

"What are you doing here?" I asked, because all that *noticing* made me completely forget my manners.

"I wanted to talk to you, but I didn't have your number. So I couldn't call. So I—"

"Charlie has our number. He calls here all the time."

Billy shifted his weight, looking uncomfortable, and fixed his gaze on the empty hummingbird feeder hanging behind me.

"Charlie's busy. He's leaving in the morning."

"Thanks to you."

Now he looked at me. "What? What is that supposed to mean? He always spends six weeks with his dad over winter break."

"But he's leaving a little early this year, isn't he?"

"He could have driven up with his mom and sister, but we really needed this game. Coach said he could still play the last game if he wanted to. If we make it. His dad could drive him down, but he's cool with missing it."

"Is he? Is he *cool* with missing the game, Billy?" I had my arms crossed tight like an angry housewife. All I needed was a rolling pin and a few curlers in my hair to make the look complete.

"Yeah." He was posturing now, too, one hand out of his pocket, flipping his leather key fob against his thumb like he did the first day we met. So, I guess he was back to not *like*-liking me again. "He's okay with it, so it's really none of anybody else's business."

"But you made it your business."

"I told him I was fine, that the team would miss him, but we'd be fine. He has a chance to work with a trainer. Plus, there's always next year."

A low rumble of thunder supplied an ominous punctuation to the idea of *next year,* and we both stood silent until it passed. Water poured in rivulets off the porch, making it seem like we were encased in a tent made of a hundred tiny streams, and I could only imagine how romantic the scene would be if I'd had a different reaction to his declaration of yesterday. Who knows? We might have been joggling on the board. Instead, we faced each other in a literal standoff, bringing me to repeat my original question.

"Why are you here? Why do you feel a need to tell me all of this? Or, were you hoping to explain this all to Jayne? Because I'm telling you, she doesn't want to hear it."

"I'm not here to talk to Jayne. I came to talk to you, but I can see it was a mistake. I won't bother you again." He turned to leave.

"It's not a bother. It's just—weird."

"Yeah, well. We've had enough of that already."

He tugged his hat on over his hair and strode out into the rain. I waited on the porch, just in case he had one of those moments. You know, where he comes to his senses, turns around, and runs back, taking his hat off right before he takes me in his arms and—

Nope. The next sound is the Camaro rumbling to life, the faint sound of AC/DC. I can't imagine how loud that must have been inside the car, for the song to carry through the storm and onto the porch. The song? "Flick of the Switch." And he was gone.

For the rest of that day I stayed home. And by home, I mean my room. And by my room, I mean my bed. Huddled under the covers while the sky continued to seep outside. Jayne did, too, and when the family came home from church, we begged to be left alone, claiming sniffles and homework and a total lack of appetite for Dad's rainy Sunday chili. Instead, Lydia was sent up with two bowls of chicken noodle soup balanced on a tray.

"Gage was at church," she said from the safe distance of our bedroom doorway. "He sat with our family and told me to tell you to get better soon."

"Thanks," I said, wiping my nose with a tissue. Jayne's sniffles were real, mine purely for show.

"Oh, and he also seemed surprised that you were home working on an English essay that he knows nothing about. So, should he be worried? Or are you just an overachiever?"

"It's not due for another two weeks," I said, thankful to have a sliver of truth to cling to. Mrs. Pierson had made some vague reference to a paper we would have to write as fifty percent of our final exam grade, but we'd yet to hear the specifics. "I'm just getting a head start."

Lydia wrinkled her nose and said, "Such a nerd," before spinning with unnecessary drama and walking away.

"I don't want to go to school tomorrow," Jayne said while flipping listlessly through her history book.

I offered a weak smile. "Maybe we can go back to home-school after all? Since we're both pretty strong with the whole readin' and writin' thing."

"What are you afraid of? Nobody knows about your awkward encounter. I, on the other hand, have been making a fool of myself with Charlie."

"What, making a fool? You like each other."

"Not enough to keep him here."

"Look. It's three days, then Thanksgiving break. Then three weeks until Christmas. And then he'll be home."

"He didn't even call me."

"The day's not over."

She looked at me, her eyes wide and blue, and I knew we were both counting all the hours that had passed, when he could have called, even for a minute, to tell her goodbye. To tell her that he missed her already. To say something sweet and goofy. To say anything.

The ring of the phone in the hallway startled both of us, sending Jayne off her bed and straight for the door, but by the time she flung it open, Lydia was already there, holding her hand over the mouthpiece and hollering, "*I got it!*" as a preemptive strike against somebody listening in. I was right behind Jayne, the two of us filling the doorway, watching our younger sister compose a conversation out of nothing more than deep, throaty giggles, and the repetition of "*Really? Really. No way. Really?*"

"She's not supposed to get phone calls from boys," Jayne said, slinking back into the room.

I closed the door behind us. "Maybe it's not a boy."

Jayne looked at me, her expression asking if I could possibly be that stupid.

"Should we find out?" I asked. "Turn her in to Mom and Dad?"

She looked like she was considering the prospect for a moment, before returning to her sweet, soft senses. "No." She climbed back onto her bed and opened her history book again. "May as well have one happy girl in the house."

conjecture: *inference formed without proof or sufficient evidence*

Once presented with additional evidence, Elyse realized her first impression was pure conjecture.

I DON'T THINK I EVER REALIZED just how much of my life-space was occupied by Billy Fitz until that Monday morning when, without any change to my routine, he was everywhere. Had he always had a locker just twelve down from mine? I don't ever remember seeing him getting a Pepsi from the machine in the alcove under the B-wing stairway, but while I was on my way to English, there he was, with only forty or so people between us.

"So, did you finish your essay?" Gage said, sliding into his seat, causing a mild panic to all within earshot.

"Sorry about that," I said, after reassuring the eavesdroppers that it was a joke. "I just didn't feel like going to church. I caught myself up on the reading, though." I flipped open our enormous anthology. "Jonathan Edwards. What a bunch of giggles."

"Indeed." Gage opened his book too. "You know, Edwards was a minister. He wouldn't approve of you using a little white lie to stay home from church."

"He was a Transcendentalist," I countered. "As long as God

forgives me, so would he. And I think God has much bigger things to worry about."

Billy and I passed each other in the hallway between every class, and when it came time for lunch, I had to sit on the opposite of my usual seat to keep him out of my field of vision.

"What's this?" Lottie said as she and Collin came up to the table. "You know Collin doesn't like to face the jock table while he eats. Inadequacy kills the appetite."

"Just for a few days." I inclined my head toward Jayne, who hadn't even unwrapped her peanut butter and honey sandwich.

"Oh, yes." Lottie set her tray down and silently instructed Collin to do the same. "I'm sorry, Jayne, but you can hardly be surprised. Everybody knows Charlie goes to Dallas from Thanksgiving to the New Year. Certainly you didn't think that was going to change just because the two of you were dating?"

"Lottie!" I intervened, knowing Jayne would never do so for herself.

"There's no insult here, just the nature of the beast. Social strata are inescapable, so if you want security in a relationship, you need to find a boy who is less likely to improve upon you as his choice." She sent Collin away to exchange her white milk for a chocolate before continuing. "Collin's family has more money than mine, so outside of school, we might never work as a couple. But he's in band and I'm in Pep Squad, so we meet the social equality standard within the school environment, see? You, on the other hand, come from an intact, middle-class family. Charlie has divorced parents, *each* with successful careers, and his father lives in a city that has a TV series named after it. So, no compatibility there. Then, while you are both equal in your academic mediocrity, he is on the Varsity Football Team. You, on the other hand, work in the attendance office, which means you are viewed either as a snitch, or as one who can facilitate truancy—each label an anathema depending on your attendance moral code. Charlie Bingley isn't capable of having an enemy. He is a hero, whose best friend is a bigger hero. You're lucky this opportunity came along for him to break it off with you. Much less messy now, before all of this becomes clear to him."

The whole time she spoke, Jayne and I could do nothing but listen in slack-jawed amazement at her calculating thesis.

Finally, Jayne came to her senses. "We didn't break up."

"Didn't you?"

Collin was back, milk in hand, and he placed the small carton silently on Lottie's tray.

"Then, tell me. How is his dad? I remember him from before he moved away. Our family bought a car at his dealership, and he threw in free floor mats because my older brother was so messy."

"He—he hasn't said." Jayne concentrated very hard now, unwrapping her sandwich.

"Really? Seems odd he would call and not talk about his father."

"He hasn't called." Jayne took a nibble. "Yet."

"Oh." Lottie took a sip of her milk, once Collin had opened the carton and inserted the straw. "Well then, of course. I'm sure everything is fine."

The one place it seemed would be impossible to avoid Billy was our Trigonometry class, as we sat across the aisle from each other, and were often paired up as a "Trig-Team" to solve complex problems. I actually had a plan for this, though, that involved skipping the dress-out for gym and getting to class a few minutes early so I could claim a seat at the back of the room, creating at least four Trig-Team pairings between us. Normally that would have meant a zero for the day at gym, but by merely uttering the magical word "cramps," I got a free pass to sit on the bleachers for an hour.

Unfortunately, there was one giant flaw in my plan, which was revealed to me the minute I rounded the corner into the classroom. Billy had thought of it too.

There we were, just the two of us, seven minutes before we would be joined by the rest of our seventh-period classmates. Mr. Venzinni was nowhere to be seen, which was nothing unusual. He didn't teach a class before this one and was reliably a good five to ten minutes late for class at least once a week. So there we were, the room lit only by the cloudy light coming through the windows, and a sea of empty desks between us.

Everything Lottie had said came rushing back, and for the first time I realized that this class—this place—had been my tiny spot of equality with Billy Fitz. We fed off each other, challenged each other, alternated higher quiz scores, talked about music while waiting for Mr. Venzinni to show up. Scooched our desks to touching when it was time for Trig-Team. Why couldn't I have remembered all of this when he told me that he liked me?

"Hey," he said from the last desk on the third row.

"Hey," I said before walking to my regular seat and turning my back, knowing he wasn't looking at me at all.

One more day, I thought. *Today, tomorrow, and three days off for Thanksgiving.*

And today was almost over.

I have no idea what happened in Trig that day. Something about simple integration, as if such a thing were possible. Mr. Venzinni loaded a new piece of chalk into the metal holder he—and of all my teachers, only he—used and promptly turned his back to us. The board filled with numbers, and I kept my notebook open, copying everything, hoping I'd be able to understand it better, later. Back in my room with my textbook. Otherwise I'd be in tutorials after school, which wouldn't be horrible, but the after-school tutorial time was also the mandatory Athlete

Study Hall time, so Billy would be in there. And Gage, but not Charlie—making that part of my life a million times more complicated than any problem on the chalkboard.

Because I wasn't paying close enough attention, I didn't hear the bell ring, and thus ruined my chance to get up, out of the room, and down the hall before any possible chance of running into Billy in the doorway. Instead, I was still trying to stuff my textbook into my backpack when an all-too-familiar set of Levi's 501 pockets stopped in front of me, eye-level. I didn't look up, and within a second they were moving on, but not before a folded sheet of notebook paper fell square into the middle of my desk.

A note. Upon close inspection—like, by picking it up—I realized there was more than one sheet of paper here. Two or three, at least. And it wasn't folded in the cute way girls do, with a fancy tug-tab. Just a few sheets of paper, folded once and over again, like they could be stuffed into a nice envelope pilfered from Typing class. My name—ELYSE—was printed in perfect, precise all-caps, and when I hazarded a quick peek at the first page, I realized the whole letter was written that way.

Billy Fitz writes in all caps. Just something for future notice.

Mr. Venzinni asked if there was something I needed to show him, and I said no, quickly shoving the papers into the front pocket of my JanSport.

When could I read this? *Where* could I read it, without risking the prying eyes of fellow students, who would probably immediately recognize the handwriting and peek over my shoulder and demand to know why I, Elyse Nebbitt, was in possession of such an epistle? At home I was Jayne's newest and bestest friend, unable to leave her side except for the necessary trips to the bathroom. And even then, I swear, she'd follow me and perch on the edge of the tub, telling me about this one time when Charlie did something so cute and romantic . . .

I had one more class after Trigonometry: Spanish, Second Year, with Señora Benavidez—a tedious way to end the day, with half an hour of verb conjugations, followed by a lecture about, for all we knew, a dozen ways to ride a bike or make a sandwich or find *la biblioteca* in Mexico City.

Jayne, however, had the perfect eighth-period class, so I turned right instead of left, and made my way to the office door marked ATTENDANCE, where my sister stood behind the counter, filing small slips of paper into a long wooden box.

"Elyse?"

I walked right up to the counter and leaned over, whispering, "I'm late for Spanish. I need a tardy slip."

"Why are you late?"

I couldn't exactly tell her I'd been wandering in the hallways, clutching a bunch of folded papers, trying to work up the courage to open them. So I used the same magic word that worked in PE. "Cramps." Because, really, I did have *something* happening in the pit of my stomach.

She gave me a look of sympathy mixed with skepticism, then leaned over the counter. "Just go. Want to know a secret? Señora Benavidez never—like, really *ever*—turns in attendance."

We'd all heard rumors of this, but it was nice to get official confirmation. "Thanks, sis," I said, hoping my eyes conveyed the depth of my gratitude before heading off in search of a place to read. Outside certainly wouldn't do, as the rain had left every inch of everywhere sloppy and soggy. The only logical choice was the library, where, thanks to my regular visits and reputation, I walked right past the librarian and disappeared into the stacks. Fiction, the *T*s, near the back. I dropped my JanSport on the ground and sat in front of it. With a copy of *Huck Finn* to give me cover, I fished out the note, opened it, and began to read:

Elyse—

*I guess you made it pretty clear that you don't want
to talk to me, and I while I really don't understand, I
will respect that. I honestly don't know what I said that
offended you,*

I had to peel my eyes off the ceiling before I could continue.
Really? He really doesn't know? Deep breath, continue.

*but it was wrong of me to assume you might feel the same
way about me as I feel about you. So, I apologize for
springing my feelings on you like that, and I promise you
this note isn't about me trying to push myself on you. At
all. I promise I won't bother you about that again, but
there are a couple of things I do want to clear up with you,
so I'd appreciate you reading this all the way to the end,
and if by then you still think I'm a horrible person, well,
there's nothing I can do about that. Please, though, just
"hear" me out.*

I read his promise again, thinking I could handle a little
push.

*First, about Gage. I'm pretty sure I know everything he
has told you about me, because it's the same story he's been
telling everyone since before he left. I just want to set the
record straight. It's true that his mom and my dad dated
for a while. I wasn't crazy about it, because he's my dad
and I still missed my mom. But Mrs. W seemed like a nice
enough lady, and my dad seemed happy with her, even
though she was nothing like my mom.*

When they started seriously dating, Dad practically moved her and Gage into our house. Gage got his own room, and I had to share all my stuff with him. Dad said it was because they didn't have as much, because she was divorced and her ex didn't help them out at all. I didn't mind sharing, really. And for a while it was cool having a brother close to my age. I mean, I was glad he wasn't a little kid, you know? So, we'd play basketball and hang out. Watch TV, whatever. But then some stuff started to go missing. Little things at first, like a couple of baseball cards, comic books. Then, my Magic Johnson poster disappeared, and I found it hanging on the wall behind the door in Gage's room. And then, he was wearing one of my favorite T-shirts. When I complained to my dad, he just said, "Son, we've been blessed with so much. It can't hurt to share. And besides, isn't it nice that the kid looks up to you so much?"

So, I got a new poster, let him keep the T-shirt, and just kept my mouth shut. But it got worse. He started stealing— outright stealing. Money, right out of my drawer, a few bucks at a time, to where I didn't even notice until I went to buy some new albums and I was $20 short of what I should have had. I told Dad, and his solution was to start giving Gage an allowance, almost equal to mine. (Plus, Dad paid me back the $20, which was cool.) Then, I found out Gage was stealing from my dad, too. From his wallet. Got money for his mom, sometimes, but mostly for him. He bought music, clothes, shoes. Skipped school and went to the movies almost every Friday.

I closed my eyes, trying to separate this behavior from the Gage I knew, but little glimpses of light came through. Things that wouldn't have meaning without this context. Like how he had new clothes every week. How he somehow managed to get called out of AP English every time we had a timed writing essay. Always had cash for the school snack bar, even though he didn't have a job and never mentioned an allowance. And once, shopping for music at Hastings, he'd said, "Do me a favor? Stand right there." Which had meant nothing at the time, but now I realize a green-aproned employee was alphabetizing the stock down the row, and I have no recollection of him actually buying the new Culture Club cassette.

I tried telling my dad, again, but he was gone a lot. You know he's this computer guru, right? And, he would go all over the country, gone for 2 or 3 weeks at a time. They'd pay him a ton of money, and we got to live here. And I liked it here. (I still do.) Anyway, when I told him about the stealing, he had a "good, long talk" with Gage, who cried and promised to do better. And Gage's mom cried, saying they'd never known what it was to have a home and be taken care of, and Gage was just acting out of fear that he'd be abandoned again, or some other psychoanalysis bull. I dunno, I think Dad wanted to somehow save this family, and every time I ratted Gage out, I ended up looking like some whiny, privileged bully. So I just shut up, figuring he'd cross a line at some point, and Dad's eyes would be opened.

Like mine.

Well, that didn't exactly happen. Not with Gage, anyway. The other part to this sad little tale is Gage's mom. Like I said, Dad was out of town, a lot. And I know she saw other guys while he was gone. I couldn't prove it, but I knew. Somehow I figured it would hurt his feelings more coming from me, so I waited. That's when I started playing football—Junior High. And track in the spring, anything to keep me busy. One day Dad came to pick me up at school. He'd been gone for a couple of weeks, setting up a system at Oxford, and he was all excited because they offered him a three-year contract for an insane amount of money, plus housing. He signed me and Gage out of school, and we picked up Chinese food from Dragon Dragon and went home to surprise Gage's mom. Turns out, we were the ones who were surprised, because she had some guy there. This Air Force recruiter guy who'd been hanging around the school, and it was pretty obvious what they'd been up to, since they were upstairs, and his uniform was downstairs.

I gasped out loud like a scandalized Victorian and slammed the letter inside my *Huck Finn* book, lest angels were reading over my shoulder. *That, Billy Fitz, is one detail you could have chosen to omit*, though I appreciated his employ of euphemism. Once my blush died down, I read on.

I've never felt so sorry for anyone as I did for my dad in that moment. His heart was broken, and his pride—he kept himself pretty together, just told her to pack her stuff and have herself and Gage out in the next three days. Then he took me on a trip to Dallas, and we went to Six Flags. I didn't even pack a bag. He still had all his stuff from his trip to London, and he bought me whatever I needed on the trip.

We didn't talk about Lorraine or Gage. Never said their names. Haven't since. He didn't want to hang around and face the gossip, so he transferred guardianship of me to Charlie's parents and took off for London. And I mean, I really love the Bingleys, but I kind of lost my dad over all of this. I miss him, and he's missing out on some important things here.

I couldn't imagine what it would be like to miss my parents. I mean, they drove me crazy with their gooberish antics, but they were *there*. Always. (Sigh, always.) Sometimes it seemed like Jayne and I and our sisters were the only kids around with both parents—the *same* parents. No wonder Billy chose to stay at Charlie's all the time. Family is where you find it.

Anyway, that's the whole truth about Gage Wickam. You can believe me if you want, or not. It's your choice. You just seem like you're too nice of a person for him. I suppose that's another thing that makes us so different. You are kind and trusting. I hold grudges, maybe longer than I ought to. For whatever reason, you chose not to trust me, though. Maybe I'm a bigger jerk than I thought.

I believed him. Not about him being a jerk, and certainly not about me being kind and trusting. But about Gage? Yeah. That all made sense. *That* was the story that made Lottie grin with hidden gossip on the night of the homecoming dance.

Sorry this note is so long. I started writing it in history, and now it's Trig, so I hope it makes more sense than whatever Mr. V is doing on the board right now. I'll have to come to tutoring for sure this week.

Oh—one last thing. About Charlie, and his trip to Dallas. Yes, I guess it would be fair to say that I encouraged him to go early.

And I could feel my cheeks burning already.

Look, you don't know just how love-sick-stupid he is over your sister. He wants to play soccer, and could probably get a scholarship, since there aren't many kids out there who know and play the game as well as he does. But he was talking about not even going to visit his dad, since he didn't want to leave Jayne. And when we were talking about college the other day, he said it would depend on what Jayne wanted to do.

Sorry, but I can't take the thought of my best friend gambling his future on a girl, when there's every chance they'll break up next week, or next semester, or even next year, when it could be too late to undo the damage. She's a pretty girl. She'll find another guy. Charlie won't find another way to get into college. Trust me, I saw his PSAT scores.

So, wait. I take it back. I'm not sorry. Not at all. I've seen how badly a relationship can screw up someone's life, even when both of the people are fully functioning adults. I'm not going to let some girl ruin my best friend's future. I hope you can understand. But if you don't, there's nothing I can do about it.

Billy

I read the last page of the letter—the part about Charlie and Jayne—three times over and then I heard the bell ring. I hadn't made it to Spanish class at all, but that was a problem for tomorrow. For today, I had enough. Like, what was I going to say to Jayne? Would she take any comfort in knowing that their love was dangerous? And what about Gage? The more I read Billy's account, the more it rang true, and I remembered the petulance in Gage's voice whenever we talked about Billy. Or saw Billy. Or heard someone talk about seeing Billy. All of it made more sense now. This was more than just an old rivalry;

Gage bore an element of resentment and shame. Billy's timeline fit the timeline of Gage's story, and maybe Gage was just trying to soften his mother's reputation. Either way, despite the fact that we barely registered as a couple, I had to break up with him. Not because of his mother's allegedly questionable morals, and not because of the evidence that he was a liar and a thief.

No, I had to break up with Gage because I just didn't like him. Not enough to want to rise to his defense against these allegations. Plus, by now I was fully convinced that I was completely in love with Billy Fitz. And I would have to use all my energy making sure he never, ever found out.

genius: *a person endowed with extraordinary mental superiority*

It is hard to feel like a **genius** *when you are wrong about absolutely everything.*

THAT YEAR, AS USUAL, we went around the table at Thanksgiving, each of us speaking aloud the one thing for which we were most grateful. Mom said she was grateful for our home, Dad said he was grateful for his job—no shocker there. Also on the predictable side, one of the Littles was thankful for the Strawberry Shortcake cartoons and the other for Halloween candy. Lydia claimed to be grateful that she'd *finally* gone up a bra size—a declaration that nearly sent my father into a mashed-potato nosedive. Jayne said she was thankful for me, her loving sister, and I said I was thankful to be out of school for a few days.

"How sad," Lydia said, "when school is, like, the one thing you're really good at."

"Well, I suppose we can't all measure our accomplishments in cup size," I retorted. Sweetly, though, because I had just been named a loving sister.

The Saturday after Thanksgiving, we won the Regional Semifinals, with an untested Sophomore kicking all the extra points in Charlie's place. Neither Jayne nor I went to the game, but we did listen on the radio, and she noticed my increased attention whenever the announcer said "Billy Fitz" in a way that seemed to give it an extra syllable. *Billy Fitz-ah.*

"You've changed your mind about him, haven't you?"

"I've changed my mind about a lot of things." I found Billy's letter, now soft along the creases from so much folding and unfolding, and handed it to her. Not the last page, though. Not the stuff about Charlie, yet.

While she read, I indulged in my favorite of the holiday meal leftovers—the last slice of pumpkin pie, broken into pieces and mixed in with the last of the Cool Whip in the container. I ate, she read, and when she was done, Jayne looked up. "What do you think?"

"I don't know."

"Billy doesn't have any reason to make this up. He's been cool about not wanting to spread unnecessary gossip, but even Charlie has told me that Gage isn't all he appears to be."

"You tried to warn me."

Jayne used her dainty fingers to extract a Cool Whip–covered chunk of pie. "I did. But people do change, you know. Maybe he has too."

"Maybe. But even so, I don't think I want to go out with him anymore."

"Because you love *Billy Fitz-ah.*" She spoke with a mouthful of pie, which looked disgusting, and made me smile.

"I don't *love* him."

"You *like* him."

Instead of answering, I dragged my spoon around the edge of the bowl.

"Admit it, Pudge!"

I gave her a look, and she deflated immediately. "Oh, I'm sorry. I forgot you asked me not to call you that anymore."

"It's okay." I studied the massive pile of Cool Whip on the spoon and handed it over to her. "It really doesn't bother me, you know."

She handed the spoon back, empty. "What doesn't bother you?"

"Being the fat sister."

She looked—stricken. We've never used *that word* before, either of us. Out loud. Ever. My mother spoke around it with eloquent euphemism. *Fat* was a curse, a swear word. Profane and ugly. Our Wednesday night Girls' Bible Study spent very little time teaching us about anything really . . . *biblical*. Even reading about Queen Jezebel slaughtering the prophets of God turned into a cautionary discussion about how wearing too much makeup can lead to deadly consequences. Miss Tammie, our leader, her body an assemblage of sharp angles and protruding wrist bones, sat at the apex of our circle of chairs and cheered on our inner beauty before mentioning that we could have our morning prayer time while doing sit-ups. *Imagine! You can have the Lord's attention and a flat stomach at the same time! You can do jumping jacks with praise!* I remember laughing along with the other girls while Miss Tammie and I worked very hard not to look at each other. I refused to believe I needed to be engaged in calisthenics while praying to God, but I walked out of that room feeling like a failure on two fronts. How was I supposed to feel like a beautiful Creation of God when I looked like . . . *this*? Why was it my sisters and I could be born of the same mother, fed from the same kitchen, inclined to the same habit of sofa-surfing TV zombie-watching, and yet I alone was burdened with all this extra flesh? Most of the time—really, honest and true, MOST of the time—it didn't bother me. God was allowed a wink every now and then.

Jayne took a deep breath. "You're not—"

"I am."

"No, you're not. You just can't *say* that about yourself. You can't believe it. Remember, Satan is the father of lies."

I pondered this for a minute. A boy I liked (yes, let's establish for good-n-all that I *liked* Billy Fitz) told me my size didn't matter, and all I heard was: IT MATTERS MORE THAN ANYTHING. So, score one for the lie. But lies can't bury facts.

"I'm fatter than you." Not even her terrible math skills could argue with this.

"I've never thought about it," she said, angling her head the way she always does on the rare occasion when she is being less than truthful.

"You don't have to. You don't have to sit back and watch other people wear all the cute clothes and get all the really positive attention. You don't have to be embarrassed by the way people *look* at you. Or wonder what they're whispering when they pass you in the hall. You don't have to dread announcing your PE uniform size or pray that there's one big enough to fit you."

"Elyse, you're not that . . . that . . ." she stalled.

"Not that what? Not that fat?"

"Stop saying that word. I mean, you're talking like you're some sort of obese monster. Like you're Jabba the Hutt or something."

Star Wars reference. Nice. "You don't have to be Jabba the Hutt to feel fat. And it's hard not to notice when you're the fa—chubbiest girl in the room. Or at the school."

"Well, you're hardly the biggest girl at school. There's—" And she started to tick a list off her fingers. And that's when I knew for sure that, of course she'd noticed. She'd thought about it. Somewhere deep in that brain of hers, where knowledge is surrounded and kept in place by kindness and affection, she'd prepared a defense specifically for this moment.

"Stop," I said, using the Cool Whip bowl to bump her hands down. "Comparing myself to other girls won't make me any thinner, right? And, really, like I said, it's okay. It doesn't bother me."

"Really? Because it kinda seems like it does."

"It didn't use to," I said—feeling all confession-y, like the suspect when the cop who has all the answers finally breaks her down—"when we were little, because we were all just kids and we never looked at ourselves, and we all wanted and got pretty much the same things. But then, you know, we grow up, and things start to *matter*. Like clothes—"

"You've never cared about clothes."

"I don't have the luxury. Mom and Dad can buy you nice stuff because it can be handed down to Lydia. I can't wear hand-me-downs, and we can't hand *mine* down, so . . ."

"Oh, gosh. Elyse. I never thought. I'm so sorry."

"You don't have to be sorry. It's not your fault I'm not a size three."

"Do you wish you were?"

And I wondered just how long she'd been waiting to ask me that question. "Sometimes," I said, giving the most honest answer I could. "But then, in a way, being . . . how I am . . . was kind of a safety thing. Like, I never had to worry about a boy rejecting me because I never thought a boy would bother to get close enough *to* reject me. Does that make sense?"

Jayne nodded.

"I mean, I never even thought about that until I realized how, like, *surprised* I was when Gage asked me out. Like part of me wanted to check and make sure he really knew what he was doing."

"I think he genuinely liked you."

"I think so, too. But then—" and this, I swear, was an understanding unfolding in the moment, like a pile of thoughts that could only have been put together through the magic of pumpkin pie and whipped dessert topping—"I think when he saw Billy at Dino's—or more like, when Billy saw the two of us, I became less *desirable*." I said this final word with a shrug. "Like, being with the fat girl would make him look like more of a loser in Billy's eyes."

"That's a terrible thing to say." But she believed it too. "Billy would never think that way."

"I know that now," I said. "I wish I would have realized it sooner."

She smiled. "Like the night of the party?"

"I'm such an idiot," I groaned, turning to the comfort of the Cool Whip once more. The pie was long gone.

"No, you're not. And I think—I *honestly* think—you mis-understood him. If you would just talk—"

Armed with knowledge she didn't possess, I said, "He's still a jerk."

"No offense, but I think I might know him a little better than you do. He's Charlie's best friend, after all."

"Yeah, best friend." And as my sister's best friend, I knew she deserved to hear the truth. From me, but not yet. There was still a chance that Charlie could find a spine, defy Billy's edict. I took Billy's letter back from Jayne. "Still nothing?" I asked as I discreetly folded it with its third page. Anything to move the conversation away from my weight.

"Nope. Not a word. Come to think of it," she said, her mind obviously miles away, "he didn't even *ask* for our address. I figured he just knew it, you know, from being here at the house all the time. I mean, it's written right on the porch, for Pete's sake."

"This is Charlie we're talking about. This is the guy who thinks whenever you're going forward, you're going north, because on the maps *north* is *up*."

(True story, that.)

Jayne smiled. "That's what I love about him. He's so sweet. And uncomplicated."

And tractable.

I handed the Cool Whip container over for Jayne to finish off and swallowed hard, preparing myself to choke out a bit of truth wrapped around a lie. "He probably just needs some time with his dad, you know? He'll talk to his dad about you, then start missing you, then call. Or write, maybe."

"Do you really think so?" Jayne had a tiny dollop of white on her lip, making her look about five years old and full of hope. Good grief, this was easy. Mom and Dad totally should have left it to me to explain the fate of our long-lost turtle. Because, despite all of Billy's meddling, there was still a chance that phone might ring, Charlie's voice penitent and pleading on the other end. But that turtle? Well, let's just say he was never coming back.

"I do. Best thing you can do now is forget about him. You have friends, you have family." *She's a pretty girl. She'll find another guy.* "We'll figure out what to do later."

But I was the one who had to figure out what to do. Billy was an easy fix. I mapped out a route that guaranteed zero across-the-hall eye contact throughout the day, and when somebody asked why he wasn't in our Trig class on Monday, Mr. Venzinni said he was tutoring Billy one-on-one during lunch, so the stress of the class wouldn't interfere with his performance on the football field. I tipped my invisible hat to the boy for killing two possible run-ins with one ruse.

As far as Gage was concerned, I decided to rip another strategy from Billy's playbook. No big breakup. No scene. No awkward conversation about how he lied, or did he lie, or how I think he lied, and this is why I think so. Once again, the broken home would work in somebody's favor. As a Thanksgiving

Day surprise, Gage's Aunt June presented him with an airplane ticket to go visit his mother and stepfather in Germany. Three whole weeks, leaving right after the last day of school, and not returning until days after we started back.

"That's going to be amazing!" I told him as we sat on the Joggling Board, watching our neighbors string up their Christmas lights. "Germany is the birthplace of the Christmas tree, you know."

He didn't say anything about missing me, and I didn't say anything about missing him. We did, however, talk about the enormous expense of long-distance phone calls and international postage, which explained both why he didn't communicate often enough with his mother, and why he probably wouldn't communicate at all with me. A little more conversation about the craziness of basketball—the practices, the tournaments—combined with the stress of final exams, and I think we both pretty much knew this relationship, whatever it had been, was over.

Jayne and I walked home on the last day of school before Christmas break much as we had walked to school on our first day. The two of us, alone. Again, with Lydia trailing behind, surrounded by an ostentation of peacocks disguised as eighth-grade boys. Every house had a GO BADGERS! sign in the front yard, some of them with the names and numbers of the players in bold, purple paint. Saturday afternoon would be the final game, the State Championship.

Who would have thought on that first day of school, when I walked through the halls, eyes glued to my schedule and the numbers above the doors, that I would have ever known, let alone *cared*, about the status of our football team? That I would wonder if the place kicker regretted his decision to cut and run early? That I would be at all concerned about the quarter-back's mental fortitude not to crack under the pressure? I've been mocking cheerleaders and have equated School Spirit with teen Black Magic since I first stepped foot inside a public school when I was twelve. Don't get me wrong—I still didn't give much of a blast whether or not we won for the school's sake. I was torn, though. Part of me wanted us to lose so that Charlie wouldn't feel left out. But I knew that would be devastating for Billy, so I wanted us to win. Just good, clean touchdowns. Six points at a time. Everybody happy, with a halftime show.

"So, should we go tomorrow?" Inside my jacket pocket were two quarter-sheets of purple paper—tickets for the Student Bus to watch the game in Arlington. They'd gone on sale a month ago, one dollar a ticket, selling out within three days at the table in the back of the cafeteria disguised as a ticket booth. I knew Jayne had bought one, and one of the ones in my pocket had ini-tially belonged to Gage, who'd bought it before he knew he'd be wishing everyone *Frohe Weihnachten* this year. We had been told that, should the team not make it all the way to State, our tickets would be good for a Student Bus for the next Away Basketball Game.

Jayne kicked at a dry leaf. "May as well. We already have the tickets, right? What else would we do with them?"

"Sell them? We have three—yours, mine, and Gage's. I could probably get five bucks apiece for them. We can go to a movie instead. Pig out on popcorn. *Starman*, maybe?"

"Too romantic. How about *Nightmare on Elm Street*?"

"It's rated R. Plus, too scary. For you, I mean."

"Scarier than going to the game?"

I knew the past few weeks had been hard for her, as she had been immediately dropped from Charlie's social circle, like they'd all simultaneously discovered she was a secret agent kitten assassin or something. For her, the hallways were filled with silence and stares, classes humming with whispers and lunches a maze of piteous glances. I hated that for her, as if she had done something wrong. As if she deserved all the unspoken *poor thing* comments, or worse, the *I knew it wouldn't last* judgments. Come to think of it, they weren't all unspoken, because that's how I knew what people were saying.

"How's this," I said as we made our way through the bed of leaves on our front lawn. "We face one set of fears and go to the game. And, I sell the third ticket at a considerable markup, and we go scarf nachos and soda at the stadium."

"I don't know . . ."

We were on the front steps by now and could hear the delighted squealing of the little sisters coming through the front door. No doubt a mad game of Chase and Climb, something Mom invented whenever she wanted Homeschool History to consist of adrenaline-fueled reenactment. Behind us, Lydia was dropping shameless hints about how *bored* she was going to be over the Christmas Holiday, and how she *hoped* she'd have a chance to go out every now and then, get some pizza. See a movie. I could hear the boys calculating their allowances.

I looped my arm through Jayne's and tugged her close. "Just think. A day—an entire day—away from these people. We'll talk Dad into taking us to buy bus snacks tonight."

She didn't respond immediately, so I had to pull out the big guns.

"Charlie would want you to go."

Now, I have no idea if Charlie would give two niblets one way or the other, but it worked. Her eyes lit up, and her skinny little body filled itself with strength and resolve. "Okay, but how are you going to sell that ticket?"

"Watch."

I turned to face the crowd now gathered on the lawn and

let out a piercing whistle that somehow managed to pull their attention away from my enticing younger sister.

"Hey!" I yelled, to garner the last bits of interest. "Which of you guys wants to buy a ticket to ride the High School Student Bus to the game tomorrow?"

"Junior High kids can't go on the bus!" one of the boys hollered back.

I surveyed the gathering. Most of these kids could pass as Freshmen. There was one who couldn't be more than twelve, and he could pass for seven, but the others were respectable enough to the untrained eye. Now, most of our bus drivers had extremely sharp, intuitive recognition of which kids did—and didn't—belong on a bus, but tomorrow, all anybody would care about was the almighty purple ticket.

"Just keep your head down, and if anybody asks for ID, tell them you left it in your locker. C-Wing, where the Freshmen are."

This sparked some response, and our leaves crunched as they shifted in their Nikes. Not wanting to lose momentum, I reached into my pocket and pulled out the ticket, holding it high above my head like a fabulous prize.

"Bidding starts at five bucks."

"Six!" one kid shouted, impressing me not only with his ready bit of cash, but his knowledge of the auction system. He was tall and would probably be handsome once the last of the baby fat got shaved off his face.

"She said five!" This from the little one, who was immediately elbowed to the back of the crowd.

"Six fifty!"

"Seven!"

"Hey!" Lydia shoved the first bidder so hard, he lost his balance momentarily. "This is only for one ticket, right? You know you won't even be able to take me."

The boy looked at her, then back at me. "Seven," he repeated.

Jayne and I laughed knowingly. "Poor little sister," Jayne said. "Don't you realize given the choice between women and sports, women don't stand a chance?"

What Lydia understood of Jayne's subtext, I don't know, but the not-so-hidden sadness in Jayne's eyes made me want to bring a swift end to this farce. So, with a lightning-quick *Once, twice, sold!* I handed my purple ticket over to the kid, and he gave me seven warm, soft dollars, straight from his pocket.

The next morning, Jayne and I arrived just as the Football and Band Buses were pulling out of the circle in front of the school. The timing was intentional, on my part at least. By the time we arrived, the opportunity for abject worship was long past, and *we* needed only to fold ourselves into the throng boarding one of the four buses and find our seat.

The single saving grace of this bus trip was that none of the kids were connected to each other enough to embark on any kind of cohesive road-trip entertainment. No ninety-nine bottles of anything. No row-row-rowing of boats. The sole foray into the sing-along came when one boy in the back commenced stomping his feet to the recognizable rhythm of Queen's "We Will Rock You." Before long, everybody on the bus was chant-singing, "*We will, we will Rock You!*" But by the time the verse rolled around, few of us knew the lyrics (besides me, and it soon became obvious no one was going to join in), so that kind of died out.

The championship game was going to be played in a huge High School stadium in Arlington. The moment it was visible, all of us kids were on our knees, craning over the seats to get a glimpse of this massive structure. Well, massive to me, anyway. Me and Jayne. Other kids had been here for other games, and someone in the back insisted over and over this was nothing like the Astrodome in Houston.

The bus stopped, and we piled out. I, for one, was grateful to the people in brightly-colored T-shirts charged with directing us through the entrance, and as one massive, purple wave, we filed in, with just the slightest bit of shoving to get to the most advantageous seats. Of course, the *best* seats were already taken by alumni and booster parents, who had paid actual stadium prices for their tickets. The band would have an awesome view of one of the end zones, and we poor students—because what did we matter, really, anyway—would have to hope for the best.

Jayne and I weren't terribly particular, and soon enough found two decent spots on an aisle, perfect for frequent trips to the snack bar or restroom without having to crawl over anybody's lap. I'd paid fifty cents for a program, and the first thing Jayne did was take it from me and open it to Charlie's picture. In the small, black-and-white, fuzzy oval photo, he looked so much smaller and sweeter than the other players.

```
Charles (Charlie) Bingley
Kicker
5'10" 175 lbs
```

I knew Charlie must have accounted for his curls in order to achieve five feet ten.

Jayne sighed over the photograph, running her pretty tapered finger around the edges of the image, whispering about how much she missed him.

"Give that to me." I snatched the program from her hands and flipped to the back. "Let's look at some useful information."

With a mathematical eye, I perused the stats for the opposing team. They were bigger, most over six feet tall, with an average weight closer to 200 pounds. They'd scored more touchdowns overall during the season, but we had passed for more yards. And run more too.

"We're faster," I said to Jayne. "Tighter, I think."

"We're gonna get plowed."

The voice of dissension came from behind, and I recognized him as the guy who'd been dancing the Cotton-Eyed Joe with Lydia at the Neewollah dance. I thought for a moment to disagree, but then I couldn't ever remember anything positive coming out of his mouth, so I just smiled and said, "We'll see," before returning to my calculations.

The band struck up a fight song, and the crowd leaped to its feet. Jayne and I joined, caught up instantly in the pageantry of the start of a State Football Championship Game.

The butcher paper tear-away run-through!

The announcement of the players!

The singing of the National Anthem by a joint coalition of both schools' Madrigal Choirs!

Coin toss!

We'll kick!

"That would have been Charlie," Jayne said as we took our seats.

I looked down at the mass of Texas Meat charging at our boys and said, "Thank goodness it wasn't."

For all I knew, there was only one player on the field that afternoon. Number 16, Billy Fitz, and he was being knocked all over the place. Sacked twice in the first, scoreless quarter. At some point, true bravery overtook me, and I stood to shout, "Come on, Billy!" I know it's crazy, but I swear he heard me. Because he *did* come on! That gorgeous arm of his threw a twenty-three-yard pass to put the first six points on the board.

Next to me, Jayne caught her breath as we watched Dennis Pratt, Sophomore, take the field to kick the extra point.

"That would have been Charlie," Jayne whined again, as if the thought hadn't occurred to every person in the stadium.

Then, from somewhere down in the good seats, a lone voice arose.

"*Let's do it, Pratt!*"

There was only a fraction of a second before our entire side of the stadium rose to witness the perfect passage of that ball through the goalposts. But that fraction was enough to put a face to the voice.

And the face was Charlie Bingley's.

rapture: *a state or experience of being carried away by overwhelming emotion*

There is no **rapture** *like that of a bunch of Texas High School football fans cheering at a championship game!*

"Well?" I asked as Jayne made her way back to our seat. I knew the answer, though, by the look of pure defeat on her face.

"I couldn't even get close. They were checking tickets at the top of the aisle."

"Did you explain that the boy of your dreams was down there? Section G, row nineteen?"

Her brows twisted in pretty suspicion. "How do you know what seat he's in?"

"I don't. But you can never go wrong with specificity and detail."

"It wouldn't have mattered." She unfolded her seat and sat down—more like, *fell* into it, her arms crossed in defiance of all future joy. "Why is he here, anyway? What about all that *time with his father and soccer coach* nonsense?"

"Could be his dad is here with him," I said. The little bit of a glimpse hadn't provided a lot of detail.

"I suppose."

The roar of the crowd clued me in that something amazing had just occurred, and I turned my attention to the field in time to see all of our guys dancing around as the announcer informed us of a fumble recovery on our twenty-two-yard line. A glance at the clock revealed less than a minute left in the half, with the score tied.

I jumped to my feet with my fellow Badgers, my voice joining theirs in hysterical encouragement, and there it was. Billy himself, faking the pass, running the ball into the end zone.

Touchdown.

The clock disappeared into zeroes, and the players ran off the field in well-earned jubilation. I joined in the cheers, of course, but experienced a momentary lapse as I wondered if Charlie regretted his decision, now that he had to sit in the stands and watch his friend, his *best* friend, shoulder all of this glory. Then again, Billy's father was nowhere nearby to share in the moment, and my sympathies shifted.

Next to me, Jayne was shifting too.

"Do you want anything?"

"Are you crazy?" I pulled my feet and legs up into the seat as the zillionth person made their way past. "This is the *worst* time to hit the concession stands. Or the bathrooms. You'll be in line forever. Everybody's going."

She winked. "Exactly. Doesn't matter where your seats are. The potty and the Pepsi are in the same place."

Her plan dawned on me, and I grinned along with her. "Tell him I said hello. Then punch him in the face."

"Do you have a pen?"

"Hey! I said punch him, not stab him. Geez, Jayne."

She punched *me*, softly, in the arm as I rooted around in my purse. Well, more like a bag, really. Soft and denim, large enough to hold the novel I'd brought in case I had any downtime, my Walkman, and five cassette tapes, because I never knew what type of music my mood would demand. Jayne, on the other hand, had this cute little rectangle on a gold chain, barely large enough for a lipstick, a mirror, and emergency quarter for a phone call.

"And some paper, maybe?"

I found the pen quickly enough, giving her four to choose from, but paper—well, somehow my notebook didn't make the transfer from my backpack. I did, however, have Billy's letter, so I fetched it out and tore off a corner from the third page.

"What do you need this for?"

Jayne was writing, quickly. "I'm going to give him our address and phone number. You know, in case he did honestly forget."

I folded Billy's note up carefully. "Jayne—"

"I know what you're going to say. And I won't bring it up first. I promise. But if we talk, and he says something like, 'Hey! I totally forgot to get your address,' well, I'll have it handy."

She joined the moving stream of humanity, soon disappearing to the concourse while the opposing team's band took the field for a medley of jazzy show tunes. The music was good enough, but the marching left much to be desired, so I took out my book—*The Clan of the Cave Bear*—and briefly longed for the simplicity of life in a cave.

I read during our halftime show, too. To be fair, I'd seen it before. Countless times, this ode to Texas, with the flag girls creating a giant yellow rose midfield. The adventures of the Earth's Children marched on in front of my eyes, but very little of the story came to life.

I checked my Swatch. Jayne had been gone for twenty minutes. Wait, make that twenty-two. Which could be a good thing, if she'd met up with Charlie in, say, the first ten or so. And they'd been talking this whole time, and maybe Charlie took her down to his section with him, trading with his old man, meaning I'd spend the rest of the game with some stranger next to me.

Or, maybe she'd simply staked out a spot outside of the men's room. Waiting, waiting—knowing he'd have to go in or come out sometime. Maybe during the third quarter. Maybe after time ran out. But men didn't take as long in the restroom. Charlie could have been in and out twelve times since Jayne had left.

I hazarded a look over my shoulder, risking another negative comment from the kid behind me. About the lame music, or the pummeling ahead in the second half, or the wonderin' about what was happenin' in that book thing. But he was gone too. Instead, I saw Jayne, her face set into a mask of bravado, and I knew something had gone terribly wrong.

"Couldn't find him?" I asked as she crawled over me to her seat. "I wouldn't worry. It's a huge crowd. He's probably—"

"I saw him," she said, staring forward.

"Well, how was it?" I sounded like that horrible relative who just made you eat a bite of something you knew would be disgusting going in. "I mean, what did he say? What did—"

"Nothing."

"Nothing?"

She looked at me. "He didn't say anything—*we* didn't say anything, because we didn't speak to each other."

"But I thought you said you saw—"

Her eyes remained void of tears, but her chin quivered, and her lips seemed to take on a life of their own, trying to control her words.

"I saw him. And *he* saw *me*. And when he saw me, he—"

A family of four, including two little boys sporting T-shirts that said Future Fitz! crawled over our laps. When they had passed, Jayne leaned forward and dropped her voice low.

"He looked right *at* me, Pudge."

I didn't bother to fuss about the nickname. She was obviously in distress, and I think she found some comfort in using it, like a soft verbal teddy bear. "He *saw* me. And then he turned around. And walked off."

"Are you sure he saw you?" Silly question. Of course he did.

"I could tell, you know? Could tell he wanted to talk to me, but he just . . . didn't."

My stomach churned with her pain. "Was he alone?"

She nodded. "At first, but then his sister came up. And—this is the worst part. She saw me, too. She looked right at me and gave me this smile. She had one of those giant pretzels, you know? And she took this big bite of it and smiled. What did I ever do that was so terrible?"

The band kicked into the school fight song, and everybody around us jumped up to welcome the players back onto the field. I knew I had to make a choice about who I would protect. If I showed Jayne the letter, the fears about her own lack of value would be put to rest. *What did you do, Jayne? NOTHING! Nothing besides be too wonderful for dumbbolt Charlie to be able to think in your presence.*

But then if I showed her, she would know not only the depth of Billy's cruelty, but the shallow ease with which Charlie could fall under his power. She would know that, no matter how much he loved her, it wasn't enough. She'd never forgive him. And if she did, I might never forgive her. I had nothing to gain by disclosing the details, and nothing to lose by hiding them. It wasn't until then that I realized I'd been holding Billy's letter all along, so I used it to mark my place in *The Clan of the Cave Bear,* closed the book, and put it back into the depths of my bag.

We were nearly two minutes into the third quarter of what was stacking up to be the longest football game in history.

"You didn't do anything," I said, finally answering her question. "Nothing terrible. He cared—*cares*—about you. A lot. And he cares about soccer, and he cares about his dad. It's a documented fact that boys can't care about too many things at once."

"I don't ever want to see him again."

"But you will, you know. He'll be back."

She leaned forward, her elbows on her knees, chin cupped in her hands, watching the game like she knew what it meant when the referee signaled that we were at first and ten. She turned to me and said, "Not for me. He'll never be back for me. You'll never have Billy. I'll never have Charlie. We may as well go shopping for our dresses to be Lydia's bridesmaids."

I laughed. "Come on." Standing, I slung my bag over my shoulder and tugged at her. "I've still got that kid's money. Let's buy every bit of food possible."

"Not a pretzel," she said. "I've lost my appetite for those. Forever."

We won. Or, to be technically correct, the Varsity Football Team from Northenfield Texas High School won. It wasn't easy, but it was beautiful. Down by three, seconds left to play, the fans on the opposing side already mid-exit, our cheerleaders standing with sagging pom-poms, and Billy Fitz lets loose this beautiful forty-eight-yard pass. It hit John Willow's hands as the clock turned into a big, red 00:00. Women held their hands to heaven. Men wept. The Future Fitz boys were confused but jumped up and down anyway.

I almost missed it completely as I was dragging the final nacho along the cardboard tray, trying to coat it with long-cold cheese. But something called to me, and with seconds to spare, I saw that arm reach back, saw the ball go—flying, in this perfect arc—and my heart raced as if I'd been the one to fire the gun.

Billy fell to his knees; my own grew weak.

He liked me, once.

The bus ride home found its passengers much more of one accord, singing—no, *shouting*—our school song in one voice over and over again. Cars with school-spirit slogans and players'

jersey numbers passed us on the highway, honking in victory, and kids leaned out of the bus windows, arms flapping in the wind. Jayne got caught up in the excitement, too, or maybe she just wanted to distract herself and avoid seeing Charlie once again driving away. In any case, she left me to join a group of girls three seats up. Their animated conversation, if I read their hand gestures correctly, had nothing to do with football. Rather, they were talking about hairstyles, makeup, and designer jeans. They stood one by one, displaying to the others the stitching of their back pockets, tracing a finger along the inside of the waistband to display each brand's ability to *fit* but not be *tight*.

I would have nothing to add to this conversation, and I'd already relived that final touchdown pass a million times in my mind, so I didn't need to be part of the reenactment as presented by Billy's newest enthusiastic fans. I had my head full of classic Golden Oldies, recorded from the Saturday Night Sock Hop on Magic 107, and I reread page after page of *The Clan of the Cave Bear*, reassuring myself that doing so didn't necessarily make me some dangerous, disconnected weirdo.

Suddenly, even the piano pounding of Jerry Lee Lewis couldn't drown out the burst of noise from my fellow passengers, as everybody ran to one side with such speed and force that, despite my pretty strong handle on physics, I worried the bus might turn on its side. My other worry was the fact that the side they were rushing to was *my* side, and so I became an unwilling participant in the throng, my body squished up to the window, pressed on all sides by sweaty Badgers.

It was the Athletes' Bus. Banners and pennants flying from the windows. For a moment, the two drivers matched each other's speed, and we drove in perfect parallel. The number of school bus safety rules in violation was staggering. Our side was piled five or six people deep in each seat, and their seats were pretty much empty, as the players, dressed once again in their dress slacks and jackets, danced in the aisle. Like, I mean really, really danced. When I slid my headphone off one ear, I could hear their music—loud. Bruce Springsteen, "Born to Run," but instead they were singing, "*Baby we were born to wiiiiin.*" And it was obvious from the cacophony that surrounded the chorus that nobody had a clue in the world about any other lyric.

Not everybody was dancing, though. Not everybody was singing. As the Athletes' Bus slowed a bit, allowing us to pull forward, I found myself window-to-window with Billy Fitz. He wore headphones, too, and seemed engrossed in reading something too. The playbook, maybe? But then I saw, no. It was the program, and I knew he was evaluating the stats of the team they'd just defeated, oblivious to the raucous celebration of victory all around him.

Right at that moment, Billy looked up, and over, at me. He rolled his eyes in an expression that decried the foolishness of his fellow players, and I answered in kind.

Kids, right? What are ya gonna do?

But I gave him a little thumbs-up of approval, and he inclined his head.

Thanks.

Then I put my headphones back on my ear just in time for "Only You" to play. Without looking away from Billy, I found the fast-forward button on my Walkman and listened to the screech of the tape, long enough to ensure that I'd passed up the song. As if in tune, our bus sped up, no doubt wanting to arrive before the Athletes' Bus so we could have a proper welcoming party. By the time we pulled ahead, my seat was once again empty, all of our fans dispersed. I'd come to the end of the tape, and instead of turning it over to the other side, I just let it sit silent, keeping my headphones on.

Chapter 17

venture: *to proceed especially in the face of danger*

Heedless of the danger or potential punishment, the three sisters **ventured** *out into the late Christmas night.*

THE TOWN CELEBRATED THAT VICTORY for a solid week—not even the lighting of the town square Christmas tree could dim the attention. The tree was adorned in purple lights and gold garland; ornaments shaped like footballs and helmets dominated the branches, along with glitter-covered numbers for each player. We sang "Silent Night" and "Hail to Thee, Northenfield" with equal investment.

Our Christmas celebration at home was blissfully football free. As it was our first Christmas in Texas, Mom went all out trying to work in local traditions, including tamales at our Christmas Eve buffet supper. For once, Dad didn't make us wait until Christmas morning to open all the gifts, allowing us just one the night before: the biggest of all the wrapped packages, with a label proclaiming it to be "From Santa" to "the entire Nebbitt family."

Mom kept up this insipid *whatever could it be?* as one of the little sisters struggled to tear off the wrapping.

What it could be turned out to be a Videocassette Recorder, and as the oldest, Jayne was given the smaller package to open—a VHS tape of *The Best Christmas Episodes in the History of Television!*

Forty minutes later, with instructions read and a new jumble of wires behind our television set, we gathered with three puffy pans of Jiffy Pop popcorn, cookies, hot chocolate, and cider, and watched a smattering of classics. Touching, funny, sweet stories all played out on various soundstages with perfect TV living rooms and their perfect TV trees. The Littles had little appreciation for the viewing, pestering us with questions about *who was this?* And, *why isn't it in color?* Once we sat through twenty-six minutes of Fred Flintstone as a BC Christmas department store Santa Claus (my attempt to argue the absolute ridiculousness of celebrating *CHRISTmas* before *CHRIST* was summarily dismissed by my mother), their attention span snuffed out, and they disappeared upstairs with Mom to read *The Night Before Christmas* and try to work themselves into a sleep.

Once Dad realized there would be no *Gunsmoke* or *The Rifleman* represented on the tape, he, too, declared he would spend the rest of the evening with a good book, leaving Jayne and Lydia and me to relive memories of shows we'd never seen.

And then, *Happy Days* happened.

Happy Days was a show I'd known and loved since I was a kid. It took place in the 1950s, spawning my love for that decade, and featured this cool character named Fonzie. Blue jeans, black leather jacket, motorcycle boots. Too-cool-for-school kind of kid, and in this episode, he's been bragging that he has some great plans for Christmas. Like, a bunch of family coming in. Ski lodge, huge meal, tons of presents. But then it turns out he's all alone in his sad little apartment above a garage eating beans out of a can.

My eyes clouded with tears, which I chalked up to the

nostalgic, sentimental schmaltz of the story. I looked over to see Lydia draped across our big, comfy chair, sound asleep, and Jayne running her fingers through the last of the popcorn.

"Remember this show?" she asked, sensing my attention. "I used to love this show."

"Me too," I said, but I was only half-thinking about the show. I was mostly thinking of Billy Fitz, wondering who he was spending Christmas with. Rumor was he'd flown to London to spend it with his father, but what if our town suffered the same delusion as Fonzie's friends? What if, instead of walking Dickens's snowy streets, he was holed up in that little room at Charlie's house? Charlie's mom and little sister were in California, at Disneyland (because life is fair), leaving Billy all alone. Maybe he invented the whole London story so we wouldn't feel sorry for him.

"Jayne," I whispered, even as the idea took hold.

"Yeah?" She barely looked at me.

"Let's go for a drive. Look at Christmas lights."

Lydia stirred a little at the sound of my voice but didn't respond.

"Are you crazy?" Jayne looked at the clock. "It's almost midnight."

"On *Christmas Eve*. We're not kids; we don't have to worry about Santa passing our house if we're not asleep."

"Naughty is naughty, Elyse. The list doesn't go away just because one of us has a driver's license. Besides, we have to worry about Mom and Dad killing us for taking the car without permission."

"Dad drank about a quart of eggnog. It's two hours past his bedtime, and Mom won't hear anything."

"We can push the car to the end of the street," Lydia piped up, sleepily. "So it won't make any noise."

"*We?*" I said.

"Take me or I tell," Lydia said, without even opening her eyes.

At Jayne's pure genius suggestion, we rewound the VHS tape to the beginning—a feel-good Christmas episode of *The Andy Griffith Show*—and let it play at a volume high enough to create the illusion that we were watching, but not so loud as to bring a parent down the steps to tell us to turn it down.

My younger sister seemed far too adept at noiselessly opening the front door and knew just how far to open the screen door as to allow enough room for escape without producing its familiar squeak.

Outside, the air was cold and crisp, enough to create puffs of steam for our silent laughter. Jayne got behind the wheel of the car and put it in neutral, while Lydia and I pushed it far enough down the street to where the roar of the engine wouldn't call the attention of Mom or Dad before jumping in, the three of us abreast in the front seat. Granted, the stealthiness of our actions gave me a bit of a pause, like we should have been dressed in all black wearing knit caps or something. But no need to rouse the whole neighborhood, right? And the three of us hardly ever did anything together.

"Now, where are we going, exactly?" Lydia asked, and it occurred to me that she was just the type of girl to jump in first, ask questions later. Dangerous. Fun, but dangerous.

"To look at Christmas lights," I said.

In fact, few houses were lit at this hour, since ours was the neighborhood where people had to balance their Christmas spirit with the expense of kilowatt hours.

"We did that a couple of nights ago," Jayne said, making it very clear she didn't believe my motivation one bit.

"And the Littles whined the whole time about being bored. Isn't this nice? Just us and some Christmas music?" To emphasize, I turned on the radio and was immediately rewarded with

Bing Crosby's "Little Drummer Boy" duet with David Bowie. "Besides, if we go to some of the nicer neighborhoods, we might see more."

"Ooh, what *kind* of nicer neighborhood?" Lydia nearly quivered in her seat. "Like, *Charlie Bingley* nice?"

"Something like that," I said, noting Jayne was already taking us in that direction.

"What happened between you two, anyway?"

I wasn't sure if I should trust the innocence behind Lydia's question. Rare were the details of our lives of which she didn't have intimate knowledge, but Jayne's love life was hardly the topic of dinnertime conversation, and she hadn't been invited into our confidence.

"He's spending the Christmas holidays with his dad," Jayne said with simple finality, as if that were the end of the story.

"Will you get back together in the spring?"

Jayne shrugged and signaled a left-hand turn. "We'll see."

"But—why wouldn't you?"

Before there was time for the awkwardness of a non-answer, I lunged for the volume knob on the radio, proclaiming, "I love this song!"

Not your traditional Christmas carol, but a song by The Waitresses, "Christmas Wrapping," and a favorite of mine and Jayne's, about a woman who found herself all alone at Christmas after a year of missed opportunities with a cute boy. Although Lydia appreciated its pop appeal, she couldn't join us in the lyrics. They required rapid-fire precision—something Jayne and I had perfected after taping it off the radio and replaying it endlessly. We shimmied in our seats and punctuated lines with pointed fingers. At some point, the song has this little instrumental break that sounds like a minihorn section. Lydia and I mimed playing trumpets, and Jayne kept her hands firmly on the wheel as we adopted a bouncing, salsa-inspired choreography that matched the music. Lydia joined in the chorus, mostly, alternating "Merry Christmas! Merry Christmas!" with "La-na-na-na! La-na-na!"

By the time we got to Charlie's house, we were laughing, our heads filled with independence. At Lydia's instruction (she really seemed to have an aptitude for this, which was something we should discuss in the future), we turned off the car at the top of the street and coasted to a silent stop in front of the dark structure. Dark, that is, except for the copious strands of white and blue lights, perfectly coordinated with the neighbors. Each house was distinct in design, but identical in color.

"Do you think they, like, planned this?" Lydia asked.

"No doubt," Jayne said. "It's kind of beautiful and sad at the same time."

"What if you don't like white and blue?" I rolled down my window to stick my head out for a clearer view. "What if you prefer red and green? Or, what if you're like, Jewish? And don't want to put up lights at all?"

"It's part of living here," Jayne said. "The price of fitting in."

"It's worth it," Lydia said, breathless with admiration.

"We'll never know," I said, opening the car door.

"What are you doing?" Jayne sounded horrified, but she followed suit, getting out of the car and running around to meet me. "Nobody's home."

"Just why are we here, again?" Lydia joined us on the sidewalk. "Are we meeting boys? Because if we are, you could have warned me. I would have totally worn something cuter."

"We're not meeting boys," I said. "Now, be quiet, would you? Before somebody thinks we're renegade elves or something." Putting a finger to my lips, I led them on a silent mission to the side of the house where a gate proved to be a harmless impediment, as I instructed Jayne to reach over to open the latch. "If anybody asks, we're here to check on the bunny."

They followed without question—a testament to my crazed sense of purpose and power. We were in the backyard, walking past the covered, dark pool. I remembered looking down on this scene when the water was lit blue, as blue as the lights strewn across the roof on the other side.

"I just want to make sure," I whispered to Jayne. "I want to make sure he's not here all alone at Christmas."

"Awww," Jayne said with sweet approval. "That is so sweet of you, but why would he be here at Charlie's?"

"Because he stays here. He said he does, most of the time."

"Who?" Lydia poked her nose between us.

"Billy Fitz," Jayne said, earning my elbow in her arm.

"Oh, him." Lydia seemed less impressed with the prospect of finding Billy than with the house itself. She let out a low, long whistle. "Geez, Jayne. Too bad you blew it with Charlie. A girl could do a lot worse than this."

Neither of us were inclined to comment. I took a few steps back to make sure the window I knew to be Billy's was dark.

"Maybe he's asleep?"

"Let's get out of here," Jayne said, rubbing her arms as if recently chilled. "It's a noble, sweet thought, Pudge, but he isn't here. He went to spend Christmas with his father."

"Are you sure?"

"Positive. He talked about it all the time."

"But London? Who flies from Texas to London for Christmas?"

"People who can, silly."

"But what if he didn't? What if he just said that so people would leave him alone?"

Jayne looked at me as if I had truly gone insane, then spoke very slowly and clearly. "Then why would he be *here* with the rest of the family gone? He has his own house, you know."

Of course he had his own house. He and his father—they

lived *somewhere*. But I only ever knew of him here, at Charlie's. With Charlie's family like his own.

"So why did you agree to come?"

Jayne glanced up at the stars. "Oh, you know. The whole Christmas miracle thing."

"So," I said, not caring that I was crashing her wistful moment, "do you know where his house is? Like, did you and Charlie ever go there?"

She shook her head. "We never went there, but—"

"It's locked," Lydia announced, tugging on the sliding glass door. Want to try a window?"

"We're not breaking in!" I lunged for her, grabbing her hand and tugging her off the porch. "We were just . . . checking on something."

"And now we're leaving." Jayne took my arm, and we made a little Nebbitt-sister chain out of the yard, through the gate, and back to the car.

To appease Lydia, thrilled to be out with her big sisters so far past curfew, we continued to drive through the neighborhoods of Northenfield, admiring the glittering displays. The radio made a nice glow in the car, too, and the DJ reminded us that he would play all Christmas, all night, old classics and new. We sang along with all of them, mumbling through the more unfamiliar verses, not talking much. Eventually, without seeking anyone's consent, Jayne turned the car toward home, where the houses got smaller and darker, until we were back on our own street where only a few of the neighbors had left their thin strands to glow into the night.

We entered our house as quietly as we'd left and were greeted by the scene we'd left—the scrolling credits of some offering from the VHS tape, and a mess of bowls, cups, platters, plates, and empty Jiffy Pop pans.

"We should clean this up for tomorrow morning," Jayne

said, eyeing the modest gathering of presents under our tree. Telltale boxes hinted at gifts of clothing for all of us girls, but there would be toys and such for the Littles in the morning. Our job would be to keep them quietly sleeping until Mom and Dad gave us the *all clear*.

Lydia yawned and stretched. "Have fun with that," she said, already halfway to the stairs. "Thanks for the fun, and Merry Christmas. Next time, though, let's have boys. Maybe New Year's?"

I didn't care about her ditching. Nothing was worse than trying to finish some chore—any chore—with Lydia. Jayne turned off the television, and we gathered the dishes and brought them into the kitchen. She ran a sink full of soapy water, and we worked side by side washing, rinsing, and drying.

"But, what?" I said, as if the last hour hadn't transpired at all.

"But, what, what?"

"You said you hadn't gone to Billy's house. But—"

"But I *do* know the address."

I pinched a few fudge crumbs from a mitten-shaped plate. "How?"

"Promise not to laugh?"

"Not unless it's funny."

"I looked it up, in his file in the office."

I gasped in mock horror. "Jayne Elizabeth Nebbitt! Are you trying to tell me you abused your power as an eighth period Attendance Office Aide?"

She nudged me with her hip. "I looked up Charlie's address too. Not here, of course. But his dad's address. In Dallas. We have to send his report card there. So, I was going to send him a Christmas card, too. But with Billy's return address, so he'd, you know, think Billy sent it."

"Because guys send each other Christmas cards all the time."

"Because he'd open it if he thought it was from Billy. He

might not if he thought it was from . . . me. Does that sound too pathetic?"

It did, but I'd never tell her so. "No, of course not. It's just pathetic enough."

She forgave me with a laugh. "I know, right?"

I worked to dislodge dried caramel corn from our Big Red Bowl. "So, I take it you didn't send the card. Any reason?"

"The game. After he didn't talk to me. I felt even more ridiculous."

"No," I said, dumping half a can of grape soda down the sink. "What's ridiculous is all this pining away we're doing for them. When has that ever been our thing? You, my sister, are far too pretty and way too sweet to waste another sad face on that shallow boy. And I—Lydia had the right sentiment, but the wrong sister. I blew it."

"Never mind Christmas. We need a new year."

I agreed and reprised The Waitresses' song, "Merry Christmas! Merry Christmas! But I think I'll miss this one this year!"

contrive: *to bring about by stratagem or with difficulty :*
MANAGE

Cursed with curiosity, Elyse must **contrive** *a way to bring*
her sister Jayne into her scheme.

I WAS GLAD, AFTER ALL, that we didn't miss Christmas, because
Mom and Dad really managed to pull through. Mom had taken
Lydia Christmas shopping with her, and for once Jayne and I
received gifts from some of the more fashionable stores in the
Abilene mall. Three pairs of designer jeans for Jayne, one of
them the color of eggplant, and four new sweaters. The same for
me, only black jeans instead of purple, and a dress that looked
like a long, heather gray sweatshirt.

"With black leggings?" Lydia enthused the moment I
opened it. "And we can go after-Christmas shopping for some
new boots? Fabulous."

Lydia got new clothes too, though without her own fashion expertise, I could tell she wasn't quite as enthused as Jayne
and I were. But it wouldn't be long before they'd be tweaked,
hemmed, sliced, and refabricated into her own designs.

The Littles got new dolls and clothes and clothes for their
dolls. And, in a moment I knew Mom had been anticipating for
weeks, the five of us simultaneously opened identical packages,

each revealing a Care Bear. The Littles squealed along with our mother, Lydia and Dad looked confused, and I don't know what was happening on Jayne's face, because I didn't dare look at her.

Mine was blue, with a blue half-moon on its tummy because, according to my mother, I always seemed a little sad. I was taken aback at her insight and felt a new spark of warmth that lasted until she patted my leg and suggested that, next time I felt blue, I should consider giving the bear a cuddle instead of having a bit of chocolate. Still, it was something. Jayne's had a bright smiling sun. Lydia's, a big red heart. I didn't pay much attention to the little sisters'. Ponies or something. Maybe a rainbow? It was the kind of silly moment our family would have, one resplendent with my mother's overzealous scrutiny and my father's mental disconnect. The kind of moment I would treasure in my mind, keeping it tucked away so deep that no one else could ever find it.

I talk all the time (really, ALL the time) about how much my family embarrasses me, and how I wouldn't wish them on any-one, but the truth is, maybe, that I'd never want to *share* them with anyone. Like, I'd never trade them away. Poor Billy was an only child with a dead mother, and Charlie wasn't even in the same *state* as his mother and sister. Gage needed a passport to see his mom at Christmas. And here I was surrounded by Care Bears and Christmas, watching Dad tramp around with a gar-bage sack to collect the wrapping while Mom screeched about saving the bows. I had never lived this day without this replay of conversation, and while I felt safe and swaddled in the routine, a part of me wondered what it might be like to have just a little something new. If I could keep this in reserve, my perpetual haven. But just the thought of it, a Christmas morning else-where, Mom and Dad absent, brought completely unexpected tears to the corners of my eyes. My throat burned, choked with senseless nostalgia for something I hadn't even *lost* yet.

Perhaps the Care Bear was perfect after all.

There were the usual peripheral gifts too. Perfume and books and scarves, and an assortment of Life Savers candy in a cardboard book. While Mom cooked breakfast, we bartered our candy, and talked louder and faster when Dad looked out the window and declared the car was in a different spot than he remembered.

The days of Christmas break stretched long and lazy. Jayne and I rarely left the house. In fact, we rarely left our room, choosing to sleep past ten, then stretch out on our beds in the midmorning light, listening to the radio and talking ourselves out of anything that might require effort.

When we did leave the room, we watched television. MTV, to be exact. Hours on the sofa, waiting to see Bruce Springsteen's "Dancing in the Dark." Again. Dancing like the lucky girl pulled onto the stage with him. The Littles whined at being denied their usual routine of all-day educational programming via puppets, but they wouldn't win this battle. Jayne and I had exactly ten days to saturate our senses with music and video, fueled by Mom's peanut butter balls and turkey sandwiches.

For New Year's Eve, Mom and Dad would be out at Dad's Obligatory Company Party. In exchange for babysitting, they allowed us to rent a couple of movies for the night. Jayne and I quickly settled on *The Sound of Music* for the Littles, but choosing for us and Lydia proved more problematic.

"*An American Werewolf in London?*" Lydia asked, holding up the plastic box.

"No," Jayne said, answering for both of us. She, I would learn later, was rejecting it on my behalf, as it might make me worry about something horrible happening to Billy while he was in London.

"*Risky Business?*" Lydia offered next, waggling her eyebrows in an attempt to appeal to our Christmas Eve adventurous spirit.

This time, it was I who said no, because Tom Cruise looked too much like Billy Fitz. Who knew the boy could have so much control?

In the end, we settled on *Poltergeist*, with Jayne and I agreeing it was much more fun to feel scared than sad.

Once Mom and Dad were out the door, we scheduled the evening so that the Von Trapps were headed out to cross the mountains at exactly ten o'clock, then convinced the Littles that the old year ended at ten, and the new one started at twelve, but just like Santa, the New Year wouldn't come unless everyone was asleep.

"Do you realize how twisted and scary that sounds?" Jayne asked as we followed them up to their room for a final story. "Like, the whole world is going to end. Time will just stop."

"Sometimes I wish it would," I said. Like maybe back on some Friday evening when your local Tom Cruise look-alike tells you he likes you.

Once we had the Littles settled, we went back downstairs to find that Lydia had actually shown a bit of initiative, rewinding *The Sound of Music,* while she herself was hunkered down in the kitchen, talking on the phone. The moment we walked in, her voice got loud and chipper, saying, "Well, Happy New Year to you, too! I'll see you at school next week." Then with a giggle, and another giggle, and a reprimand to whoever was on the other side of the line to *stop it, already,* she hung up.

"Who was that?" I asked, cutting into the pan of brownies baked fresh for the occasion.

"Just a boy from school," Lydia said. "I know I'm not supposed to have phone calls this late, but it's New Year's Eve, right? So, please, don't tell Mom and Dad?"

"No problem." I had no burning desire to get Lydia in trouble, especially with nothing to gain. Better to bank the knowledge for now, in case it came in handy later.

We started watching the movie, Lydia on the stuffed chair, Jayne stretched out on the couch, and me on the floor, with a pyramid of pillows and cushions surrounding me. Within the first thirty minutes, we were huddled together on the couch, trying not to scream out loud and scare the Littles. Lydia was watching through a curtain of curls; Jayne kept her face buried in my shoulder, begging me to tell her when the scary part was over. And the scary part after that.

I, however, watched every minute of it. The scary clown doll. The tree branch bursting through the bedroom window. The tennis ball covered with gross ghost goo. Long-buried bodies lurching up and out of the empty swimming pool. Sure, my pulse raced, and there were moments when I jumped with a bit of a squeal, but it felt good to face the fear.

January 3 marked exactly six months before my sixteenth birthday, the day my father had promised me we could begin my driver's training. But it was also a Thursday—a workday for him, a headache day for Mom, and the day Jayne and I were about to lose our minds with school break boredom.

Go! Mom had said from the couch, a cold washcloth covering her eyes and brow. The Littles were contented with finishing their Christmas-themed coloring books, Lydia had left the house at ten that morning to practice makeup with a friend two blocks over, and Jayne and I had done little more than wander into the kitchen to open the refrigerator and declare that there was nothing to eat, nothing to do, and nowhere to go.

When Mom issued her plaintive command, I immediately interpreted it as permission for Jayne to give me my first day of instruction. Actually *clarifying* this with Mom seemed cruel, given her weakened state, and Dad had always made it very clear that phone calls to his office had to be reserved for emergencies only.

"Absolutely not," Jayne said at my suggestion. "You have to be with a licensed driver—"

"*You're* a licensed driver—"

"Over the age of eighteen. Or a parent, or something."

"Just, like, around the block."

"We don't even have the car here. Dad has it at work."

"So? We walk to his office. Take it from there. An hour, hour and a half, tops, and it's back before he leaves."

Jayne narrowed her eyes. "How long do you take planning these things?"

"I'm bored!" To emphasize, I flopped on my bed and made a quick mockery of suffocating myself with a pillow. "I have to get out of this house. *We* have to get out of this house. It's not healthy. How are we going to get on with our boyfriend-less lives if we spend every waking moment hiding out in our room?"

"I don't know," she said, but she seemed to be on the slippery slope of consent.

"Besides, I need some new stuff for school. Pencils and a notebook. We can go to Walgreens? You can look for a new lip gloss? Come on, you *love* Walgreens."

By the time I finished wheedling, she was smiling, and from there it was just a matter of slipping into the kitchen and getting Mom's keys and leaving with a vague report of our intentions. I changed into one of my new Christmas outfits, you know, to break everything in. Stretch out the jeans a bit, make sure the sweater landed below the waistline. My hair poufed around a matching headband, and I took a few minutes for mascara and lip gloss before meeting Jayne at the front door.

"Well, look at you," she said, more surprised than impressed.

"Just felt like looking human," I said. "New Year, and all that."

It was a gray, damp winter day, so pretty much like any other, with soft leaves and dead grass. Every now and then a house had its abandoned Christmas tree languishing on the curb, with bits of tinsel still clinging to the dry needles. Sometimes there was an ornament, too, and these Jayne would rescue and place safely within the residence mailbox.

The walk to Dad's office took a little more than half an hour and might have been much quicker had Jayne and I shown the gumption to speed our steps. Somehow, though, having escaped the confines of home, we managed to find so much more to talk about, beyond Billy and Charlie and the fragility of our own hearts. Trash bins were stuffed with Christmas wrappings and soggy Northenfield Texas High School football signs. While there were still plenty of houses with strands of lights attached, none of the windows were painted to support the players, not even when we emerged from the residential neighborhood onto our main street. The whole town had regained its senses, taken a new breath. No reason we couldn't take one too.

Dad's office was part of a four-business complex, and to our relief, the car was in the parking lot.

"Go in," I said to Jayne. "Ask if we can take it."

"Oh, so we're asking, all of a sudden? What happened to my sister the criminal?"

"Think how much worse off we'd be if he walked out to go see a client or something and it was just . . . gone."

"Is that what he does? Visit clients?"

"I don't know, but he might. Just go? I'll wait in the car."

"I'm taking the keys with me," she said, shaking them for emphasis.

I'd been in Dad's office before. The walls were covered in dark wood paneling, and the whole place smelled like cherry cough drops. The men (including our father) wore short-sleeved dress shirts, and the women all had their hair clipped in huge barrettes. The place muffled everyone's voice, and the sound of the constantly running printer left a ringing in the ears. I hated that place. Besides, I had business to do.

As soon as Jayne walked in the door, I went to the car, pleased to find it unlocked, and took out the folded map of Northenfield roads and streets. I knew it would be here because yes, of course, Dad used the car to meet with clients, and even if our town could be crossed from end to end within half an hour, I have no doubt he had to consult this resource every other time he left the office.

I, on the other hand, had a memory that might not be technically photographic, but worked well under the conditions of desperation and desire. And while I wasn't anywhere near desperate, and I'd talked myself into squelching my desire, I'd been plagued with a certain curiosity for nearly a week.

Jayne knew where he lived.

Thanks to a quick look through the common area of the desk in our room, I did too. Or, at least, I knew the address, as it was printed in her symmetrical, curly script on the back of a discarded tardy slip.

1813 Pember Lane.

It was an unfamiliar street, and a quick study of the map revealed why. None of my normal comings and goings around Northenfield would bring me anywhere near it. This was out of town—like, way out of town. Fifteen miles, at least, and an exit to a private road. We passed it every time we drove to Abilene and I never knew. Never thought to know, until now.

"Dad gave us five dollars for lunch," Jayne said, sliding behind the wheel with triumph.

"Sonic?" It was a brilliant suggestion on many levels. Not only could we feed ourselves with Dad's money, but the drive-in was close to the edge of town—the edge leading, eventually, to Pember Lane. "We can eat in the car and then switch."

"Determined little thing, aren't you?"

But she was game. We navigated the streets and parked the car in one of the few empty slots. Our standard order—one cheeseburger, one order of french fries, one Coke, one Sprite. When the carhop on roller skates brought our order out, we split the burger straight down the middle and divvied up the fries. The restaurant always attached small plastic animals to their large drink lids. Today, Jayne got a little orange monkey, and I got the rare blue marlin.

"Like *The Old Man and the Sea*," I said, making it jump invisible waves between us.

Jayne dipped a fry into a puddle of ketchup on a napkin. "We don't read that until next semester."

"Well then," I said, lodging the little plastic spear in the top of my cup, "you have something to look forward to."

As soon as we finished eating, we gathered our trash and dumped it en route to switching seats.

Now, it's not like I'd never been behind the wheel of a car before. Even on the drive to Northenfield from Arizona, Dad gave me a turn at the U-Haul, just for a three-mile stretch on a deserted highway. And, on three occasions, at least, when Mom had declared her head ached to the point of incapacitation, I had driven us home from Kroger. So the mechanics of it, the gas, the brake, the mirrors—all of that was familiar enough. The only true difference here was the fact that I had to back out of a drive-in, with cars parked fairly close on either side. Jayne and I each rolled down our windows and hung our heads out, ignoring the terrified expressions on the faces of our fellow patrons. Once I was declared *safe!* it was smooth sailing—er, driving—around the restaurant and out the exit.

"Blinker," Jayne said, unnecessarily. I knew exactly where I was going. I put her in charge of the radio, and she flipped the dial until Cyndi Lauper's "Girls Just Want to Have Fun" came on. It only took a few erratic swerves of the vehicle for me to learn that I was not yet adept at singing and driving—something I would make a point of practicing. The music mellowed into the Commodores, then the Eagles, as if the old Station Wagon herself was urging me to slow down and pay closer attention to the road, and when I saw the small, subtle sign, nearly hidden by brush, I obeyed, bringing the car to a creeping speed as I eased onto the shoulder.

"What are you doing?" Jayne twisted in her seat, looking behind us as if we were being followed.

"Just . . . feeding my curiosity."

"Curiosity? Pudge, what—"

"Don't distract me." I executed the turn as smoothly as my inexperience would allow, and found myself navigating a narrow, single-lane, paved road. "Get the map out, would you?" My memory was good, but not that good.

"Map?"

"In the glove box. We left straight north off Main. And turned"—she had the map out, and I took my eyes off the road long enough to find the intersection—"here."

"And just what am I looking *for*?"

I navigated a hairpin turn, quite expertly, even as I muttered, "Pember Lane."

"You *snoop*!"

"I stumbled across the address—"

"In *my address book*!"

"On *our* desk. Come on, Jayne. It's an adventure. Or it will be, if you'll let me know . . . do I turn left up here?"

"This is crazy. I'm not going to help you."

"Then I'll read it myself."

I reached across to snatch the map and nearly drove us off the road when she held it aloft. She was about to reiterate her command for me to stop the car, probably turn it around and switch places, but her breath got caught up in a gasp as her eyes filled with awe. In response, I *did* bring the car to a speed so slow we were barely moving, all the better for me to concentrate on the mansion splayed out in front of us.

Okay, maybe not a *mansion*. But something certainly unexpected, especially tucked away in the hills on the side of a Texas highway.

"Do you think that's it?" Jayne asked.

I looked at the house numbers etched into a giant piece of granite at the edge of the drive.

"No. We're not even on the right road yet, I don't think."

In that moment, Jayne fell prey to her own curiosity and became more cooperative, taking on the lion's share of map-reading and direction-giving. I had her turn down the radio so I could pay closer attention to the unfamiliar turns in the road. In retrospect, it might have made more sense for us to switch places, as I knew how to read a map, and she knew how to, well, drive. But we'd come this far, and I was afraid that even the slightest hint of a second guess might throw the entire mission off course.

One dead end, three U-turns, and two close encounters with a couple of trees, and there it was. A low rock wall surrounded the front of the property, encompassing a circular drive that bisected a conglomeration of tailored hedges from a massive brick structure with a four-car garage. We didn't take our car onto the drive, of course—I had a feeling the oil leak alone would have set off some sort of intruder alert—but we did pull over and park, and without a second's hesitation, I got out of the car.

"Elyse! What—"

I slammed the door on her question and took a first tentative step toward the wall. The only sound was the crunch of my steps on the gravel road. That, and the rumbling of the car, which was soon joined by the sound of Jayne's voice, muffled through the window.

"Are you crazy? Get in the car."

I held up one finger, asking for just a moment to—what? I didn't know. I *don't* know. My stomach and brain were all twisted up with what might have been, had I not been so quick to assume the worst about his feelings for me. I stood in a daze, staring at the garage doors, thinking, behind one of them, Billy's Camaro waited for his return. A basketball net stood over on one side of the house, and I imagined him and Charlie engaged in good-spirited games of Horse.

Then, behind me, a car honked. *Our* car—and the sound of it nearly knocked me out of my skin. I jumped, twisted, and glared at Jayne, whose expression was an unlikely combination of impatience, discomfort, and triumph. She'd moved herself behind the wheel and leaned over the bench seat to open the passenger door and give it a no-nonsense nudge.

"Get in."

"I'm getting," I said, sliding in and giving the door a purposeful slam.

"Honestly, Elyse, the ideas you have in that head . . ."

I tilted my head to watch the house disappear. "That's it. He's out of my system now. Completely. I mean, I thought we were incompatible on the *school* social level. I didn't even know real people lived in houses like that."

Jayne sniffed. "It's just a house."

"*Just* a house. Just a house?"

"We saw bigger than that back in Phoenix."

"Yes, and we gazed upon them with a sense of awe and wonder."

"No house is worthy of that kind of reverence. No person is, either."

"Speaking of wonder," I said, drawing on the remaining

dregs of my Coke, "I wonder just how big that place is? Outside looks can be deceiving. Like, how far back do you think the property goes?"

I felt the car slowing as I spoke.

"Jayne? Come on, I'm kidding. No need to go back there."

"I'm not going back," she said.

"Then why are we stopping?"

"Because." Her voice was suddenly tiny. "I think we're out of gas."

endear: *to cause to become beloved or admired*

Somehow, the sight of Billy's baby pictures **endeared** *him to Elyse even more.*

"How did this happen?"

Jayne looked at me accusingly. "You were driving. You didn't check the gas gauge?"

"No, but—" My mind traveled back to a moment that had given me too much joy to have seemed suspicious at the time. "Are you sure the five dollars Dad gave you was for lunch? Not for gas?"

Jayne scrunched up her face, remembering, and I pretty much had my answer. "He said, 'Here. The girl's going to need some fuel if you have plans for the afternoon.'"

I smacked my forehead and groaned. "And you thought that meant lunch?"

"We're girls. Food is fuel."

"Let me ask you—were his coworkers around? Is there any chance that he was trying to be clever?"

Now it was time for Jayne to smack her own forehead, but softly, so as not to leave a mark. "What are we going to do? We're, like, a hundred miles from home!"

Adorable, really, the math and the geography . . .

"We could get back to town on half a gallon," I said. "We're surrounded by people of means and—hopefully—philanthropy. We'll just ask."

"Yeah, right. Because people just keep gallons of gasoline sitting around."

"As a matter of fact, they do. For their lawn mowers and their golf carts. And boats. And—"

"In what, buckets?"

"In gas cans. Stay here. I'll go ask."

"Wait, you aren't going—he's out of town, you know. Nobody home."

"Somebody's home," I said. "There was a truck parked around the side of the house. A work truck, so maybe a landscaper? If I'm not back in twenty minutes, come break into the house and call the police."

"Elyse . . ."

I patted her arm. "I'll be fine. Just stay here and listen to the radio."

"But we're out of gas."

Somehow, I didn't sigh. "There's no connection between—" but I dropped it. With my luck, listening to the radio might leave us with zero gas *and* a dead battery. "You just listen to your own thoughts."

Before she could stop me, I was out of the car and walking back to the Fitz house. We hadn't driven far, so it was just a matter of minutes before I turned up the drive, this time walking purposefully to the front door. If my landscaper theory held true, I might be better off poking my head around to the backyard, but I figured, with the Young Master away, there would be a whole staff of people scurrying around, dusting and mopping and whatnot. I rang the bell and tried to pick out a tune from the heaviness of the chimes within. No sooner had they died away than the door opened, revealing a small, round woman with red hair and gray roots.

"Yes?" she said, holding the door at a wide, welcoming angle.

"Um," I stammered, surprising myself with my nerves, "my sister and I? We were driving? And our car? It, um, ran out of gas. Just up the road."

"Oh, my." She opened the door a little wider. "Would you like to use the telephone?"

"Actually? Ma'am? I was wondering if you might have a gallon or so of gasoline? Like, for your lawn mower? Or your golf cart? Or your, um, boat? I could pay you—" I fished out the wadded dollar bill from our change at Sonic. "And my sister, I think, has more in the car . . ."

She waved dismissively at my money and stepped back to allow easy access. "Come inside. Wait here, and I'll go find Mr. Hank. I'm sure he'll be able to help you."

Wait here.

Now, logically, I should have realized that I had given the same directive to my sister, and in doing so I expected her to comply. I, too, should have taken the nice lady at her instruction and waited. Here. Inside this foyer with a vaulted, echoing ceiling and a little table with a silver orb-type thing sitting on top of it.

Instead, I moved *here*. Just a few steps over to where the ceramic tile of the entryway met up with plush carpeting that looked like oatmeal. Then, *here*, into a room with butter-yellow walls and wide beams across the ceiling. Then, *here*, to a spot where the entire wall was covered with pictures of a growing Billy Fitz.

An infant, holding a giant plush football.

Three years old, wearing a little football jersey, staring intently into a helmet.

Kindergarten, framed in a border of brightly colored books.

Second grade, toothless. Cute, but toothless.

Fourth grade, braces. And glasses.

Sixth grade, football uniform, posing with his helmet tucked under his arm.

Ninth grade, pudgy? Yes, definitely. A little something we had in common.

Eleventh grade, a pinch to myself to keep breathing.

Next to the pictorial ode to growing was a glass case full of trophies—little golden boys playing football, baseball, running, bowling. (*Bowling?*) Ribbons for Attendance and Honor Roll. Certificates for Kindness and Character. Newspaper clippings; yearbooks opened to *his* page. Then, family photos: a young boy with his mother beside a Christmas tree; a teenager and his father holding a giant fish between them. And then, unframed, casually propped into the glass, the Billy I knew, haircut and shoulders and 501 jeans, standing with his arms folded in front of the statue in Rockefeller Center, New York City.

"He's a handsome boy, isn't he?"

She was back, looking at the pictures of Billy with the affection of a mother. Or grandmother. Oh, no—was this Billy's *grandmother?*

"I've been working for the family since before his mother passed on. Such a good, good boy."

"I—I don't really know him? We go to school together, but . . ."

She smiled, clearly not believing a word. "I talked to Mr. Hank. He's finishing up something and then he'll be right in."

"Should I go ahead and wait outside, then?"

"Don't be silly. Have a seat, and I'll see if William is ready to come down."

Her words made no sense. "William?"

She smiled. "Sweet girl. I forget you all call him Billy. He's always been William to me. He was out in the pool earlier, but I thought I heard him go upstairs to shower."

"Wait—he's *here*?" In the shower?

Then, from a place not nearly far enough away, his voice was calling, asking Darlene (Hank's wife? Mrs. Hank?) if the doorbell rang. If somebody was here, and before I could conjure up whatever magic might be necessary for the carpet to open up, swallow me whole, and belch me out onto the ocean floor, *he*, William (Billy) Fitz, was here.

Chapter 20

totally endear

I SAW BILLY FITZ.
   I saw Billy Fitz wearing nothing.
   Nothing but a dripping wet bathing suit.

solicitude: *attentive care and protectiveness*

He walked beside her with solicitude, and she felt very calm and safe.

I HAD TWO CHOICES—cover my eyes to shield myself from the vision of the shirtless, sculpted torso just a leap away, or cover my mouth to keep myself from saying something stupid. Knowing full well this was one of those sights I might never see again—like the Grand Canyon or a Muppets Holiday Special—I kept my eyes open. Wide open, actually. I could feel my lids stretch until I must have looked like some crazed cartoon character.

"Elyse?" Billy's hands sat comfortably at his waist, confident against the power of my gaze. "What are you doing here?"

"Isn't it too cold to go swimming?" Because *that's* what mattered in this moment.

"Our pool's heated." Because, of course it is.

I clapped a hand over my mouth and turned around before I asked him another stupid question.

"William Matthew Fitz!" Darlene chastised. "What are you thinking? You're dripping all over the floor. Go get dressed."

Ignoring Darlene's cruel directive, I turned again, keeping my eyes averted as I dashed out of the room saying, "I'm sorry—I'm so sorry." My apologies echoed in the entryway, overpowering Billy's request that I stop. *Wait!*

I opened the massive door and stepped out onto the circular drive, momentarily unable to remember which direction I needed to take to head toward the car. I didn't run, though, for fear Billy might be watching from one of the windows, and I couldn't let his last sight of me be me running away. Not that I feared any appearance of cowardly panic; I just knew it wouldn't be the most attractive of exits. I mean, I've never seen myself run, but I've seen others, and I've always managed to add superfluous motion to my body. It was bad enough enduring the snickers of the other girls who lapped me on the track in PE. I did, however, walk swiftly. The way the old ladies in jogging suits do when they walk around the neighborhood.

"Elyse!"

Don't turn around. Don't turn around.

Then, footsteps behind me.

"Elyse! Wait a minute. Hold up!"

Just a few more steps, and I'd be gone. Well, as gone as one could get sitting in a car with an empty gas tank. At least here, I might have a scrap of dignity left.

He came up beside me and tugged on my sleeve. "Hey, so what are you doing here?"

In what must have been the fastest act of obedience on record, he was dressed. Sort of. Jeans, yes—his favored pair of 501s, sitting perfectly on his hip. No shoes, though, which was fine for their smooth driveway, but would have stopped him from following me all the way to the car. Hindsight, right? And, in what could be nothing less than the universe rewarding me for some long-forgotten good deed in my past, he was still shirtless, too. That condition was soon to be remedied, as he was holding a shirt in his hand, but I was given another blissful opportunity to study the beauty of his bare chest for a complete nanosecond while he put it on. Once the long-sleeved black thermal was in place, my power of speech returned.

"Well, good," I said. "Now you can get halfway into a restaurant."

He looked confused. "What?"

"You know how they always have those signs that say, "No shoes, no shirt, no service"? I mean, you still don't have shoes on, so . . ."

He raked his hand through his wet hair and laughed. "Yeah, sorry. I was just about to hop in the shower and—wait, *why* are you here?"

Only the truth could save me from evil thoughts of Billy Fitz in a shower. "I was driving—like, a driving lesson with my sister. And we ran out of gas."

"But you don't live anywhere near here."

"We went out on the highway a little, and then I thought I'd practice on some highly dangerous and unfamiliar roads."

He smiled again. The sun had come out, but the day was still a little cold. That's what it feels like to have Billy Fitz smile at you. A bright, perfect chill.

"Now you see why I stay at Charlie's house during school. Can you imagine driving this every morning?"

This time it was my turn to laugh as I gestured back toward his house. "Honestly? I can't imagine any part of this."

Then I felt bad, because he looked a little embarrassed.

"So," he said, obviously changing the subject, "where's Jayne?"

"She's in the car. Just a little ways up. Your—Darlene? She said Mr. Hank? He was going to be able to help us out. I should go . . ."

"Wait here while I go get some shoes. I'll go with you."

Billy ran back to the house—which was very nice to watch. Inch by inch, I took baby steps back toward the door, not sure what it was about this place that made me unable to stay where I was put. If I were to be totally honest with myself, I wanted to meet up with Billy at the door so we would have a little longer to walk together.

Minutes later, one of the garage doors rumbled open, and Billy emerged, newly shod with an old pair of loafers and carrying a red gasoline can.

"Hank says there's a full gallon in here," he said, hoisting it. "Should be plenty to get you back home."

"Thanks," I said, reaching for it, but he playfully held it out of my reach.

"I got this! What kind of a gentleman would I be if I handed off a gas can to a girl?"

One who recognizes a girl as his equal, I thought. But I said thanks again, because I am brilliant.

Billy reached inside the garage and pressed a button to bring the door down, and we started walking. Slowly, stroll-like, as if neither of us were in any hurry to complete the errand at hand. I hooked my thumbs in the front pocket of my jeans and attempted a casual air.

"So, I really didn't expect to see you here."

"That's odd," he said, "considering that I live here."

It was the kind of comeback that, months ago, when we had a semblance of an uneasy friendship, I might have answered with a slug to his arm.

"No, I mean—I heard you were in London. To visit your dad?"

"Ah, rumors. They're a wonderful thing. I did go see my dad, but not all the way to London. We met in New York."

"Christmas in New York? Cool."

"More like *cold*." (Another punch-worthy comment.) "But,

yeah. It was fun. We stayed at this really nice hotel and had dinner with some of his friends. Went to a few shows."

"Like, Broadway shows?"

We'd come close to the end of the drive, and I swear he slowed his steps.

"Yeah. We saw *Cats*. Had really good seats for that one, and it was really cool. No plot or anything, just a bunch of people in cat costumes dancing. But the dancing was good."

"I have the tape," I said, not mentioning that I could sing just about every song on it.

"You should see it sometime."

"I hope to."

It was a pure moment where it seemed like we both forgot who we were. I wasn't a girl who would probably never get a chance to go to New York and see *Cats*, and he wasn't a boy who did such things over Christmas break. It was like, *Hey, you know that new Jamocha Shake they're serving at Arby's? You should try that. / Yeah, I'm going to try to get there this week on my lunch break.*

That easy.

"What else did you see?"

"Something called *La Cage aux Folles*, which was weird. And then a production of *Much Ado about Nothing*."

"That's my favorite. My favorite Shakespeare, I mean."

"I can see why. It kind of reminds me of you. It's funny. And smart."

We'd turned a corner. Literally, I mean, because we'd come to the end of the driveway and now had to turn onto the gravel road where our steps took on a unison crunching. I took one last glance over my shoulder, thinking, *This could have been my boyfriend's house.* I had brief, fleeting images of summer afternoons hanging around at the pool, long nights renting movies while Darlene brought in snacks. All appropriate. All chaperoned, even if by no one other than Jayne and Charlie on the other side of a foosball table.

But we'd turned some other corner too. He'd complimented me, in his own way. Granted, not a lot of girls would be over the moon about a guy calling them *funny* and *smart*. But those two words summed me up perfectly. And, as more evidence of a new path, I took them as they were meant. Not insulted because they didn't speak to some subjective assessment of beauty, and not all gooberish at the joy of his attention.

Fact: I am smart and funny.

Fact: Billy thinks I am smart and funny.

Nothing more to add.

"Oh, by the way," I said as the car came into view. I could see the fuzzy blonde bump of Jayne's head above the seat, waiting. "Great play. You know, the one? In that game? Remember?"

He laughed, deep and genuine. "Vaguely."

Jayne must have seen us approaching in the rearview mirror, because her door opened and she got out of the car saying, "Well, hello, Billy!" as if this were the most natural thing that had ever happened to us.

"Have you thought about what you're going to do as a follow-up?" I asked him, dreading the moment our conversation would end. "Establish World Peace? End Hunger?" We were at the car, and after an obligatory *hey* to my sister, he flipped open the little door to the gas tank and unscrewed the cap.

"To tell you the truth? I'm just glad it's over."

Chapter 22

abominable: *worthy of or causing disgust or hatred :*
DETESTABLE

Caroline stared at Elyse with distaste, obviously finding
her to be just as abominable *as she had the last time they*
were thrown together.

REMEMBER? Remember how I dreaded that first day of school, being the new girl, not knowing anybody? Wondering who I would eat lunch with, what my classes would be like, if I would ever make any new friends? When I walked up the long, wide steps to the front doors of Northenfield Texas High School on that first day after Christmas break, I found myself plagued with the exact same questions. Except for lunch. That would be with Jayne and Lottie and Collin. But how was I going to face English class, knowing Gage would be sitting right behind me? And Trigonometry, with Billy "Friendly" Fitz?

I'd taken some extra time that morning, working myself into my new jeans, figuring I would do all of my deep breathing later, when I got home. A new sweater had a black-and-red diagonal zebra stripe, and it was long enough to disguise the little *pouf* that rimmed my waist. I'd contained my hair in a wide, red headband, pegged my jeans and tucked them into a pair of thick red socks, and completed the outfit with a pair of high-top canvas sneakers I'd fished out of a giant barrel of shoes on a visit to Thrift Mart the last Saturday of vacation. When I came downstairs for my hot breakfast Pop-Tart, the look was met with Lydia's approval.

"See? There's jeans and a shirt. And *jeans* and a *top*. You're half the schlump you used to be."

I thanked her, despite the lingering judgment, and hollered up to Jayne to hurry, or we'd be late.

"It's barely seven thirty," she said, dragging herself into the kitchen, shoes in hand.

"I need to get there early. Make sure nobody tries to start the year off by stealing my desk."

"You just want to get there before Gage does," Jayne said, in that all-knowing way she has. There's no keeping anything from that girl.

Lydia paused in her effort of picking every last raisin out of her cereal. "So, you guys, like, broke up?"

"I'm not sure how much there was to break." My Pop-Tart jumped from the toaster, and I wrapped it in a napkin to take on the road. "But, yeah. I don't think he's the guy for me." *Or for anyone*, but I kept the last thought to myself.

Jayne grabbed a banana and pocketed the lunch money Mom had left on the counter the night before, and we were off, leaving Lydia behind in charge of pouring cereal for the Littles, who were currently in the living room watching a Spanish-language children's show. They'd discovered it the first morning of the school year and could already sing the opening song with an accent that would earn them extra credit from Señora Benavidez.

The sidewalk was covered with soft, lifeless leaves, and we trudged along in silence for the first half of the block before Jayne said, "I wonder if Charlie is going to be there today."

It was one of those statements that might have been a question or might just have been a thought. And if it was a question, there was no telling if she was expecting an answer or just posing it to the morning mist, so I let it linger for a few steps before she spoke again.

"I mean, school *is* back in session, so he should be here, right? New semester and all."

"Should be," I echoed.

"Not that it matters. To me, if he's there or not. I was just wondering, is all."

And then I didn't say anything, because my mind was clogged with my own questions—all of which seemed more complicated than whether or not Charlie Bingley would be ignoring Jayne here at school, rather than from afar.

For instance, did something *happen* in Billy Fitz's driveway?

And if something *happened* was it likely ever to happen again? Say, across the aisle in Trigonometry? Or maybe a glance in the hallway?

And, if nothing *happened*, then what accounted for the warmth of his smile, or the genuine nature of our conversation?

And, again, if nothing *happened*, then what were the expectations for that moment across the aisle in Trig? Or that glance in the hallway? Do we just act as if I never saw him shirtless?

Our questions hovered above our heads, unanswered, for the entirety of the fifteen-minute walk. We dragged them up the stairs and into the empty halls. Jayne peeled off to volunteer her services in the front office—there was always some kind of note or folder to deliver—and I made my squeaky way (new shoes, clean floor) to Mrs. Pierson's room. The door was open, but the lights were off, and I chose to leave them that way since the light from the windows created the perfect shade of gray for an empty January morning. My desk waited, and I slid into its comfort before pulling my copy of *Great Expectations* out of my JanSport. I'd found the perfect copy at the used bookstore in the strip mall behind the theater—wide margins, slightly yellowed pages, and the smell left behind by years of lingering. In fact, that's what I was doing—fanning through the pages and bringing them up to my nose to inhale—when Gage walked into the room.

"I've heard reading's easier if you do it with your eyes," he said, easing past me to his desk.

"I like to engage all my senses whenever possible," I replied, and just like that, whatever had or hadn't happened between *us* was put away.

The morning classes passed with little fanfare and lots of homework. Not until I found myself at a lunchroom table with Lottie and Collin and Jayne did I learn the answer to the first question from our morning walk.

Charlie Bingley was not at school. Not at the athletes' table, not with the rich kids, not anywhere. Jayne's face confirmed it.

"He withdrew," she said, poking her plastic fork into a pile of mashed potatoes. "I saw the paperwork in the office this morning."

"Are you kidding?" Horrible sister that I am, my thoughts bounced immediately from her hurt to wondering how Billy would get along without his best friend. How he'd be hanging out in his giant house, all alone, and might need someone . . .

"But he's not, like, transferring," Jayne said. "So I don't know what that means."

"It's the privilege that comes with privilege," Lottie said before sending Collin off to the snack bar to buy a cup of french fries. "While the rest of us are relegated to obligatory Public School, kids like Charlie Bingley can breeze in and out on a whim. A few years ago, before his parents divorced, they took him out of school for two weeks to take a Greek island cruise. Who knows but he and Daddy Bingley are taking a tour of the great southern golf courses? I'm telling you, girls. Don't reach for what you can't have. There's nothing wrong with settling for a below-average boy who you can count on to be where you need him, when you need him."

Right then the below-average boy returned with a tall wax cup, bits of grease from the school's fresh french fries spotting through.

"Ketchup?" Lottie said in lieu of *thank you*, and Collin was off again, his unkempt black hair bobbing in apology.

"I'll see Billy seventh period," I said, pilfering a fry from the cup. It was hot and salty and didn't need ketchup at all. "I can ask him if you want."

Lottie gave a dismissive snort at the hopelessness of it all, but Jayne ignored her.

"Thanks, but I'm fine. Really, really fine."

"Well, I hope so," Lottie said, leaning on her elbows across the table as if something of great conspiratorial import was about to be disclosed. "Prom might not be until May, but it's the only other monumental event at this school. I'll be going with Collin, of course. And *you*"—she pointed straight at me with a naked fry—"aren't expected to go since you're just a Sophomore. But you, Jayne. You're a Junior. It's *your* prom. Set your sights a little lower. I'm sure there's someone out there who would be more than happy to pick up what Charlie Bingley left behind."

I'd like to think that she was trying to be encouraging, and Jayne even offered up some kind of a smile, but I thought it best to change the subject.

"Wait," I said, speaking quickly because the boy himself was in view with a tiny paper cup of ketchup, "you and Collin are Sophomores, too. How is it you're going? I thought at least one of you had to be a Junior or Senior to go?"

Lottie leaned closer and whispered, "He may not look like much, but he knows people. Important people."

"Like who?" I was whispering now too. Ridiculous.

"Like Katie Berg."

Ah, yes. Of course. Queen Katie, our resident royalty.

"Junior Class President?" Lottie was saying, mistaking my silence for ignorance. "Head of the Prom committee? He lives right next door to her. They actually *talk* sometimes. Plus he mows their lawn and cleans their pool during the summer. He's pretty sure he'll be able to get us in."

I took another fry and scooted over to make room for Collin on the bench beside me, thus bringing me into perfect view of Billy Fitz. It wasn't the first time I'd seen him that day, but it was the first time I'd seen him without a cloud of students between us. Most importantly, it was the first time he'd seen *me*, because he paused his steak finger midair, looked *right* at me, gave a nod of his head so slight it would have been imperceptible to anyone not looking for some sign of recognition, then returned his attention to dunking the aforementioned steak finger into a generous puddle of white gravy.

I reached across the table and gave Jayne's hand a reassuring pat. "It's going to be okay. I'll talk to Billy."

But I didn't. Couldn't, not really.

I got to Trigonometry before he did, which was no great feat, considering I didn't have throngs of adoring fans to wade through. I took my usual seat and constructed a mental "Billy Only" force field around the one across the aisle, which held strong until Billy himself walked in. He sat down, looked over, and said, "Hey."

Hey.

Hey.

And then, class started. Class continued. And then the bell rang. And he left.

So, no. I didn't get a chance to ask about Charlie. Or about anything. Not even about Trigonometry, because Mr. Venzinni lectured the whole time. We didn't get a chance to be problem partners, or anything that would have given Billy Fitz and me an opportunity to scoot our desks together and work equations side by side.

In Spanish, I sat in my usual spot in the back of the room and copied the new vocabulary list into my notebook. Mindless work, and before I knew it, I was humming the tune from the children's program my little sisters were watching earlier. When I say *before I knew it*, what I mean to say is that Everybody knew it before I did, because all of a sudden everybody was turned back to look at me, including Señora Benavidez, who was walking down the aisle, headed straight for me.

"So you're a fan of *Aprendamos, muchachos*?" She'd stopped in front of my desk. Arms folded, head cocked, with one giant hoop earring dangling free.

"My sisters are." And then, "*Mis hermanas disfrutan de ese programa.*"

"*Yo también.* But right now—" Her tapered, painted nails made a motion to zip her lips, and she strode back to the front of the room.

But the song wouldn't leave my head, compiling one frustration on top of the other. That—knowing, but not knowing. The tune, yes. But not the lyrics. And even if I *did* know the lyrics, not knowing what they meant.

Like a whole world full of . . . *Hey.*

Hey.

The greeting extended to a friend. A buddy. A pal. Or, what you would say to the guy working behind the counter at 7-Eleven right before you ask him to make you a cherry-blue Slurpee.

I copied the vocabulary list. All words for the New Year.

Esperar—To Hope

Pensar—To Think

Aceptar—To Accept

Aprender—To Learn

And then, just like that, one of the words of the song came clear to me. *Aprendamos.* I could hear that group of children chant-singing it over and over. *¡Aprendamos! ¡Aprendamos! ¡Aprendamos!* Let's learn!

It might have taken me a while, but I'd finally learned. Finally accepted, too, what kind of a chance I had of being girlfriend to Billy Fitz. Or, maybe, to anyone. And that chance? *Nada.* Same chance Jayne had with Charlie. She was now the girl who ran boys out of town. I was the girl who used to kind of date the guy Billy Fitz hates. Combined, we were—nothing.

I skipped two lines and started my conjugations. By now my jeans were cutting into my waist, and I didn't want to hope, or learn, or think, or accept anything. All I wanted was to go home, back to our ratty house, change clothes, lie on the couch, and watch MTV videos. I completed the assignment ten minutes before the end of class, and when the bell finally rang, I stuffed all my books into my JanSport and practically knocked kids over on my way to my locker. Jayne met me at the school's front door, her face reporting a day that had been just as stellar as mine.

"Can we go?" I said, hooking her arm as I passed by, like we were some sort of trapeze act.

"What about Lydia?"

"She knows the way home."

"It's the first day back. We should walk with her."

I exhaled and craned my neck toward the Junior High School building. "Five minutes. Then I'm leaving. Come on, we'll wait at the Tree."

Jayne followed me, and we sat on one of the stone benches, watching kids pile onto the buses. It was colder now than it had been when we left the house this morning, and I'd worn a jacket recommended by Lydia for its fashion rather than its warmth. The sky held on to its iron gray—like something out of a Dickens novel. Like the very one in my JanSport. To make matters worse, tiny flecks—not snow, but crystalized rain—were drifting around, occasionally landing on my cheek. My eyelashes and hair. They were light enough, and sporadic enough, that I thought for a moment I might be the only one who felt them. But then I saw Jayne lift her head and stick out her tongue. Such a Jayne thing to do.

I, on the other hand, peeked above the crowd and grumbled for my curly-haired sister. "Three more minutes."

Just then a burst of distinctly male laughter drew my attention, and I saw Billy Fitz and company—all boys wearing their letterman jackets and 501 jeans—moving as one mass toward the student parking lot. Puffs of steam came out with their laughter, making me think, *It must be cold.* Like I didn't realize it until I saw proof.

"That's it." I stood up. "We're starting home. Lydia can catch up, or not. I don't care."

"Let's give her—"

Whatever else Jayne said to me was lost, because at that moment, Billy Fitz broke away from the pack and started a slow jog right in my direction. Surrounding students turned into a blur of colors, but somehow each of those icy crystals took on a distinct form. I saw every one of them. Counted them, in fact. Thirteen, fourteen, fifteen—floating between me and Billy. One landed in the corner of my eye, and I might have lifted my hand to wipe it away, but I didn't want Billy to think—

I don't know. I don't even know what I wanted to hide. I stood there, and it burned. Another one, right on top of my lip. And then, he was right in front of me, and I saw one light on the collar of his jacket. He had one hand in his pocket, the other held his car keys, and he was flipping the leather fob in the way that was now so familiar.

And, he was talking, because I saw the steam puffs coming from his mouth.

"I'm sorry—what?" Rude, I know, but somehow when Billy Fitz is around, it's hard to get all of my senses to work together.

"I asked if you were waiting for a ride."

"No, we're waiting for my sister."

He looked at Jayne.

"My other sister," I said. "Lydia? She's in eighth grade."

"Oh."

"And then we're walking home, so I guess we're waiting for a walk." One of those things that sounds so clever before you actually *say* it out loud.

"Oh." *Again.* "Well, I guess I was going to ask if you wanted a ride? Because it's pretty cold."

"It's not that bad."

"I'm giving my buddy a lift home, but I could probably squeeze all three of you in the back seat."

I knew my face was red—red enough to match my sweater. It got that way sometimes when it was cold, or when I might be within minutes of dying from joy. Or embarrassment. Or indignation, whatever. Dying. It occurred to me that I'd been *this* close to Billy—meaning, this *physically* close to him before— with my heart swelling in hope for another such moment. Once in the darkness of a dance floor, with lyrics of longing swirling around us. Once on my porch, with rain pouring from the sky. Once at his house, with sunshine beaming between us. And now, in the steel-gray cold of a winter afternoon, with intermittent stinging ice. And what if—*what if*—I got in that car, me and my sisters? With his buddy in the front seat, and the three of us in the back.

No—better, if the buddy sits in the back, with Lydia and Jayne, because Billy told me to hop in beside him. And the ride to my house is only long enough for a single song on the radio.

But one perfect enough for me to show off what I know, a bit of trivia about the album or the band. Or, since it was a Tuesday, meaning Two-for-Tuesday, when the radio station always played two songs in a row from the same artist, we might hear the first of a pair. Then speculate what the next would be. Then, he might decide to drop his buddy off first. You know, so we could see who was right. And when we get to our house, Jayne will cunningly take Lydia inside, and we—Billy and me—might sit in his car. Listen to music and talk, while steam builds up on the window. Or decide to drive to Sonic for ice cream, joking about eating ice cream in this cold weather, but he'll remember something from Boy Scouts, about how you should eat cold food when it's cold and hot food when it's hot.

Or something.

I'm not sure, because I won't remember the conversation, because all I'll remember is what happens when he takes me back home. How he might put the car in neutral, set the brake, lean over, the sleeves of his letterman jacket crunching against the upholstery. How he might kiss me. Then pull back and say—

Hey.

Hey—like this afternoon in Trigonometry, when he didn't even know me. After . . . everything.

I couldn't take that risk again. Couldn't risk that hope of being close—*this* close—and then dropped. No ride home was worth it. No warmth could tempt me. It wasn't *that* cold. I wasn't weak. Home wasn't far.

"No thanks," I said, after what I hoped wasn't an eternal stretch of time.

He looked shocked at my response. Actually took a step back, as if a new perspective would change my answer. "Are you sure?"

"We're fine. It's not far." I saw my little sister's curly head, miraculously styled where the rest of us were quickly falling victim to the frozen, falling mist. "Besides, my sister Lydia? She's not supposed to ride in a car with boys."

"Not even if you're all out together?"

I shrugged, hoping I looked adorable. "Our family, what can I say?" From the corner of my eye, I could see Jayne mercifully intercept Lydia.

Billy glanced their way, then looked at me a little harder, like he was waiting for a last-minute change, before he took a few steps back. "Okay. Some other time, then?"

"Maybe?" I nodded furiously for emphasis. Deep down, though, I knew he wouldn't ask again. If there was one thing Billy Fitz and I had firmly in common, it was that neither of us was likely to pursue rejection. Again.

disconcert: *to throw into confusion*

Elyse was amused when she realized how **disconcerted** *the boy sounded on the phone.*

ALL THE CLASSICS talk about *winter's icy grip.* I'd read the phrase a dozen times, but never understood how a season could have an actual hold on you until that winter of my Sophomore year.

Having lived in Phoenix all my life, the *feel* of this winter was sometimes paralyzing. Knowing the walk to school would require layers of clothing, a hat, gloves, and scarf made me want to stay in bed as long as possible just to avoid the hassle of getting dressed. Then, the walk itself, step after step in the cold. We talked very little, because every breath meant a little sting in the lungs. I guess I should clarify that Jayne and I talked very little; Lydia wouldn't shut up about the cold. About how she was *freeeeeeeeeeeeeezing c-c-c-c-c-cold.* She'd sniffle and wrap her scarf halfway up her face, put her head down, and hug her arms tight. Her steps slowed until it seemed she was about to freeze in place.

So when, on a particularly sleety Thursday, Gage Wickam, driving his aunt June's Gremlin, slowed down beside us to offer a ride (as he did almost every day), we finally granted Lydia the grace to disobey Mom and Dad's rule and get in a car. With a boy. A High School boy. Alone.

"Sure you don't want a ride?" Gage was leaning forward, looking at us (me) over the form of my younger sister, who was already comfortably settled in the front seat. I could feel the heat emanating from the car, and the sound of Culture Club's "Do You Really Want to Hurt Me" straining weakly through the speakers. The cassette I'm pretty sure he didn't pay for. Still, I considered Boy George's question: Did I really want to hurt him? I didn't, but I'd decided a definite loyalty in the Gage vs. Billy Battle for Truth. Even though Billy would never know (or, frankly, probably care) that I took a ride with Gage, *I'd* know.

Not that Gage appeared to be in danger of any pain as a result of my refusal. When I repeated, politely, "No thanks," he shrugged, reached across my sister, and closed the door.

"Do you think that was a good idea?" Jayne asked as the cloud of Gremlin exhaust dissipated. "You know Mom and Dad wouldn't approve."

"She'll be fine," I insisted. "Gage might be a liar, but he's a gentleman. Just doing a good deed for a friend."

We fell in a slow step together, and by the time we got to school had come to the conclusion that today's indulgence had to be a one-time event. Unless it was snowing. Or we rode with her—both of which seemed unlikely.

The icy grip of winter didn't loosen one bit at school. I walked around feeling like I was held in an ever-tightening fist. It made a kind of buffer around me, loosening up only when I was with Jayne, or Lottie and Collin. Sounds were muffled, the atmosphere cold. If I had a carrot nose and button eyes I couldn't have felt more temporary and out of place. When the final bell rang in Spanish class, I was ready—JanSport over my shoulder. Halfway to the door before the end of the tone. Ready to face the trudge home.

I stopped off at the attendance office to meet up with Jayne and found her speaking on the office telephone, looking upset.

"It's okay," she was saying, though her face didn't match her words at all. "No, really, Mrs. Bingley"—she noticed me then, and made a gagging motion—"I understand. Not a problem at all. Bye."

She hung up the phone, gently, then stamped her feet in display of the prettiest temper tantrum known to humanity.

"What was that all about?" I asked, helping myself to a mint from the dish on the counter.

"She needs me to babysit the monster."

My jaw dropped, but then I popped the mint in and closed it. "You're kidding. *You*? Does she know that her son, um, broke your heart?"

"She was all apologetic, 'I know this is perfectly awkward.'" Jane captured Mrs. Bingley's affected voice beautifully. "But she's in a jam, stuck in a meeting until late this evening, and the brat needs somebody at home."

"Why you?"

"Truthfully? I think because she doesn't have any of her other sitters' numbers with her, and she just called the school."

"So you said yes?"

Jayne shrugged. "What was I supposed to do?"

"Well, say *no*?"

"She's in a bind. So, look. I have to hurry so I can catch the bus to their neighborhood."

My sister. My sweet, good-hearted, generous, forgiving sister.

"Let me go," I said, momentarily surprised at the words as they exited my mouth.

"You? Why should you go?"

Mrs. Rocha was signing the blue bus pass, obviously paying no attention to our conversation.

"For one thing," I said, even though I considered the matter settled, "I'm not allergic to the cats. For another, they have a better TV, and tonight's all the good shows. Hopefully she won't be home before *Cheers*."

"She said around nine o'clock." Already Jayne seemed relieved, then turned serious. "You know Billy won't be there, right? He's been staying at his dad's—*his* house—since Christmas break."

"Well, now it's more than settled." I snatched the bus pass out of her hand.

"You don't think she'll mind?"

Frankly, I didn't give a care if she minded or not, so I ignored the question. "I'll call you when she gets home, and you can come pick me up? I don't want to be alone in the car with her and Caroline if I don't have to."

Once outside, Jayne pointed out the bus to me, and I had to run to catch it. The bus driver ignored my pass, and for the most part, the kids ignored me. I passed five seats before the bus's lurching motion dropped me into a blessedly empty one. I wanted to pull a book out to read but was terrified I'd get absorbed and miss the stop, so I put my headphones on instead and watched the town unfold outside the window.

The tape in my Walkman was one fished out of the used tapes bin at the library, a group called Bread, a *best of* compilation. It immediately plugged its soft rock sounds into my life. The chords—warm and easy—brought a thaw to the frigid winter days, and the song filled my head, blocking out the unfamiliar conversation around me. He, this long-haired man, sang of life being emotions passing by. About wanting and needing this woman. Fleeting.

That's the way I felt, the way I'd felt since turning down

Billy's offer for a ride home. I'd been right in feeling I was passing up a final chance. He'd barely acknowledged my existence since then. I mean, he was polite, I guess, saying my beloved *Hey* every day in Trigonometry, but then seemed content to tap his pencil and stare straight ahead during those endless moments while we waited for Mr. Venzinni to get the warm-up problem written on the board.

I wished the icy grip of winter would numb my heart and not just my extremities.

Jayne had written the name of the intersecting streets for "my" bus stop on the back of the pass. Three stops in, I confirmed with a surly seventh-grader and disembarked to see the Bingley home about five houses down. I was the only High Schooler on the bus, as all the kids in this neighborhood had their own cars, but I kept my headphones on and eyes aimed forward, making my way with all the confidence I could summon.

At the house, I found the spare key hidden beneath a barrel-shaped planter (as per Jayne's instruction too) and let myself in. The elementary schools released half an hour later than we did, so Caroline wasn't due to be here for at least thirty minutes. My arrival wasn't totally ignored, however, as two of the Bingley cats sat perfectly still in the entryway. They—like so much of the house—were pristinely white. Who knew you could get pets to match your decor?

"Hey, kitties," I said, dumping my backpack on the sofa. The shorter-haired of the two greeted me back by nudging its head firmly against my shin. The other simply sat and stared. Blinking.

I folded back the doors of the giant armoire in the living room and turned on the TV. The first image to appear was the face of Sally Jessy Raphael—a woman who wore enormous red glasses and gave advice to women whose husbands were cheating, or to men whose wives were cheating, or to kids who were growing up to be hoodlums. None of that interested me in the least. I found the remote control, pushed in the numbers for MTV, and was immediately rewarded with the video for "Take on Me" by the band a-ha. A favorite. I plopped myself down on the white sofa and indulged in the story of a comic character come to life, reaching through the panels of a comic book and pulling our beautiful video star into his animated chase.

I wished I could be pulled into a story. Have some hero reach out, grab my hand, and take me into some other dimension for a while. Because life here had become equal parts tedious and complicated. More than that, I didn't feel like I belonged any-where. Not at school, where my entire social circle could fit at a single lunch table. And certainly not at home, where my only true ally—Jayne—shared my misery. We were like two stranded muskrats on a log, floating down a river of disregard.

Not to be too dramatic or anything.

What would it be like to be pulled into one of those TV shows that I watched all the time? Like *Family Ties*, where I might get some tough but sage advice from a man of wisdom? To sit on a couch in the middle of a perfect little living room and have a mother listen to me spill the whole story about Billy—how he liked me then didn't then might have and now doesn't?

But I couldn't talk to Mom, because she'd just say something about thinking I was seeing that nice Wickam boy, and what-ever happened with that? Before leaving to make sure the Littles hadn't spilled their poster paint on the carpet.

And Dad? In the approximately thirty-two minutes that passed between his coming home from work and his disappear-ance in front of the television, he ate dinner, discussed the news, complained about his job, and warned Lydia that something she was wearing was too short. Occasionally, if I wandered into his sight line, I might get an inquiry about my grades.

How could I live in a house so full of *people* and still have it feel so empty? We literally walked over each other getting from one place to the next. Our laundry ended up in each other's closets. We sometimes had to share a dinner plate if Mom got behind on dishes. And yet, when I was home—even with Jayne there, sometimes—I felt as alone and stranded as I did occupying the Bingleys' high-ceilinged, perfectly furnished, empty tomb-like place.

I wondered what it was like for Caroline and her mother these days—just the two of them with Charlie gone. If they had late nights of girl talk. If they ate ice cream directly from the carton, sharing a spoon. But then, I realized—Mrs. Bingley hadn't even bothered to arrange for a babysitter. Not a real one, one that Caroline knew. The little girl was coming home to a virtual stranger. And what she did know of me, she didn't like.

It became very important to me, all of a sudden, to make some kind of a new impression. I thought about all those TV moms, greeting their kids in the kitchen, taking cookies off a baking sheet—and while I wasn't sure I could commit to stirring up an actual batch of cookies, surely there had to be something I could present as an after-school snack.

The Bingley kitchen was as perfect as I remembered it being the first time I saw it, and much less chaotic than the last time, when hordes of teenagers had gathered around its island. I checked the refrigerator and found a full carton of milk and a crisper drawer with apples and carrots. I took out an apple, intending to slice it up and serve it with a peanut butter sandwich, cut in triangles, and a big glass of milk. Just a snack to tide her—us—over until dinner, since I had no idea what dinner would actually be.

When I closed the refrigerator, a certain note magneted to the door caught my eye.

Emergency Numbers

Mom (work): 555-3435
Dad (work): 214-555-6821
Dad (home): 214-555-9325

And then some names—maybe neighbors—of people I didn't know. But, written in pink felt-tip pen, the name CHARLIE in rounded, childish letters, and a looping arrow drawn to the dad's home number.

Charlie's number.

It was one thing for the coward to duck Jayne's letters, never responding. But what would he do if he picked up the phone to hear her voice on the other end? Then—*then*—we'd know if that mop of golden curls was really nothing more than the mane of a cowardly lion.

I found a pen in a cup next to a pad of paper with an embossed *B* on the top of each page. (Really, how classy is that? At my house, we write messages on cereal boxes.) I copied the number, and as I scrawled the final digit, the front door opened, and a rather timid *Hellooooo* sounded from the front door. Quickly, as if committing some act of romantic espionage, I ripped the paper from the pad and was stuffing it into the back pocket of my jeans when Caroline Bingley came into the kitchen.

"Oh." She actually, literally, totally wrinkled her nose. "It's you."

"It is!" I tried to force some sort of cheer into my voice, which kind of made me sound like I was trying to sell the ten-year-old a bottle of new and improved floor cleaner or something. "I was just making you a snack."

"I don't want a snack. And no TV until after homework. That's a rule."

She turned on her heel and went back into the living room. Immediately, the TV went silent. Then she was back, flopping her backpack on the kitchen island and rummaging through it until she produced two workbooks and a Trapper Keeper featuring dancing blue dolphins.

"Do you need any help?" I offered, noticing one of the books was titled *Adventures in 5th Grade Math*.

"No."

"I'm pretty good at math."

She clamped a pencil between her teeth and muttered, "So am I."

I went into the living room and recovered my own JanSport. "Well, I have homework too. Maybe you can help me."

Caroline looked at me, her eyes holding all the humor of a forty-six-year-old public servant. *Such a beautiful girl*, I thought. *Like a baby shark.*

"I don't understand why you are here."

"Your mom had to work late—"

"But why *you*? I thought we were done with you."

In my life, there have been very few questions I couldn't answer. But that was one of them. Done with me—*done with me?*

"She called the school for Jayne."

Caroline opened her math workbook, using it as a tool for social warfare in a way no other turquoise-colored paperback had ever been used before. "I thought we were done with her, too."

I wanted to ask her exactly what she meant by that, but some small voice reminded me that she was only ten. Vicious and black-hearted, but still young enough to be struggling with long division. Her first problem was 764 divided by 92. Her answer was completely, laughably wrong, but I kept my laughter—and the correct answer—to myself.

For the longest time, the only sound in the room was the scratching of pencils, punctuated by occasional exasperated sighs on the part of Caroline. I could smell the flakes of her pink eraser—she'd nearly rubbed a hole through the page in her math workbook. Her pretty brow was furrowed in frustration, but if I so much as leaned in her direction, she glowered at me, effectively putting me back in my place.

"Sure you don't want me to check your work?" I asked when she finally slammed the book closed.

"I'll have my mom check it."

"She might not be back until late." Without incurring further conversation, I slid the book away from her and flipped open to the page, still marked by her now eraserless pencil. "Recheck number one, number five, and number seven. They're wrong."

I could tell she wanted to ignore me, but when I handed her the big pink eraser from my bag, she took it, rubbed away the incorrect problems, and started again.

By now more than an hour had passed, and I began to rummage around for dinner. There were pizzas in the freezer, and without asking her input, I started the oven to preheat, feeling an odd sense of déjà vu in the process. Thankfully, Caroline was too absorbed in her own problems to ask me why I was staring wistfully at the image of the Red Baron on the box. Once finished, she shoved her book into her backpack, declared she would do her reading later, and stomped out of the kitchen, blonde ponytail swaying in her wake.

I was in the middle of making a face when the phone rang. Most likely Jayne, checking in to make sure Caroline was still alive and well.

"Bingley residence," I said, picking it up on the second ring.

"H-h-hello?" The voice was masculine, sweet, and familiar.

"Hello?" Not the most useful conversation thus far.

"Who's this?"

"It's—um. Elyse?" Then, because who knew the state of the boy's long-term memory, "Elyse Nebbitt."

"Oh, hey, Elyse." *Hey.* It's a thing with them. "This is Charlie. Charles Bingley?"

"Yes." I tried not to roll my eyes into my voice. "I figured as much. How are you?"

"I'm—I'm good, I guess. What are you doing there?"

"Your mom had to work late, and needed a sitter? So, she called Jayne, but Jayne . . . um, couldn't. So I volunteered."

"Oh." Silence fell on the line for an uncomfortable moment, but I wasn't about to be the one to break it. "So, how is everyone?"

"Like, your sister and mother?"

"No. I mean, I hope they're okay. I was asking about everyone with . . . you."

Everyone? "We're fine."

"Your family? Everyone good?"

"Yep. We're good."

"Your sisters?"

"They throw up every time they eat citrus, but I think they're just trying to get out of eating fruit."

"They—what?"

"And Lydia's probably going to be expelled from school for dress code violations."

"Wow." Bless his heart. He seemed to actually be trying to care. "And, everyone else?"

"Like my parents?" Cruel, maybe. But like most sport, highly rewarding.

"Like—"

"Jayne?"

"Yeah." Nonchalance was not his strength. I could hear the relief in his voice. "So, how's Jayne doing?"

Now here's where I should have been awarded a Nobel Prize for kindness or something, because what I really, really wanted to say was that, if he truly wanted to know how Jayne was, he would have called, or written, or sent a telegram, or placed a cryptic message in the personal ads like in that Madonna movie coming out. But since no international recognition would be forthcoming, I had to let decency be its own reward.

"She's fine, Charlie."

"Good."

One word, but enough. He cared, a lot. And for the sake of my sister's pride, I left off the part about her being sad. Lonely and heartbroken.

"How are you?"

"Good," he said, and I could tell he'd left off a lot too. "I just usually check in with my mom around this time. Let her know how my day has been and stuff."

"Well, I can take a message. How has your day been, Son?"

I heard him smile. I know people say you can't really hear that, but I did.

"It's been good. I—um, I call here every day, right about this time."

"So, does your mom need to call you back?"

"No, no. Because I'll talk to her tomorrow when I call—"

"About this time?"

"Yeah. Even if she's, you know, working. I'll still call."

"I'll make a note of that. In the meantime, do you want to talk to your sister?"

"*Your* sister?" His voice was filled with so much actual hope, I almost hated to disappoint him. Almost.

"No, silly. Your sister, Caroline. She's right here."

And indeed, she was, having come running in midway through our conversation.

"Give me that," she said, grabbing for the phone.

"No!" Charlie was saying on the other end. "That's okay. Just tell her I'll talk to her later."

"Are you sure?" I stretched myself to keep out of Caroline's reach. "Because she seems pretty insistent."

"I'm sure," he said. "Just tell her I said hi."

"He says hi," I said, planting my hand on her shoulder and not quite pushing her away. Back to him—"Anything else?"

"Tell everyone for me, will you? That I said hi."

I wanted to tell him that if he wasn't such a coward, such a pushover, he could tell *everyone* that himself, but the line went dead on his end, so I hung up on mine, much to Caroline's seething disappointment.

She planted her hands on her skinny little hips. "You don't have any right to talk to him, you know."

"I answered the phone."

"Well, you don't have any right to answer the phone, even. This isn't your house. And I don't care if your sister was my brother's girlfriend, or if Billy used to like you, or anything. Everything was perfect before you came along. Now you've ruined everything!"

She stamped her foot and ran out of the kitchen, and a few seconds later I heard a door slam upstairs. I remembered being upstairs. Thinking back, I had to grudgingly agree with the kid. I had ruined everything. More than she knew, maybe, though I had a feeling Caroline Bingley knew just about everything. She knew that Billy used to like me, and it wasn't until I heard it come out of her bitter little mouth that I ever truly believed it.

The oven *beeped* that it had finished preheating, but I couldn't face the thought of baking, slicing, and sharing a pizza. Silly, right? The things that can trigger sadness and regret. So

I put the box back in the freezer and found a couple of frozen dinners—chicken pieces for Caroline, Salisbury steak for me. Mashed potatoes for both. Because the two of us were more alike than I ever could have imagined. Two broken hearts— perhaps hers worse than mine, because she'd held the dream of loving Billy Fitz a little longer, and much closer, than I'd ever allowed myself.

We ate in silence, on TV trays, watching *Wheel of Fortune*. Then the Thursday shows. When Mrs. Bingley called and said she was on her way, I called Jayne to tell her to come get me. The two pulled up in front of the house at the same time, and I met Mrs. Bingley on the front porch.

"Thank you so, so much," Mrs. Bingley said, looking remarkably put together for a woman who had just spent thir- teen hours in a real estate office. She rummaged in her purse and came up with a ten-dollar bill. Caroline stood on the other side of the threshold, flanked by both cats. She held her arms crossed in front of her, and I was suddenly loathe to participate in any gesture that would relegate me to hired help.

"No, thank you," I said, easing my way down the steps. "I just did my homework and fixed my dinner. No trouble at all."

"Are you sure?"

By this time I was on the walkway. "Positive!"

I slid into the front seat of our Station Wagon and immedi- ately turned up the radio. I didn't tell Mrs. Bingley that Charlie had called, but I did tell Jayne. I wanted to tell Jayne everything, but for now, this would be enough.

enumerate: *to specify one after another : LIST*

Lydia wandered up and down the aisle, enumerating all the boys who would receive a Valentine's Day card.

PROM. Prom, Prom, Prom, Prom, Prom. Even though the night itself wouldn't happen until Spring, posters advertising the event popped up in the hallways the week before Valentine's Day, in hopes that the holiday would prompt ticket sales and net the Junior Class enough money to have a soda fountain *and* rotating disco ball in the gym. I knew this because Jayne had been recruited to the committee back when she was one half of one of Northenfield Texas High School's beautiful, powerful couples. The fact that Katie Berg hadn't invited her to a single meeting since school resumed after Christmas Break did nothing to quell my sister's dutiful commitment. All official school event planning meetings had to be approved and posted on the all-school calendar, and Jayne's Office Insider privilege alerted her to every one of them. As for the secret, off-campus meetings Katie Berg tried to arrange at her house, at Dino's, or in the dark corners of the Junior High cafeteria—well, we had Collin and Lottie to tip her off to those.

The theme? Endless Romance.

"Like the movie," Jayne explained when she came home from the heated negotiations. "And the song, you know. The duet?"

"That's 'Endless Love,' I said, already set to gag on the schmaltziness of it. "And whose idea was it?"

I immediately regretted my question as Jayne's head dropped.

"Mine, actually. But to be fair, I suggested it at our very first meeting before—everything happened. I think Katie approved it just to be cruel."

"What were some of the other options?"

"Hello, Hollywood! A Night in Paris. Werewolf in London."

The last one not only made me laugh, but inwardly vow to join the committee next year to see it through.

The posters consisted of various life-sized silhouettes of dancing couples, each a product of a magical process involving students and an overhead projector. Some profiles were recognizable. Katie Berg, of course, in the dark, featureless arms of Frank Churchill. Collin and Lottie, deemed attractive enough for a shadowy profile, though I noticed Lottie's glasses weren't a part of the picture.

Right at the entrance of the school, between the trophy case and panoramic picture, the full-size depiction of Billy Fitz. Fitting, due to his football hero status. He held an anonymous girl in his arms—respectfully, though. Like a waltz. Their profiles—his, unmistakable, hers, obscure—gazed at each other surrounded by an ocean of stars dotted on a background of purple butcher paper. The first time I saw it, I lingered a little too long, staring. I'd danced with Billy once before, and I allowed myself a moment of triumph remembering that he'd held me much, much closer than he did the nameless girl on the poster.

"Who *is* she, anyway?" I'd asked Jayne later that day at lunch.

"Nobody," Jayne said mysteriously. "Do you know Harriet

Smith? She's, like, the best artist in school. She did it freehand, so that every girl in school could imagine herself dancing with Billy. Isn't that the silliest thing?"

"Ridiculous," I agreed, then concentrated on my pudding.

Endless Romance had a subtitle: *A Night of Love and Friendship.* The word *Friendship* was spelled *Freindship* on at least half of the posters and, apparently, on the first run of tickets. It had been initially misspelled and sloppily corrected for the banner to be hung on the ticket-selling table in the cafeteria.

"It's supposed to make people want to go even if they aren't part of a couple," Prom Agent Jayne informed us all. "For people like me, I guess."

Not to be outdone by their older, sophisticated counterparts, the students at the Junior High School had successfully petitioned for a winter dance of their own. Scheduled for the Friday night between Valentine's Day and President's Day, the event was spearheaded by my sharp sister Lydia, who buzzed on and on about nothing else.

So, I was surrounded. At home, at school—nothing but talk about this dance or that one. Conversations about dates and dresses and dinners. The Junior High would serve sandwiches and chips, but Jayne had been tasked with approaching local businesses to create a special Prom Night dinner menu. The winner? Dragon Dragon, where the evening's theme of Endless Romance would kick off with an Endless Chinese Buffet for $20 per couple.

As a Sophomore, I was left out of all of this. High School students weren't allowed at the Junior High Dance (not that I was about to embark on some torrid affair with a seventh grader), and I could only go to our Prom with a Junior or Senior as my date. Also a freakishly unlikely scenario.

So I drowned out the conversations around me by clamping

on my headphones and listening to the kind of music that would never find its way onto a Northenfield Texas High School Prom Dance Floor. The Clash, the Ramones—anything that would make a wall of sound fuzzy and interesting enough to fill the times when I had nothing to say. To anybody.

Mrs. Bingley never called again for either Jayne or me to babysit Caroline after school, probably at the insistence of the girl child. Charlie's number remained on the wadded-up sheet of Bingley stationery in Jayne's address book. Unused.

"You could ask someone else, you know," I told her once as we lay head to head listening to the soundtrack of *West Side Story* on a Friday night. "It's the eighties, you know? Make Women's Lib count for something."

"Don't be silly. Who would I ask?"

I named of a list of eligible boys, culminating in an ironic recommendation for Gage Wickam. "He'd be flattered. And honored. Flonored."

"And I'd be—no offense, he's a nice enough guy. But he's a Sophomore."

"How about Billy Fitz? Charlie's best friend. Serve him right for skipping town the way he did."

"I'd never do that to you." We'd been speaking to the ceiling, but now she turned her head. I did, too, and she was so close I could only see one eye. But it was sincere. "Besides, I know for a fact he hasn't asked anyone else. There's still hope."

"There's still two and a half months."

"See? Hope."

That's why I love her, my sister Jayne.

In the first week of February, the cafeteria was festooned with all manner of crepe paper drapes and cardboard cutouts of hearts and cupids and arrows. Replica candy hearts cut from construction paper appeared on random lockers, with phrases like "Be Mine" and "Hot Mama" written in bubbly letters. All of this putting the *endless* in the idea of Endless Romance.

Jayne and I had been charged with doing all the Valentine's Day shopping for the homestead. Even though Mom homeschooled the Littles, they had friends from the neighborhood and Sunday school, and we all had teacher gifts to buy. So it was that the five of us sisters piled into the Station Wagon to drive to Kmart with a blank check and a strict budget.

Once we parked, the Littles hopped out like birds from a cage, ready to do battle for the last box of Barbie Valentines. Lydia followed, her pretty brow furrowed as she studied her list, reprioritizing boys' names like a chess master. Jayne and I lingered at the back, trying to convince each other that it was a good thing, really, to be free of the responsibility of buying a Valentine for a boy. Or to expect one, for that matter.

"It's the eighties, after all," Jayne said, echoing my pragmatism. "If I want chocolate, I'll buy it myself."

"Or a stuffed bear," I countered.

"Exactly."

Once inside, we set everyone free, with strict orders to meet us at the cash register in exactly fifteen minutes. Jayne even gave her watch to the Littles, explaining multiple times what the hands would look like in fifteen minutes, then hoping for the best.

Free from responsibility, Jayne and I took a slow turn through the Juniors clothing department before heading to the snack bar for the signature Kmart ham sandwich and a blue Icee. We sat on round swivel stools at the counter, watching one harried mother after another buy bags of popcorn and hot dogs in an effort to appease children who had no desire to be in Kmart, Valentine's Day or not. A familiar whiny voice wafted above the throng, intensifying the pain of the brain freeze I'd just encountered after a too-fast sip of Icee.

"Did you hear that?" Jayne asked, her whole body alert.

"No," I said, more in the sense of denial than dishonesty.

Jayne swiveled her stool just enough to look beyond me, then met my gaze in confirmation.

"It's her."

"The monster?"

She swatted my arm, as if she hadn't called the girl the same name just weeks before. "Be nice."

Turning back around, Jayne leaned closer to me, as if we could somehow meld ourselves into one incognito being, and we listened. Caroline Bingley wanted something. To eat. A snack. Because she was hungry, and breakfast was forever ago. And there was nothing at home for lunch, nothing good anyway. She just needed some popcorn. Or an ice cream.

But Mama Bingley was having none of it. *No,* emphatically. Over and over. Because Caroline had eaten enough junk food at the school party yesterday. Because they were having pizza for dinner tonight. And soda. Which reminded her, she needed to get some Orange Crush, since it was Charlie's favorite.

At the sound of his name, Jayne froze mid–Icee sip, her lips pursed around a solid blue straw.

"What do you think it means?" Jayne asked, whispering, even though Mrs. and Daughter Bingley had moved on.

"No reason to buy Charlie's favorite soda if Charlie isn't here in town." My sense of caution would only allow me to state the obvious.

"Probably just here for a visit. After all, a boy can miss his mother, can't he?"

"Mother, yes. Sister? Not so sure."

"What am I going to do?" She braced herself on the countertop and rose from her stool, looking around, then immediately hunkering down again. "You don't suppose he's *here*, do you?"

"Would any red-blooded American boy willingly come to Kmart if he didn't have to?"

She handed the Icee over, clearly uninterested in another sip. "I wonder if he's in town. At his house, you know? Or just, I don't know. Hanging around."

"Should we drive by on our way home? Maybe run out of gas in front of *his* house for a change?"

She laughed—sounding nervous, but almost giddy. "Has it been fifteen minutes yet?"

I shrugged. "You're the one who gave your watch away."

"What if *she's* at the register?"

"We can stop by Clearance, see if there are any Halloween masks left over. Or maybe there'll be a Blue Light Special on oversized sunglasses and hats."

She laughed again, with a bit more warmth. My old Jayne seeping back. "Come on. We have just as much a right to be here as they do. More so, really. We're poor."

Now it was my turn to laugh, and I slurped the last of the Icee before wadding our sandwich wrapper and stuffing it in the empty cup.

The Ladies Bingley had disappeared into the Blue Light bowels of the store, at least for the moment, so when our younger sisters appeared, we hurried them to the shortest checkout line, paid with Mom's check and Jayne's driver's license, and herded ourselves back to the car. The drive home lasted the same fourteen minutes as the drive to the store, but it seemed infinitely longer. Every song on the radio was stupid, every commercial annoying.

"If I ever get my own car," I muttered for the thousandth time, "the first thing I'm going to do is put a tape player in."

Jayne drove with careful precision, her fingers tapping on

the steering wheel, even during some incessant Climax Blues Band ballad. The Littles had been forbidden to divvy up their Valentines in the car, lest any of them go flying out the window, so when we finally came to a stop in front of our house, they went flying out the door, one of them screaming, "Dibs!" on any card featuring a pony.

"I'll be in my room," Lydia said. She'd insisted that her stack of cards be bagged separately from the rest and clutched the package to her sweater protectively. Even in this cold weather, her belly button winked from the expanse of flat, white belly beneath.

"And what are you going to do?" I asked Jayne as we plodded up the steps.

"Not wait by the phone," she said. "Not wait anywhere."

Not waiting meant the two of us slouched on the living room sofa watching an old movie on TV. *Sabrina*, in which a young Audrey Hepburn falls in love with the much older Humphrey Bogart. We decided it was a shame the two of them never had a torrid affair and love child in real life, because if it had been a boy, she could have named him Humphrey Hepburn. You know, one of those conversations that you have when you're trying to distract each other from the thoughts at hand.

We could hear Mom at the kitchen table, negotiating the Great Valentines Divide of 1985, and Dad was—somewhere. His office, probably. Who knew the world of property management would call for so many working Saturday afternoons? In fact, of course he was in the office, because he called. Three times. Each ring of the phone brought Jayne clear out of her skin, and it took a lot of long, lingering gazes on the part of Audrey Hepburn to get her put together again.

Then, Lydia's voice from the top of the stairs calling, "Jayne!" Followed by Lydia herself running down the stairs.

"Jayne! Jayne!" She came to a skidding halt between us and the TV. "They're here."

"Who's here?" Jayne asked, all cool. Like she didn't know. Or care.

"Who else? Charlie!" She looked at me. "And Billy, if you care. Charlie's car just stopped in front of our house. Quick!" She handed Jayne a hairbrush, which was immediately put to good use spinning a fluffy cloud of golden beauty around her face. I could only smile wide and ask for confirmation that my teeth weren't Icee blue before the doorbell rang, bringing Mom and the Littles into the room, chorusing, Who is it! Who is it?

Mom, taking charge as if some kind of grand dame of the premises, waved the Littles to sit in Dad's big chair while she opened the door. There, she exclaimed greetings to the boys the way one would to conquering heroes who had just sludged through mud and snow to collapse on the doorstep, urging them to come in! Out of the cold! Such a frosty day, such a winter she never would have imagined! And could she take their coats? Get them some Hot Chocolate? Maybe they would like to watch some nice musical videos with the girls?

Charlie and Billy stepped over the threshold, taking it all in good-sportsman stride, but in that instant, the room became electric. I half-expected Jayne's newly brushed hair to rise from her head the minute she and Charlie looked at each other. There was, I swear it, a buzz. At least a hum, though that might have just been coming from one of the Littles.

Jayne stood, tugging down her T-shirt under Charlie's hungry gaze. There were eight of us in the room—six mere humans to witness this reunion of pure carnal attraction. I felt compelled to cover the Littles' eyes. Lydia's, too, lest she get ideas that would get her permanent status on the bathroom walls of Northenfield Junior High. Even Mom seemed, momentarily, at a loss for words, probably regretting the offer for Hot Chocolate.

When I finally tore my eyes away, I looked at Billy. *He* was looking at *them* with an air that could only be described as proprietary. Satisfied. And immediately, I knew. He'd done this. Said what he had to say to make this happen.

He looked at me, raised one eyebrow, and cocked his head toward Jayne and Charlie, saying, *See?* Confirming.

"We just wanted to stop by," Charlie said, his eyes full of Jayne, his mouth full of smile, "to say hello to everybody."

Mom made a half-hearted offer for lunch, which was politely declined on the part of Billy.

"We have to go," he said, already inching toward the door. "But his mom's throwing kind of a welcome-home party tonight."

"And you should come," Charlie said, a towering blond tremor of eagerness. "At six. At my house. All—well, both of you."

This, I'm assuming, extended to me.

Bored, the Littles slid out of their chair and wandered back to the kitchen, demanding Mom's presence. Lydia, in an unaccustomed act of social awareness, excused herself, too, stating she had scads of Valentines to write—a shocking number of them, really—and seeming quite disappointed when none of the company bothered to inquire as to the exact amount.

That left the four of us—an assembly of the most angst-fueled of couplings—standing in an awkward shapeless gathering at the foot of the stairs.

"So, Charlie. You're back?" Thus continued my never-ending quest to provide the most obvious comment to any situation.

"He is," Billy answered, because the power of Jayne's presence seemed to have put Charlie on a three-second delay. Like when foreign diplomats are interviewed on TV.

"For, like, the weekend?" I pressed. A valid question, this one, and I looked straight to Billy for the answer.

"For as long as he wants," Billy said.

Charlie's curls bobbed in agreement. "Forever."

elude: *to escape the perception, understanding, or grasp of*
Although Elyse understood the words on the note, the
identity of its author eluded *her.*

As it happened, I didn't go to Charlie's Welcome Home shindig, for fear it would be little more than an Endless Romance
preview. I would never begrudge my sister a moment of happiness, but neither did I feel obligated to magnify my misery.

"Who was there?" I asked when she crept into our room just
past midnight.

"Everyone." She perched on the edge of her bed and began
unlacing the cute suede boots she'd worn with thick socks
poufed around the cuffs of her jeans. "Like, almost the entire
Junior class. The usual. You would have been fine."

"I was *fine* here at home. Read an entire Danielle Steel novel.
So, you know, time well spent."

Indeed, the accomplished library book still sat on the end of
my bed. Jayne picked it up.

"*Full Circle*? Seems appropriate."

She draped her nightgown over her arm, went across the hall
to the bathroom, and came back moments later, her hair caught
up in a ponytail and strategic swathes of pimple cream on her
face. Like she needed it or something.

"So," she said, climbing into bed with me, "should I tell you everything?"

"As long as you can keep it rated appropriate for audiences of all ages," I teased. Her Clearasil tinged pink.

"He was waiting for me. On his front porch, even though it's freezing outside. He said he didn't want to take a chance of not seeing me immediately. Or of somebody else finding me first, and not getting a chance to talk."

"So, it's true," I said, adopting a mock tragic tone. "He's lost all capability of using a telephone. Poor, poor boy."

She nudged me, hard. "The very first words out of his mouth were, 'I'm sorry.' If he said it once, he said it a million times, and that if I never forgave him he would understand. And that he didn't deserve even this moment. That he'd been a fool, an idiot—to take off like that without a word."

"And ignoring you at the football game?"

"Both his mom and his dad thought we were just getting too serious. Too fast. Like, they were afraid we were going to run off together or something."

"But you—"

"Not because of *me*. Not really, I don't think. Unless he was trying to spare me or something. But him. He says he loves me, Pudge."

"Of course he does."

"But, like, really. *Really.* And I guess his parents got married young, and they started to freak out. So his dad came up with this amazing opportunity to train with a club soccer team over Christmas. And they gave him this sort of ultimatum. He'd only get the sessions if he broke up with me. Completely. He said his dad checked the phone records and the mail and everything."

"So," I said, not so quick to forgive, "he did, in fact, choose soccer over you?"

"It was an amazing opportunity. The exact right priority. This is something he wants to do with his life, and I'm a High School girlfriend."

"That doesn't sound like Charlie."

"No." Here, she got uncomfortable. "That was Billy. He— he encouraged this. All of this."

"I know."

How—how could I have forgotten? I'd never told Jayne of Billy's role in this separation. And here I'd dropped it, like a bomb in a peanut factory.

"You *know?*"

I nodded. "Billy told me. Wrote me, in that note? Forever ago."

"And you never said anything?"

"I didn't want to hurt you any more than you already were. Thinking that Charlie would hold Billy's opinion in such high regard."

"And that's why you didn't—"

"Didn't, what?"

"Oh, I don't know. *Pursue* him? Out of some loyalty to me?"

I pulled my knees up to my chin. "There was nothing to pursue."

"I think you're wrong. Charlie would think so too."

"You *talked* about this with him?"

"Briefly. And, no, Billy was nowhere around. He stuck mostly with the other guys from the football team, watching the State Game. Over and over."

"Charlie didn't watch the State Game?"

"He'd already seen it, remember?"

"So," I said, preparing to get to the most important matters at hand, "where did you and Charlie spend the bulk of the evening? Surely not in some crowded kitchen where people could slip on the heart spilled all over the floor."

Jayne giggled. "No. We went to his room—door open, of course. The whole time. But we could be alone, and talk."

"And talk."

"Yes." But the way she blushed and looked away, I knew they did a little more than talk.

"And kiss? Maybe? Just a little?"

"A little," she said. "Yes. But not much, really. He—he asked me to forgive him. Like, on his knees asked me."

"What did you say?"

"What could I say? I said, 'Yes, of course.' Then he asked if I would ever consider being his girlfriend again."

"Let me guess. Yes to that, too?"

She fiddled with the buttons on her flannel nightgown. "I know it sounds silly, but I love him. As much as I know what such a thing could possibly mean. I knew the minute I saw him—again, today at the house. And it was like the last few months never happened."

"But they did happen."

"But they won't again. Not like that, anyway. I'm sure of it."

"I hope you're right."

She gave me a quick hug and a kiss on my cheek, leaving a residue of cream, which I blended into my skin as she scuttled across to her bed.

"Besides the novel," she said while burrowing under her covers, "any other exciting news here?"

"Somewhat, actually," I said, having nearly forgotten. "Remember all those phone calls from Dad all afternoon? He was making plans with Mom. Seems next weekend is some big conference in San Antonio, and he wants to take her. Property Management seminars by day, romantic strolls along the River Walk by night. A sweethearts' getaway on the company dime." The last bit was a paraphrase of the gag-inducing dinner conversation.

"Sounds fun," Jayne said. "But, wait. We don't have to go, do we? Charlie just got back, and—"

"*We* are not invited, hence the romantic strolls. You and I are in charge. All weekend. They leave Friday morning and get back late Sunday afternoon."

"Oh. This'll be a first."

It would be. Our parents had no problem leaving us in charge for long evenings or all-day excursions. But overnight? This was new, and probably only considered due to Jayne's ability to drive one of us to a hospital should we fall victim to a stray butcher knife or dog or something. Of course, they'd have the car . . . but, a minor detail.

"There's one more thing," I said, trying not to sound ominous. "It's the same weekend as Lydia's dance, and Dad was about to say that she couldn't go—not while they were out of town. But I said we'd make sure everything went okay. Like you would be sure to talk to the parents of the lucky boy who gets to go with her and make sure they aren't whiskey runners or anything before handing our precious Lydia over to them."

Jayne yawned, long and loud, saying something about all of that sounding fine.

"It means no date with Charlie next Friday night. We have to stay home, by the phone, in case the school is overrun with escaped criminals. Or if her date's parents are too hyped up on goofballs to drive her home. But mostly to make sure she doesn't break curfew. And we're sworn to tell them if she does."

Another yawn. *Fine, fine.*

"And the next morning, you have to drive us all to Denny's for breakfast. And you have to give me all of your hash browns." There had been no promise for Denny's; I was just checking to see if she was still awake. She was, but just barely. I could have gotten her to promise me anything at that moment. Instead, I listened as she fell asleep before turning on the radio to keep me company late into the night.

A new light permeated the school upon Charlie Bingley's return. Sunshine poured through the cafeteria windows, glinting off his golden curls. Sometimes he sat with us, he and Jayne splitting a cup of Snack Bar fries or sharing a Wednesday Warm Cookie. Other times, she joined him at a more popular table. Most days, though, since Juniors were allowed off-campus lunch during the second semester, they disappeared altogether and came back breathless at the bell, with Sonic cups and half-eaten chili dogs. On those occasions, Jayne brought me tater tots, since I'm the one who convinced Mom and Dad that the occasional drive-in lunch probably wouldn't result in having to send her away to a home for wayward girls in the fall.

Because it was the second week in February, and the school's Valentine's Day decorations were beginning to fade, the crowning of a new couple seemed to lift everyone's spirits. Give us hope that we might too, someday, find a love befitting an endless array of pink and red tackiness. Honestly, when the two of them were together, you could almost see a cloud of animated, dancing hearts floating above their heads. A smug, smiling Cupid perched on Jayne's shoulder, his arrow notched right between Charlie's eyes.

I, too, basked in the light of this hope. Seeing Jayne and Charlie reunited loosened a grip I hadn't realized was so strong upon my heart. I'd been hurting for two. Three, maybe, if I wanted to count Charlie. And in an amazing twist I never could have imagined, the lifting of my sister's burden gave weightlessness to mine.

So I didn't have a boyfriend. So what? I didn't have one

before, not really. Gage could never have borne the title the way Charlie did for Jayne. I had no right or reason to feel emptiness or loss. Now, Jayne didn't, either, and that void I felt on her behalf was now filled—twice over, with a seriousness and commitment that would terrify *all* of our parents if they ever got a glimpse of it.

So I didn't have a date to prom. So what? The very definition of Endless Romance meant that time would stretch in possibility. I mean, it wasn't Finite Romance. Or, April-or-Else! Romance. I preferred to think of it as Democratic Romance—free for all who would partake but limited in scope.

So my younger sister had a poster-board-sized chart listing the benefits of every possible date to her Junior High School Night of Wonder. So what? Did I really want to judge my beauty, my worthiness, my Future Wonder of Endless Romance by the likes of my sisters?

If I hadn't been through the roller coaster of Billy and me and Charlie and Jane, I wouldn't care a bit about the who and what and when of this dance. And I didn't care now, but my *not caring* was different. Not apathy, but acceptance. A weird bit of incomplete peace. My size, my face, my hair—we were all well on our way to becoming friends with each other. That misdirected pride I'd carried for so long, the one that led me to hide behind an almost aggressively plain appearance, was being chipped away with every bit of color I allowed in my wardrobe, my accessories, my tinted lip gloss. I was finally comfortable enough with myself to *highlight* myself. Like in the books I love. The ones I've read a dozen times. The ones I combed through the bins and shelves of used bookstores to buy because the library copy was so frustratingly not mine. I'd hunt and save for a copy of my own, so I could run a pink highlighter over the words I wanted to return to again and again, the ones that rose to the surface from the thousands and thousands around them.

Somehow, since that first day of school—maybe since that first day of *ever*—I belonged to myself, and I was finding more than a few bits to embrace. I was clear and important to myself, and I wanted to be easy to find.

Thus, I made it through Thursday, Valentine's Day, with my spirit intact, watching girls walk through the hallways, barely able to see over the tops of their teddy bears. The very air squeaked and rumbled with balloon bouquets bumping into each other at the end of the long ribbon tethers, and *actual* bouquets of fresh flowers perfumed the classrooms—as much as white carnations and grocery store roses can perfume anything. Boxes of candy were passed across the aisles, something the teachers allowed as long as they got their own taste.

The French club delivered *Notes d'Amour* to kids in home-room. These were slips of paper with various French phrases, attached to a chocolate rose on a stick. Lottie was in French club and charged with delivering the *Notes* during morning announcements. To my surprise, when she showed up in my class, she walked straight toward me, two chocolate roses in hand. The first was from Jayne, with the message, "*Pour ma petite soeur. Je t'aime beaucoup!*"

The second, though, unsigned, bore a much different message.

Pour elle avec les yeux brillants.

Displaying illogic at its best, I looked around the classroom, as if the sender would take to his feet and proclaim the brilliance of my eyes. When no such proclamation came forth, I carefully untied the ribbon and removed the note. Studying the hand-writing meant nothing, as the messages were dictated to vari-ous French Club students at lunch, translated, and scripted in something meant to look like seventeenth-century calligraphy.

When she passed by me in the aisle, I grabbed the hem of Lottie's red sweater and whispered, "Who sent this?"

"I don't know. I'm only in French I. My job was to tie the ribbons. Besides, there was a box where you could paper clip the message to a dollar if you wanted to keep it secret."

I unwrapped the rose on my sister's message and nibbled at the chocolate. Who thought my eyes were brilliant? No, not brilliant. Bright. Bright eyes. Had Gage ever said anything like that? Surely Collin wasn't brave enough to harbor a secret admiration. There was this boy in Chemistry who sometimes seemed a little flustered around me, so—maybe? Would this broker an invitation to meet Frank Churchill?

I put the slip of paper inside my current novel—*The Hobbit*—because it seemed the safest shelter from romance. For the rest of the day, I looked at everyone as a suspect. Looked at them with my bright eyes. Of course, there was only one person I wanted the *Note d'Amour* to be from, and I mentally combed through every compliment he'd ever given me, trying to find some memory of a similar flattering remark. *Sharp*, he'd called me. And *witty*. But nothing that put those words in his mouth. Or even in his head.

My plan was to stare him down in Trigonometry. Bore a hole to his very soul with my laser-like vision. *Brilliant!* Or drop *La Note* itself in the aisle between our desks, ask him to pick it up for me, and see if he squirmed. Just because he could throw a forty-eight-yard pass under pressure didn't mean he stood a chance against a French Club fund-raiser.

Alas, I would have no such opportunity. He wasn't in class. Turns out, he wasn't at school at all—a major disappointment to at least a dozen girls, according to Lottie at lunch.

"He had ten *Notes d'Amour*," she said. "Ten. And I could sit here right now and name at least five girls who brought him candy."

"Mayhap he's diabetic," Collin offered, exceeding pleased with his humor, despite Lottie's glare.

"I'm just saying," she continued, speaking right over his soft laughter, "if you ever had a chance with him, it's over."

I choked on my fifty-cent cupcake, purchased from the band bake sale table. "What are you talking about? What chance?"

"Nothing. Only that it's been bandied about that he might have had a bit of a thing for you. Silly, I know."

"Yeah. Silly. So there's probably no chance he sent me a note."

"What note?"

"This." I handed it over, wishing it didn't look so worn. I mean, how many times a day could a little slip of pink paper be folded and unfolded?

"Hmmm. Bright eyes." She lowered her glasses and looked at me like a witness studying a lineup. "I suppose you do have really pretty eyes. The dark lashes help."

"Like an outline," Collin said. "A frame for the mirror of your soul."

"The eyes are the *window* to the soul," Lottie said with condescending patience.

"And I like how yours are magnified behind your glasses," Collin replied. "Like double-paned, to keep your soul warm." He seemed just as pleased with this as he had his earlier joke, though this was delivered with the solemn precision of a rehearsed compliment.

Lottie blinked exactly three times and sent him on a mission to find a center-piece brownie at the bake sale table.

"He's really very sweet," I said, watching him scuttle away. I turned back to Lottie when I knew he was out of earshot. "So, do you think Billy sent it?"

"Maybe." She examined the note from different angles, as if an answer would tumble out. "It could just as well be him as anybody. But let me just say this: it really doesn't matter if

Billy Fitz thinks you have bright eyes. There's very little chance that he'll ever see anything beyond them."

I'd just taken a bite of cupcake and wished beyond anything I could put it back.

"No," she continued as if I'd spoken, "I'm not talking about your weight. Honestly, that is something we are all going to have to accept and get over. We all have our flaws, and I must say you've made some admirable progress in overcoming yours. You're not any thinner, but you seem to be, well, embracing what you cannot change. Good for you."

"Thank you?" Because, really, what else was there to say?

"And if you can't land Billy Fitz as a boyfriend, it has nothing to do with your weight. Attractiveness is hardly the biggest hurdle for a boy to overcome. Look at Collin and me. We are neither of us an ideal. What matters is, we are each entire, whole people. You, Elyse, are a whole person, no matter what anybody thinks about your . . . eyes. Just let this go."

"So . . ." I busied myself folding my cupcake's paper wrapper, "for the record, you don't think Billy sent it?"

"*For the record*, I'm saying it doesn't matter who sent it if he's not strong enough to sign his name. And, for your own happiness, you need to stop wanting it to be Billy."

"But I have to know."

"No, my friend, you don't. If you're going to survive all of this, you have to stop caring so much. Try assuming it's from somebody whose love—or lack of it—won't break your heart."

There was only one other boy who fit that description.

Near the end of Spanish class, claiming an upset stomach after too much chocolate, I asked Señora Benavidez if I could be excused to *el baño, por favor*. It wasn't a total lie—there'd been a bit of churning all day. Still, I packed up my JanSport and took it with me, right past the girls' room, to the gym hallway, where Gage Wickam was on his way to basketball practice.

"Hey!" I called out, like we saw each other here every day.

"Hey," he said, looking startled. He moved toward me, cautiously, as if a trap was going to snap up from the purple floor tiles.

I waited until he was close enough to hear me without my voice echoing in the hall.

"Did you"—I stopped, feeling the ridiculous shortsightedness of my plan, then started again—"Did you by any chance send me something?"

"Something . . . like . . . what? Exactly?"

Stupid. "Um, a note? Like, one of those French Club notes? I got one, and it wasn't signed, and I just wondered . . ."

He looked more and more uncomfortable with each word, and I wanted to crawl into a locker and die. And that's just with what *I* said. His reply made me want to revive, come out, and go back to die again.

"Look, Elyse. I'm sorry. I didn't know you still had, like, feelings—"

"I don't—"

"Because, I've kinda moved on, you know? And it might be weird—"

"No, it's fine. It's good. I was just, like, narrowing down the possibilities . . ."

I backed away, banging into the lockers for added smoothness in the moment. Should have listened to Lottie. She was right. I should have let it go. But she was right about something else, too. My heart wasn't broken, not in the least. Sure, the moment was awkward, but I emerged from it just fine. Maybe the note was from the elusive Frank Churchill. Or Pete Pacheco. Or countless other boys at Northenfield. At this moment, Billy Fitz was a name tossed in among them. Not the only contender but, until I had empirical evidence otherwise, certainly the favorite.

tumult: *disorderly agitation : COMMOTION*

The parents worried their house would fall into tumult *when they went out of town for the weekend.*

OKAY, CONFESSION: I DIDN'T LET IT GO. Not at all, not even a little bit. I didn't exactly moon or mope, but my mind never stopped perseverating. I spent the evening with Mom, wandering around the grocery store, stocking up on frozen pizzas and cereal and canned spaghetti—all meant to keep us girls fed while the parents were away at play. The Valentine's Day candy was already slashed to half price, and I talked Mom into letting me toss a couple of battered heart-shaped boxes into the basket. She wasn't happy about it, telling me that too much chocolate might chase away a sweetheart, but I prevailed.

Jayne was out on a date with Charlie, so it fell to me to get the list of instructions and restrictions, most of which boiled down to keeping Lydia out of trouble and the Littles out of poison. We still didn't know the name of the lucky Junior High School boy who would be escorting my younger sister to the dance.

"I'm trying to maintain an air of mystery," Lydia said as she trailed sullenly behind us in the grocery store, mortified that she hadn't been allowed a date on this all-important evening. "But don't worry, he's somebody I know you'll approve of."

Perhaps it was the preoccupation with the idea of a few nights away in the big city, but Lydia's explanation satisfied Mom, and to date I'd only heard Dad mutter three sentences about the dance, all of them some variation of *How much will it cost?*

Meanwhile, I kept *La Note* wrapped around my subconscious. Questions filled my mind. I'd moved beyond *Who sent it?* to far more punishing queries, like, *What kind of person sends an anonymous love note?* And, *Why did I take Spanish instead of French?* Because then, I might have some real inside information. *What if the translator got it wrong, and it really was about my intelligence, and it came from a teacher?* I tried to picture Mrs. Pierson, all warm and smiley, drafting a quick message to her favorite student. Just, you know, to make her feel better.

But I didn't let myself wonder about Billy. Too cruel—on his part, for teasing my affection, and mine for entertaining a fantasy. Too close to forbidden heartbreak territory.

Because it was a special occasion, Jayne was allowed to stay out until ten o'clock—unheard of on a school night. Upstairs, when I heard the rumble of Charlie's car, I turned off my bedside lamp and stole a quick peek out of the window. Sad, yes. Pathetic? Maybe. But watching him get out of his car, walk around, open the passenger door, and extend his hand to Jayne—it made me such a believer in love. Even though they'd had so many weeks separated by silence, at least it was a silence they carried equally. Like, a common longing, and it brought them back stronger than before.

That was the problem with me and Billy. (*Me and Billy!*) We were too unbalanced. He liked me for a nanosecond. I liked him for all of time stretched back. He could speak; I couldn't. We both reached, but neither of us reached back.

Out on the sidewalk, Charlie could have been kissing Jayne. But he wasn't. They were facing each other, holding hands. The type of holding that couples do at weddings. She was wearing a long, white wool coat, he a black Members Only jacket, with the red carnation she'd bought for him tucked into the front pocket.

They're going to get married. I knew it, as much as I've ever known anything. Ever. Maybe not for years down the road, after college or whatever, but my head filled up with the idea.

I'd been listening to a tape—the soundtrack to *The Hobbit*, as a perfect accompaniment to my reading of *The Hobbit*. The final notes strained away as the tape clicked off. Popping the tape out of the player, I opened the case, but before putting the tape away, I scribbled a brief message in the liner notes.

February 14, 1985
Jayne is going to marry Charlie.

I wish I could have written the note in the book itself, but it was a library loan. Such an act of vandalism might mean a whopper of a fine. By the time Jayne came into our room, I'd stashed the tape on the shelf above my bed and had my nose innocently buried with Bilbo Baggins.

"Fun night?" I asked, moving my *Note d'Amour* to mark my place.

"Perfect," she said. Even in the shadows, her smile held a secret. At least, I'm sure she thought it did.

The next morning dawned and dropped us all into a swirl of confusion. Mom and Dad were up and out and headed south to San Antonio before the sign-off of the morning news. Jayne and I were left in charge of getting everybody up and ready for the day. For us and Lydia, that meant nothing unusual, but for the Littles? They were set to spend the day with another homeschool family who would be picking them up before we left for school. Unfortunately, a lifetime of homeschool with Mom meant the Littles had never been required to be up, out of bed, and dressed at any decent hour, ever. So there were tears and promises—on their part and ours. Lydia, furious at the idea of being late to school on *dance* day, was excused from the struggle and released to walk to school on time. Jayne and I stayed behind, shoving dead-weight little arms into jacket sleeves and sending our little sisters down the frozen sidewalk clutching day-after Valentine's treats in one hand and their shoes in the other.

So I was late to English, which was really okay, since that spared me from awkward idle chat with Gage. He was absent, probably in an attempt to avoid me. Weird, because I could have sworn I'd heard the rumble of his car outside our house when I was trying to stuff a Little into her coat.

Everything for the rest of the whole day was off. I took my Chemistry book to History, sat out in PE when I accidentally locked my dress-out clothes in someone else's locker. I spent the lunch hour in the library, frantically finishing my Spanish homework—a ten-point list of what would make *un novio perfecto* (a perfect boyfriend).

A sample:

Un corazón amable
Buenos pantalones vaqueros (cinco cero uno)
Ojos brillantes

True, I could have finished my Spanish homework in the cafeteria at our table, but that might put Billy Fitz in my line of vision, and it was bad enough that he took up all the space on my list.

Because I was in the library, I didn't hear the bell, and since I didn't hear the bell, I was running like a crazy girl to get to Trigonometry. Mr. Venzinni had come back from Christmas break a tardy slip machine. Must have been a New Year's Resolution or something. Any dream I had of a smooth, understated entrance was shattered because, in a weird trick of timing, I found myself one of two parties in a mid-doorway collision. The other person? None other than Billy Fitz. Like, we slammed through the doorway together, neither of us paying attention until we were wedged against each other, backpacks entangled.

"Sorry," I—*we*—said, to each other, without actually looking at each other. Which was too bad, considering we both have such bright eyes.

For the next twenty minutes I knew nothing beyond the formula on the board and the mad attempt to re-create it faithfully in my notes, because I knew I wouldn't remember a word of what Mr. Venzinni was saying. I barely heard the knock on the classroom door but did welcome the break from Mr. Venzinni's teaching when he went to open it. After a terse conversation with the person on the other side, he came back to my desk and dropped a folded note. Not just any note—something official. From the office, with the message to report to Attendance.

"At the end of class," Mr. Venzinni said. I swear, I could have been bleeding from my eyes and he wouldn't have excused me to the nurse's office until he'd finished his lecture.

The rest of the class was a blur. Several glances over to Billy showed him to be glancing at me, looking concerned. A note from the office could be anything—somebody found your textbook in the hallway, you were due for a vision test with the nurse. Family emergencies were handled with a bit more urgency, usually a call over the intercom to report to the office. This was Attendance. *Attendance?* Probably to do with my first period tardy.

When Mr. Venzinni announced that, in deference to yesterday's holy day of Love, and the extended weekend in honor of our former Presidents, there would be no homework, I raised my hand and asked to be excused. He checked the clock and nodded, and I gathered my book and notebook, shoved them into my JanSport, and left without a glance back. Keeping the note handy as my pass, I rushed through the empty halls and into the Attendance office, where Jayne was waiting behind the counter.

"What are you doing here?" An honest question, since she wasn't an aide until next period. Another moment of the day's wacky timing. "Is it my tardy to first period? Can you, like, fix that for me?"

It was like she didn't even hear me. "Lydia hasn't been at school all day."

It was so far from what I expected to hear, I couldn't come up with a response beyond, "Okay."

"We just got the attendance slips from the Junior High, and Mrs. Rocha called me down to ask, since I hadn't brought a note in for her."

Jayne looked sickly pale, and she was actually wringing her hands. I'd never seen anyone do that before. Then, a tiny, dark thought niggled at the base of my brain.

"Did Gage ever come to school today?"

"Let me ask Mrs. Rocha." She came back from a brief, whispered conversation, shaking her head so gravely her hair didn't move. Together, we silently assembled these two bits of information and formed a new, unsettling truth. "Do you think they're together somewhere?"

"What do you think?"

"I don't know," Jayne said, but her face betrayed her worry. "I only know she's not where she's supposed to be."

"So, what should we do?"

"Find her?" The quiver in Jayne's voice manifested in her chin, and her eyes sparkled with tears.

Ignoring all protocol, I strode through the little swinging gate and met Jayne behind the counter, gripping her hands in what I hope felt like reassurance.

"She's fine. In a massive amount of trouble, but fine."

"Even if she's with *him*?"

Him. Gage, and thinking back, I began to think this wasn't the first time Lydia'd had some secret such-n-such with my former maybe-boyfriend.

"She's fine," I repeated. "He's—nice?" But he was a High School boy, one who'd kissed me on our *first* date. And if whatever was happening between them was a date, then he might have kissed her already. "Besides, we don't even know for sure if they're together."

Mrs. Rocha kept one eye on us and clucked her tongue in a way that spoke great, silent judgment on the character of our younger sister.

The bell rang, not nearly as loud in the office as it sounded in the classrooms and halls.

"You'd better go," Jayne said. "We'll go looking for her right after school."

"Go where? How? Mom and Dad have the car, and we need to be home for the Littles."

"I don't know." She looked at Mrs. Rocha and lowered her voice. "If she is off . . . somewhere, with him. Oh, Pudge—people are going to think that she's . . . that they're . . ."

"Nobody's going to think anything," I said. But that wasn't true. Kids would talk, and Lydia would ride the wave of gossip all the way into High School.

"I'm really worried."

"I am too. But only because we don't know anything. She's not stupid. She'll be here after school to walk home with us. Or she'll be at home. She probably—I don't know. Went to the mall? Maybe someplace to get her hair done for the dance?" The more I spoke, the more it made sense, and a picture started to form in my head of Gage chauffeuring Lydia around town while she readied herself for her Night of Memories.

Jayne caught the same vision and seemed somewhat relieved. "Maybe. I'll head straight home after school—unless?" She looked over at Mrs. Rocha, her blue eyes china-doll wide. "Maybe I could leave now? Go home, to check on my sister?"

The second bell rang, signaling the beginning of class.

"Me, too?" I tried to affect the same expression of poignant desperation. Anything to get out of Spanish.

But it was made clear that the school wasn't about to allow all three Nebbitt sisters to run truant all over Northenfield, Texas. I was lucky to extract a tardy pass for last period.

I took the long way, though. Veering my path toward the gym, thinking that, no matter how powerful Lydia's wiles, Gage wouldn't miss out on basketball practice. With each step, my mind flitted over the past few months, like a music montage in the middle of a movie, underscored by "Careless Whisper" by Wham!

Lies. Deception.

Gage, earning honor society points by tutoring at the Junior High School; Lydia's English grade, skyrocketing.

The two of them, walking together to school. From school.

The Woodsman turned back to a Wolf.

Dad always says that the whole world started going to h.e.l.l. when the atheists and Democrats took prayer out of school. But Charlie told Jayne that the football players prayed in the locker room before every game, and there was always a group of kids with apple juice and Honey Buns gathered at the corner table in the cafeteria before first period. Plus, we had a minute of silence between the Pledge of Allegiance and the Pledge of Allegiance to Texas, so that was two times every day I acknowledged that I was here under the guidance and protection of God. But right then, in that empty hallway, my head filled with nightmares about my wayward sister, I felt so helpless and small. Like I was literally *under* him—a fleck of a girl he could—even should—disregard while he worked on bringing rain to Africa or something.

But despite this, I prayed. Prayed that my stupid sister would remember that she was really not stupid. Like, at all. Prayed that she was somewhere safe, just hanging out and waiting for Jayne and me to get home so she could tell us about her adventure in that way she has of making us feel like we are in the presence of greatness. Prayed that, if she was with Gage, she was with the boy who took me on my first date, and not this shadowy figure formed from secrets.

I didn't pray out loud, though I probably should have because, as it was, my mind kept jumbling my prayer with the lyrics of the George Michael song. *Guilty feet. Should've known better. Waste the chance. Never gonna dance again.* As in, she was absolutely *not* going to that dance tonight. I might have actually been humming the song—maybe singing softly, I don't know. The cloud that had settled over this day since its first hours completely enveloped me, and for the second time that afternoon, I collided with the increasingly present form of Billy Fitz. This time, though, there was no awkward untangling. I looked up, and everything this guy had told me about Gage came crashing to my consciousness.

"Hey," he said, one hand on my shoulder to steady me. "I was coming to find you. Is everything okay?"

Hey. And I immediately knew he could help.

"It's my sister."

"Jayne?"

"My younger sister. Lydia?"

His face grew more concerned. Totally worried. "What's wrong?"

"She's—she hasn't been in school all day. Skipped, because she left for school this morning. And we're—Jayne and me—worried that she might be with someone."

"Like, one of her friends?"

"No. Like, Gage."

"Wickam?" His eyes darkened. Another one of those moments where you get to see what you read about all the time. I've always wondered how that works. How can somebody's eyes get darker? But they did. Maybe because they got narrow. Smaller, condensing the color. But the soft brown turned to something deeper, and I immediately knew I had a very real reason to be freaked out.

"Have you seen Wickam today?"

I shook my head. "He wasn't in first period, and Jayne says he's been marked absent in every class. All day. I mean, I know we joke about how my little sister acts like a twenty-five-year-old man magnet, but she's just a kid. I don't think she realizes, exactly, how older boys might—"

"That creep." Billy's nostrils flared (Yes! I know! Like in the books!), and I had this very real tingle from being in the presence of power. "I'll find him. We can go right now and look—"

"I have to go to class. Then home. Right after school, to take care of the—my littlest sisters. Plus, I'm sure Lydia won't be silly enough to stay out later than that."

"I'll ask around here. See if anybody knows anything—"

"Don't." I reached out, touching the sleeve of his letter jacket. "I'd just rather not a lot of people know—you know?"

"I get it." And I ~~loved~~ liked the fact that I didn't have to explain.

Then, I said the six saddest words of my life: "I have to go to Spanish."

"Can I call you? I mean, if I find out anything?"

"Yes, please." We stood for just another moment, and then I waved my tardy pass. "Gotta go."

"Yeah." We took a few steps before he said, "Hey, Elyse?"

I turned back. "Yeah?"

"If it turns out Wickam has done anything to hurt your sister, I'll probably pound his face. Is that going to be okay with you?"

"That'll work. Just not if Lydia's there. She throws up at the sight of blood."

Billy laughed. I did too, and it felt good. Probably made my eyes really, really bright.

surmise: *to form a notion of from scanty evidence :*
IMAGINE, INFER

Seeing her sister's tears, Elyse could only surmise *that*
something horrible had happened that afternoon.

"He's ruined me!"

For a full five minutes, those were the only words Lydia seemed capable of saying as she sobbed uncontrollably, face-down on her bed. That's where Jayne and I had found her when we came rushing through the front door. We'd waited for fifteen minutes at the Tree, and when she wasn't a part of the giggling throng of Junior High School students exiting the school, we practically ran all the way home.

"Ruined you, how, exactly?" I was perched on the side of her bed while Jayne stood by, arms folded, fingers tapping. "Did Gage . . . *do* anything?"

Lydia might be young, and Jayne might be sweet, but we all knew I was asking about a very particular three-letter word in that moment.

I was torn between wishing *very much* that our mother was there, and being very, very glad she wasn't. Honestly, I don't know how helpful she would have been since she—and *for sure* our father—had never said a single word to any of us about sex. Even when Mom said, Be careful! whenever Jayne and

Charlie left for a date, she meant the kind of careful associated with driving the speed limit and Just Saying No if someone offered up a beer at a party. Definitely not the same kind of *Be Careful* admonition we got in Health class with graphic slide-shows about pregnancy and disease. We didn't learn about sex at home, we didn't talk about sex in church, and we couldn't avoid learning or talking about it in school. Even poor Mrs. Pierson had to stammer through what just might be happening on those moors in *Wuthering Heights*. A few years ago there was a commercial on TV where Brooke Shields was reading the last line of *Great Expectations* and saying something like, "Reading is to the mind what Calvin Klein jeans are to the body," and even though I was younger than Lydia, I remember thinking, *What does Charles Dickens have to do with tight-fitting jeans?* (Plus, it gave away the ending of *Great Expectations*, but I might be the only person to worry about that.) Then she came out with another ad where she says, "Nothing comes between me and my Calvins," and the whole world finally caught on to what teenagers had known forever. We all know about, talk about, joke about, and wonder about sex. Rich and poor, good church kids and good non-church kids. Nerds and jocks. Popular and not.

But just because sex was, literally, *everywhere*, that didn't give it a place in our shabby little corner of Northenfield, Texas. None of us girls had taken any kind of a pledge or anything—*I pledge allegiance to my virginity, and to the virtue for which it stands.* But we—at least Jayne and I—had a clear understanding of what breaking such a pledge would mean. Breaking it would be a disappointment to Mom and Dad, a sin against God, and the risk of succumbing to all those Health Class warnings. Even more, there was the hallway stigma of whispers and snickers. The things boys said. Even worse, the things *girls* said. What everybody assumed. And if Lydia and Gage did *do* anything, well, everybody would be saying and assuming all the same things about Jayne and me, too.

"Lydia?" I prompted, feeling all of our reputations hanging on her response.

Lydia popped up her tearstained face, curls matted to her cheeks. "Don't be stupid. We didn't *do* anything. I'm not—I'd never, and he wouldn't either."

"Oh, thank you, God," Jayne said, looking like some woman from a TV church.

"So, where were you all day?"

She twisted her body and sat up, making room for Jayne to sit on the other side of her. "At the mall. And around."

"Around . . ." Jayne and I chorused.

"Okay, I, like, told everybody I was going to go to the dance tonight with a High School boy. Gage said he'd take me."

"Wait," I interrupted. "What about all those boys who were on some kind of waiting list to take you?"

"Boys my age are just so"—she searched her room, as if she might find the right answer on one of the *Tiger Beat* magazine photos pinned to her wall—"ridiculous."

"You can't take a High School boy to a Junior High dance," Jayne said, sounding official enough to write the rules for everything.

"I know." Lydia sniffed; Jayne and I looked at each other, perplexed.

"You *know*?"

"I told him I had this great plan, like he did for Neewollah."

Ah, yes. The Wolf-turned-Woodsman. "So what was your plan?"

"My plan was to wear a fabulous dress, get my hair done, and my makeup. At Sweet's Salon. And for him to be in a tuxedo. *Rented.*" She said the last word like he was going to be renting it from the back of some guy's Volkswagen.

"Wait a minute," Jayne piped up. "I thought you were going to wear one of my dresses. Where are you getting the money for all of this stuff?"

"I've had the dress on layaway at Bealls forever—practically since we moved here. Because I knew there'd be *sometime* to need it. And I got my hair and makeup done for free at Sweets, as long as I told everybody that's where I got it done and convinced at least ten High School girls to get theirs done there too."

This is where I took a longer, closer look at my little sister's face, and it became clear that the makeup now smeared from a tragic collision of pillow and tears had once been a very intricate, frosty masque of perfection. A few pins remained in the complicated updo of her normally cascading curls. Much as I hated to admit it, Lydia was kind of a Machiavellian Genius of Manipulation and Beauty.

"Anyway," she continued, "I was going to show up to the dance, looking fabulous, with my handsome High School boy in a tuxedo. Let everybody see me and get all jealous, you know? Then, when the chaperones wouldn't let him in, I'd be all pouty and sad. Beautiful and alone."

"Why would you want to be alone?" Jayne asked, because she still believed in the fundamental goodness of the human heart. Even Lydia's. I, however, knew better.

Lydia looked at her the way I sometimes do when I'm helping the Littles with their homeschool worksheets. "Because then, silly, I could be, like, *everybody's* date. At the dance, at least. But Gage would still be honor bound to bring me home. After."

"So," I ventured, "he would just, what? Wait outside in the parking lot? Go to Denny's and hang out with the moms and dads?"

Lydia shrugged. "I don't know. What do I care?"

"So . . ." this time it was Jayne. "What happened?"

"Gaaaage." She stretched his name along four notes of disappointment. "We had this all planned—well, the part he knew. But then it turned out he didn't have enough money to get a tuxedo. And I said, 'Fine. Wear a suit, like all the other boys.' Then, I think he sort of figured it out, because I wasn't all that upset. He said he wasn't going to take me at all—that he wouldn't waste his Friday night on a girl like me. And now I can't even *go!*"

She wailed and threw herself facedown on the bed again, nearly knocking Jayne to the floor in the process.

"You wouldn't be able to go anyway," Jayne said, her voice stronger now that the danger seemed to be clear. "After skipping school all day? Mom and Dad are going to ground you forever."

A wary, smudgy eye peeped from the pillow. "You're going to tell them?"

"Of course we're going to tell them!" But when she looked to me for solidarity, I must not have looked convinced. "Aren't we?"

I shrugged. "Well, no harm done, right? I mean, not really."

"Right!" Lydia was somehow, somewhat healed from her despondency.

"And no need to say anything at all until they get home. We don't want to ruin their weekend away. But the minute they get back"—I gave Lydia my sternest look—"we're going to sit them down and tell them everything."

Jayne looked ready to jump in, but the sound of the front door opening and the clattering of the Littles' feet commanded her attention. She left the room to greet them, leaving me alone with the girl who would probably marry a shifty senator and become coleader of this free, corrupted world.

"That was a totally crappy thing you were going to do to Gage," I said. As much as I might have misgivings about his character, nobody deserved that level of disregard.

"I know, but I was going to make it up to him."

"How?" I tried not to sound suspicious, but must have failed, because she rolled her eyes at me like I was a paranoid parent or something.

"Nothing *bad*. Just a movie sometime. He's not so bad, you know."

"He's a Sophomore. In High School. He's sixteen. So it really doesn't matter if he's *so bad* or not. You know you can't date him."

She pouted. "I know. But, maybe next year? When I'm in High School?"

"Next year is next year. For now—wait." A horrible thought seized me, and it involved Billy Fitz's fist and Gage Wickam's face. "Where is Gage now?"

"Home, I guess. He brought me here because I didn't want any of the kids at school to see me before tonight. Then, well, *everything*. And he left."

The phone rang at that moment, and I was in the hallway with my hand on the receiver even before Jayne hollered up could I get it, because she was making the Littles' snacks. It had to be Billy, and I could only hope I wasn't too late to stop him from inflicting pain.

"Hello?"

"Can I talk to Elyse Nebbitt, please?"

I exhaled. It wasn't him. The voice on the other end was impatient and unfamiliar.

"This is she."

"Hello, Elyse. This is Katie Berg." As in Katie Berg, Prom Committee.

"Oh, you must want Jayne. I'll get her—"

"No, I don't want Jayne, or else I would have *asked* for Jayne. I need to talk to *you*."

"Okay." I sat down in the chair next to the telephone table, took a nubby pencil from the cracked coffee cup stuffed with old pens and the family thermometer, and found the back of an envelope with a bit of clean space on it. Certainly a Katie Berg conversation required a few notes.

"Well," she started, "you might be tempted to tell me this is none of my business, but since it's about Prom, everything is my business. Even this."

"Even . . . what?"

"Well, again, I'm hoping this is just a rumor. Like, a sad, silly rumor, but I have to know. Are you going to Prom with Billy Fitz?"

The shock of it, the very *idea*, made me glad I was sitting down, because my entire body filled with something like frozen fog. I could barely keep my grip on the phone.

"Am I . . . *what?*"

"It's all very unofficial on our end. Just some conversations we overheard that he likes you." She said it as if announcing the discovery of a new and dubious amphibious species. "Then, we know he gave you a note once, sent you an anonymous French Club Valentine, and was seen talking with you—*intimately*—during eighth period today."

Katie Berg listed each social infraction with the conviction and precision of a TV detective. The evidence added up. I was charged with a circumstantial case of Prom Date Inequality.

Of course, all I cared about was the next-to-last accusation.

"So, he *did* send it." I didn't even try to keep the triumph out of my voice.

"Answer my question." Katie would not indulge my victory. "Are you going to Prom with Billy Fitz? Did he ask you?"

"How, again, exactly, is this your affair?"

"First, I need to know if there *is* an affair."

"Why?"

"Because it can't happen."

"What can't happen?"

"You can't go to Prom with Billy Fitz."

Funny how, just a few months or minutes ago, that would have been the most obvious statement in the English language. Of course I wasn't going, and he hadn't asked me, so the idea itself remained in the Land of Ludicrous. But it was fun listening to her protests. I'd never been accused of anything quite so wonderful before.

"Why can't I? I paid my activity fee, just like everybody else. I'm a student in good standing."

"You're a Sophomore."

"Sophomores can go."

"Only with a Junior."

"Billy's a Junior."

"And you're—look, I don't want to hurt your feelings or anything." *Duly noted.* "But Billy is probably going to be named Prom King this year."

"Is he? He hasn't said a word to me about it. Not in any of our intimate conversations."

She plowed on. "We like it if the King and Queen are each other's dates. For the inaugural dance, and the Yearbook Picture, and . . . everything."

"Oh, I know I can't be Queen. Since I'm—as you say—a *Sophomore.* But I'd be more than happy to share my date with the Queen. One dance, one picture."

"Stop it! Stop acting like—like, this is *happening.* Look, no offense or whatever, but if anything, you're some charity case so that his best friend's girlfriend will have somebody to talk to."

So, yeah. Not offensive at all.

"You see?" Now her voice had taken on a tone that she probably thought sounded like comfort. "You deserve better than that. You deserve a date who is more your . . . style? Because you're somewhat brainy, right? I could introduce you to some boys in National Honor Society, and maybe next year—"

"Now *you* stop it!" My voice was loud enough, my emotion strong enough, to bring Lydia's moppy head poking out of her room, and Jayne's concerned face to the top of the stairway. "It's not up to you—or any sort of *committee*—to decide who I go to the Prom with, if I decide that I'm going to go at all. It's months away, for Pete's sake."

"But there's a lot of planning to do. A social order of things—"

"And I am quite capable of making my *own* plans. And following my own social order. Or, better yet, showing the social order to be absolutely insane. Crazy with stupidity."

"*Pssst!*" Jayne hissed at me from the stairs. "You should—"

But whatever route of graceful protocol my sister would urge me toward mattered little in the midst of my battle against this insult. "I don't know why people like you think you can talk to people like me—wait! I don't even know why I'm even considered a different type of *people*."

"I know it might not seem like it," she said, now sounding more irritated than compassionate, "but I really am speaking for your own good. You need to know when you're out of your league."

"*Pudge!*" Now Jayne was at my side, hissing into my ear, but I was too entrenched in the conversation with Katie-Social-Nazi-Berg to worry about the level of my voice, or the hatefulness of my words, or the fact that the Littles were probably huddled downstairs, wondering why their big sister was screaming into the phone. I turned my back, making a quick note to yell at Jayne for speaking the nickname close enough to the phone that my newest (and so far, only) archenemy could someday use it against me. Like, have it printed on my actual Prom Ticket, should I choose to go. Should I be asked. By anybody.

"Listen to me, *Katie Berg*. If I want to go to Prom with Billy Fitz, I'll go to Prom with Billy Fitz. Maybe he'll ask me, maybe I'll ask him. Or maybe not. On either score. But hear this—if I *don't* go to Prom with Billy Fitz, it won't be because you, or your cronies, or your outdated sense of sensible coupling had any part of the decision. If I don't go to Prom with Billy Fitz, it's because I don't want to. Because I never did want to, and never intended to, and probably wouldn't go just to have the opportunity to stand tall in my opinion. Do you understand?"

"So . . ." I could hear Katie's wheels turning like a Spirograph, "you're *not* going?"

I hung up.

"Elyse?" Jayne seemed much less flustered now. Calm, and kind of smirky.

"What?"

"There's someone downstairs waiting to see you."

And that someone, according to a peek down the stairs, was Billy Fitz.

forbearance: *the capacity to endure what is difficult or disagreeable without complaining*

With great **forbearance,** *Elyse kept a smile on her face as her sisters went to the dance, leaving her behind.*

"OH, HEY, BILLY." Because what else could I say to the not-so-smirky face looking up at me over the bannister? Never before have I been so grateful to have a dozen steps to take—slowly, so I wouldn't fall on my face—before starting a conversation. By the time I got to the bottom, I was doubly glad to have had the time to compose myself, because not only was Billy Fitz standing in our entryway, he was wearing a suit. Dark—black wool, with a silvery-gray shirt and impressively silky tie. Wait, not a suit. A tuxedo, creating a whole new category of clothing Billy Fitz looks good in.

Breathe. Breathe, and pretend the last ninety seconds never happened.

"What are you doing here?"

"I found Wickam," he said, stepping back as I descended. He kept his head cocked, studying me like I'd just sprung a new head. "He explained everything."

"Good." He looked like such a lovely, fancy thing standing in the middle of the shabbiness of our house. And with the franticness of this afternoon, and who knows what all Gage had told him—he must think we were the biggest mess of a family in Northenfield. "I mean, I don't know what Lydia must have been thinking."

"She's something," he said, sounding positively indulgent.

"So, I mean—why . . . Why are you here? Looking so spiffy?"

Spiffy. When no other word will do.

"Well," he actually looked a little awkward. Nervous, even. "With your permission, and yours, too, Jayne—I'm here to take Lydia to the dance."

I couldn't help it. My cheeks flushed, and Jayne, newly arrived behind me, made the same sound she'd make if a little puppy were to suddenly stick its sleepy head out of his pocket.

"Are you nuts?" I asked, somehow missing the cute factor.

"Probably," he said, and then hit me with that sideways grin he has that makes me forget I have bones. "But apparently she's told *everybody* that she was going to this thing with a guy from the High School. She's a lot better off with me than with him."

"You know she's in eighth grade, right?" I asked in a tone that implied a question about his intentions.

"I'm there to be an escort, nothing more. Like, an uncle or something."

No uncle ever looked like Billy Fitz. But, whatever.

"That's the sweetest thing I've ever heard," Jayne said, now speaking from behind clasped hands.

"Between you and me," Billy said, dropping his voice, making Jayne and me both lean in a little closer. Well, me, more than a little. "I don't think Gage ever really intended to follow through. Just was leading her on, getting some kind of thrill from spending time with her right under our noses."

Our noses. The thought produced an image of our noses touched together. What one might call canoodling.

"What a creep," Jayne said.

"Maybe," Billy conceded, "but I don't think any real harm was done. Anyway, I'd like to do what I can to help save your sister's reputation."

"Her reputation?" I asked, worried that he knew something I didn't.

"It's a small town, in case you haven't noticed." That smile, again. "If the kids in that school see her as some kind of a liar, it'll haunt her. Gage knows that, and I think he was ready to let her suffer with it. I don't think we should."

We. I turned to Jayne. "What do you think?"

"I think it's a very kind and generous gesture. But that doesn't change the fact that you're a High School student. They won't let you in."

"Oh, please." I knew Billy was probably too modest to voice what I was about to say. "Look at him. He's Billy Fitz. She'll be the firstborn daughter of the entire eighth grade."

Billy himself bowed with self-effacing humility. "That's what I kind of figured."

"But do you think it's right for her to be rewarded for such a mean-spirited scheme?"

"No," I said. "It's not right. Or fair. But sometimes life isn't right or fair. Think about her having to face all those kids next week. She's a monster, but . . ."

"She's not a monster," Billy said softly. "She's a kid. Now, this thing starts at six, and I don't want to be so fashionably late that nobody sees us walk in. So, why don't you go tell her to get ready?"

Jayne offered up one last avenue of reason. "Mom and Dad would never approve."

"She would if you went with them. Junior chaperones."

"I thought of that," Billy said, stepping back to the door and pulling the curtain aside to reveal a familiar blond head in the passenger seat of his Camaro. "I have Charlie with me. I thought Lydia and I could double with him and Jayne. For the ride there and back, anyway. I remember what you said about her not being able to ride in a car with a High School boy."

He winked, for the benefit of all.

"What about during the event?" I asked. "Are they just going to sit in the parking lot and make out?"

"*Elyse!*" Jayne looked delightfully mortified.

"Whatever they want. Just have the car back to the school by ten."

"And home by ten thirty," I chided with a wagging finger. "No after-dance Denny's for you."

"Right." Jayne said. "But what about the Littles?"

I sighed. "I guess that makes me babysitter for the night. Now, go tell Lydia she has exactly fifteen minutes to make herself beautiful."

It took less than ten. Probably because Lydia began the primping process the moment she heard Uncle Billy's proposal. Still, that meant a not-so-insignificant amount of time to entertain our guest. *Guests*, that is, once Charlie was invited in from the cold to wait with us. As I was the only grown-up girl in the house with no reason to crowd the bathroom mirror and curling iron, I invited them into the living room, shooed the Littles off the sofa and closer to the TV, and turned down the volume on the evening rerun of *I Dream of Jeannie*.

"So," I said, just in case we needed a repetition of the obvious, "this really is nice of you."

"I am capable of being nice on occasion."

"It's a much more civilized approach than just punching Gage in the nose, I guess. I mean—you didn't punch him, did you?"

"Tempting, but no. Don't get freaked out, but I think those two might just be made for each other."

I gave a mock shudder and watched a pillar of pink smoke dance around on the television screen. My sisters were entranced.

Apparently, so was Charlie, but not by anything on the screen. The moment his face lit up, I knew Jayne had walked into the room. I turned, following his gaze, and was right. She looked beautiful, as always. Her hair fluffed, makeup touched up, fresh gloss on her lips. She wore the same jeans as earlier but had changed into a black sweater with a slight puff at the top of the sleeves. She lifted her arm in a total car show model pose and announced, "Here she is!"

There she was, indeed. Lydia, creating enough of a vision to capture the attention of everyone in the room. Even the Littles, who scrambled to their feet and made gleeful sounds, as if a doll had come to life.

Her dress was a deep rose color, with a sweetheart neckline and huge puffy sleeves. The perfect number of curls fell across her shoulder, and her makeup had achieved a new perfection. No one would believe she'd been a sobbing, soggy mess half an hour before.

Perhaps spurred by the Littles' reaction, we all stood, the jaunty theme music of sixties television filling in the background. Billy walked straight to Lydia, took her hand, and kissed it, inventing the persona of the Gentleman Quarterback.

"You look lovely," he said, in the single most gallant moment our home has ever hosted.

Lydia covered her mouth with her free hand and giggled in gratitude.

Then, in a moment I think went unnoticed in the room, Billy looked right at me. He wasn't doing this for Lydia—not to save her reputation or to heal her feelings. He wasn't trying to rub Gage's face in his misguided courtship. He was doing this for me. For my sister, because I loved her.

And because of that, I loved him. So much, my heart hurt. Like, an icy grip squeezed around it, ready to split it in two. Half that would survive if he ever loved me back, and half that would die after this moment.

Jayne beckoned me back to life with the instruction to "Get a picture!"

"My camera's upstairs," I said, weaving my way through the tableau of beauty assembled at the foot of the stairs. Once in my room, I went to my desk and found my camera in the top drawer, with three flashes left on the bar. I breathed deep, deep, deep, and allowed myself a quick check in the mirror before going back down. Hair half-in, half-out of scrunchie. Face, pale. Jeans, cute. Black-and-pink gingham blouse, perfectly fine, if a bit wrinkly.

Eyes, brilliant.

"I have six pictures left on my film," I announced on my way downstairs, "but only three flashes, so we have to get this right."

At Jayne's direction, we took one picture of Billy and Lydia, to be shown to Mom and Dad sometime in the 1990s. Then, one of Jayne and Charlie, and then the two couples—out for the night in the Junior High gym.

"That's it," I said in the fading of the final burst of light. "Have fun, kids."

amends: *compensation for a loss or injury : RECOMPENSE*

A love song, a sip of Sprite, a moonlit drive, and Elyse was ready to make amends.

THE LITTLES AND I HAD FUN TOO. Hot dogs and macaroni and cheese for dinner, ginger ale added to the Kool-Aid for extra zip. While brownies baked in the oven, we played Candy Land, then Sorry! Then, Old Maid. I tried to stretch each game into an hour, to fill the evening, but by nine o'clock the girls were tired, whiny, and cranky, so I let them skip their bath and read *The Secret Garden* with them in my parents' bed until they fell asleep.

When Mom and Dad called to check in, I told them as much truth as I could. That the Littles were asleep after an evening of minimal TV, and Jayne and Charlie drove Lydia to the dance, and I was fine. Really, really fine. And not upset about anything at all.

I went into my room and, out of habit, shut the door, even though I was essentially the only one home. It was almost ten o'clock, and for the first time that evening I had nothing to distract me from thinking about the Junior High School's Night of Memories. Or Billy. Everything I knew about him, everything about what he thought or didn't think, felt or didn't feel—all of it clumped together in my head. Like a nest, and I couldn't decide which twig to take out first.

The silence made me crazy, but I didn't want to be the girl sitting in front of the glowing TV when all the others got home. I'd listened to all my tapes a million times and needed the spontaneity of the radio. Our most local station played dedications on Friday nights, which meant one love song after another. Punishment upon punishment. Salt in the wounds.

So, you know. Perfect.

But the song that was currently playing—Culture Club's "I'll Tumble 4 Ya"—was fun and upbeat.

I hummed along, dancing a little, kicking off my shoes, and found a pair of sweatpants and sweatshirt as the song faded out, when the DJ's voice came on again, all Friday-night smooth.

"And now, something special from a boy named Bill to a certain bright-eyed girl."

Bill. Bright-eyed girl.

"With a special request to play it at ten o'clock. Sharp."

I dropped my sweatpants and turned up the radio. Wishing there was some way to hear it again. Verify it, so I'd know it wasn't just my crazy, twiggy brain. Sometimes the DJ had a whole story to tell. A message, or a letter, and I waited to hear—

But nothing. Just the opening notes of something familiar. Something beautiful, and I sank down to the floor, grabbing my sweatpants again, because I needed something to clutch.

Stuck on you
I've got this feeling down deep in my soul
That I just can't lose . . .

Lionel Richie's voice filled my empty room like a warm, comforting breeze. I clung to each word, getting carried away with each lyric. One phrase repeated itself.

Guess I'm on my way.

I didn't move. Not an inch. Not a breath, until the final line trailed off into a commercial for a local hardware store.

I looked at the clock. He was on his way. At this very moment. And I wasn't about to be wearing sweatpants. I jumped up, yanked the scrunchie from my hair, and ran to the armoire.

"Something, something something . . ." Something he hadn't seen before. Something cute. Something that would make him glad I'd heard the song. Glad I stayed.

My fingers found something soft. Fuzzy. I pulled out a long, lapis-blue sweater. Angora, according to Lydia, fished out of a bargain pile at Joske's. Marked down to almost nothing, then an extra ten percent taken off because of one missing button and a rip in the lining. I remember her carrying it to the counter like an Olympic torch, then handing it to me since it was way too big for her.

I checked the clock, then ripped off my current shirt. Before putting on the sweater, I bent at the waist, brushing my hair from the root, then flipping up to witness its soft fall into place. Well, most of it. I squirted a dab of mousse into my palm and ran it through the curls, twisting and scrunching, until I'd created—*something*.

Another commercial on the radio, then another love story, then another love song. I spritzed myself with Gloria Vanderbilt perfume, smoothed the front of my Gloria Vanderbilt jeans, and pulled the sweater over my head. Mascara, lip gloss, a touch of blush, and then the familiar rumble of a Camaro.

"How did it go?" I practiced out loud, studying myself from all angles. "How was it? Did you have fun? Did you have a good time?"

Shoes? No shoes?

The front door opened.

No shoes.

The front door closed, and within seconds, I was running into Lydia on the stairs.

"How was it? How did it go? Did you have fun?" Three more unnecessary questions have never been spoken. Lydia was glowing. Beyond smiling—the joy of an evening rose from her very flesh, like an aura.

"Perfect. I danced with every boy there. At least once, some twice, while the girls lined up to dance with *my* date."

"Well," I said, not knowing how to respond to such a run-down. "Looks like a happy ending for you, at least."

"Looks like you're wanting one of your own," she said, looking at me from the top of my curls to the tips of my toes. "It's about time you wore that sweater. Now, if you'll excuse me, I have about a chapter to write in my diary."

She shouldered past me, and four steps down, Jayne waited, smiling in some sort of triumph.

"Did you already drop Charlie-boy home?"

"We did."

"So." I fiddled with the hem of my sweater. "I guess Billy went home too?"

Jayne shook her head. "He walked Lydia to the door and told me to tell you—to ask you, I guess—if you'd be okay to talk to him for a little bit."

"Oh."

"Are you? Or should I tell him to—"

"No, I'm good." I moved down, she moved up, and for a moment we were on the same step.

"I'm going to be upstairs, in our room. Door closed. And I'll make sure Lydia stays upstairs too."

I clutched the banister. "Jayne, what if—"

"Don't make me push you down the stairs. Go."

I opened the door to find Billy, hands thrust deep into his pockets. Tie loose, jacket open, hair and face perfect.

"Hey," I said. Because, as we have established, I am brilliant.

"Hey."

"Do you want to come in?"

"Actually, I was wondering if you'd come out. Maybe go for a drive? Get something to eat?"

"It's almost ten thirty." Again, the brilliance.

"I missed dinner."

"My parents aren't here."

"Which means they aren't here to say no."

He looked up over my head, and I turned to see Jayne, in complete violation of her promise to lock herself in our room, standing with my loafers and coat.

"Midnight," she said. "Now, go."

I slipped into my shoes, thankful Jayne hadn't brought anything that required me to bend over to tie or buckle, but opted to hold my coat. It was big and puffy and noisy, and holding it gave me something to do with my hands. Moving like I was under some alien power, I followed Billy out to his car, where he opened the passenger door for me, saying, "Here you go," as I slid into the seat.

He brought the car to roaring life and flooded it with soft light from the dashboard.

"You cold?" He moved the lever to turn on the heat before I could answer.

Warm air blew on my feet, and I smoothed my coat over my lap. I wished I'd been brave enough to imagine this moment for myself, because then I might have rehearsed something to say. Muscle car trivia, perhaps. All of the obvious topics—questions about the dance, observations on the chill of the night—seemed too banal for consideration. Oddly enough, the silence didn't feel uncomfortable. We'd spent countless hours (quick calculation: 167) in silence next to each other in Trigonometry. It wasn't the lack of conversation that made the moment squirmy, it was the swelling music. Something about love lifting us up where we belong.

Billy glanced over, and I swear there were a million eagles flying between us.

"Friday night dedications," I said. Cautiously, in case it wasn't him, after all.

"Were you listening?" he asked. "Earlier?"

I nodded, very casually, while somewhere near the base of my spine, an explosion of paralyzing joy threatened to send me into seizures. "I never picked you for a Lionel Richie guy."

"Yeah? Well"—he put the car in gear—"I'm a man of many surprises."

A three-word conversation brought us to the drive-through at Wendy's. Caroline Bingley would have been appalled at the blatant disregard of the *no food in the car rule* as we left the drive-through window. Cheeseburger and chocolate shake for him, a Sprite for me. That's what Mom always gave us when we had an upset stomach.

The burger stayed untouched in the bag while Billy expertly drove us back out onto the street with one hand.

"Thank you," I said after swallowing the first sweet, fizzy sip. "I mean, for everything tonight. I hope Lydia wasn't too . . . *Lydia.*"

"She's something." He spoke around his straw. "Sweet kid, though. Those poor guys don't stand a chance."

"I have a feeling they'll be willing victims."

He chuckled. "Where do you want to go?"

"Nowhere. I mean, wherever. Whatever." *Sprite. Sprite. Sprite.*

We drove, slow and purposeful, down Northenfield's main

street, in full view of every other High School student out for a cruise. I wondered if Katie Berg was out there, somewhere. In a nondescript Toyota parked at Sonic or something. If tomorrow morning she'd get a flood of phone calls about the latest sighting of Billy Fitz and Elyse Nebbitt cozied up by the dashboard light.

"So, earlier?" I ventured, because it had to be mentioned at some point. "Before you came to pick Lydia up? I got the weirdest phone call."

"I heard." He stopped at a red light, setting the engine to purring. "I mean, I literally heard your side of the conversation. What was that?"

"Some insane rumor that we're going to Prom together. I just want you to know, I didn't start it. I have no idea—"

The light turned green and we roared forward.

"That *is* crazy."

Remember that half of my heart? It began this long, slow crawl to death.

"I mean"—he took an endless sip of his shake—"we aren't even going out. We should do that for a while first. Right?"

He kept driving, one-handed, as if the entire world hadn't tilted on its edge. Like, I know the *earth* is round, but the *world*? It's shapeless and spreads out in all directions. All the days we've lived, and all the ones we're going to, with surprises on the side.

"Elyse?"

Thus I realized his question was not rhetorical.

"I—I suppose so."

He clamped his lips shut, signaled, and changed lanes, ready to turn left. Toward home.

Neither of us said another word. Billy had turned down the radio when he was ordering his food, so the current song was almost too faint to be heard. But I knew it. Another Billy—Billy Idol, "Eyes without a Face." *Les yeux sans visage.*

"I hate this song," he said. "Do you mind?" And then before I said anything, he popped in a cassette tape, filling the car with something rich and heavy. The Pretenders. Perfect.

"I love her voice." Because it was true, and I had to say something.

Billy felt no such compulsion. The five-minute drive to Wendy's turned out to be a 972-hour drive home. He brought his car to a stop in front of our house, switched off the lights, and then the engine. Instantly the car took on a new chill.

He put his cup on the dashboard and tossed the burger into the back seat. "I'll walk you to your door."

I sat in the brief dome light as his door opened, then took advantage of the few seconds of darkness after it closed to take one deep breath after another.

It seemed like he—

It sounded like he—

But then I—

Had I learned nothing?

The light came on and he was offering me his hand. Mine was cold and damp from holding my drink, for which I apologized.

"It's fine," he said.

Once I was standing, he took my drink and my coat, somehow managing to drape the latter over my shoulders without spilling a drop of the former.

"Warm enough?"

I nodded, and when I did, my chin touched his hand where he was clutching the collar of my coat.

He dropped his grip, then turned toward the front porch. I took the first step, and he followed. Well, not quite *followed*. He was beside me, his hand on the small of my back. I mean, I think it was. Between the jeans and the sweater and the maddening fluffiness of my coat it was hard to tell. All I know is that I felt like I was being *steered* into my own house. I guess I was the one who was following.

We climbed the steps, and there the front door loomed. If I opened it, this night would be over. And I didn't want it to end.

"Jayne's still up," I said, glancing around his shoulder toward the silver-lit window. "Probably watching *Friday Night Videos*. Would you want to"—*deep breath*—"come in and watch?"

"No thanks."

"Because you could bring your burger, and we probably have chips, or something."

"I don't want to watch *Friday Night Videos* with you and Jayne."

"Oh." Suddenly our doorknob was the most fascinating thing on the planet. I reached for it, ready to say good night, but he caught my hand. His, still, somehow warm. Mine still icy, so I was glad he held it all the way over to the Joggling Board, where he sat, then scooted, making a place for me. Then let it go.

"Look." He put the cup on the porch at his feet. "I know I wasn't always the greatest guy—"

"You are." I turned to face him and somehow joggled us a little closer. "What you did tonight? For Lydia, that was—"

"I didn't do it for Lydia. I did it for you."

Another confirmation, and while up to now, everything he said made me feel alternately flippy and breathless, this brought everything into a state of perfect rhythm. My breath, my heart, my thoughts—all in a steady pace. For the first time, there was balance between what I wanted and what I knew to be true. All questions, answered.

Billy, intrigued by the physics, joggled the board, scooching me closer. I smiled, and joggled too, and then our knees were almost touching.

"That time back?" Billy said, "At Charlie's? I screwed everything up. Said everything wrong, obviously. I should have just said that you are the single most interesting, captivating girl I have ever met. Instead of saying it was weird—"

"But it *is* weird, isn't it? A little?"

"I thought so then. But I don't now. Not even a little. I just—you're so . . ."

Close. That's what I was. Close to jumping up from this board and running inside, just to preserve this moment of hope. To maybe come back to it, again. When I'd assembled all the little pieces together.

As if he sensed my fears, Billy took my hand, then turned himself fully to face me, and took the other.

"When I think back to what I said that night—how I said it." He dropped his grip and stood, leaving me to brace my feet against the porch to counteract the joggle. "I know this is going to sound like I have the biggest ego in the world, but it's not easy being me."

"Oh, I can imagine. With all the good looks, and talent, and money. That house—"

He'd been speaking with his back to me, but now he turned around, and the look on his face—the utter, genuine *sadness* on his face—silenced me.

"That house," he said, strengthened after a few deep swallows and a drum solo with his key fob, "that house is empty because some woman wanted it more than she wanted my dad and me."

"I'm sorry."

"Don't be. It's nothing to do with you. But it's just another example of why it's so hard for me to ever really trust anyone's feelings. Or actions. Or motivations. Do you know why I've never had a girlfriend?"

I held back an avalanche of disbelief. "Never?"

"Because I never felt like I could truly trust a girl's feelings. Like I'd never know if she liked *me* or if she liked *Billy Fitz.* Does that make sense?" He'd been pacing but stopped right in front of me with his question. I had to look up to see him, and it didn't help his case one bit that he had a star-studded stretch of black velvet behind his head.

"Sort of?"

"Think about it, all those girls going around with my name—*my name*—on their T-shirts. Girls I don't even know, let alone like, and they've attached themselves to me. You know, it's hard enough to have friends, let alone a girlfriend. It's just easier to keep everyone at a distance."

"Except Charlie." And I realized how hard it must have been for him to be so separated from his best friend.

"Except Charlie." He came back and sat down, closer than he'd been before. "And, somehow, you. The first day I met you—I mean, nobody ever *talks* to me the way you did. And I guess I'm just so used to being—"

"Worshiped?"

He laughed. "Here's the deal. I pretty much hate most of the people who would consider themselves *in my circle*, and I've never paid much attention to people outside of it. I just didn't know where to put you."

"I didn't know there were circles."

He cocked his head. "Yes, you did. And you do now. It's an ugly truth, but it's true."

I looked down at my knees, *our* knees, really. One good joggle would bring them together. Now I really wish I'd put my coat on—like, arms through the sleeves—so I could close myself within it. "Here's the deal." I stole his words and looked up to find his gaze full of enough warmth and strength to carry them across. "It's hard for a girl . . . well, like me . . . it's hard to be in *any* circle." He started to speak, but I lifted up a hand to stop him. When I did, my coat slipped off my shoulders, leaving my back totally exposed to the cold. "And I know you said it didn't matter."

"It doesn't—"

"And I know you think you're super brave or whatever to even entertain the *thought* of liking me. And I know part of me should have been flattered at the attention, and then for a while I felt so stupid for making such a show—"

"You were hurt."

"I wasn't hurt." No, that was a lie. Start over. "Okay, I was, but mostly I was angry. At the time I thought I was just angry *because* I was hurt." My hands found his, and I held on tight, needing him to feel this truth. "But it was also because it's not up to you to decide whether or not any of this *matters*. Your Fitzness, my—"

I was going to say *my fatness*, because sometimes, well, you know, I can get caught up in the waves of my own words—but he stopped me. Like he was protecting me from giving that word the power of my identity. He let go of one hand and touched my face, tilting my chin so I could look into his eyes.

"You were hurt. I hurt you, and I'm sorry. I know I said in my letter that I would never bring it up again. Liking you—but I do. I like you, Elyse. A lot. More than any girl I've ever met. I was a jerk about Charlie and Jayne, and I've tried to make up for that. But if you still feel like you did that night, if you still hate me, or if you're still angry . . . I promise you, I'll leave you alone. I won't—"

"Hey." Because I had to stop him from talking. "I don't."

"You don't . . ."

"I didn't hate you then, that night. And I don't now. At all. In fact, what I feel, and what I've always felt, is probably the most opposite of hate."

He dropped his touch, but I didn't look away.

"*Most opposite of hate?* That's a great sentence for an AP English student."

"You know I'm in AP?"

"I know everything about you, Elyse. I know that you go to your first period class early to read, and that you can uncap your highlighter without ever taking your eyes off the page."

"It's a gift," I say, thankful more than ever for my desk by the window.

"And I know you hate science, because every day before you walk in the door you sigh like you're carrying the weight of the world in your JanSport."

"My lab partners. They are such idiots—you can't even know . . ."

"You only buy school lunch on spaghetti and pizza day—"

"There's something about pizza in a rectangle shape. Makes me happy."

"And you get a warm cookie every Wednesday."

The realization hit me—lots of what he was talking about involved food. What I ate, and how much and when. I tried to move away, but he brought his arm around me. Divested of my coat, I could feel it this time. Definitely. He could pull me closer—if I wanted to be pulled closer. I wasn't sure yet. For the moment, it was enough to know his hand felt nothing but the softness of my sweater on the polar opposite side of my pounding heart.

"In Mr. V's class," he said, "when you're thinking, you push your pencil into your cheek."

"I do it with a pen sometimes too."

"I know. I've seen the mark. And, you have the most unpredictable dimple."

"Unpredictable?"

"*Here.*" He touched the place right below the corner of my mouth. "It only happens when you smile just right."

I smiled, just right.

"Like now," he said, pulling me close. And he kissed me.

For the first time in my life, music was playing, and I didn't know the song. It was coming from inside. His mouth was warm on mine. His hands, too, when they came up to frame my face, and hold me there, as if I would ever run away. We were bathed in silver television light—I know, because I let my eyes flutter open, just for a second, just to see.

Billy pulled back and looked at me. "I think I've been wanting to do that since the first day I met you."

"No, you haven't." I sat back, just a little, to bring his face into focus.

"You're right. I don't know when, exactly—when you started to mean *more* to me. My mind woke up in the middle of liking you. I should have—"

"That's okay." Hey, I'm a girl who enjoys a good conversation, but . . . "It's enough that you want to now. And that, maybe, you'll want to again?"

Before he could decide, I kissed him, and in that kiss were all the days to come. Saturday nights in the couples' booth at Dino's. Spring Break at Six Flags with Charlie and Jayne and the pesky Caroline, who I swear tried to push me off at the top of the Texas Cliffhanger. Prom night in a midnight-blue dress, color coordinated to the bow tie and cummerbund of his tuxedo, standing on the side while Prom King Frank Churchill dances with a triumphant (but probably inwardly seething) Queen Katie Berg. Running into Billy's arms after he hits the winning run at the tri-district tournament. (Did I ever mention he plays baseball too? He does.) Blowing each other a kiss before diving into the Trigonometry final exam.

Summer.

And that's when the story gets interesting.

THE END

ABOUT THE AUTHOR

A. K. PITTMAN is an award-winning author of thirteen novels, including the Christy-nominated Sister Wife series and the critically acclaimed *The Seamstress*. An enthusiast for all things writing, she leads two different writers' groups, helping to bring new voices to the world of books. When not writing, Allison teaches middle school English, working as a conduit to introduce her students to new, fresh literature. You can follow her around on Instagram (@allisonkpittman) or Twitter (@allisonkpittman) and keep up with her writing news on her Allison Pittman Author Facebook page. Here you'll learn what's going on with new books, next books, and day-to-day life with Allison and her husband, Mikey. You'll also get a peek at Snax, the world's worst dog.